8-19(91)

JUN 1 1 1997

T-90

2015-2
2016-2
2017-6
L 8/17
2 15

DATE DUE

LONG AFTER MIDNIGHT

*Also by Iris Johansen
in Large Print:*

The Ugly Duckling
Midnight Warrior
The Beloved Scoundrel
Strong Hot Winds
Wicked Jake Darcy
York, The Renegade
   (Shamrock Trinity)

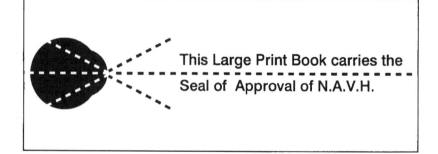

This Large Print Book carries the
Seal of Approval of N.A.V.H.

LONG
AFTER
MIDNIGHT

IRIS JOHANSEN

G.K. Hall & Co.
Thorndike, Maine

Published in 1997 by arrangement with Bantam Books, a division of Bantam Doubleday Dell Publishing Group, Inc.

G.K. Hall Large Print Romance Collection.

The text of this Large Print edition is unabridged.
Other aspects of the book may vary from the original edition.

Set in 16 pt. Plantin by Al Chase.

Printed in the United States on permanent paper.

Library of Congress Cataloging in Publication Data

Johansen, Iris.
   Long after midnight / Iris Johansen.
    p. cm.
   ISBN 0-7838-2040-2 (lg. print : hc)
   1. Large type books. I. Title.
  [PS3560.O275L66   1997b]
  813´.54—dc21
                                         96-54266

Now hast thou but one bare hour to live
And then thou must be damned perpetually
Stand still, you ever moving spheres of heaven
That time may cease and midnight never come

— Christopher Marlowe
The Tragical History of Dr. Faustus

Acknowledgments

My sincere thanks to Asst. Professor Dale L. Vogelien, Ph.D., for her help in overseeing my journey through the maze of genetic science.

"I can't do it." Kate's hand tightened on her father's with desperation. "I don't want to even talk about it. Do you understand? Don't ask me, dammit."

"I have to ask you." Robert Murdock tried to smile. "There's no one else, Kate."

"There could be a cure. New cures are developed every day."

"But not in my foreseeable future." Wearily he leaned back against the pillows of the hospital bed. "Be merciful. Do it, Kate."

"I can't." Tears were streaming down her face. "This isn't why I became a doctor. You don't mean it. If you were yourself, you wouldn't ask me."

"Look at me." She met her father's eyes. "I've never been more myself. Do I mean it, baby?"

He meant it. She searched frantically for a way to sway him. "What about Joshua? He loves you."

He flinched. "He's only six years old. He'll forget."

"You know better than that. Joshua isn't like other kids."

"No, he's like you." His tone was loving. "Bright and loyal and ready to fight the world. But he's too young to be forced to carry around any kind of baggage. If you don't want to do this

7

for me, do it for my grandson, do it for Joshua's sake."

He had thought it all out, she realized in despair. "I don't want to let you go," she whispered.

"You won't be letting me go." He paused. "I've been lying here thinking about the time when you were a very little girl and we'd walk through Jenkins's woods. You used to be sad when autumn came and the leaves fell. Do you remember what I told you?"

"No."

He shook his head reprovingly. "Kate."

"You said that each leaf was a link that could never really be broken or die," she said haltingly. "It would curl and fall but it would return to the earth and the chain would go on brighter and stronger than ever."

"A bit profound but absolutely true."

"Bullshit."

His face lit with laughter and for a moment he was once more that younger, stronger man in Jenkins's woods. "You believed it then."

"It's easier to accept fate when you're seven years old. I'm different now."

"Yes, you are." He reached out and gently touched her damp cheek with an index finger. "Twenty-six and one tough cookie."

She didn't feel tough. She felt as if she were breaking apart inside. "You bet I am," she said shakily. "These days I'd get a ladder and nail those leaves back on their branches or find a way of keeping them from falling in the first place."

His smile faded. "Maybe someday. Not now, Kate. Don't try to nail me back to my branch. I've no taste for crucifixion."

Pain stabbed through her. "You know I wouldn't — I love you."

"Then let me go. Help me. Let me keep my dignity."

"I don't know — I can't even think of — Please, don't make me." Her head sank to rest on their joined hands on the bed. "Let me *fight* for you."

"You will fight for me."

"No, you want me to give you up. I can't do that."

She felt his hand lovingly stroke her hair. "You can do it. Because you're one tough lady . . . and you wouldn't want to be crucified either. We've always understood each other, haven't we?"

"Not in this."

"Even in this."

He was right. She did understand. If she had allowed herself to think about it, she would have realized he would come to this decision. "To hell with understanding. I *care* about you."

"And that's why I know you'll do it. I've tried to live my life with dignity. Don't let it end like this."

"You're not being fair."

"No, I'm not. Will you let me be selfish? Just this once?"

She could barely hear his words through the sobs that were shaking her body.

9

"Thank you, baby." His hand continued to gently stroke her hair as he said softly, "But you'll have to be very careful. I don't want you hurt. No one must ever know."

One

Dandridge, Oklahoma
Three years later
Saturday, March 24

"You're not concentrating." Joshua lowered his bat and frowned at her reprovingly. "Get a grip, Mom. How will I learn if you make it this easy for me?"

"Sorry." Kate grinned at him and sprinted to retrieve the baseball that had bounced off the high wood fence. "I forgot I was dealing with the next Fred McGriff. I'll try to do better." She wound up, lifted her leg, and released the ball.

Joshua connected with the ball and it soared over the fence. He grinned at her. "Home run."

"But that was a good pitch," she said indignantly.

"Great pitch, but you signaled a fastball."

She wiped her palms on her jeans and looked at him in disgust. "How?"

"You always lift your leg higher when it's a fastball. You ought to watch it."

"I will next time." She made a face. "You could have gone easy on me. I have to work this afternoon. I don't have time to search the neighborhood for that blasted ball."

"I'll help you." He dropped the bat and came

11

toward her. "If you give me another fifteen minutes' practice."

"Get one of your friends to pitch to you. Rory's the team's pitcher. He must be pretty good."

"He's okay." He fell into step with her. "But you throw a better slider."

She opened the gate and preceded him to the front of the house. "You're darn right."

"And you learn quick. You don't make the same mistake twice."

"Thank you." She inclined her head gravely. "I appreciate the kind words."

His freckled face lit with a sly smile. "I'm buttering you up."

"I suspected as much." She made a half motion toward him and then caught herself. Joshua was an affectionate child but he was a very dignified nine. It was Saturday afternoon and the suburb was brimming with neighborhood kids. It wouldn't do to have one of them see her son submit to a hug. "We've been practicing two hours. I don't have any more time."

He shrugged philosophically. "I thought I'd give it a shot."

"Like you gave my fastball."

"Yep." He glanced away from her. "You brought home work from GeneChem again?"

"Uh-huh." She glanced around the postage-stamp front yard. "Where is that ball? Do you see it?"

He didn't seem to hear her. "Rory says his dad said the people who work at GeneChem are building Frankensteins."

She stiffened and turned to look at him. "And what did you tell him?"

"I told him that he was stupid. That you're trying to save lives, and monsters are only in books and movies." He looked away from her. "Does it make you mad that people lie about you?"

"Does it make you mad?"

"Yes." His hands clenched at his sides. "I want to punch them in the nose."

She smothered a smile. This was serious stuff. It was the first time Joshua had faced the controversy surrounding her work, and she must handle it as diplomatically as possible. Unfortunately, diplomacy wasn't her forte. "It's better to try to explain and make them understand. It's not really their fault. What we're doing in genetics is fairly new, and a lot of people don't understand that by studying and attempting to alter gene structure, we're only trying to fight diseases and make life better."

"Then they're stupid. You wouldn't hurt anyone."

"I guess they think I may not do the right thing, that I won't be careful enough."

Joshua made a rude noise.

She wasn't reaching him. She had an inspiration. Joshua was a computer fanatic, like all the kids these days. "I'll buy you a computer program that explains DNA and what medicine is trying to do. Maybe you could show Rory."

13

He instantly brightened. "But what if he still doesn't get it?"

Then you punch him in the nose, she wanted to tell him.

Diplomacy. She wouldn't have Joshua suffer for her impatience and frustration. "Then you come to me and we'll map out a new plan."

"Okay." He studied her, and his face suddenly lit with mischief. "And don't worry, I won't tell you when I punch him in the nose."

Shrewd little rascal. He was entirely too perceptive for his age. Perceptive and bright and totally lovable. She felt herself melting as she looked at him. Small, sturdy, with sandy brown hair and an untamable cowlick, he was nearly irresistible. She quickly turned away and started back to the house. "Just for that, you can find the blasted ball yourself."

"That's not fair. You're the defense. If you didn't catch it, you should be —"

"Telephone." Phyliss Denby stood on the front porch. "Long distance. Noah Smith again."

Kate frowned. "You told him I was home?"

Phyliss nodded. "I got tired of making excuses."

"Will you help me find my ball, Grandma?" Joshua asked.

Phyliss smiled at him as she came down the steps. "You bet."

Kate gave Joshua a mock scowl behind Phyliss's back. They both knew his grandmother would jump over the moon if Joshua asked her. He

14

smiled innocently back at Kate and turned to Phyliss. "I hit a home run. Fastball."

"She kicked her leg too high again?"

"Yep."

"You knew I was doing it too?" Kate asked indignantly. "Why didn't you tell me?"

"Why should I tell you? I'm no pitching coach," Phyliss said. "Go answer the phone."

Kate moved reluctantly across the porch and into the house. She didn't want to talk to Noah Smith again. She usually had no problem asserting herself, but the man's confidence and persistence were overwhelming and annoying. At first she had been flattered that Smith had wanted to hire her. J. and S. Pharmaceuticals was a small but prestigious company, Smith himself a famous research scientist, and the money he had offered more than generous. But the man couldn't seem to take no for an answer. It was as if he didn't hear anything he didn't want to hear.

"Sorry to bother you on a Saturday." Noah Smith's deep voice was layered with silken sarcasm when she answered the phone. "It was necessary. I never seem to catch you at home . . . or the office. Strange."

"Not so strange. And just how did you get my home phone number, Dr. Smith?"

"Noah. I told you to call me Noah."

"How did you get my home number, Noah? It's unlisted."

"But nothing's really private any longer, is it?

Who answered the phone? I've talked to her before."

"My mother-in-law. It's very flattering that you would go to the trouble of calling me at home, but I prefer to keep my home and work separate."

"Your mother-in-law? I understood you were divorced."

"I am but she still cares for my son. Phyliss is —" She stopped. "How did you know I was divorced?"

"I'd hardly try to hire you without knowing all I could about you."

That made sense. "Then you must know I'm providing a very stable life for myself and my son and wouldn't consider uprooting my family to take a new position."

"Oklahoma doesn't have the monopoly on stability. Seattle has a lot to offer. We need to work together. Do you want more money?"

"No." She was suddenly tired of his bulldozer tactics. She said with precision, "I don't want more money. I don't want to move. In fact, I don't want to work with you, Dr. Smith. Is that clear?"

"Perfectly. I'll up the offer another ten thousand a year. Think about it. I'll get back to you."

He hung up the phone.

She gritted her teeth in frustration as she returned the receiver to the hook. Impossible. The man was impossible.

"You know it might not be a bad idea if you

took the job," Phyliss said from the doorway. "You need a little shaking up."

"I'm happy where I am." She made a face. "And you'd yell bloody murder if I took Joshua across the country."

"Not if you took me with you."

Kate's eyes widened. "You'd leave Michael?"

Phyliss smiled. "I love my son but I'm not blind to his faults. He has a habit of pigeonholing people and then getting upset when they won't stay in their niche. He saw you as his wife, mother of his child, keeper of his home. You divorced him because you're more than that and you had to break out of the pigeonhole. He sees me as just good old Mom, his father's widow, Joshua's grandmother. I'm more than that too."

Kate looked at her affectionately. Slim, tall, with short curly brown hair, Phyliss appeared younger and possessed far more vitality than many of the women Kate worked with every day. "Yes, you are." She had been astonished and pleased when Phyliss Denby had moved in with her after the divorce two years ago. She had thought there was every chance her friendship with Phyliss would go down the drain with the marriage. Instead, her mother-in-law had taken over running the house and caring for Joshua when Kate was at work. Independent, brusque, and energetic, she had been a blessing for both Kate and Joshua. "But you wouldn't want to move. You've lived here all your life."

"Maybe it's time I was shaken up a little too."

17

She came forward. "If this is a good job, don't let it go by."

"It's not that good. Noah Smith is . . . eccentric. We probably wouldn't be able to work together."

"Eccentric?"

"Genetic research is a slow, methodical process of trial and elimination. He goes off on tangents."

"And the result?"

She shrugged. "He's brilliant. Naturally, he's had his successes."

"Then maybe tangents are the way to go."

"Not my way." She turned and moved toward the door. "And there's no use talking about it. Even if I thought I could work with him, I can't leave here."

"Can't?" Phyliss looked at her curiously. "One of the things I've always admired about you is the fact that you didn't seem to know the meaning of that word."

"All right. Won't." Kate smiled at her over her shoulder. "Did you find Joshua's ball?"

"I take it the subject's closed," Phyliss murmured. "The ball was under the rosebush. Joshua says you have to work this afternoon. Should I take him out to the movies?"

"If you like. It doesn't matter. Once I start work, I don't hear him anyway."

"I must have lost it for a minute. When you're working, you wouldn't hear a volcano erupting."

Because every minute brought her nearer to the answer, and the anticipation was becoming unbearable. The last experiments had been wonderfully promising. She said lightly, "There aren't any volcanoes in Oklahoma."

"But there are volcanoes near Seattle. It could be exciting for you."

Kate glanced around the small, cozy living room, at the comfortable sofa and chairs with faded upholstery, the old oak coffee table where Joshua could safely prop his feet when he was watching TV. She and Phyliss had carefully made this house a home. Even if she could have left, she would not have chosen to go. She needed the stability and roots she had here.

"I can do without excitement," she said firmly. "I'm staying here."

"She turned you down again?" Anthony Lynski asked as Noah turned away from the phone. "Stubborn lady. Are you sure you need her?"

"I need her." Noah sat down at his desk. "I want the delivery system and she's got it. Or she'll have it soon."

"I read that last article she wrote for the medical journal too, and it seemed pretty speculative to me."

"Did you expect her to detail the process before it was patented?"

"Then why did she write the article at all?"

"Sheer excitement. I could almost taste it while I was reading the article. I felt the same way when I had the first breakthrough on RU2 three years ago. She wanted to share, to talk about it, but it wasn't safe to confide in anyone."

Tony raised a skeptical brow. "How do you know? You've never met the woman."

Noah pulled the manila folder out of his top desk drawer and flipped it open. "But thanks to your pet detective Barlow, I have an excellent profile on her." A photograph of Kate Denby preceded the report. Short, silky ash-blond hair framed a face that was an odd combination of strength and vulnerability. A square jaw, a large mouth that still managed to look sensitive, wide-set hazel eyes that stared boldly — these features seemed to jump out at them. "Or, at least, I thought I did. There's nothing in here about her mother-in-law taking care of the child."

"Barlow's a good man. He probably thought you wanted him to concentrate on her professional qualifications." Tony picked up the dossier and scanned it. "Seems pretty thorough. Daughter of Robert Murdock, a distinguished physician. He died of cancer three years ago. She was something of a child prodigy, graduated from college at sixteen, from medical school at twenty-two. She has a string of degrees in genetic sciences. Worked at Breland's lab in Oklahoma City and then took a job across town at GeneChem. They offered her less money but a contract that allowed her to do private research on her own time, using their facilities. She's divorced and has custody of a nine-year-old son."

"I knew almost all of that before I asked for a dossier. Her background was on her credit line with the article," Noah said. "What I didn't know

20

was that she was still on good enough terms with her mother-in-law to let her take care of her son."

"It's not exactly important data, is it?"

"It's important if it contributes to the comfortable nest Kate Denby's built for herself."

Tony lifted his brows. "Oh, the nest you want to jerk her out of and burn down behind her?"

Noah looked up with a grin. "You malign me. I've been very gentle with her . . . for me. Nary a jerk. I've wielded only persuasion, bribery, and persistence."

"So far," Tony said dryly. "But you're getting impatient."

Noah's smile faded. "You're damn right."

"Have you told her anything about the project you want her to work on?"

"I can't risk it. I have to wait until I have her here." He scowled. "And time's running out."

"Maybe faster than you think." Tony paused. "I was followed this trip. Since London, I think."

Noah muttered a curse. "You're sure?"

"I'm sure. You expected it, didn't you?"

"I expected it but not this soon. I wanted to have everything in place." His voice held a thread of desperation. "I'm not *ready*, dammit. Do you know who's paying him?"

Tony shook his head. "Hey, I'm a lawyer, not a fortune-teller. Do you?"

"Maybe. Raymond Ogden called me yesterday."

Tony gave a low whistle. "Big stuff. He owns one of the largest pharmaceutical companies in the world, doesn't he?"

Noah nodded. "And a bag of dirty tricks to go along with it."

"How do you know?"

"He tried to take over my company six years ago." Noah smiled crookedly. "He tried everything from seduction of stockholders to launching an ad campaign that hinted that our production line was careless."

"But he didn't succeed in taking you over."

"No. He changed his mind."

Tony didn't ask what methods Noah had used to change his mind. Noah was one tough bastard and almost feudal in his possessive attitude toward his company. "So he can't be much danger to you."

"He barely flexed his muscles on the takeover attempt. J. and S. was too small to be worth his personal attention."

"But this will be different?"

"Oh, yes. I'll definitely have his full attention. Which means you're out of it, Tony."

"What?"

"You heard me. It could get nasty from now on."

"You're overreacting. I haven't made the Washington trip yet. Ogden may not know anything. He's probably grasping at straws."

"God, I hope so."

Tony looked at him in surprise. Hope wasn't Noah Smith's usual modus operandi. He preferred to make his own luck, mold circumstances to suit himself like the modern-day buccaneer Tony knew him to be. The weary heaviness and uncertainty in his tone were uncharacteristic of him. But then, Noah's entire handling of RU2 had been unusual. He had kept his reckless streak firmly in check. He had been careful, painstaking, and relentlessly protective. "You're really worried." He paused before asking the question he'd kept himself from asking for the last ten months. "What the hell is RU2?"

Noah shook his head. "You don't want to know."

"If I didn't want to know, I wouldn't have asked. I've been your friend for sixteen years and your lawyer for eight. I think I deserve your trust, Noah."

"My lawyer shouldn't ask me questions I don't want to answer." He met his gaze. "And my friend should believe me when I tell him he doesn't want to know more than he has to know. It's not safe."

"Professionally?"

"It's not safe," Noah repeated. "Back off, Tony."

"I doubt if Ogden's going to blackjack me in some dark alley."

"Not personally. Why should he? He can hire someone to do it."

Tony shook his head. "I can't see Ogden regarding your RU2 as that much of a threat. He's a major player."

"Then think of Ogden Pharmaceuticals as Hiroshima and RU2 as the first atomic bomb. That should make it clearer."

Tony started to smile. "You're joking. You can't be —" Then he realized Noah was dead serious, and for the first time he was shaken. "You're not being paranoid?"

"I'm being careful. For God's sake, I'm trying to keep you out of this." Noah's voice roughened. "I let you help me because you're the only one I could trust, but now I want you out. I knew that someone like Ogden was bound to surface as soon as the sharks found out about RU2."

"Found out what?"

Noah was silent.

It was no use. "You always were a selfish bastard," he said lightly. "We haven't done any shark fishing since Grenada and now you want to keep them all to yourself."

Noah relaxed. "With any luck I'll swim away before they know I'm in the water."

"Not likely. You usually make a pretty big splash."

"Well, go away to the mountains for a week or so until I see what's happening with Ogden." He opened the desk, pulled out a key ring, and tossed it to Tony. "I've rented a lodge in the Sierra Madres for you. The address is on the ring. Don't tell anyone where you're going, not even your secretary. Okay?"

"Whatever you say." He got up to leave. "I could use a little vacation. I have to bring by those Amsterdam contracts for you to sign. They

24

should be ready by Monday and I'll leave by the end of the week."

"Leave Tuesday."

"Okay. Okay. You'll call me if you need me?"

"Loud and clear."

Tony moved toward the door.

"And Tony." Noah's brow was knitted in thought. "Get in touch with Seth. Ask him to come."

"He won't do it."

"Ask him."

"For God's sake, Noah, you don't need a mercenary. This isn't a war."

"Not yet."

"He may not even be alive. He hasn't surfaced in the last five years."

"He was alive eight months ago. He spent a week with me on the *Cadro* sailing in the Caribbean."

Tony's eyes widened in surprise. "You didn't tell me."

"I don't tell you everything, Tony."

"It seems you tell me precious little."

Noah smiled. "Are you disgruntled because I didn't invite you along? You and Seth are hardly bosom buddies."

"The bastard has always needled the hell out of me."

"True. I think your newfound respectability annoys him. He doesn't like lawyers."

"No, he prefers smugglers, killers, and sundry riffraff," Tony said sourly.

"Riffraff." Noah savored the phrase. "Where the hell did you come up with that word?"

"It comes to mind every time I think of Seth."

"You must try it on him next time you see him."

"I don't want to see him. Hell, I don't even know where to contact him."

"South America."

"Thanks for narrowing it down."

"Pedro Estaban's hotel in Venga, Colombia. Leave a message with Manuel Carrerra. Tell him it's time. Get Seth for me, Tony. Right away."

"I'll try," he said grudgingly. "You won't let me help, but, dammit, you don't mind putting his neck on the line."

"It's his area of expertise. He has an edge." He smiled slyly. "He's not a lawyer."

"You bastard." Tony paused at the door and glanced back at the dossier on Noah's desk. "You're so concerned about keeping my ass safe. What about Kate Denby's?"

Noah's expression became shuttered. "I can't allow myself to worry about her. She'll have to take her chances."

"Why?"

"I need her," Noah said simply.

After the door closed behind Tony, Noah flipped shut the Kate Denby dossier. He didn't want her face gazing up at him. Over the last few weeks he had become too familiar with that face. He had become familiar with *her.*

26

And that was a mistake.

When he finally persuaded her to join his camp, he'd have to distance himself. Not an easy task since they'd have to work closely together, but he knew himself too well. He couldn't let her close, couldn't let her become a friend. If he started to worry about Kate Denby, RU2 would be endangered, and that mustn't happen. He had to be able to use her and not worry about the consequences.

And the consequences were beginning to loom on the horizon. He could put off Ogden for a little while, but he was like a tribe of Indians circling the wagon train. Sooner or later he'd swoop in and attack.

And Noah had to sit on his butt and watch it coming. Wait, instead of attack. Evade, instead of rushing in and grappling toe to toe.

He stood up and moved restlessly to the window and gazed down at the factory yard. It was almost deserted this Saturday afternoon. Only a skeleton crew was working in the east wing of the plant, where most of the production took place. J. and S. Pharmaceuticals was small but very prosperous for its size, a family business started by his grandfather and built upon by his father. A good many of the employees who worked in that building had been here while he was growing up. As a kid, he'd taken his lunch bucket and eaten down there in that yard with Pauly McGregor, who now headed production. In a changing world, this plant was a bedrock.

His bedrock. His people.

But RU2 might change that too. It could twist and transform everything that was important to him.

Why was he second-guessing now? he wondered impatiently. He had made the agonizing decision two years ago when he'd realized RU2's potential.

There was no way he could back down now.

RU2 must survive.

Sunday, March 25
South America

Seth knew that smell.

It was a smell you never forgot.

Goddamn Namirez.

He moved quickly through the rain forest toward the village. No need to be silent now. Not when the smell was this strong.

The village was silent.

Bodies lay everywhere. Men, women, children, babies.

Death. Mud. Stinking decay.

Christ, even the babies.

Namirez, you lying son of a bitch.

A yellow-brown mongrel pup crept out of a hut, wagging its tail. It came closer, sniffing at Seth's combat boots.

He was surprised Namirez hadn't butchered the animals as well.

Son of a bitch.

"You have acquired a pet, senor?" Manuel shook his head as Seth came into the lobby of the hotel a day later. "Very scrawny. I can get you a much finer animal."

"I like this one." He handed Manuel the rope with which he'd haltered the mongrel. "Feed him, will you? Is Namirez in town?"

Manuel nodded. "In the back room. Sergeant Rimilon is here too. He's in his room." He handed Seth a folded slip of paper. "That's a message for you. Mr. Lynski wishes you to call him right away."

"Later." He stuffed the message into his shirt pocket. "Call the *policía* and then tell Sergeant Rimilon to meet me in the lobby. Get the helicopter gassed up."

"You are going somewhere?"

"Yes." He went around the desk and opened the door to the back room.

Namirez was sitting at the desk. He looked up and smiled. "Ah, Drakin, all is going well for us. You've done what you promised."

"You haven't." He drew his pistol from its holster. "I told you. No reprisals."

He shot him squarely in the center of the forehead.

"What are we supposed to do now?" Rimilon shouted, trying to keep pace as Seth ran toward the helicopter behind the hotel.

29

"Did you have to kill him?"

"Yes." Seth jumped into the helicopter and set the pup on the floor beside him. "Disband the men and get the hell out of here. Namirez's partners aren't going to like losing him at this point. Everything's going to fall apart."

Rimilon swore long and emphatically. "All you had to do was ignore what happened in the village. Now how are we going to get paid? I saw the *policía* rifling through his safe."

"But I got there first." Seth tossed him a bundle. "Pay the men off and scat. I'd leave S.A. for a while. I'll be in touch." He closed the door and the helicopter lifted off.

He didn't unfold the slip of paper he'd put in his pocket until he was out of Colombia and heading for the Caracas airport. It was only one line and a telephone number.

Noah says it's time.

It was what he expected to see. Noah had told him everything would be coming to a head soon. Another war. Another place.

God, he was tired of it.

But this would be different. It was Noah's war and Noah was one of the good guys, the white hats. Maybe it wouldn't be so bad.

The pup at his feet whimpered.

He glanced down and saw the pup had peed on the floor. Great. The noise and vibration of the helicopter had scared him. Seth understood fear. You got used to it, but it never went away.

He reached down and patted the pup on the head. "Take it easy. We'll be down soon." He shouldn't have brought the dog. What the hell was he going to do with him? He could have trusted Manuel to take care of him.

But he wasn't long on trust, and the pup had survived the massacre and deserved to live. So he was stuck with a mongrel who was going to prove inconvenient as hell.

Which might be the least of his worries. Noah was smart and he thought he was prepared, but he hadn't gone to war since Grenada. He didn't think like a soldier anymore.

But it was Noah's war, Noah's call. Seth didn't have to run the show on this one. It would be good to relax and take a backseat for a while.

If he could do it. He was having a harder time unwinding lately. Every year the edge got sharper, the tightness got —

The pup was trying to climb into his lap, and Seth pushed him back to the floor. "Sorry, you'll get in my way. You wouldn't want to see this bird go down in the jungle. You've been there."

And so had he. Jungle, desert, islands . . . they all became a blur after a while. Nothing was different but the people, and they tended to fade too.

Except for sons of bitches like Namirez and Noah of the white hat.

The white hat and RU2 that could send them all to hell.

TWO

Dandridge, Oklahoma
Monday, March 26
10:35 A.M.

"Murderess!"

"Filthy butcher!"

"Get the demon!"

Kate flung open the glass door at GeneChem's front entrance, watching grimly as Benita Chavez bolted from the parking lot and down the walk followed by the howling mob.

"Do you think she'll make it?" Charlie Dodd murmured in Kate's ear.

"If she does, I'll murder her myself," Kate said. "Where the hell is Security?"

"I don't know. We were all supposed to be in the building before eight. It's almost eleven."

"Well, ring the buzzer for them."

"I already did. As soon as I saw Benny get out of her car."

Benny Chavez waved cheerfully as she saw Kate. Her jean-clad legs took the stone steps two at a time; her long black hair streamed behind her.

"She's laughing," Kate said between her teeth. "The idiot thinks this is a big joke."

"It won't be so funny if they catch — Damn."

32

One of the signs carried by the protesters had descended on Benita's head. She staggered, stopped, and caught her balance. It was too late. She was engulfed in the screaming horde.

"Hold the door open." Kate flew down the steps toward the knot of humanity surrounding Benny. She grabbed a sign away from a gray-haired harridan on the edge of the crowd, turned it around, and started wielding the wooden pole like a staff, clearing the way before her until she caught sight of Benita.

Benny's shirttail was out of her jeans, her hair covered her eyes, and she was no longer smiling.

"Run for the building." Kate jabbed a potbellied man in the abdomen, forcing him to back away from Benny. "Now."

"I can't leave you. I won't go until you — Ouch."

Kate had jabbed her with the pole. "Now, damn you. I'll be right behind you."

Benny hurried up the steps.

"Bitch." The snarl came from the gray-haired woman from whom Kate had taken the sign. "Murderess."

Blinding pain struck her temple.

She was going down. . . .

The hell she was. They'd be on her like a pack of hyenas. She fought back the darkness, striking blindly to the right and left with the pole.

She heard wood strike flesh, a shrill scream, a pained grunt.

Someone grabbed her hair from behind and

tried to pull her down the steps.

Her head snapped back as agony jarred through her. She swiveled and swung the pole.

A scream and the grip on her hair was suddenly gone.

Good. She hoped she'd knocked the —

"Hurry, Dr. Denby." A man in a gray uniform with *GeneChem* embossed on the pocket was beside her. She recognized Cary from Security. "Get inside." He was pushing her up the stairs while two other security men battled the crowd. "You know you shouldn't be out here."

Her relief turned to annoyance. "I didn't have much choice, since you weren't. Why the devil did you have to —" She broke off. She wasn't being fair. The building was secure, and everyone had been warned to come in early to avoid contact with those idiots out front until Administration could find a way to reason with them. "Sorry. Events just escalated."

"You should have waited. Why did you go out there?"

Kate glanced at Benny standing in the doorway beside Charlie Dodd. Evidently Security had arrived after Benny had reached safety and had no idea of her involvement. Charlie shrugged and raised his eyebrows, leaving it up to Kate. That scene outside might well escalate into a major public relations nightmare. As head of her project, Kate could survive the bureaucratic fallout, but Benny was only a lab assistant and would be considered expendable. "It was a mistake. I should have known better." She saw the relief in Benny's expression and added deliberately, "It's always foolish to try to stop idiots from making asses of themselves."

"Right." Benny stepped forward and took Kate solicitously by the arm. "You look like you've been through a hurricane. Come on along to the washroom and I'll get you cleaned up."

Cary was uncertain. "Maybe she should go to the infirmary. Her temple's bleeding."

"It's nothing," Kate said. "I'll be fine, Cary."

"Sure you will." Benny was guiding her down the hall. "Tell them at the lab that I'll be there as soon as I finish helping Kate, will you, Charlie?"

"And of course they can't expect you to be on time when you're playing Florence Nightingale," Charlie said dryly.

She winked at him over her shoulder. "It would be totally inhumane of them."

Kate heard Charlie chuckle and she knew he would cover for Benny just as she had done. Why did they do it? she wondered in exasperation. Benny was always late, recklessly impulsive, sometimes manipulative.

She was also the most thorough technician in the lab, generous and boundlessly good-humored.

And Joshua adored her. He would be heartbroken if anything happened to Benny. So, for Joshua's sake as well as her own, Benny must be protected.

"Sit down." Benny pushed her into the chrome seat in front of the long mirror, turned to the basin, and dampened a paper towel. "You look like hell."

"I wonder why."

"Because you're a pushover." Benny grinned as she began to dab at Kate's temple. "And you rush in where angels fear to tread."

"You're no angel and you were in the middle of that mess."

"You should have let me battle my way out. I'm better equipped for the job. I'm a strapping five foot ten and you're five foot nothing."

"Five foot two," Kate corrected. "And you'll notice I was more successful than you were."

"They caught me by surprise." She wiped the smudges off Kate's cheeks. "I couldn't believe they'd actually go for me. For God's sake, it doesn't make any sense. Do they think we're performing abortions here?"

"They're fanatics. They believe what they want to believe. They get bored with attacking abortion clinics so they target genetic research."

"But GeneChem isn't even involved in fetal research. We're searching for a single vaccine for all the influenza strains."

"We're all monsters as far as they're concerned." Kate took the towel from Benny. "I can do that. Clean yourself up."

"I thought you'd be taking over pretty soon." Benny made a face. "No one's allowed to take care of you for very long, are they?"

Kate looked at her in surprise. "Why should I let you do what I can do myself?"

"No reason. I just thought you might relax for a change. You don't have to be Wonder Woman every minute of the day. Brilliant Scientist meets Super Mom. It must be exhausting."

Kate smiled. "Not nearly as exhausting as playing Little John with that makeshift staff. If you want me to relax, get here tomorrow morning at eight like you're supposed to. Okay?"

"Okay. So I overslept. I had a date last night." She raised a brow. "You should try it sometime."

"It would get in the way of my being Super Mom." She added flippantly, "I don't need a man. I've been there, done that."

"Some things bear repeating." Benny hesitated. "But maybe you'd rather really do a repeat. Are you still seeing Michael?"

"Every Wednesday and Saturday afternoon." She held up her hand as Benny opened her lips. "When Josh plays in Little League games."

"So that your son will see a united front. It's nice seeing a happy, civilized divorce."

"No divorce is happy." Kate stood up and straightened her white lab coat. It had survived miraculously unscathed. She looked almost normal. "But it doesn't have to destroy everyone around it."

"No danger. You wouldn't allow it. You always have everything under control." Benny washed her face. "Do you still sleep with him?"

Kate made a face at her. "That's none of your business."

"Well, actually it is." Benny looked a little sheepish. "I kind of . . . like him."

Kate went still. "Michael?"

"He dropped in at the house a few weeks ago when I was babysitting Joshua. Remember the night you worked in the lab until after midnight and Phyliss was at her accounting class?" Benny was talking fast, avoiding Kate's eyes. "What can I say? I've always liked cops. Authority figures. It must come from having a father flit out when I was a kid. But if you still have a —"

"How does he feel about you?"

"He likes me." Benny turned to face her and added baldly, "We've been out a few times. I won't go again if you don't want me to."

Why did she feel so betrayed? Kate wondered. Michael had a right to form new attachments. They had been divorced two years, and the only bond between them now was Joshua. "Was it Michael you were with last night?"

Benny nodded.

No, it wasn't betrayal. It was loneliness . . . and plain dog-in-the-manger envy. "Do what you like. We don't sleep together. It's over." She straightened her hair. "It should never have begun. You'd suit Michael much better than I did."

"I think so too," Benny said with a sigh of relief. "I know I'm not as smart as you, and I don't look like an angel on the top of a Christmas tree, but I have my points."

Yes, Bennie had her points. She was twenty-two years old to Kate's twenty-nine, and in the mirror she appeared even taller and more vivacious standing next to fair and delicate-looking Kate. Kate automatically squared her shoulders. She had been fighting and compensating for that fragile image for most of her adult life. "You're not dumb and you have to know you're attractive, Benny."

"I'm not so bad." Benny rushed on, "And Michael's an old-fashioned guy. It must have been hard for him being married to a workaholic."

Benny was already aligning herself with Michael, Kate realized with a pang. "Yes, it was very hard for him. But being married to a police detective working Narcotics wasn't a piece of cake for me either."

"I didn't mean it was all your fault." Benny looked stricken. "It's just you expect a man to —" She shrugged. "I was brought up in a Latino household. I guess I'm old-fashioned too."

"How nice for Michael."

"You *do* mind."

Kate wearily shook her head. "I don't have the right to mind anything Michael does. I suppose I should feel lucky he chose someone Joshua likes."

"It's not as if we're an item," Benny said quickly. "But if you really don't care about —"

"It's okay," Kate interrupted. "Thanks for telling me."

She walked quickly out of the washroom. It was

stupid to feel this hurtful sense of loss. Benny and she were friends, but Kate's work had prevented them from becoming really close.

It must have been hard for him being married to a workaholic.

She blocked the words out as she opened the door of the lab. All right, she wasn't a fifties sitcom mom. She and Michael had realized the marriage was a disaster from the beginning, and only Joshua's birth had made it last as long as it did. She was no more a failure than Michael.

Failure? She had Joshua, respect in her field, and work she loved. Not bad for a woman of twenty-nine. Many women had far less.

She sat down at her desk and eagerly reached for the results of yesterday's tests.

"Noah Smith called again." Charlie tore off the number on his notepad and tossed it on her desk. "He wants you to call him back."

"Thanks." She absently pushed aside the message and went back to the DNA pairing on the chart. She felt a leap of excitement. Eighty-seven percent. Close. My God, she was close.

"It's the fourth time," Charlie said. "Didn't you return his call?"

"Once."

"The great man's nose must be out of joint."

"Maybe."

"If you don't want the job, you might recommend me." Charlie sat on the edge of her desk. "I've no prejudice against working with a Nobel Prize contender."

"Talk to him. You've a better background in cancer research than I have."

"That's what I told him just now when he called." He sighed. "He says you have certain credentials that I lack."

"Bull."

"Have you ever met him?"

She shook her head. "We were at the same conference a year ago, but I saw him only at a distance. The reporters were clustered around him like flies." She had a sudden memory of Noah Smith cleaving his way through the crowds like a scimitar: forceful, totally assured, dynamic. "He was there for only one day. I guess he found us lacking in inspiration."

"Ouch," Charlie said. "I take it you don't care for him."

She shrugged. "I suppose he's okay. I just think he's a bit of a hot dog."

"Well, he's a colorful character. Special Forces, yachtsman in the America's Cup . . . Newspapers love to write about scientists who don't wear horn-rimmed glasses and tote microscopes in their back pocket. So he likes to have a good time. Give him a break."

Kate knew that Charlie was right. Noah Smith was a reporter's dream — a war hero, sportsman, and scientist who had carved a brilliant career. And he had yet to turn forty. Her antagonism was completely unreasonable. No, it wasn't. He was making himself a major pain in the ass to her. "You give him a break."

41

"He won't give me the chance," Charlie said mournfully. "If you won't put in a word for me, you could at least take the job he's offering so I could take over yours."

"Sorry. I'm not going anywhere. I like it here." She smiled. "Now get off my desk and let me get back to work."

Charlie's gaze fell on the chart. "I bet that's not an influenza statistic. Your private project?"

She said evasively, "Just a few comparisons."

"Rudy?"

"Yes."

"You lit up like the Fourth of July when you saw them."

"Did I?"

"My God, you're cautious." He looked hurt. "Don't you trust me?"

"You're impossible." She shook her head in amusement. "You just tried to bounce me out of my job."

"Well, I guess I can see where that might give you pause."

She chuckled and waved a dismissing hand. "Get out of here."

The phone on her desk rang.

"Opportunity calling," Charlie murmured. "Smith's not a man who gives up."

"It's probably Public Relations reading me the riot act for causing an 'incident.' " She picked up the phone. "Kate Denby."

"What the hell is going on out there at GeneChem?"

She sighed. "Hello, Michael."

Charlie shrugged and ambled back to his own desk.

"What are you doing beating up on those nut-cases?"

"Trying to keep them from beating up on me. Administration called the precinct?"

"They want police protection out there tomorrow. For God's sake, are you an idiot? You could have been hurt."

"But I wasn't." She paused before saying deliberately, "And neither was Benny."

There was silence on the other end of the line. "She told you?"

"Was it a secret?"

"No, I just — I don't know. It's damn awkward. I need to talk to you."

"No, you don't." She felt raw and vulnerable, and the last thing she needed was to listen to Michael make excuses for becoming involved with one of her friends. "It's all been said."

"I'll pick you up at four out front and drive you home."

"I can't leave my car here. There's only a skeleton Security crew at night. It would probably be trashed."

"I'll bring Alan. He can drive it home for you." He hung up.

She should have kept her mouth shut. She should have known Michael would react like this. He had always insisted on having every issue on the table and shredded into neat pieces. Well, four o'clock was hours away, and she couldn't let her dread at the coming meeting with Michael distract her.

She lowered her gaze to the report, and the excitement flared again. "We did it, Rudy," she whispered. "I think we did it." She stood up and walked quickly to the adjoining room. Rudy was scampering about his large cage, alert and bright-eyed and . . . healthy. So healthy she wanted to hug him. A white lab rat wasn't precisely huggable, so she fed him a piece of lettuce instead. "Eighty-seven percent," she told him. "I think it's time you retired from this job. There's not much future in it. How about coming home with me next week? Joshua would love you."

Rudy didn't appear too excited at the prospect. Well, she was excited enough for both of them. She'd study the comparisons for a few more minutes, then put them aside. It was time she set herself to the work for which GeneChem paid her.

God, she hated to do it.

She was coming so close.

Seattle
3:35 P.M.

"You wanted me," Seth said as soon as Noah picked up the receiver. "So here I am."

"Just where are you? Venga?"

"My condo in Miami. Venga became difficult. I had to crush a local insect and thought it best

44

to leave. I flew in late last night."

"Christ, I don't need this. Legal trouble?"

"No, actually, the local *policía* declared Namirez had suffered an unavoidable accident."

"What kind of accident?"

"He fell face forward into a bullet," Seth said cheerfully. "Funny how that could happen. Must have something to do with equatorial balance."

"Who was Nam— Never mind, I don't want to know. You're sure the police aren't after you?"

"They wanted to give me a medal. Maybe even put up a statue in the town square."

"Then why are you on the run?"

"I don't run. That's undignified. I just walk quickly, very quickly. Namirez had partners who wouldn't appreciate his demise at a very sensitive time in their endeavor." He paused. "Why did Tony call me? RU2?"

"Things may be coming to a head. I wanted you where I could get in touch with you."

"In Seattle?"

"No, stay where you are. I'll call you when I need you."

"Good. I could use some R and R after being in the jungle for the last six months. Hey, do you want a puppy?"

"What?"

"Well, not right away. Customs didn't like the fact that he didn't have shots and I found him running around in the jungle. I had to put him in quarantine."

"I don't want a puppy."

"I think you should have a dog. It goes with pipe and slippers and hearth and home. He'd be an asset to a sedentary type like you. Maybe stir you up a little."

"*No, Seth.*"

"I'll try you again when he gets out of quarantine. Give a holler when you need me." He hung up the phone.

Noah found himself smiling. Where the hell had Seth picked up a dog? He probably wouldn't find it so amusing when the pup was cleared from customs, he thought ruefully. If Seth had gotten it into his head that the dog was going to belong to Noah, then he'd shake the earth on its axis to make Noah accept it.

But he did find it amusing. Seth always made him feel safer, lighter, better able to cope. Though God knows Seth's method of coping wasn't always to be recommended. It was too simplistic.

I had to crush a bug.

Well, that was certainly simplistic enough.

The phone rang again.

"You've been avoiding me, Noah," Raymond Ogden chided when Noah picked up the receiver. "Is that kind?"

All amusement vanished. "I have nothing to say."

"But I do." He paused. "You don't have the facilities and contacts to produce RU2. I think you need to sell out to me. It would be much better in my hands."

Noah's hand tightened on the receiver. "I don't know what you're talking about."

"Really, Noah. Do you think you could work on something like RU2 for six years and not have it leak?"

"You're admitting to industrial espionage?"

"Why, that's illegal." He paused. "I wasn't worried about it at first. I didn't think you could pull it off."

"What makes you think I did?"

"Let's call it intuition."

He could be bluffing. Noah had kept close rein on every aspect of the testing, never letting one department have more than one portion of the whole. Ogden's call could be a reconnaissance ploy to see if Noah would confirm his suspicions. "Just what do you think RU2 is, Ogden?"

"Don't play with me. Will you sell or not?"

"Let me think about it."

"You're stalling," Ogden said softly. "I'm not going to sit and let you ruin me, Noah. Sell me RU2."

Ogden wasn't bluffing, Noah realized. He knew exactly the threat RU2 posed to him. "And what would you do with it?"

"What do you think? Make a potload of money."

"I don't think so. I think you'd bury it."

"So? You'd still have the millions I'd give you for it."

"True. And what will you do if I don't sell it to you?"

"Destroy you," Ogden said casually. "And your friend Lynski and your little cohort in Oklahoma. I won't hesitate to wipe all of you out of my path."

Oklahoma? Shock rippled through Noah as he realized Ogden was talking about Kate Denby. How the hell had he found out about —

"I want an answer, Noah."

"Give me time to think."

"I can't oblige you. You've been moving too fast lately. You've made me feel most insecure." He paused. "I think you're trying to buy time and play me for a fool. I was afraid that you'd take that path. In fact, I expected it. I've always known that beneath that bad-boy persona, you were something of an idealist. Are you at your desk?"

"Yes."

"Look out the window." Ogden hung up the phone.

Noah slowly returned the receiver to the hook and stood up.

He was knocked to the floor.

Glass shards from the broken window pelted his back.

An explosion. Some kind of explosion . . .

He crawled toward the window. He could hear screams.

He pulled himself up by the windowsill.

"My God," he whispered.

The east wing of the plant was engulfed in

flames. People were running from the ruins. His people . . .

He had to get down there. His plant . . . his people . . . He had to help. . . .

The floor was heaving beneath his feet.

Another explosion. He hadn't heard it.

Damn you, Ogden.

Searing heat.

Pain.

Darkness.

Dandridge, Oklahoma
4:10 P.M.

"Hi, Kate." Alan Eblund got out of the Chevrolet, a smile illuminating his dark brown face as he watched Kate coming down the steps. "Good to see you again." His gaze went to the crowd cordoned off several yards from the GeneChem building. "What you doing stirring up all these nice folks?"

"Those 'nice folks' were trying to take my scalp." Her gaze went beyond him to Michael sitting in the driver's seat. He was frowning. Not good. "I'm sorry Michael thought it necessary to inconvenience you, Alan."

"No problem. What's a partner for?" Alan opened the passenger door for Kate. "Much nicer work than that drug buy we staked out yesterday."

"Thanks . . . I think." Alan had been Michael's partner for the last six years, and she had always

49

liked him. "How are Betty and the kids?"

"Great. Betty's always talking about calling you and asking you to meet her for lunch."

But the call would never come. Her friendship with Betty Eblund had been one of the casualties of the divorce. Betty was a policeman's wife, and her loyalty was with her husband's partner. "That would be nice." She handed Alan her car keys. "Third row back. You'll recognize it. It's the same gray Honda I've been driving for five years."

"Right. I'll see you at the house." He loped away from the car.

"Are you trying to make me look bad?" Michael asked moodily once Kate had settled herself in the passenger seat. "I send you child support every month, and you return the checks. You could have gotten a new car."

She sighed. "I didn't want child support and I don't need a new car. The Honda runs fine. And I had no intention of making Alan think you weren't a good provider."

"Just because we're divorced is no sign that I intend to evade my responsibilities. Nothing will change that."

"I know that's the last thing you'd do." Michael had always been arrow straight and almost fanatically conscious of his duty. He had been very upset when Kate had refused child support. "I just didn't need it. Can we go?" She nodded at the crowd. "I'm tired of looking at those vultures."

"Then you should get a job where they don't

target you." Michael started the engine and backed out of the parking space. "And they must not pay you much if you can't afford a new car."

He seemed fixated on that blasted car. "They pay me enough. The fringe benefits are worth it."

"You mean they let you work yourself into a stupor," he said sarcastically. "Joshua says you work every weekend at home now."

Bristling, she said, "I don't neglect Joshua. You know I always put him first. It's just like you to —" She broke off as she realized she hadn't been in the car five minutes and already he had put her on the defensive. "Stop it, Michael. I'm not going to let you upset me just because you feel guilty." She gave him a weary glance. "Particularly when there's no reason for you to feel you've done anything wrong. You're free to form new relationships. For God's sake, we've been divorced for two years."

"I don't feel guilty. The one has nothing to do with —" A reluctant smile curved his lips. "Smart. You always did see right through me." He paused. "I didn't mean it to be like this. I wish it had been anyone else. I know Benny's a friend of yours."

"These things happen." She looked away from him. "Is it serious?"

"I don't know. Maybe. I like her and it's been a long time for me. She makes me feel good, Kate. She makes me feel ten feet tall."

She forced a smile. "I'd say that's a great start."

"Yeah." His hands tightened on the steering

wheel. "If I'd thought there was a chance for us, I would never — It's really over, isn't it, Kate?"

"You knew that."

"With my mind, maybe." He shook his head. "I did love you, Kate. I just wish you weren't so damn smart. Did you know that you intimidated the hell out of me?"

"What?"

"You scared me. In college you were some kind of whiz kid and I just plodded along."

"You didn't act scared." She added dryly, "As I recall, you tried to lure me into the sack on our first date."

He grinned. "Well, I'm never that intimidated. You were little and cuddly and sexy, and we had great chemistry."

"Cuddly?" she repeated indignantly. "Teddy bears are cuddly. I am *not* cuddly."

"Sorry, but you are. I wanted to snatch you up and take care of you."

Which only showed how faulty Michael's image of her had been, she thought sadly.

He said, "Hell, we had some great times together."

"But I never made you feel ten feet tall."

"Only in bed." His smile faded. "But then it was over and you went your way. I was never important enough to you."

"You were important. I just couldn't make you the lodestar of my existence, and you wouldn't accept that. I wasn't the wife you wanted." She turned to him. "We made a mistake. Don't make another one because you think Benny's my opposite. Make sure this time."

"We've not gotten that far along." He paused. "But she's crazy about Joshua. I wonder if you'd mind if she came along with us to his game tomorrow afternoon."

She felt a flare of anger. It was all very well for her to give up Michael to Benny, but she'd be darned if she'd give her Joshua. "Let's take it slow. You take Benny to the game instead of me. We'll sit together in the bleachers to show Joshua that her being there with you has my stamp of approval and then I'll drive Joshua home after the game."

"If that's the way you want it." He drew up to the curb in front of her house. "I want to make it as easy as possible for you." He turned to face her and said haltingly, "You know I want the best for you, Kate."

The exasperation she felt with him faded as she gazed at him. With his sandy hair rumpled and his brown eyes slightly squinted, he looked like Joshua in one of his more earnest moments. It was hard to hold on to anger when Michael didn't even realize he had been clumsy and tactless. In many ways he was like a big kid, and the boyishness that had first drawn her to him softened her now. "I know you do. I want the best for you too, Michael. You deserve it." She opened the car door and got out as Alan pulled into the driveway. "The coach will be driving the team from school to the field so they can get in some batting practice before the game. You can pick up Benny from work. I'll see you there."

Michael was frowning. "You're sure it's okay?"

"It's okay." She turned away and walked quickly toward Alan, who was coming down the driveway. It wasn't okay. A door had closed and she felt sad and alone and a little inadequate.

Was that how Michael had felt when he was married to her? What a ridiculous notion. He had always been confident in his professional abilities and totally stubborn in his belief about where men and women belonged. She had always known she was more clever than most people in abstract studies, but her father had made sure she realized that there were all sorts of intelligence in the world. The mechanic in the garage she frequented was a genius at what he did. Michael was a wonderful police detective. She had assumed Michael knew she respected him and thought of him as an equal.

Benny would have told him. Benny made him feel ten feet tall. Perhaps it was Kate's fault that she had been impatient about — No, she wouldn't blame herself. Michael's insecurities were his own, just as Kate's were her burden. Still, that knowledge didn't make her feel less sad . . . or uneasy. Things would be different now. If Michael didn't marry Benny, he'd probably form another relationship. If he married again, he'd have a more stable life and want Joshua more often.

"Okay?" Alan was looking at her in concern.

54

She nodded and took the keys. Alan probably knew about Benny and Michael. Partners usually were aware of everything that went on with each other. "I'm fine."

She continued up the driveway. Joshua should be home by now. She'd ask him if he wanted to go out in the yard and have her throw a few balls. She'd look at him and see him smile and maybe find a reason to hug him. She would have to be careful; Joshua was sharp and mustn't suspect anything.

Joshua was still her own. She needed Joshua now.

Phyliss met her at the door, her gaze going to the car at the curb. "Isn't Michael coming in?"

"He's in a hurry. Where's Joshua?"

"I sent him out to play. I didn't want him watching TV. I thought the explosion might upset him."

"Explosion?"

"You didn't hear?" Phyliss closed the door. "I've been watching the story on CNN. Noah Smith is dead."

"What?" Shock riveted her in place. "How?"

"There was an explosion at his pharmaceutical plant." Phyliss went over to the TV and turned on the set. "Actually, several explosions."

"What happened?"

Phyliss shrugged. "They don't know. There are all kinds of combustible chemicals at pharmaceutical plants, aren't there?"

"Yes." Kate walked slowly across the room and

sank down on the couch, staring at the horrible images on the screen. A woman weeping, huddled in a corner. Firemen, gurneys racing with the casualties to the ambulances, buildings in flame. "My God."

"They don't have any idea how many are dead. They think it may climb to over a hundred," Phyliss said.

"And they're sure Smith is one of them?"

"They haven't found his body yet, but he was in his office at the time of the explosion." She nodded at the center wing of the plant that was being devoured by flame. "The firemen haven't been able to get in there to check for survivors."

Kate felt sick. No one could survive in that inferno. "It's terrible." She felt sorry for those poor people who worked in the plant, but she had just spoken to Smith two days ago. He had called her this morning.

And now he was gone.

Noah Smith's face suddenly flashed on the screen before her.

CNN had chosen a picture of him on board his yacht, *Cadro*. He was laughing, his light brown hair wind tossed, dark eyes gleaming with vitality and intelligence. He looked strong and bold and unconquerable.

CNN cut to the burning building.

She couldn't take any more. "Turn it off."

Phyliss pressed the remote button and the screen went dark. "Sorry, I didn't think you'd be this upset. You didn't seem to like him much."

"I didn't know him well enough to like or dislike him." But she had felt as if she knew him. She hadn't realized that a bond of intimacy had been formed by those calls she had found so exasperating. She had grown to recognize his voice, to picture him as they talked. "He was a brilliant man."

"I'd never seen a picture of him. He looks so . . . alive."

"I'm sure that's what CNN was aiming for." She rose jerkily to her feet. "I think I'll go find Joshua."

"He's in the backyard."

Kate moved down the hall toward the kitchen. Only moments before, she had wanted to see Joshua to reassure herself that she wasn't alone. Now that reason seemed petty and selfish. But she still wanted to see her son. Those scenes of death and destruction had shaken her.

She needed to celebrate life.

Three

"Did you hear about Noah Smith?" Charlie Dodd asked as soon as she sat down at her desk the next morning.

"I would have had to be lost at sea not to have heard about it. There's been nothing else on the radio or television since it happened. Tragic."

"The death count has risen to ninety-two."

She stared blindly down at the report in front of her. "What about Smith? Have they found his body?"

"No, but they're looking damn hard through the ruins. They need to rule him out on the bombing."

Her head lifted swiftly. "Bombing?"

"You didn't read this morning's paper?" He nodded at the newspaper on his desk. "There were four bombs set at the plant. That's what caused the explosions."

"But why?" Kate asked, stunned.

"Who knows?" Charlie grimaced. "Who knows why we have forty raving lunatics camped outside? But GeneChem's upping security now. Good thing you didn't take that job, huh? Hell, what am I talking about? It's a good thing I didn't steal it away from you."

She nodded absently, her mind on those horrific scenes of devastation on CNN. "J. and S.

wasn't involved in any government research?"

"You're thinking terrorists? Not as far as anyone can find out." He sat down at his desk. "They're looking closer to home."

"What do you mean?"

"Insurance. J. and S. was reportedly in financial straits the past year. That's why they're combing for Smith's body. They think they may find some kind of igniting device by —"

"They're assuming he blew up his plant *and* himself? That's crazy."

Charlie threw up his hands in mock defense at the harshness of her tone. "Look, I don't know what happened. I only know what I read in the paper."

"Sorry." She didn't know why her reaction had been so violent. But suicide was a surrender, and the Noah Smith she had come to know would not have surrendered. "It's just unfair and the man's dead and can't defend himself."

"Did you hear about Noah Smith?" Benny had appeared at Kate's desk.

"We've already gone through that scenario," Charlie drawled and gave a melodramatic shudder. "Watch it."

"Oh? Well, I really don't want to talk about it anyway. Those poor people . . ." Benny lowered her voice to a tone inaudible to Charlie. "Michael called me last night. You're sure my coming to the game this afternoon is all right with you?"

"I'm sure."

"You know how crazy I am about Joshua, Kate."

"I know." Kate wished she'd just go away. She didn't want to think about Michael or Benny right now. She felt shaken and outraged and she didn't know how much of it was for Noah Smith and how much was for herself. "I'll see you at the game, Benny."

"Right." Benny smiled and turned away. "I'll be there rooting up a storm."

"I was good, wasn't I?" Joshua asked, elated. "Did you see that last double?"

"I saw it." Kate knelt to help him on with his Braves' baseball jacket. "Stand still. It's getting chilly now that the sun has set. I saw everything. You were the hero of the game."

He grimaced. "No, I wasn't. We lost. You can't be the MVP if your team loses."

"My mistake. You looked like an ace to me."

"That's because you're my mom." But he still looked pleased. "Did Dad say anything?"

"Why not ask him yourself?" She stood up and watched Michael and Benny make their way through the crowd of parents gathered in the center of the ball field. "I'd say he looks pretty proud."

"Great game, champ." Michael was grinning broadly as he clapped Joshua on the shoulder. "If you'd had a little help, you'd have slaughtered them."

"Shh." Joshua glanced worriedly at a dejected

group next to the wire batting cage. "Rory did the best he could."

"Sorry." Michael lowered his voice. "But you outclassed them, kid."

Benny nodded. "I jumped up and nearly knocked your mom off the bleachers when you hit that double. Pow!" She smiled at him. "Your dad and I are going to Chuck E. Cheese's for a pizza. How about coming along?"

Kate stiffened, her gaze flying to Michael.

He almost imperceptibly shook his head. No, he'd accepted her decree to go slow. It was probably one of Benny's impulses to ask Joshua.

"Sure." Joshua glanced at Kate. "You coming too?"

Kate shook her head. "I have work to do. I'd better go on home. You run along."

Joshua frowned uncertainly. "You sure it's okay?"

She squeezed his shoulder. "It's okay." She glanced at Michael. "Have him home by nine. It's a school night."

"Right." He looked over Joshua's head at Kate. "Thanks. Come on, slugger." He started across the grass toward the open field designated as the parking lot.

Benny smiled and waved at Kate before falling into step with Joshua.

Kate watched them go. Get used to it. Make it easy for Joshua. This is what divorce is all about. Someone usually gets left alone.

Joshua was looking back over his shoulder.

She smiled with an effort and waved at him.

He didn't wave back. He stopped in his tracks.

He said something to Benny and came running back to her.

"Did you forget something?"

"I'm not going." He jammed his hands in his baseball jacket. "I'm going home with you."

"Why?"

He scowled. "I'm just going home with you. I'm tired of pizza."

He was never tired of pizza. "Benny and your dad will be disappointed."

"Maybe we'll all go next time. Come on, let's go home."

Benny and Michael were looking back at her. Michael shrugged philosophically, took Benny's elbow, and turned away.

Evidently she hadn't handled this right. Joshua must have sensed her loneliness, and it had triggered that fiercely protective streak. She started toward the parking lot. "You'll be bored. Why don't you try to catch up? Benny was looking forward to seeing you tonight. You know you like her."

Joshua fell into step with her. "Sure I like her. She's funny." He looked straight ahead as they left the ballpark. "Dad likes her too, doesn't he?"

"Very much," Kate said. "And that's good. Your dad's been lonely."

"You don't mind her —" He stopped.

"I'd be pretty selfish if I minded your dad being

happy." She stopped at the Honda and got out her keys. "And so would you. So why don't you go to Chuck E. Cheese's and have a great time." She glanced over at Michael, who had settled Benny in the passenger seat of the Chevrolet on the far side of the parking lot. He slammed the door and ran around to the driver's seat. "You still have time."

He shook his head. "I'll stay with you."

God, she was tired of being noble. Why couldn't Michael fight his own battles? One more try. "It's really okay with me if —"

She was knocked against the Honda with bone-cracking force.

"Mom!"

"I'm okay." She reached out blindly to steady herself against the hood, then turned around toward Joshua, who was picking himself up off the ground. "Are you hurt? I don't know what happ—"

The door of Michael's car was lying on the grass only a few feet from where they stood. The car itself was a mass of flames.

"Michael?" she whispered.

Joshua was looking at the flaming wreckage in bewilderment. "But where's Dad . . ."

And then Joshua screamed.

"How you doing?"

Kate looked up to see Alan Eblund climbing the bleacher steps. She drew Joshua closer and wrapped the blanket tighter around both of them.

Cold. She couldn't seem to get warm, but the blanket helped. Someone had given the blanket to them, she remembered dully. That's right, Rory's mother. She had gotten it out of her trunk. Kind. Everyone had been kind.

Alan sat down beside her and said heavily, "You know how I feel, Kate."

Yes, Alan would feel as if he'd lost a brother. "Joshua needs to go home. The police wouldn't let us leave."

"I know."

"He needs to go home."

"I brought Betty, she's waiting in the car. We'll take him home with us."

Her arm tightened around Joshua. "No."

"Listen, Kate, you're almost in shock and so is Joshua. You can't take care of him." He paused. "And he shouldn't be there when you tell Phyliss."

Phyliss. Oh God, she had to go home and tell Phyliss her son was dead.

Michael was dead. Fresh pain washed over her, raw and piercing through the shock.

Alan turned to Joshua. "I know you want to be with your mom, but she needs to be alone with your grandmother for a while. Betty's waiting outside the gate. Will you let her take you to my house?"

"No." Joshua's arms tightened around her. "I've got to stay with Mom."

Alan looked at Kate.

She wanted to keep on holding Joshua, to try

64

to make everything all right. But how did you go about making the sight of your father being blown to pieces go away? Joshua would need her more when the numbness wore off. She nodded. "I'll be okay, Joshua. Please go. I'll pick you up in a few hours."

"But what if —" He reluctantly released her, stood up, and started down the steps. He stopped and whirled on Alan. He said fiercely, "You take care of her."

"You bet," Alan said gravely.

They both watched him as he descended the stairs.

"He saw it?" Alan asked.

She nodded. "We were both in the parking lot."

"He's taking it well."

"The hell he is. He couldn't stop shaking for an hour." She shivered. "And neither could I. What happened, Alan?"

"We think it was a car bomb wired to the ignition." He put his arm around her. "He started the car and . . . boom."

"A car bomb," she repeated. "Who?"

"Michael was a narcotics detective. You know the risks. We were closing in on a big operation. The Bochak combine had made threats to both of us." He shrugged wearily. "Or maybe it was someone he fingered in the past. I'll look into both possibilities. I hope we'll know more when the lab boys get through going over the car."

She felt sick as she remembered that blazing

funeral pyre. "I don't see how there could be anything left to go over."

"You'd be surprised. Michael came to these games every Tuesday?"

She nodded. "And Saturday."

"So, he had a routine going? Someone watching him would know he was going to be here?"

"I guess so." She shook her head dazedly. "It seems impossible. At a Little League game? It shouldn't have happened here. How did they plant the bomb? There were people coming and going all the time."

"Except during the last innings of the game. No proud parent is going to walk out on his kid. The parking lot would have had to be deserted for only a short time. It doesn't take long for an expert to rig a bomb."

"But there were other cars around . . . kids in that parking lot. For God's sake, Joshua almost went with them in the car." She had to stop to steady her voice as that horror overwhelmed her. "It's a wonder someone else wasn't hurt. Whoever did this must be some kind of monster."

"No doubt about it." He looked away from her and the next words came awkwardly. "According to the witnesses, there was a woman in the car."

"Benny. Benita Chavez. She worked at GeneChem."

"Did she have family here?"

That's right, Benny's family had to be notified. Poor Benny. Kate felt a flare of guilt that she

66

wasn't as devastated by Benny's death as she was by Michael's. Benny had been young and full of life. She had a right to be mourned.

"Miss Chavez's family," Alan prompted.

She tried to remember. "No, she had an apartment of her own here, but she mentioned that her mother lived in Tucson. I don't know the address."

"We'll find out from GeneChem." He stood up. "Come on. I'll take you home."

Home to face Phyliss. She got to her feet, her gaze going to the parking lot that was ablaze with blinking lights from the police cars and coroner's van. She didn't want to see that coroner's van at closer range and she didn't want to see the hideous wreckage of Michael's car again. "Where are you parked?"

Alan instantly understood. "You won't have to go back out there. After we checked out your car, I hot-wired your Honda and pulled it around to the other side of the ballpark. I'll have a squad car follow us."

"Thanks." She squeezed his arm. "Thanks for everything, Alan."

"No problem." He hesitated. "The reporters got here the same time I did. I'd advise you not to take any calls. They might upset you."

"More than I am already? I doubt it. But I've no desire to talk to the press."

"There may be innuendos . . ." He sounded uneasy. "You know, divorced wife . . . new girl-friend."

She stared at him, shocked. "You said Michael's death was drug related —"

"Sure," he interrupted. "But you know how reporters are always digging, looking for an angle. I'll handle them for you. Just don't answer the phone."

"Don't worry, I won't. I'll turn off the ringer," she said grimly. "That's all Joshua would need."

"We'll watch over Joshua." His hand on her elbow was firm but gentle as he helped her down the bleacher steps. "You just take care of yourself and Phyliss."

Kate stared at the front door.

She didn't want to go in. If she went in the house, she'd have to see Phyliss and tell her —

Alan opened the passenger door. "I'll call you tomorrow."

She nodded. She had to get out. She had to go in the house. Someone had to tell Phyliss. Someone who loved her and had loved Michael.

Michael . . .

Oh God, don't fall apart now. "Thanks, Alan." She got out of the car and walked toward the house.

Michael laughing, Michael passionate, Michael angry.

Michael proud and tender at the hospital when Joshua was born.

Michael alive.

She could feel the tears running down her face as she opened the front door.

Phyliss was watching TV. "Good game?" she asked without turning around.

"Phyliss."

Phyliss's head jerked around. "Kate?" She saw Kate's face and jumped to her feet. "What's wrong? Joshua?"

"No." Hold on tight. Don't break down. She had to get the words out. She moved across the room and took the other woman in her arms. "Not Joshua, Phyliss."

"I keep remembering him as a little boy," Phyliss whispered. "His first day at school. Christmas . . ." Tears flowed down her cheeks. "Isn't that silly? I can't think of him as a grown man. All I can think of is that little boy." She closed her eyes, her face twisted with pain. "They killed my little boy."

"Phyliss . . ." There wasn't anything Kate could say to ease her agony. She could only hold her and weep with her and try to make her feel that she wasn't alone.

It was hours later when Kate was able to leave Phyliss and go to Alan's to pick up Joshua. He was tearless and silent on the way home. Shock? If it was, she would have to deal with it tomorrow. They all needed to go to bed and try to rest.

She didn't get Joshua and Phyliss settled until nearly midnight. Finally she was able to close the door of her own room behind her. But she knew she wouldn't be able to sleep. The hurt was still raw and burning though the tears had been exhausted.

Or maybe not.

She could feel her eyes sting as the desolation washed over her again.

Michael . . .

"We have to go back to the house now." Kate gently nudged Phyliss away from the open grave. "Some of Michael's friends are dropping in to see you and pay their respects."

"Yes." Phyliss still didn't move. "It's not fair. He was such a good man, Kate."

Kate blinked back a hot rush of tears. "Yes, he was."

"We didn't always agree, but even when he was a kid he tried to do what he thought was right. That's why he became a policeman."

"I know."

"And they killed him for it."

"Phyliss."

"I'll shut up. I'm making this hard for you."

"Talk all you please. Just come away from here now."

Phyliss looked around her and said dully, "Yes, everybody's gone, aren't they? Where's Joshua?"

"Alan Eblund and his wife took him back to the house."

"I always liked Alan."

"We should go too. I'll bring you back tomorrow."

"In a minute." She looked back at the grave.

"You go back to the car. I want a little time alone to say good-bye to my son."

Kate didn't want to leave her alone. Phyliss had held up wonderfully during the three days since Michael's death, but Kate could tell she was very delicately balanced. "I'll wait."

Phyliss's gaze never left the grave. "I don't mean to be unkind, Kate. You've been wonderful to me, but I don't want you here right now."

Kate flinched and then nodded jerkily. "I'll wait at the car." She strode away from the grave and down the path toward the cemetery gates, eyes stinging. Phyliss hadn't meant to hurt her, but the hurt was there. Hurt and guilt. Phyliss was right. She didn't belong. Michael was her first love, the father of her child, and she had let their marriage splinter. She should have tried harder. She should have listened instead of gotten angry when he —

A hand encircled her wrist and she was jerked behind a huge oak tree bordering the path.

Her heart leaped with fear as a hard callused palm covered her mouth.

"Don't scream." The voice was hoarse, masculine. "I'm not going to hurt you."

She didn't scream. Instead she sank her teeth into the hand pressed to her lips. At the same time she kneed the bastard in the groin.

He grunted with pain. "Christ." He sank against her, but his hold didn't loosen. "Listen to me."

"Let me *go*."

"Just listen to me." He pushed her back against the tree, glaring down at her. "And, by God, if you knee me again, I'll strangle —" He drew a deep breath. "I didn't mean that. I'm not going to rob you or rape you. I just had to —"

"My God," she whispered, staring up at him incredulously. "But you're dead."

"I would have argued that with you a minute ago. Until you almost killed me with that knee," Noah Smith said.

There was no doubt about it, she realized dazedly. He was dressed in jeans and a gray sweatshirt, not a business suit or yachting outfit. His left cheek was bruised, there was a cut at his hairline, and his hands were bandaged. But the man standing before her was definitely Noah Smith. "You jumped out at me. I thought you were going to —" None of that was important. "What are you doing here?"

"I have to talk to you." He scowled. "And I couldn't get near you, dammit. Do you think I wanted to lurk in a graveyard like some kind of ghoul? You weren't answering the phone and your house was crawling with cops and well-wishers."

She was jolted out of the shock that held her immobile. "I have to get back to the house. I don't know why you're —"

"I won't take long." He spoke quickly. "I want you to meet me at the King Brothers Motel on Highway 41 tonight. Room 24. Come as soon as you can get away. I'll be there all evening. Bring your son and pack enough for an extended stay."

"Why should I do that?"

"To save your life." He paused. "And maybe your son's life too."

Her mouth dropped open. "You're crazy."

"Park your car around the corner from your house and be careful when you leave. If you see anything strange, go back in the house and call me."

"Take Joshua? My son is mourning his father's death. I'm not dragging him out of the house on a wild-goose chase."

"Okay, leave him. We'll try to go back for him. It might be safer for him anyway. Just come yourself."

She shook her head. "Why doesn't anyone know you're alive?"

"I'll explain that to you tonight."

"Explain it now."

"Because I want to stay alive," he answered simply. "And I want you to stay alive."

"But I have nothing to do with you and your problems."

"You have everything to do with me." He paused. "And our problems are showing a remarkable similarity. My plant was blown up. Your ex-husband's car was blown up a day later. According to the papers, the police said if you'd followed your usual custom, you and your son should have been in that car."

"Michael was murdered by drug dealers."

"Was he? I think he was an innocent bystander.

You were the target."

"Bull."

"All right. I know it sounds crazy unless you know — Let me think."

"I can't waste any more time. My mother-in-law will be —"

"Okay, I've got it. According to the newspapers, the timer that set off the bombs at my plant was Czechoslovakian built. Ask the police about the timer that destroyed your ex-husband's car." He glanced beyond her. "Someone's coming. I've got to go. Don't tell anyone you've seen me." He released her wrists and stepped back, his gaze holding hers. "And come tonight. I'm not lying. I'm trying to keep you alive. You've *got* to live."

He turned and walked away quickly.

She stared after him. The man must be totally insane.

"Who was that?" Phyliss was standing beside her, her gaze on Noah Smith's retreating back.

"Just someone from the lab expressing his condolences." The lie tumbled out before she had time to think. Why was she protecting him? His story was a wild hodgepodge of crazy —

"He looks familiar." Phyliss was frowning. "Have I met him?"

She was too upset and confused to deal with Smith or his story. She had no intention of going to him tonight, and there was something distinctly fishy about his not wanting anyone to know he had survived the fire. Still, the raw urgency of his appeal had shaken her.

But worrying about Noah Smith's wild accusations would have to wait. Right now there were people at the house for the wake, and she had her final duty to perform. "I don't think you know him." She took Phyliss's arm. "Come on, let's get home to Joshua. He needs us."

"The kid seems to be holding up pretty well." Charlie Dodd awkwardly balanced his coffee cup in one hand and a sandwich in the other. "How you doing, Kate?"

Kate's gaze followed his to Joshua sitting across the crowded room with Alan's oldest boy, Mark. He looked so pale and grown-up in his blue suit, she thought with a wrenching pang. For once, his hair was neatly combed and he'd tried to plaster down the cowlick. He hadn't worn the suit since Christmas, and he'd almost outgrown it. She'd have to buy him a new one soon. "We're both doing well, Charlie. Thanks for coming."

"Hey, I just wish I could do more. Benny's being buried in Tucson, but did you hear there was going to be a memorial service for her here on Tuesday?"

She nodded. "I'll be there."

"I heard you were taking a week's leave. I just wondered if you were planning on going away."

"Familiar surroundings are always a comfort. I just need to spend more time with Joshua and Phyliss right now."

"Can I do anything? Take over any of your work? Bring anything home for you?"

"No, I'm pretty caught up. I may stop by the office to pick up a few reports later." Her gaze returned to Joshua. "Not now."

"Well, just let me know."

"I will." She turned and smiled at him. Tall and lanky, Charlie always reminded her of Disney's rendition of Ichabod Crane, and in his dark suit, he looked even more awkward than Joshua. She could tell this type of situation wasn't easy for him, and he was really being very thoughtful. Everyone at GeneChem had been very understanding. "But there's really nothing you can do."

He gave a sigh of relief as he set the cup of coffee down. "Then may I go? I know I should stick around and be comforting but I'm really lousy at it."

She waved her hand. "Go."

"Thanks." He bolted toward the door.

Kate set her own empty cup down and glanced at the clock. It was only a little after five. When would they all leave? God, she was tired. Phyliss looked exhausted too. There was such a thing as too much kindness.

"Should I start the mass exit?" Alan was beside her. "I think you need to be rid of the lot of us."

"You've been wonderful, Alan." Her eyes filled with tears. "You and Betty both. I don't know what I would have done without you."

"You'd have managed. No matter how tough things got, you always managed. Michael was always boasting about how smart you were."

"He was?" She shook her head. "I don't think 'boasting' is the word you're looking for."

"No, he was proud of you. And he always cared about you. You can still admire what you have trouble living with." He squeezed her shoulder. "But sometimes we all need a little help. If Betty or I can give a hand, call us. Maybe Joshua would like to spend a few days with us."

"I'll ask him." Her gaze went to Joshua. "I'm worried about him."

"I thought he was acting pretty normal."

"Too normal. I haven't seen him cry since you brought him home."

"You know the department has a psychologist who can help if either you or Joshua have trouble with . . ." He stopped. "Witnessing the death of a loved one is pretty traumatic. Particularly when you see . . ."

"Them blown up before your eyes," she finished when he broke off again. "I hope that won't be necessary, but I won't hesitate if Joshua starts having trouble." She paused. "Have you found out anything?"

"The school security guard knows most of the parents and saw no one suspicious arriving before the game. Whoever did this must have arrived after everyone was in the bleachers."

"No leads?"

"We're exploring the drug connection and

we're rounding up anyone who might have had a grudge against Michael."

"Any evidence from the explosion?"

"Not much."

"Did you find the timer?" She hadn't known she was going to ask the question until it came out.

He nodded. "Very sophisticated."

"Can you trace it?"

"We'll trace it. It may take a little time. It's not a local product. It was made in Czechoslovakia."

She felt as if she'd been punched in the stomach. It could have been coincidence. It didn't mean that Noah Smith's ravings had any basis in fact.

"We shouldn't be talking about this. You look like you're ready to pass out." He turned away. "I'm going to clear these bozos out so you can get some rest."

"Thanks," she said faintly.

Czechoslovakia. It didn't have to mean anything. Michael had died because of his job. It had not been because of her. No one would want to kill her.

"Tough day." Kate sat down on the bed beside Joshua and carefully tucked him in. "Thanks for being a trooper."

"S'okay." Joshua's eyes were closing. "It will be better tomorrow, won't it, Mom?"

She nodded. "With each day it'll get a little better." Lord, she hoped she was telling the truth.

"I'll miss him. He was one of the very brightest links."

"What?"

"Your grandfather used to say that nothing is ever lost, that nothing really fades away, that it comes back brighter than ever."

"You hardly ever talk about Grandpa."

"Because it hurts, not because I don't remember him. He's always with me." She brushed her lips across Joshua's forehead. "Just as your dad will always be with you as long as you remember him."

"I'll remember him." He turned his head and looked at the wall. "Why do people have to die? It's not fair."

What could she say? "Sometimes bad things happen." Great, Kate, very profound. That explains everything. That will be a great help to him.

"But you won't die, will you?"

Her arms closed tightly around him. She whispered, "Not for a long, long time."

"Promise?"

"Promise."

Don't make me a liar, God. He can't take it right now.

She felt him relax against her. "Shall I turn out the light?"

"Can I have it on tonight? I had a dream last night."

"Why didn't you call out? I would have come to you."

"You were sad."

"That doesn't mean I don't want to be with you." She paused. "Do you want to talk about it?"

"No," he said sharply. "It's over. Dad and Benny are dead. What's there to talk about?"

She felt a ripple of shock at the harshness of his voice. "Sometimes it makes things easier to talk about bad things."

"It's over. I don't want to think about it anymore. I'm not going to ever think about it again."

Denial. She should have known he was being too controlled. No wonder she had not seen him cry since that day it happened. She must have been blind not to have seen the wall he had built around himself.

"Well, if you do want to talk, and not to me or your grandmother, Alan will take you downtown to see someone at the precinct."

"A shrink," Joshua said with disgust.

"A doctor, like me and your grandfather," she corrected. "A doctor who helps you understand yourself and what you're feeling."

"A shrink."

"Whatever." She stood up. "I'll leave my door cracked open so I'll hear you if you call out. Good night, Joshua."

"G'night, Mom."

She paused a moment outside the door before she went back to the living room to join Phyliss. She wished she could just go to bed, cover up her head and go to sleep and forget about Michael and that closed casket. She couldn't really blame Joshua for not wanting to face it.

Only a little while longer.

"How is he?" Phyliss asked when Kate joined her in the living room.

"Hurt. Sad. Scared." Kate grimaced. "Like us."

"It will take time."

Kate nodded. "But he's not making it easy for himself. He's trying to pretend he's not feeling anything."

"Maybe he's the smart one," Phyliss said. "We all have our own way of adjusting to the unacceptable. I wish I could close it out."

"This way may come crashing down on him and everyone around him. If he's too much for you, let me know."

"It will be good for me to be busy." Phyliss stood up and wearily arched her back. "And Joshua's always a blessing. We'll help heal each other."

Kate watched her as she moved toward the front door. "Where are you going?"

"Just to turn out the porch light. Time to go to bed." She opened the door and took a deep breath. "It smells good out here. Spring is coming. The house is so stuffy. All those people . . ."

"Nice people."

"One of those nice people left their car at the curb down the street."

"What?"

"There were so many of Michael's friends from the precinct. Maybe one of them decided to go somewhere with one of his buddies."

"And maybe it belongs to one of the neighbors."

Phyliss shook her head. "I know all the neighbors' cars. No, it's one of Michael's friends."

Kate slowly moved toward the door.

The car parked in front of the Brocklemans' home was a late-model Ford. At least, she thought it was a Ford. The car was parked three houses down from the nearest streetlight and was only a shadowy form.

And there was another shadow. Someone sitting behind the wheel.

She hurried to the hall closet and reached up for the safety gun box Michael had given her.

"What are you doing?" Phyliss asked.

"There's someone in that car. It won't hurt to check it out." Kate punched in the combination and drew out the Lady Colt. She grabbed a raincoat from the closet and draped it over her arm, hiding the pistol. "You know all those stories Michael used to tell us about thieves targeting homes where there have been bereavements."

She moved out of the house and down the steps.

"Kate." Phyliss was standing on the doorstep behind her.

"It's okay." She grinned at her over her shoulder. "I'm not going to shoot anyone."

"You have no business going out there. It's foolish."

It was foolish, Kate thought, even as she moved down the street toward the car. She should have called Alan. He would have sent someone. The man out there might be perfectly innocent, a friend of the Brocklemans. It was Noah Smith and his crazy insinuations that had prompted this idiocy.

The car window was rolled down and she could see sleek dark hair pulled back in a long ponytail, concave cheeks, silver gray eyes sunk beneath bushy black brows.

"Hi," Kate said after she stopped beside the car. "Nice evening."

"Real nice." The man smiled. "A little cool. You should put that raincoat on if you're going for a walk, Dr. Denby."

She relaxed a little. "You know me?"

He shook his head. "But I knew Michael. I worked with him a few times. A great guy."

"You're with the force?"

"Oh, sorry, I should have introduced myself. I thought Alan told you who was going to have first watch." He nodded. "I'm Todd Campbell."

He didn't look like a Todd. Now that she was closer, he appeared even more exotic than at first glance. Except for the gray eyes, he looked Native American. Dark hair, aquiline nose. He even wore some kind of beaded necklace around his neck. Not that his apparel should mean anything, she told herself. Cops on stakeout had to look like everyone else, and the faded jeans and chambray shirt he wore appeared clean and commonplace. "Alan sent you?"

"He wanted to make sure you weren't bothered by reporters or any other scumbags."

It made sense. The man was affable and appeared to be genuine. "Then you won't mind if I check your credentials."

"Mind?" He smiled and reached into his pocket. "I wish I could get my wife to be as careful. She lets anyone in the house."

She took the badge and ID, scanned them, and handed them back to him. "Thank you." She turned away and started back to the house. "You won't care if I call Alan and check?"

"No way. I'd be disappointed if you didn't. Michael taught you right." Todd waved cheerfully at Phyliss, who was standing in the vestibule, before bending down and turning on the radio. "You go to sleep and have a good night. I'll be here to protect you."

Phyliss was frowning as Kate reached her. "Everything all right?"

"Probably." Of course it was all right. She was just being paranoid. "He says Alan sent him to watch the house."

"That was nice of Alan." She shut the door behind them and took the raincoat from Kate. "Now will you put up that gun? You looked like Sam Spade striding out there."

"Who's Sam Spade?"

"Forget it. Generation gap." She took down

84

the safety box and stared pointedly at the gun. "Let's get that thing out of the way."

"In a minute." She reached for the phone on the hall table, opened her phone directory, and found Alan's number. "I just want to check with Alan."

"At this hour?"

"I'm sure everything's all right. I'll just feel better if I check." She punched in the number. "It's only a little after ten."

"Hello," Alan answered.

He sounded drowsy. Guilt flooded her. "I didn't want to disturb you, Alan."

"No, it's okay." He was obviously smothering a yawn. "Do you need to talk?"

"No, I just wanted to thank you for the man you stationed outside the house."

There was a silence. Then, "What the hell are you talking about?" Alan sounded wide-awake now.

Her hand tightened on the receiver. "Todd Campbell. The officer you asked to watch over the house."

"I don't know any Todd Campbell." He paused. "I don't like this, Kate."

Neither did she. She was suddenly scared to death. She looked at the front door. Jesus, had Phyliss locked it? "Lock the door," she whispered.

Phyliss didn't question. She was at the door, turning the bolt the next instant.

"He told you he was with the department?" Alan asked.

"I saw his credentials."

"Christ, Kate, you know credentials can be faked. What kind of car did he have?"

"Late-model Ford."

"Did you get his license number?"

"No." And she thought she had been so careful. "But I went out and talked to him. He knew you. He knew Michael."

"The hell he did. He could have found out a lot of information from the newspapers. That's usually how they zero in on a victim. I don't think you're in danger now that he knows you're aware he was casing the place. It was probably one of those ghouls who prey on bereaved families."

"That's what I told Phyliss."

"I want you to go to the window and see if the car is still there."

She took the portable phone with her as she crossed to the window in the living room. Relief poured through her at the sight of the empty street. "He's gone. The car's gone."

"Good. Now make sure all the doors and windows are locked tight. I'm going to send a black-and-white to watch the house tonight. He'll be there in a few minutes. You'll be perfectly safe. Do you want me to come out?"

"No, go back to sleep, Alan. Thanks for everything. I feel much better now."

"Okay, I'll phone you tomorrow morning. If you get nervous, just give me a call."

"Don't worry, I will." She hung up the phone

and turned to Phyliss. "He's sending a black-and-white to watch the house, but he doesn't believe it's really necessary. He thinks we were being cased for a robbery."

Phyliss shook her head. "How can people be so terrible? To try to invade a house of mourning."

"He said to lock up the house, just in case."

"It's already locked up."

"Then go to bed. I'll wait here until I see the black-and-white." She brushed a kiss against Phyliss's cheek. "Try to sleep."

Phyliss turned away and moved heavily down the hall toward her room. "Terrible . . ."

Kate's hands clenched in helpless rage. Phyliss, whom Kate had never associated with age, at this moment looked like an old woman. It wasn't enough she'd had to face Michael's funeral today, but that creep had —

She stiffened. Headlights were spearing the street outside.

The black-and-white.

She relaxed as the police car slid to a stop at the curb outside the house. Safe. A young officer got out of the car and waved at her. She waved back and turned away from the window. Everything was all right now. She could go to bed . . .

The hell she could. She wasn't going to be fooled again. She took down the license number of the black-and-white and called the station to verify it.

It checked out.

She still didn't go to bed. She went to Joshua's room.

She checked the locks on the window and then stood looking down at him. He was sleeping deeply, thank God. She could feel tears sting her eyes. She had almost lost him. If he'd obeyed her urging to go with Michael and Benny, he'd be dead too.

To save your life. And maybe your son's life too.

She wouldn't think about Noah Smith's words. No one had a reason to kill her.

The timer that set off the bombs at my plant was Czechoslovakian built.

For all she knew, that could be coincidence.

And the thief with amazingly authentic credentials who had staked out her house?

All the more reason for her to stay here safe and sound and not tear across town on a wild-goose chase.

Joshua stirred and turned on his side.

Oh God, she had almost lost him.

Jonathan Ishmaru punched in Ogden's number on the Ford's car phone.

"Ishmaru," he said when Ogden picked up the phone. "It can't happen tonight."

"Why not?"

"I had to leave the neighborhood. She came out and questioned me." He stared ahead at the lights streaming down the highway, remembering Kate Denby standing only inches from him. He had been tempted to get out of the car and finish her, but that would have meant getting only one of his targets. "And then she said she was going to call Eblund."

"Where are you?"

"About twenty miles from the house. I'll go back tomorrow night."

"And get your ass thrown in jail?"

"I'll be prepared."

"So will she. The place will probably be crawling with cops." Ogden paused. "A bomb worked before. We'll find a way of making it look like some kind of mob hit. It's not unusual for them to make an example of the whole family. It will be safer than trying to go inside and kill them. That's what you're to do."

He had expected this from Ogden, Ishmaru thought contemptuously. He always chose the coward's way to vanquish enemies. "I gave you your bombs in Seattle. I even planted one here. You promised me the next one I could do my way."

"You bungled it. I want you to change cars and go back tomorrow and plant a device. But don't let her see you, for God's sake."

"My way. I'll go in and kill the grandmother and the child and then make Kate Denby's kill look like a suicide because she murdered the others." He added regretfully, "But it would have been more effective tonight after the funeral."

"You stupid Indian, who do you think is paying you?" Ogden hissed. "You'll do what I tell you."

Ishmaru smiled. It was Ogden who was stupid

for thinking that he did this for the money. Ogden didn't understand the glory. He didn't understand the triumph.

He didn't understand coup.

"I'll call you tomorrow night," Ishmaru said. He hung up the phone, reached into the glove compartment, and drew out the Polaroid he'd taken of Kate, Joshua, and Phyliss Denby at Michael Denby's funeral. He propped it on the dashboard where he could occasionally catch glimpses of the three as he drove. It always gave him pleasure to anticipate the coming triumph.

That Kate Denby had not been in the car that he'd rigged with the bomb was actually a good thing. On no account would he use a bomb again. It was too frustrating. All those lives gone and not one coup.

But he would have three tomorrow night. A knife for the child and the grandmother and a bullet for Kate Denby. Pity. He regarded using his hands as the ultimate coup, but he had to give Ogden something. Ogden wanted no questions asked, and Ishmaru tried to comply as long as he was given what he wanted.

And he wanted Kate Denby. She had been a surprise to him when she had marched out to confront him with that gun held ready under the raincoat. She had been unafraid, like a warrior going into battle. There were few warriors left in the world. It had pleased him to find one facing him tonight. Even if she was a woman and probably not worthy of the title. But in this day and age one must accept warriors where one found them.

He frowned as his gaze fastened on her figure in the picture. She reminded him of someone but he couldn't quite . . . Oh well, it would come to him.

It did come to him. Emily Santos. Twelve years ago . . . A small, unimportant job. It was before he had become recognized as the warrior he was. Her husband had paid him to kill the woman for the insurance money. She had been small and blond and had fought him like a tiger. He reached up and touched a small white scar on his neck. Yes, he could see Emily in Kate Denby.

Really see her? he wondered suddenly. Had Emily's spirit come back to take revenge? The thought intrigued him. If such a thing was possible, then Kate was indeed worthy of his attention. What a battle could rage between them.

He reached out and touched the photograph. "Emily?" It sounded right. But he must be sure. He would think about it.

He smiled at Kate/Emily in the photograph. She had a lovely throat. He almost hoped things would not go well tomorrow night so he could tell Ogden that the suicide scenario had been impossible to maintain.

He had not had his hands on the throat of a warrior in a long time.

Four

"Okay, talk to me," Kate said as soon as Noah Smith opened the door of the motel room. "I'll give you thirty minutes. I have to get back to my son."

"Nothing like pressure." Noah stepped back from the door. "What if I can't talk that fast?"

"I don't think you'll have any problem." She entered the motel room and glanced around her. Shabby, clean, impersonal, like a million other third-rate motel rooms. "You did pretty well at the cemetery."

"I was motivated. I didn't know when I'd get another chance at you." He pulled back the curtain at the picture window and looked out into the parking lot. "I don't suppose you noticed if you were followed?"

My God, he was acting as if he were expecting a commando raid, Kate thought. "I noticed. I was careful. Nobody followed me."

He let the curtain swing closed. "I'm surprised. I didn't think you believed me."

"I didn't believe you. I still don't believe you."

"Then why are you here?" His gaze narrowed on her face. "Something happened?"

"The timer was Czechoslovakian."

"And?"

"There was a man outside my house tonight.

He had police credentials but he wasn't police. He knew about Michael. He knew about Michael's partner, Alan. Alan thought he was staking the house out for a robbery."

"But you don't?"

"He could have been."

"But you're suspicious enough to have come here."

"Those credentials were very good. I saw my husband's badge and ID for years, and I'd be hard to fool."

"I'm glad to see you're being logical."

"I don't feel logical. I feel very emotional." She met his gaze. "You said my son was in danger. If I decide you're lying, I'm going to walk out of here and tell the world Noah Smith is alive and definitely up to no good."

"Good and bad are always relative." He held up his hand. "Okay, I won't wax philosophical. Neither of us is in the mood for it."

He looked tired, she noticed suddenly. Not only tired but bone weary. "Were you hurt in the fire?"

"Minor concussion." He glanced down at his bandaged hands. "First-degree burns. I'll take these bandages off tomorrow."

"How did you get out? That office building was in flames. I saw the film of the explosion on CNN."

"So did I." His lips tightened. "Two days later, after I woke up."

He still hadn't answered her. "How did you get

out?" she repeated.

"My friend Tony Lynski had just come into the building. When he heard the first explosion in the east wing, he ran up to my office. He was in the outer office when the second bomb went off on the floor right below mine. He found me unconscious and managed to get me down the back stairs."

"Then why weren't you in the plant yard with the other wounded survivors?"

"Tony thought it best to bundle me into his car and take me away."

"Why?"

He smiled lopsidedly. "He said that he remembered something I'd mentioned about RU2 and Hiroshima and the comparison leaped out at him after the explosions. He wasn't sure I'd be safe in a hospital. Tony has very good instincts."

She stared at him incredulously. "You're saying that your plant was blown up just to kill you?"

"And to wipe out every vestige of RU2. Judging by the pictures I saw, I'd say he succeeded."

"He?"

"Raymond Ogden. You've heard of him?"

"Of course. Who hasn't?" Smith's story was becoming more and more bizarre. "You're accusing *him?*"

"Damn right." He studied her. "You're having trouble taking all of this in."

"You might say that." She added ironically, "I wonder why?"

"Because you don't know the key pieces. It's like working on a puzzle with only the outside edges finished."

"And is Michael's death one of the key pieces?"

He shook his head. "I told you, he wasn't involved at all. He died only because it was convenient."

She flinched as though the words had struck her. "Convenient?"

"They wanted to make your death look like an accident. He was a policeman in a very dangerous job. If you died with him, it would be assumed that the bomb was meant for him."

"It *was* meant for him."

He shook his head. "It was meant for you."

"No."

"Yes." He shrugged. "Ogden found out about you."

She stared at him. "Found out what?"

"That I needed you. Maybe Ogden thinks you're working with me already. He probably does or he wouldn't place so much importance on you."

"How would he know that you've even contacted me?"

"I thought about that. I had an expert come in and check my phones for bugs every week. She never found any. So I know Ogden didn't have a transcript of our conversations. But he did know enough about you to jump to conclusions. The only thing I can think of is that he probably bribed someone at the phone company to give him a list of my calls. Over the last month you'd appear very frequently. Once he found out your profession, you were targeted too."

"Just like that?"

"Just like that."

"And what about Joshua?"

"Joshua is like your ex-husband. If it's convenient for him to die, he will die."

"A little boy?"

"He will die," he repeated. "Just as ninety-seven of my people died in that goddamn explosion."

My people. The words were laden with both possessiveness and passionate bitterness. No matter what else she doubted, she couldn't disbelieve how strongly he felt about this.

A chill went through Kate as she realized that if one part of his story was true, then the rest might also be true. Michael might have died because of her. Joshua could still die because it was "convenient."

"I'm telling the truth." His intent gaze was on her face. "What reason would I have to lie to you? What reason would I have to come halfway across the country when I'd be safer hiding out?"

"I don't know." She jammed her hands into her jacket pockets so he wouldn't see that they were shaking. "I don't know why you'd have to hide. I don't understand any of this. I don't know why anyone would want to kill me just because they thought I'd been hired by you."

"RU2."

"What the hell is RU2?"

He shook his head. "I think you've had enough to digest for right now."

"The devil I have. You say I'm going to be killed because of RU2 and then you're not going to tell me what it is?"

"I didn't say I wasn't going to tell you." He picked up an army green windbreaker from the bed and pulled it on. "I said I was going to give you a little time. Come on, let's go."

"Go? I'm not going anywhere."

"Just down the highway a mile or so," he said. "There's a truck stop and I need a cup of coffee."

"Then get one after I leave."

He shook his head. "Now." He opened the door. "I still have ten minutes left and we'll spend them at the diner."

She stared at him in frustration. It would probably take ten minutes just to get to the diner. But extending the thirty minutes she'd agreed to give him wasn't what bothered her. She felt frightened, uncertain and about to lose control. It was as if she'd fallen into quicksand the moment she'd walked into Smith's motel room.

"Stop fighting me," he said wearily. "We'll take both cars so that you can leave when you like. What's one cup of coffee?"

He was right, she was fighting over a triviality, she realized. It was the fear that had made her instinctively strike out. She didn't like being afraid. If you were afraid, you couldn't think, and she had to think and make judgments. For herself and for Joshua.

She brushed by him on her way out the door. "Okay. *One* cup of coffee."

"One cup of coffee?" she asked sarcastically as she gazed at the empty plates in front of Noah. "You must have ordered half the menu."

"I was hungry," he said simply. "I had to hang around the motel room all evening. I didn't want to miss you." He lifted his fork with the last bite of apple pie and grinned at her. "And it was partly true. You had one cup of coffee." He waved his hand at the waitress. "And it's time you had another."

"Do you always have this big an appetite?"

He nodded. "I like good food."

But he looked as compact and tough as barbed wire. She said sourly, "And I suppose you're one of those disgusting people who never put on a pound."

"Sorry." His gaze ran over her. "You can't have any problems with weight."

She scowled. "I run every day. If I didn't exercise, I'd be a blimp."

"But an interesting one." He turned to the waitress who was hovering at his elbow. "Could we have more coffee?" He smiled. "And one more piece of pie, Dorothy?"

She smiled back as she served them. She'd been smiling at Noah since they'd walked into the diner, Kate thought. Women probably always smiled at Noah Smith. He had animal magnetism and charm. For the few minutes he'd spoken to Dorothy, he had made her feel as if she were the most important woman in his world.

His brow lifted when he saw Kate watching him. "What?"

"Nothing." She grimaced. "I was just wondering if Dorothy was going to stick to you all night or give us some privacy."

His gaze went to the waitress who was now drawing coffee at the urn. "Nice woman." He lifted his cup to his lips.

"Will you answer my questions now?" Kate asked.

"Drink your coffee." He attacked the pie. "I'll be with you in a minute."

She deliberately pushed her coffee cup away. "Now."

He looked up and studied her. "Okay, I guess you don't need the coffee. You've stopped shaking."

She hadn't realized he'd noticed. "I was cold."

"You were scared. You were starting to believe me and it scared the hell out of you." He pushed the pie plate to the side and gazed wistfully down into his coffee cup. He said, "You know, I quit smoking two years ago and the only time I miss cigarettes is after a good meal."

She stared at him in astonishment. "You're an expert on cancer research and you *smoked?*"

"Pretty dumb, huh? I was always going to quit tomorrow." He grimaced. "But tomorrow caught up with me. Two years ago I discovered

I had lung cancer."

Her eyes widened. "I hadn't heard."

"I didn't go public with it." He took a sip of coffee. "And you don't have to look at me so hesitantly. I don't have it anymore. My lungs are clear now."

"I'm glad for you," she said sincerely.

"Me too. Stupidity isn't often so generously rewarded." He smiled. "But it did give me a renewed appreciation for the pleasures of life. Though I wouldn't prescribe the malady for the side effect."

"No." She found it hard to imagine Noah Smith sick or dying; he was too alive. And sitting across from her, looking very relaxed, he seemed very . . . human. Nothing at all like the aggressor he came across as at the medical conference. She found herself pushing his pie plate back in front of him. She said gruffly, "You might as well finish it. Dorothy will be upset."

"Ah, I've aroused your maternal impulses. And all it took was a fatal disease." He dove into the pie again. "Are you a good mother, Kate?"

"Damn good. That's why I'm here."

"For Joshua's sake." He finished the pie and leaned back in the booth. "A good kid?"

"The best."

"But good kids get sick, good kids have accidents, wounds become infected." He looked at her. "Good kids die."

She stiffened. "Are you threatening my son?"

He shook his head. "I wouldn't dare. Even in

a lighted diner, I'd be afraid for my life."

"Then what the hell do you mean?"

"I'm trying to tell you why ninety-seven people died in Seattle and two were killed here in Dandridge."

"Then you're not telling it very well. Why?"

"RU2." He held up his hand as she opened her lips. "I know, I'm getting to it. I was trying to prepare you."

"I don't need preparation. I need answers. What's RU2 and what does it have to do with Joshua?"

"It could save his life," he said simply. "RU2 is a universal immune cocktail. I've developed a drug that will strengthen the cellular immune system enough to repel almost any attack."

She stared at him in shock. "That's not possible," she whispered. "We're twenty years away from anything close to that."

He shrugged. "So I leapfrogged. Six years ago I was studying interluken genes and went down a path that intrigued me. I ran into a treasure trove."

Then maybe tangents are the way to go, Phyliss had said.

She shook her head dazedly. "It's not possible."

"I did it," Noah said. "I couldn't believe it myself at first. And it took another four years of testing and refining to convince me that it wasn't a fluke." He held her gaze. "It's not a fluke. RU2 works, Kate."

"That means . . ." The possibilities were tumbling through her mind. "Alzheimer's, AIDS, cancer . . . You're sure it's universal?"

"If the immune cells are strong enough and the disease isn't in its last stages, RU2 can lick anything I've thrown at it."

"But that's a miracle."

He inclined his head. "Saint Noah, at your service."

"Don't joke, you've done something . . . wonderful."

"I've done something dangerous as hell. At first I was pretty puffed up, and then I became uncharacteristically humble. It was only after I had time to get over the euphoria that I realized what a powder keg I was sitting on. Think about it."

"All I can think about is the lives it will save."

"Ogden can think of something else. About the billions of dollars that are spent on medicines every year that will vanish if sickness virtually disappears. And what about the insurance companies? They're one of the financial behemoths of our society. How do you think they'll like taking a gigantic hit on health and hospital insurance? Religion. They're screaming now that we're violating nature with the small steps we've taken. They'll go ballistic at any major intervention. Shall I go on?"

"Not right now. I'm having trouble assimilating."

"You're doing fine. Take it slow."

"And Ogden killed to prevent you from going

public with RU2?"

"Yes."

"You're sure?"

"He as much as told me he was going to do it only minutes before the explosion."

"He must be a complete bastard."

"Complete."

She was silent a moment, trying to gather her thoughts. "If you already have the cocktail, why did you need me?"

"Present tense, not past. I do need you."

"Why?"

"I need a delivery system for the serum. I think you've got it."

She stiffened. "Why would you think that?"

"You wrote an article for the medical journal."

"Pure speculation."

"Bullshit. You've isolated a gene that keeps cells from rejecting. You've been working on a foolproof plasmic delivery for medication that the cells will accept without throwing them into shock. In your paper you called it a Trojan Horse because it would sneak up on the cells and deliver before they could reject. How close are you?"

She didn't answer.

"Dammit, tell me. Do you think I'm going to steal your patent?"

"I haven't applied for a patent yet." Her reaction had been purely instinctive. Noah had been very open with her, he deserved equal honesty. "But I'm very close."

"How many weeks?"

"Four, maybe five. I have to work on it on my own time."

"Then three if you devote your entire time to it?"

"I can't do that. I have a living to earn."

He leaned forward, his expression intent. "What's your success rate on the last results?"

"Eighty-seven percent."

He slapped his hand down on the table. "My God, that's fantastic."

She could feel the flush of pride warm her cheeks. "I thought so."

"But you'll have to bring the rate up to ninety-eight."

"What?"

"It has to be as close to perfect as possible. RU2 has the wallop of a nuclear missile."

"I wasn't working to provide you with a carrier."

He grinned. "No, but isn't it great that you came along at just the right time?"

"Wait a minute." He was going too fast for her. "How did you do testing if you didn't have an anti-rejection element for the drug?"

"I thought I'd built one into the formula. It worked fine in animal testing. Smooth. No side effects at all." He shrugged. "Unfortunately, chimps aren't people."

"My God," she whispered. "You've tested RU2 on people?"

"One person." He tapped his chest. "Two years ago."

She suddenly understood. "When you were ill?"

"I would have died within six months anyway. I figured I didn't have much to lose." He made a face. "But the cure damn near killed me. I went into shock."

"What saved you?"

"RU2. It grabbed hold in time. I survived and it did the job." He took a sip of coffee. "But it's too rough a ride. It would probably kill a good percentage of those inoculated with it. RU2 will be under fire from the moment I go public. It has to be super safe."

"But my formula and procedure may not be compatible with RU2."

He smiled. "We'll have to see, won't we? It shouldn't take long. Three weeks for you to complete your work. Another month for me to experiment with the best way to combine it with RU2."

"A month? It could take years."

"We don't have years." His smile vanished. "We may not have months. Ogden will eventually find out I'm alive, and the hunt will be on. He's already set his dogs on you. He tried to kill you once. He'll try again."

"If he did try to kill me. I can see how your RU2 could put you in danger, but my connection to you is too tenuous. I've no proof that —"

"If you wait for proof, you'll be dead."

The starkness of his words shook her. "And what am I supposed to do? Call the police and tell them I'm being stalked by a murderer hired by —"

"The police can't be trusted when there's this much money involved," he said flatly.

"The police can always help."

"Look, did you hear the report that J. and S. Pharmaceuticals was in financial trouble?"

She nodded.

"It wasn't. We were doing fine. But there was enough money spread around to assure that the accounting firm who handled our books would issue a false statement."

"Why would anyone pay them to do that?"

"To make it look like I needed the insurance money. If I wasn't killed in the explosion, I'd have to untangle fraud and murder charges before I could move with RU2. Ogden went to all that trouble as a backup. How much do you think he'd be willing to spend when he's on the attack?" He shook his head. "No police. The stakes are too high. We're on our own."

"I lived with a policeman for eight years. I believe in the system. I know it works."

"And your husband never mentioned bribery in the ranks?"

"Of course. There are always a few dirty cops. That doesn't mean I should distrust all of them." She paused. "Or that I should trust you."

"But you do trust me."

She shouldn't trust him. He was a stranger who had told her the wildest story on the face of the earth. Yet she didn't distrust him. She shook her head wearily. "I'm too confused to think right now."

"Then let me do it for you." He took her hand and said softly, "I know what to do, Kate. I've made plans to keep you and Joshua safe."

"While you use me to make your RU2 perfect?" she asked dryly.

"Hell yes, do you expect me to deny it?"

"I don't know what to expect anymore." She pulled her hand away and put on her jacket. "But I'm not going to leave either my or my son's fate in someone else's hands."

"Listen, Kate, the only way you'll be safe is to help me go public with RU2. Once we do that, there's no percentage in killing either of us. Until then Ogden will throw everything he can at us to —" He stopped, studying her. "I'm not reaching you, am I? Okay, go away and think about it. If you change your mind, I'll be at the motel for the next few days."

She nodded and scooted out of the booth.

Noah frowned. "I don't like the idea of you going alone. Why don't you let me follow you home?"

She shook her head. "I told you I wasn't followed."

"Wait."

She looked back at him.

"What did the man outside your house look like?"

"Why?" she asked, surprised.

"It helps to know your enemies. Besides, I have

a few friends I can contact. I might be able to find out who he was."

"Long dark hair worn in a ponytail, high cheekbones, gray eyes. He looked . . . maybe he was Indian. Maybe not. All that Southwest stuff is popular now." She tried to think. "He wore some kind of beaded necklace. I don't know how tall he was. He never got out of the car. He didn't look very big."

"Okay, I think I'll remember." He paused. "Don't go to the police, Kate. It could be dangerous for both of us."

"I'll do what I think best." She hesitated and then said haltingly, "But I don't want you hurt. If what you've said is true, then you've done something extraordinary for all of us."

"Then may I take it you're not going to turn me in?"

She shook her head. "Whatever I do, I'll try to leave you out of it."

"You can't do that." He met her gaze and his tone was almost sad when he said, "You still don't understand, do you? Whether we like it or not, from now on, we're in this together."

He hadn't played her right.

Noah watched Kate walk out of the diner and get into her car. Dammit, he wanted to run after her and shake her, argue with her instead of sitting here on his ass. She didn't come close to knowing the odds against her. He'd only managed to confuse and frighten her, when he'd hoped to sway her to his side.

Not bloody likely. Kate Denby was pure steel and used to making her own judgments.

No, not pure steel. When she had spoken of her son, she had changed, softened. That might be something he could use, a button he could push.

Use.

He wearily leaned back in the booth. So what was the problem? He had known it would come to manipulation, had even planned on it.

But she had been clean and sharp as a scalpel, cutting through the bullshit to the truth. She had sat there across from him with shaking hands and bold, clear eyes. She had been frightened but never lost control. She had attacked when she felt the most vulnerable.

A unique woman.

He only hoped to hell he could find a way of keeping her alive.

He took out his wallet, threw some bills on the table, and rose to his feet. He would go back to the motel, call Tony and see if he'd found out anything more about the victims of the plant explosions. Three of his people were still on the critical list as of yesterday.

"Lars Franklin died," Tony said when Noah reached him fifteen minutes later. "Clara Brookin and Joe Bates are still alive."

"Shit." He closed his eyes, trying to absorb the blow. He had known Lars Franklin since Noah was a boy, and he had been desperately hoping the older man would recover. He had given Lars's daughter a job in his office a few years ago, and her name was on the missing list.

"I'm sorry, Noah. I know he meant a lot to you."

"They all meant a lot to me," he said dully. "All of them."

"I'll keep abreast of the developments. How do I get in touch with you?"

"You don't. I'll call you."

"Dammit, aren't you going to tell me where you are?"

"I've got to hang up now. There's a chance your line might be bugged. I want you to switch to a digital system tomorrow. It's near impossible to trace."

"Why? You made sure no one knows about the lodge and everyone thinks you're dead."

"I told you, Ogden wants everyone connected with RU2 put down. He mentioned your name. Just stay where you are, out of sight. Okay?"

"I can't see why —"

"I have to hang up." Noah pressed the disconnect button and returned the receiver to the cradle.

Lars Franklin. He had thought he was over the worst of the pain and shock, but evidently he was not. It had just been lying in wait.

Go to bed. Go to sleep. Don't think about it.

He couldn't go to sleep. He had something else to do.

He called Seth at his condo in Miami.

A woman answered, her voice breathless. "Hello."

"Let me talk to Seth."

"Is it important?" she asked, annoyed.

"Noah?" Seth came on the line. "Dammit, this isn't a convenient time."

"I'll let you go in a minute. Ogden's man has surfaced. Kate Denby saw him tonight. I need to know what I can about him."

"Name?"

"I don't have one." He rattled off the brief description Kate had given him.

"Sounds familiar. Let me think about it for a while. It will probably come back to me."

"I need it now."

"Too bad. You'll get it when I get it."

"By all means, don't let me disturb you," Noah said sarcastically. "Go back to what you were doing."

"Who stopped?"

Noah heard a woman's giggle before he hung up the phone.

"Ishmaru," Seth said when Noah picked up the phone an hour later. "Jonathan Ishmaru. Crazy son of a bitch but good. Very good. I heard about him down in Mexico three years ago, so I called Kendow."

"Who's Kendow?"

"Information broker. Lives in L.A. Ishmaru thinks he's some kind of Apache or Comanche warrior. Something like that."

"He's Indian?"

"Half Indian, half Arabic. Grew up in East L.A. Hell, that's enough to drive anybody crazy."

"Ogden wouldn't have given the job to someone who wasn't stable. He'd have protected himself with a professional who had all his ducks in a row."

"If they're caught, sane men make deals. Ishmaru would consider captivity a trial by fire."

"And wouldn't bring Ogden down?"

"There's a story about the time he was jailed down in a little southern town after he'd assassinated the town mayor, who was the brother of the sheriff. The sheriff wanted to know who hired him real bad. Before Ishmaru managed to escape, every fingernail on both his hands was torn out. He didn't talk."

"Could he have planted the bombs?"

"Not willingly. He likes to work up close. Real close."

"But he could have done it?"

"Oh yes, he's multitalented. It depends on what he was given as an incentive."

"Does he work with anyone else?"

"No one would work with a crazy bastard who would kill you as soon as look at you. Anything else?"

"Yes, I want you to go to the cabin tomorrow and wait for us."

Seth hung up the phone.

Ishmaru. Noah went into the bathroom,

stripped off his clothes, and turned on the shower. He would have to call Kate tomorrow and tell her what he'd learned. That's all she needed — to know a crazy man was assigned to kill her. He should be glad; this could be the impetus for her joining his camp.

He stepped beneath the warm shower and let the pounding water ease a little of his tension.

He wasn't glad. He was mad and sad and a little jealous of Seth, who had nothing to worry about but pleasing the woman in his bed. He didn't want this guilt and responsibility. He didn't want to scheme to frighten a woman he respected. He didn't want anyone else to die.

So what if he didn't want any of those things, he thought impatiently. There was only one direction he could go now. He would call Kate and hope he frightened the hell out of her. Time was running out. When he moved, it would have to be fast.

And Kate Denby had to be with him.

The black-and-white was still parked in front of the house when Kate pulled into the driveway. She got out, crossed to the front door, and stood under the porch light for a moment so that the officer could see that she was the same woman who had left three hours ago. He waved his hand in acknowledgment. He was a nice young man. He hadn't wanted her to leave the house he was guarding tonight.

Three hours. It seemed more like a century.

She unlocked the door, went into the house, and closed the door softly. She mustn't wake Phyliss. Phyliss had buried her son today and didn't need to worry about why Kate had been wandering around the countryside in the middle of the night. She locked the door and shot the bolt.

Safe.

But she didn't feel safe. A friend and lover had died, a man had stalked her home, and Noah Smith had told her that she and Joshua would be killed if she didn't work with him. Talk about forced labor, she thought tiredly.

Well, it was too much for her to deal with now. She would think about it after she'd had a good night's sleep.

She turned out the lights and moved down the hall. Joshua's door was ajar and she peeked in. She hoped he hadn't called out while she had been away from the house. She hated the thought that she might not have been there for him.

Joshua was sprawled on his stomach, and his cover was on the floor. He didn't stir when she went in and tucked the covers over him again. The threat that had seemed so frightening was fading away as she stood in this room. It was the quintessential Joshua room. A baseball glove hung on a bedpost, faded Star Wars drapes framed the venetian blinds at the window, a Dave Justice book bag lay in the far corner.

I don't know what's best, Joshua.

I think Noah Smith is trying to do something

wonderful. It could help so many people, maybe even you. But it's a dream.

Joshua was her reality.

And she had to protect that reality. Aligning herself with Noah Smith might be the worst thing she could do to keep her son safe. Perhaps it would be better for them to take a trip, disappear for a while until RU2 went public.

She turned away from the bed and left Joshua's room.

She went to the hall closet, got down the safety gun box, opened it, and drew out the Colt. Dammit, she *hated* guns. When Michael had brought the gun home for her, she had agreed to learn how to use it but refused to have the weapon anywhere in the house except in the safety box. Now she slipped the gun in her leather shoulder bag and then carried the purse to her bedroom. She set the bag, flap open, on the floor beside the bed.

My God, a week ago she would never have dreamed she would sleep with a gun within reach.

She could feel tears sting her eyes as she lay down on the bed and nestled her head into the pillow.

Things are crazy, Daddy. I'm so tired of trying to be all things to everyone. I'm not good enough. I'm not smart enough. I need you.

I feel so damn alone.

Marianne was asleep. Seth could hear the soft sound of her breathing.

He rolled over and sat up in bed.

Ishmaru.

Not good.

He got up and moved toward the open glass door leading to the balcony. The soft, warm wind felt good on his naked body. He stared out at the surf below. He'd always liked the freedom of the open sea, and this condo was as different from the crowded houses where he'd grown up as night was from day. God, how he'd hated those places. Funny that he hadn't been able to keep himself from fighting like hell to belong in them. But then he'd been such a contrary little bastard, clawing for a place . . . Thank God, he'd learned to let go and walk away.

But some part of that hungry, desperate kid must still have survived, because one of the first things he'd bought was this condo. He'd kept it all these years. A place to come back to, a haven.

Did Ishmaru have a haven?

He didn't like what Kendow had told him about Ishmaru. He wasn't a man Noah would be able to handle easily.

Seth wouldn't find him easy either, but at least he was used to dealing with vermin. Noah didn't have his experience.

Even when they were in the Special Forces together, Noah had never been cautious enough. He lacked the basic cynicism that made a good fighting man. He always wanted to believe in the best scenario.

Seth didn't believe in much of anything and

knew that most scenarios had to be molded to the shape he wanted.

Yet it was Noah's very lack of caution that had led him to rush in and drag Seth out of the line of fire when he was wounded at Grenada. Seth owed him.

But he had been going to relax and let Noah run the show.

Dammit, Noah was his friend. He couldn't let him blunder in and get himself killed.

He was doing Noah an injustice. Noah wasn't a blunderer. It would be okay. Noah had said he was to go to the cabin and wait.

"Seth . . ."

Marianne was awake again and he knew that tone. He smiled as he turned and moved toward the bed. Marianne never asked for more than he wanted to give. She was usually available when he came back to Miami and asked no questions. She liked sex and a few laughs and then moved on to someone else. So give her what she wants. Take what you want. Forget about Ishmaru.

Let Noah run the show.

Five

"The man's insane?" Kate repeated.

"Sounds like it to me," Noah said. "Doesn't it to you?"

"It may not be the same man. He didn't seem — He was very . . . normal."

"All I'm telling you is what I found out from Seth. Your description rang a bell with him."

"Who is Seth?"

"A friend." He paused. "Can't you see this changes the picture, Kate? Any threat is doubled when you're dealing with someone who won't do the expected."

Kate shivered and closed her eyes. The idea of criminal insanity had always terrified her. How could you protect yourself from a man who had no reason? "His name is Ishmaru?"

"Yes," he said. "I'll be at the motel. Call me."

She stared at the phone after she'd hung up. *Clever, Noah. Tell me just enough to scare the socks off me and then go away and let me brood about it.*

"You're up early, Kate." Phyliss came into the kitchen, dressed in her chenille robe. "Didn't you sleep well?"

"No." She crossed her arms across her chest to ward off the chill that refused to go away. "I've been thinking, Phyliss. Maybe it would be a good idea if we all went away on a little trip."

"Just can't keep away from us, huh?" Charlie Dodd straightened his glasses on his nose as Kate came into the lab. "Or maybe it's me. Have you been harboring a secret passion all these years?"

"That's right, Charlie." Kate smiled as she opened her top desk drawer and rifled through papers for the test results she'd done the day before Michael's death. She was sure she'd put them there. "I just can't help myself."

"I thought as much." He got up and strolled over to her. "What are you doing? I told you yesterday that I'd bring you anything you needed."

Where the hell were they? "I know but I wanted to get these right away." They weren't in the drawer. Maybe she'd stuffed them in her briefcase before she left that day. She'd been pretty upset. "I must be losing it. I guess I took them home."

"Anything else?"

"No." The computer disk with the formula and records was locked in the trunk of her car with her laptop. "I just wanted to study those reports." She picked up the phone and dialed Alan's number at the precinct. It took her a few minutes to get through to him. "Hi, I have a favor to ask."

"That's what I'm here for."

"Could I have the black-and-white at the house again tonight?"

"Sure. I'd already planned on it." He paused. "Any problem?"

"No, I'd just feel better. And could you have a car cruise by every now and then and keep an eye on the house for the next few weeks? I'll be gone for a while."

"Where?"

"I'm not sure. Tomorrow I'm just going to bundle Phyliss and Joshua into the car and take off. It may do us all some good."

"You're not going because you're afraid? There's nothing to be afraid of, Kate. I'll make sure you're safe."

"I just want to get away."

A silence. "Well, keep in touch. I'll make sure everything stays safe and sound here."

"Thanks, Alan." She hesitated. "Have you ever heard of a man named Ishmaru?"

"Don't think so. Should I?"

"I don't know." She didn't know anything, she thought in frustration. That might not even be the man's name. She had only Noah's word for it. "Could you run a check on the name?"

"What's this about, Kate?"

"Could you just do it?"

"Okay. Right now?"

"Whenever you can."

"It will take a little time." He was silent and then said, "You're keeping something from me. I don't like it."

She didn't like it either. "I have to go now, Alan. Thanks for everything."

She hung up.

"I guess you won't be at Benny's memorial

service," Charlie said. "I thought you were staying in town."

She had completely forgotten the service, she realized. She would have to remember to send flowers. "I decided it would be better to have a change of scenery."

"That's what I told you."

"And you're always right."

"Mostly always."

"There's something seriously wrong with that phrase."

"Well, I had to throw in a qualifier. I didn't want to sound too egotistical."

"Perish the thought." She turned to go. "Bye, Charlie. See you in a couple weeks."

"Right. Too bad about Rudy."

She stopped in mid motion and faced him. "What?"

"You didn't hear? Rudy's dead."

"How?"

He shrugged. "Don't worry, it didn't have anything to do with your experiments. It happened two nights ago."

"How can you say that? It could have been a delayed reaction."

He shook his head. "It was a broken neck."

She stared at him in bewilderment. "Broken neck? Was he out of his cage?"

"Nope, must have been some kind of freak accident." He raised a brow. "Hey, don't go into shock. It was a lab rat, not your best friend."

But, dammit, she had *liked* that lab rat. She

had conducted the last four experiments using Rudy, and she had felt as if he somehow shared her pride and excitement as she had closed in on the final solution. "You're sure he wasn't out of his cage?"

"The lab technician said she fed him at six-thirty two nights ago and he was in his cage and happy as a clam." He smiled. "Don't worry. Before you come back, I'll make it my personal responsibility to get you an A1 lab rat with all Rudy's doubtful charms."

"Thanks," she said absently as she headed for the door.

Missing papers. A dead lab rat.

The plant was blown up also to wipe out every vestige of RU2.

Maybe Ogden thinks you're working with me already.

But to kill a lab rat because she was using it for experiments? And GeneChem's security was superb. How could someone have gotten into the building and located her office and lab without anyone knowing about it? It was probably a freak accident, as Charlie had said. Any other explanation was ridiculous.

No, any other explanation was terrifying.

"You have lousy taste in motels," Seth said when Noah opened the door. "I bet it has bugs."

"What the hell are you doing here?" Noah asked. "I told you to go to the cabin."

"I got to thinking about Ishmaru." Seth moved

into the room and shut the door. "I decided you need me here."

"I can handle Ishmaru."

Seth shook his head. "You just think you can." He threw himself in the chair and draped his leg over the arm. "You're not qualified anymore. Maybe you never were. Not to deal with Ishmaru."

"What's so special about Ishmaru?"

"He's crazy . . . and you're sane. You don't understand him."

"And you do?"

"Hell yes, I have my moments of madness too." He grimaced. "Or I wouldn't be here offering to smash the rat." He glanced around the room. "No coffeemaker. Now I know this is a lousy motel. Let's go get some lunch. I haven't eaten since dinner last night."

"I can't leave. I have to wait in case Kate comes." He gazed at Seth. "Go on to the cabin. I mean it, Seth. You should never have come here. I don't like interference with my plans."

Noah's tone flicked like a scourge, and Seth slowly straightened in the chair. "And I don't like orders. In the old days we used to make plans together."

"Not this time. It has to be my way."

"Your way . . ." He studied him. "You know, something just occurred to me. We hadn't seen each other in over six years when you stirred yourself to look me up five years ago. That was after you'd developed RU2."

Noah stiffened. "So?"

"I just wonder if it was auld lang syne or if you were planning to use me even then."

Noah was silent.

It was true, Seth realized. Noah had never been able to lie worth a damn. "You spent a lot of time preparing me to join the show. Talking about the old days so that I'd remember what I owed you. All those weeks on the *Cadro*, the hunting trips that —"

"Don't be a fool. You're my friend. I'd probably have looked you up eventually anyway."

"You just found a reason to do it sooner. I hate to be used, Noah. It leaves a bad taste in my mouth."

"Does that mean you're opting out?"

"No." He smiled crookedly. "You did me a big favor once. I made you a promise and I'll keep it. But that damn RU2 must mean a hell of a lot to you." He rose to his feet and started for the door. "So I'll hurry obediently to the cabin and wait for you."

"Seth." Noah was frowning. "You are my friend. My best friend."

"I know. It snuck up on you, didn't it? My fatal charm." Seth opened the door. "Don't worry, I can't afford to jettison you. I don't have that many friends." He gazed into Noah's eyes. "But I never use the ones I do have. Don't try to manipulate me again, Noah." He started to leave and then paused. "If you want Kate Denby to stay alive, I wouldn't sit on my butt and wait for her. Get moving and keep watch on her, because you can damn well believe Ishmaru will."

"One of her police friends has a black-and-white guarding the house. I have to stay here in case she comes." He added, "And I'm not one of your men, Seth. This is my game."

One that might blow up in his face. Well, what the hell should he care? He'd tried to tell him. "Sure. Your game."

Seth closed the door and moved quickly toward his rental car. He'd been a fool to come here. He should have known Noah would dig in his heels.

And he'd learned more than he wanted to know.

Forget it. It didn't change things for him to know that Noah's white hat was a little dingy around the edges. He still owed him. He was still his friend.

He glanced at his watch. Three thirty-five. He could be on a plane out of here tonight. He washed his hands of Ishmaru. Good luck, Noah.

And good luck, Kate Denby.

The rays of the late afternoon sunlight dappled the path in front of Ishmaru as he ran swiftly through the woods. He always chose a motel that opened onto a wooded area. It was necessary for the preparation for the kill.

He ran faster. His heart was pumping with fierce pleasure.

He was fleet as a deer.

He was unstoppable.

He was warrior.

But warriors should not be guided by fools like Ogden. The kill should be made in a burst of glory, not cool calculation. He had lain awake a long time last night thinking of the kill tonight, the disturbance growing within him.

He reached the summit and stood there, gasping for breath. Below him spread a subdivision with neat, small houses like the one in which Kate Denby lived. If he shaded his eyes, he could see her subdivision just on the horizon. He had been pleased that her house was so close to the others in the neighborhood. It was an exciting challenge for him to move like a shadow among these sheep, to strike boldly.

But Ogden did not want him to strike boldly. Ogden wanted him to hide the act behind lies and deception.

Since it disturbed Ishmaru, there must be a reason. His instincts had told him from the first moment that Kate Denby might be special. Was she Emily sent to challenge him? He would meditate and wait for a sign.

He fell to his knees and dipped his finger into the dirt of the path and painted streaks on his cheeks and forehead. Then he threw out his arms. "Guide me," he whispered. "Let it become clear."

The ancient ones used to pray to the Great Spirit, but he was wiser. He knew the Great Spirit was within himself. He was both the Giver of

Glory and the Punisher.

He stayed kneeling, arms thrown wide for one hour, two, three.

The rays of the sun paled. Shadows lengthened.

He would have to give up soon. With no sign he would have to submit to Ogden's will.

Then he heard a giggle in the shrubbery to his right.

Joy tore through him.

He didn't move. He kept facing straight ahead, but he slanted a glance toward the bushes from the corner of his eye.

A small girl was watching him. She was no more than seven or eight, wearing a plaid dress and carrying a backpack. His joy increased as he realized she had fair hair. Not the same ash blond as Kate Denby's but pale yellow like Emily Santos's. It could be no coincidence; his power must have pulled the child to him.

She was the bearer of the sign. If he could count coup on her, then that must mean he could ignore Ogden and follow the true path.

He slowly stood up and turned to the little girl.

She was still giggling. "You have a dirty face. What are you —" She broke off and her eyes widened. She took a step back.

She felt his power, Ishmaru exulted.

She whimpered, "I didn't mean — Don't —"

She whirled and ran down the path.

He started after her.

It would do no good for her to run.

He was fleet as a deer.

He was unstoppable.

He was warrior.

"Did you pack my laptop and my video games?" Joshua asked.

"They went in the trunk right after your bat and catcher's mitt," Phyliss said. "And don't ask us to stuff one more toy in this car. There's barely enough room for the suitcases."

"All we've got in there are clothes," Joshua said. "Who needs clothes for sleeping? We could take out my pajamas and —"

"No," Kate said firmly and shut the trunk. "Now go into the house and take your bath. I'll be in as soon as I check the tires and oil, and you'd better be in bed."

"Okay." Joshua made a face at her before loping toward the front door.

"He's perking up," Phyliss said. "I think this trip will be good for him."

"I hope so. Will you hold the flashlight for me? It's getting too dark to see."

"Sure." Phyliss took a step closer and aimed the beam of the flashlight as Kate opened the hood and took out the oil stick.

"It's a quart low. We'd better stop at a gas station before we get on the road tomorrow."

"You made up your mind in a hurry," Phyliss observed. "It's not like you."

Kate grinned at her. "Slow, boring, methodical Kate?"

"You said it, I didn't."

"I have a right to an impulsive moment now and then."

"Maybe." Phyliss paused. "And it's not like you to run scared just because some young hoodlum decided to rob us."

"I thought we'd all had enough."

Phyliss's gaze searched Kate's expression. "Is something wrong, Kate?"

She should have known Phyliss was too perceptive not to be aware of Kate's tension. "Of course there's something wrong. We're a house of mourning." She knelt and began checking the air in the left front tire. "Will you go in and see if you can keep Joshua from smuggling his tennis racquet into his pillowcase? He was entirely too sentimental about taking his very own pillow along."

"I thought so too." Phyliss chuckled. "What a schemer." She went into the house.

Joshua was always a good distraction, Kate thought. Or maybe Phyliss had merely allowed herself to be distracted. She had a great respect for personal privacy, both her own and —

"What you got there?"

Kate's heart leaped to her throat and then quieted when she looked up and saw that the man who had spoken wore a blue police uniform. She hadn't seen the police car draw up to the curb, but there it was.

"I didn't mean to scare you." He smiled. "I'm Caleb Brunwick. You're Dr. Denby?"

She felt foolish. No one could look less frightening. Caleb Brunwick was a heavyset man, with gray-flecked dark hair and a lined face. She nodded. "You weren't the one on duty last night."

"No. I just got back from vacation. I took my grandkids to the Grand Tetons. Beautiful country, Wyoming. I've been thinking of retiring there." He squatted beside her and took the tire gauge. "I'll finish this for you."

"Thank you." She stood up and wiped her hands on her jeans. "That's very kind of you. May I see your ID?"

"Oh, sure." He handed her his badge. "Here's my shield. Smart of you to check."

"I'll return this to you after I call the precinct."

"No problem." He moved to the next tire. "Sorry I'm late. There's a little girl missing from the Eagle Rock subdivision about ten miles from here. Since I was going to pass it on the way here, they asked me to stop and make out the report."

"A little girl?"

He nodded. "She missed the school bus."

My God, what a terrible world when a child could be put in danger because she missed a bus. It came too close to home. Joshua took a bus from school every day. "Why didn't one of the teachers take her home?"

"She didn't ask. The subdivision where she lives is right over the hill from the school." He glanced at her. "I know how you feel, but they're searching for her now. She might have just gone to a friend's house. You know how kids are."

Yes, she knew how kids were. Thoughtless.

Trusting. Impulsive. Defenseless.

"You taking a trip?" he asked.

She nodded. "Tomorrow morning."

"Where are you going?"

"I haven't decided."

"You ought to try Wyoming." He bent his head over the tire. "Great country . . ."

"Maybe I will." She smiled and held up his badge. "I'll bring this back in a minute."

It took more like ten minutes to check with the precinct and return his badge to him.

Joshua was in his pajamas and looking extremely disgusted when she entered his room. "I need my tennis racquet."

"You're taking enough equipment to open up a sports store."

"My tennis racquet goes wherever I go."

"I'll make you a deal. Leave your baseball glove and you can take the tennis racquet."

Joshua's eyes widened in horror. "Mom!"

She had known he would never leave that treasured beat-up glove. "No? Then give it up, kid."

He studied her and then nodded. "Okay, now I'll make a deal with *you*. If I need a tennis racquet, we'll go to a store and you can buy —"

She threw a pillow at him. "Brat."

He grinned. "I had to give it a try." He hopped into bed. "Grandma says we have to get up at five."

"Grandma's right . . . as usual." She drew the covers over him and brushed her lips on his forehead before straightening. "Joshua, what would

131

you do if you missed the school bus that brings you home?"

"Go back in the school and call Grandma."

"You know we wouldn't be mad at you. You *would* call us?"

He frowned. "Sure, I told you I would. What's wrong?"

"Nothing." She prayed for the sake of that little girl's parents that she spoke the truth. "Good night, Joshua."

"Mom?"

She turned back to him.

"Will you stick around for a while?"

"You can't put off —" She broke off as she saw his expression. "What's wrong?"

"I don't know — I feel — Will you stick around for a while?"

"Why not?" She sat down on the edge of the bed. "You've been through a lot. It's natural to be a little nervous."

"I'm *not* nervous."

"Okay, sorry." She took his hand. "Do you mind if I say that I'm nervous?"

"Not if it's true."

"It's true."

"It's not that I'm scared. I just feel kind of . . . creepy."

"Do you want to talk about the funeral now?"

His brow immediately furrowed. "I *told* you I wasn't thinking about that anymore."

She backed off. It was clearly still too soon to approach him. It was just as well. She was probably too raw herself to maintain any degree of control. All he needed was to see her break down. "I was only asking."

"Just stick around for a while. Okay?"

"As long as you want me."

She didn't look like a warrior, sitting there on the boy's bed, Ishmaru thought in disappointment. She looked soft and womanly, without spirit or worth.

He peered through the narrow slit afforded by the venetian blinds covering the window of the boy's room.

Look at me. Let me see your spirit.

She didn't look at him. Didn't she know he was there, or was she scorning his threat to her?

Yes, that must be it. His power was so great tonight, he felt as if the stars themselves must feel it. Coup always brought added strength and exultation in its wake. The little girl had felt his power even before his hands had closed around her throat. The woman must be taunting him by pretending she was not aware he was watching her.

His hands tightened on the glass cutter in his hand. He could cut through the glass and show her he could not be ignored.

No, that was what she wanted. Even though he was quick, he would be at a disadvantage. She sought to lure him to his destruction as a clever warrior should do.

But he could be clever too. He would wait for

the moment and then strike boldly in full view of these sheep with whom she surrounded herself.

And before she died, she would admit how great was his power.

Joshua remained awake for almost an hour, and even after his eyes finally closed, he slept fitfully.

It was just as well they were going away, Kate thought. Joshua wasn't a high-strung child, but what he'd gone through was enough to unsettle anyone.

Phyliss's door was closed, Kate noted when she reached the hall. She should probably get to bed too. Not that she'd be able to sleep. She hadn't lied to Joshua; she was nervous and uneasy . . . and bitterly resentful. This was her home, it was supposed to be a haven. She didn't like to think of it as a fortress.

But, like it or not, it was a fortress at the moment and she'd better make sure the soldiers were on the battlements. She checked the lock on the front door before she moved quickly toward the living room. She would see the black-and-white from the picture window.

Phyliss, as usual, had drawn the drapes over the window before she went to bed. The cave instinct, Kate thought as she reached for the cord. Close out the outside world and make your own. She and Phyliss were in complete agree—

He was standing outside the window, so close they were separated only by a quarter of an inch of glass.

Oh God. High concave cheekbones, long black

straight hair drawn back in a queue, beaded necklace. It was him . . . Todd Campbell . . . Ishmaru . . .

And he was smiling at her.

His lips moved and he was so near she could hear the words through the glass. "You weren't supposed to see me before I got in, Kate." He held her gaze as he showed her the glass cutter in his hand. "But it's all right. I'm almost finished and I like it better this way."

She couldn't move. She stared at him, mesmerized.

"You might as well let me in. You can't stop me."

She jerked the drapes shut, closing him out.

Barricading herself inside with only a fragment of glass, a scrap of material . . .

She heard the sound of blade on glass.

She backed away from the window, stumbled on the hassock, almost fell, righted herself.

Oh God. Where was that policeman? The porch light was out, but surely he could see Ishmaru.

Maybe the policeman wasn't there.

And your husband never mentioned bribery in the ranks?

The drapes were moving.

He'd cut the window.

"Phyliss!" She ran down the hall. "Wake up." She threw open Joshua's door, flew across the room, and jerked him out of bed.

"Mom?"

"Shh, be very quiet. Just do what I tell you, okay?"

"What's wrong?" Phyliss was standing in the doorway. "Is Joshua sick?"

"I want you to leave here." She pushed Joshua toward her. "There's someone outside." She hoped he was still outside. Christ, he could be in the living room by now. "I want you to take Joshua out the back door and over to the Brocklemans'."

Phyliss instantly took Joshua's hand and moved toward the kitchen door. "What about you?"

She heard a sound in the living room. "*Go.* I'll be right behind you."

Phyliss and Joshua flew out the back door.

"Are you waiting for me, Kate?"

He sounded so close, too close. Phyliss and Joshua could not have reached the fence yet. No time to run. Stop him.

She saw him, a shadow in the doorway leading to the hall.

Where was the gun?

In her handbag on the living room table. She couldn't get past him. She backed toward the stove. Phyliss usually left a frying pan out to cook breakfast in the morning. . . .

"I told you I was coming in. No one can stop me tonight. I had a sign."

She didn't see a weapon but the darkness was lit only by moonlight streaming through the window.

"Give up, Kate."

Her hand closed on the handle of the frying pan. "Leave me *alone*." She leaped forward and struck out at his head with all her strength.

He moved too fast but she connected with a glancing blow.

He was falling. . . .

She streaked past him down the hall. Get to the purse, the gun.

She heard him behind her.

She snatched up the handbag, lunged for the door, and threw the bolt.

Get to the policeman in the black-and-white.

She fumbled with the catch on her purse as she streaked down the driveway toward the black-and-white. Her hand closed on the gun and she threw the purse aside.

"He's not there, Kate," Ishmaru said behind her. "It's just the two of us."

No one was in the driver's seat of the police car.

She whirled and raised the gun.

Too late.

He was on her, knocking the gun from her grip, sending it flying. How had he moved so quickly?

She was on the ground, struggling wildly.

She couldn't breathe. His thumbs were digging into her throat.

"Mom." Joshua's agonized scream pierced the night.

What was Joshua doing here? He was supposed to be — "Go away, Josh —" Ishmaru's hands tightened, cut off speech. She was dying. She had to move. The gun. She had dropped it. On the ground . . .

She reached out blindly. The metal of the gun hilt was cool and wet from the grass.

She wasn't going to make it. Everything was going black.

She tried to knee him in the groin.

"Stop fighting," he whispered. "I've gone to a great deal of trouble to give you a warrior's death."

Crazy bastard. The hell she'd stop fighting.

She raised the gun and pressed the trigger.

She could feel the impact ripple through his body as the bullet struck him.

His grip loosened around her throat. She heaved upward, slid out from under him and struggled to her knees.

He was lying on his back on the ground. Had she killed him? she wondered numbly.

"He hurt you." Joshua was beside her, tears running down his face. "I was too far away. I couldn't stop him. I couldn't —"

"Shh." She slid an arm around him. "I know." She started coughing. "Where's Phyliss?"

"She's using the Brocklemans' phone. I ran out of the house —"

"You shouldn't have done that."

"And you should have come with us," Joshua said fiercely. "He *hurt* you."

She could hardly deny that when she couldn't muster more than a croak. "It's not as bad as it —"

"It's bad enough." She turned at the voice to see a lean, dark-haired man running up the driveway.

She instinctively raised the gun and pointed it at him.

"Easy." He held up his hands. "Noah Smith sent me."

"How do I know that?" How could she believe anything? she wondered dazedly.

"You don't. Just keep the gun pointed at me and you'll feel better. I'm Seth Drakin."

Seth. Noah had mentioned a Seth. "What are you doing here?"

"I told you, Noah thought you might need some help. I was protecting you." He added, "Though I seem to be a little late." He turned Ishmaru's body over with his foot. "This is the same man who was here last night?"

She nodded.

"I don't think there's any doubt it's Ishmaru."

"Is he dead?"

He bent down and examined the wound. "No. Nasty flesh wound in the right side. It doesn't look like you've cut an artery. Extremely painful but not serious. Pity. Do you want me to finish him?"

"What?" she asked, shocked.

"Just a thought." He turned to Joshua. "Go get your grandmother, son."

Joshua looked at Kate.

She nodded. "Tell her to call an ambulance."

Joshua streaked across the lawn.

"An ambulance for a man who just tried to kill you?" Drakin asked.

"No, for me. I don't want to be responsible for killing a man if I can help it."

"Noble," he said. "I'm afraid I wouldn't be as generous." He glanced away, his gaze raking the dark houses along the block. "Nice supportive neighbors you have. Someone must have heard that shot."

"Most of them know how Michael died, and they've seen a police car here for the last two nights. Naturally they're afraid." She shuddered. "I would be too."

He studied her and then smiled. "But I don't think you'd be hiding behind closed doors if you thought a neighbor was in trouble. I'll be right back." He disappeared into the house and returned with a length of drapery cord. He swiftly tied Ishmaru's hands behind him.

"What are you doing? He's helpless."

"You won't let me kill him. I need to make sure of him. Ishmaru has the reputation of being always more than expected." He pulled her to her feet. "Come on, we have to get out of here before the police and ambulance come."

"Run away?" She shook her head.

"You just shot a man."

"It was self-defense. They won't hold me."

"Maybe not for an extended time, but do you want to leave your son alone and unprotected while you make explanations down at the police department?"

"He's safe now."

"Really? And where's the officer who was supposed to be protecting you?"

She glanced at the black-and-white. "I don't know."

"Probably somewhere spending Ogden's money. Suppose the police send your officer to protect Joshua while they're holding you?"

"Stop it. I'm not going anywhere with you. You could be lying. I don't even know you." She ran her fingers through her hair. She couldn't think. "And you're confusing me."

"You don't have to go with me. Go to Noah at the motel. Now's not the time to make a mistake. You wouldn't be the one to pay for it."

Joshua would pay. Joshua must be protected. Maybe Drakin was right. At any rate, she needed time to sort things out. She nodded jerkily. "I'll go to the motel."

"Good. I'll phone Noah and tell him you're coming. Do you need anything from the house?"

"No."

"Don't change your mind." His gaze searched her face. "Don't get halfway there and decide to take off. You need all the help you can get."

"I'll go to the motel," she repeated. She turned and watched Joshua and Phyliss coming across the lawn toward her. She was still clutching the gun, she realized. She picked up her purse and stuffed the weapon inside. "That's all I'll promise."

"Hurry. You've got to move fast." He glanced

at Ishmaru. "And don't untie him. I have a hunch he's playing possum. Are you sure you don't want me to send him to the happy hunting grounds?"

So casual. So cool. What kind of a man was he? She shivered. "I told you no."

"Just asking." He hesitated. "I don't want to leave you alone. Suppose I wait until you take off before I go."

"And what will you do to him after I leave? Kill him? You go first. I don't trust you."

He nodded approvingly. "Good, you shouldn't."

"Leave."

"Promise you won't untie him."

"I promise," she said through clenched teeth.

"Then I'm on my way." He strode down the driveway.

She stared after him. The appearance of this stranger had been as bewildering as everything else this evening. Bewildering and terrifying. He had seemed to know just what buttons to push to get her to do what he wanted.

"Emily . . ."

At the whisper she went rigid and then swung around to look at the man on the ground.

His eyes were open and he was staring directly at her. How long had he been conscious?

"I knew it was you, Emily."

"My name is Kate."

"Yes, that too." He smiled. "You're . . . wonderful, Kate. You did . . . well."

A chill went through her. He was lying there

with a wound she'd inflicted and there was genuine admiration in his voice. Noah was right, the man had to be insane. "Why did you do this?" she whispered.

"Coup . . . I will have three when you are all dead." He closed his eyes. "But you alone will bring me great honor, Kate. I can hardly . . . wait."

She took a step back before she realized what she'd done. There was no reason to be afraid. He was no threat. He was wounded, bound, and soon the police would be here. She could hear the sirens now. She would call Alan from the motel and tell him what happened, and he would make sure this scum was kept in jail, away from them.

She turned her back on him and went to meet Phyliss and Joshua.

Ishmaru opened his eyes and watched the taillights of the Honda move down the street away from him.

Happiness flooded him, warming him. The woman had brought him down but he felt no shame. The women were always the coldest, the fiercest. That's why warriors always gave their prisoners to the women for torture. This wound she had given him was great torture. Every breath he took was pain, and she had known it. When the man had asked if he should finish him, she had said no and the man had thought her merciful.

Ishmaru knew better. She had wanted him to

suffer. She wanted him to lie here and know she had done this to him. He had been right about the strength he had sensed in her.

Sirens . . . far away . . .

It made no difference what she had said. She had called an ambulance to heal him so that he would be well enough to face her again. She had realized that he was her destiny.

But the police would also come. A gauntlet for him to run before he could get to her.

Clever, Kate. She was testing him to see if he was worthy of meeting her again.

He was worthy.

He rolled over and began to crawl up the driveway toward the open front door. He would get a shard of glass from the window he'd cut and slice through these bonds, then go out the back door and lose himself in this suburban wilderness of tract houses.

He was bleeding and each movement was agony. It didn't matter. He was used to pain, he welcomed it.

He was in the shadows at the side of the house.

The sirens were closer.

He must move faster. He pressed his back against the brick wall and pulled himself up to a standing position.

Dizziness swamped him and he swayed.

He fought it back and staggered toward the front door.

You see, Kate, I'm coming.

I'm worthy of you.

Six

"She's coming," Seth said. "And she thinks you sent me. Since I behaved in my usual heroic fashion, I wouldn't disillusion her."

"Damn you, Seth. I told you not to interfere."

"I was sitting at the airport. I was bored and got to thinking. You know that's one of my fatal flaws. Now say 'Thank you, you were right, Seth,' and I'll hang up."

There was a silence on the other end of the phone. "Thank you."

" 'You were right, Seth,' " he prompted.

"I suppose you were. How much did you scare her?"

"I was tame as a pussycat. Well, almost. I guess I'll have some bridges to mend. Call me back on my cellular when you finish talking to her. She's not an easy sell. You may not convince her to go to the cabin."

Noah was waiting on the walkway outside the motel room when Kate drove up.

"I rented the two rooms next door to mine for you," he said as Kate got out of the car. "I don't think we should stay the night, but you all can get some rest while I finalize plans." He opened the passenger door for Phyliss. "I'm Noah Smith, Mrs. Denby. I know this is upsetting for you.

145

How much has Kate told you?"

"Not enough," Phyliss said grimly. "That maybe whoever blew up your plant may have killed Michael. That doesn't explain why we're running away when we should be talking to the police."

"There wasn't time," Kate said. "I'll call Alan later." She opened the back door. "Come on, Joshua."

"I don't like it here," he whispered as he got out of the car. "How long are we staying?"

"Not long." Noah smiled at Joshua. "We haven't been introduced. I'm Noah Smith and I'm going to make sure you and your mother and grandmother are safe from now on."

"Are you a policeman?"

"No, but I can still help you."

"You can't be very good. You weren't there to help Mom. She almost died."

Noah grimaced. "I know. It won't happen again." He handed a room key to Phyliss. "Will you take him inside and make him comfortable? I need to talk to Kate."

Phyliss looked at her daughter-in-law, eyebrows lifted in question.

Kate nodded. "Please. I'll be with you soon and explain everything." She gave Joshua a little push toward Phyliss. "Go with her, honey."

"No." His hands nervously opened and closed at his sides. "I'm not leaving you. What if that man comes after you again?" He glared contemptuously at Noah. "He's no good. He almost let you die."

"He won't come after me. He was badly hurt. I shot him."

"But you didn't kill him. You should have shot him again. Or let that Seth kill him like he wanted to do."

"I promise you that I'm in no danger, Joshua. I'll be right next door."

Phyliss came forward and took his hand. "Come on, Joshua, let's get out of this wind. I'm getting cold."

He didn't move. "You promise you'll come right away, Mom."

"I promise."

"And call if you need me?"

Kate nodded.

"I won't go to sleep." He let Phyliss lead him away. "I'll be waiting for you."

"Smart kid," Noah said as the door closed behind Phyliss and Joshua. "Excellent instincts." He opened the door of his room and let Kate precede him. "Except about me, of course."

"He's very protective." She shut the door. "But children have the instincts of savages. Grown-ups are supposed to guide them away from barbarism, not encourage them. I didn't appreciate you sending a man like that Seth Drakin to show him just how barbaric we can be."

"Barbarism has its place. Joshua was right. You'd have been safer if the threat was eliminated entirely."

"It will be eliminated — by the police. The way it should be." She sank down in the chair. "I don't even know why I'm here. I should have waited for them."

"Because you have good instincts too. You're just fighting them." He leaned back against the door. "Seth said you were all very close to dying tonight."

"It was a nightmare," she said wearily. "Ishmaru regained consciousness before I left. He called me Emily but I think he knew who I was. Anyway, he's not sane."

"What did he say?"

She smiled without mirth. "He wants to count coup."

He went still. "You know what that means?"

"Oh yes, Joshua was into cowboys and Indians before he discovered baseball. I tried to stress the splendid integrity of the Native American culture, but all he was interested in were battles and coup. It's a charming old custom. It means to get close enough to your enemy to kill by hand weapon and gain some sort of mystical honor." She gripped the arms of the chair to keep from shaking. "He wanted me and Phyliss and Joshua. All of us."

He crossed the room and knelt before her. "But he didn't get you and he won't," he said softly. He took her hands and held them tightly. "Not now. You're safe here with me."

She could almost believe him. His fingers were strong and warm and he was holding her gaze with the same strength of will. She wanted him to pull her into his arms and cradle her as she did Joshua when he woke from a bad dream.

"Now will you let me tell you what I've planned?" he asked.

She nodded.

"Four months ago I rented a place in the mountains near Greenbriar, West Virginia. I visited there once with an old friend. It's completely off the beaten track, even fifteen miles from the nearest general store. I had a fully equipped lab and computer linkup installed and stocked it with enough food to last six months. I've buried the paperwork on the place to make sure it couldn't be traced to me."

"Four months ago?" she repeated slowly.

"I knew we'd need a private place when you agreed to work with me."

"But I had no intention of working with you four months ago."

He was silent.

She felt a sudden surge of uneasiness that was close to fear. Staring at him, she knew she had never encountered a more relentless man. "I suppose I should be grateful you didn't kidnap me and carry me to your lair," she said dryly.

He shook his head. "You had to come willingly."

"So that I'd accommodate you by working on your miracle project." She shook her head. "Incredible."

"None of that matters. What's important is that

I have a safe place to take you and your family. I'll arrange to have you guarded day and night. Will you come?"

"Don't rush me. I haven't decided." She reached for the telephone on the bedside table. "But right now I have to call the police and tell them why I ran away."

"They'll come and get you. Joshua will be alone with just your mother-in-law to care for him."

Fear rippled through her. Seth Drakin had used the same argument, the one argument Noah knew would shake her. "It won't be like that. I'm calling a friend with the force."

He shrugged. "Be my guest."

She quickly dialed Alan's home number. He answered on the second ring.

"Where the hell are you?" he demanded. "I've just come back from your house. What happened out there?"

"I shot him, Alan. He tried to kill me."

"Who?"

"The same man who came last night. I shot him. I don't know where Officer Brunwick went, but he —"

"Brunwick is dead. We found him on the floor in the back of the police car with a broken neck."

"Broken neck?" She lifted her hand to her bruised throat. For an instant she could again feel those fingers digging into her flesh. "Is he in the hospital?"

"I told you, Brunwick is dead."

"No, the man I shot. Ishmaru."

"The only man we found was Brunwick, plus a little blood on the grass and in your living room, and the glass that was cut out of your window. We also heard some pretty wild tales from your neighbors."

Her hand clenched so tightly on the phone that the knuckles whitened. "He's gone? But he couldn't be. He was hurt. I shot him."

"Listen, Kate, I don't know what the hell has happened, but a policeman is down and you know what that means. Every cop in the city, including the captain, wants answers. You have to come in and talk to us."

Coup.

I can hardly wait.

"He can't be gone. You have to find him, Alan."

"Tell me where you are. I'll send a car for you."

Panic surged through her. "I'll call you back," she whispered. She hung up the phone.

"I take it your problem has escalated," Noah said behind her.

"He couldn't have just gotten up and walked away."

Coup.

"The alternative is that he had an accomplice who picked him up and toted him away. Did you see anyone else?"

"No." If there had been anyone but Ishmaru, she doubted if she'd have been aware of him anyway. Ishmaru had totally dominated the picture from the moment she had seen him outside her window. "And Officer Brunwick didn't sell out. He's dead. His neck was broken." He would never see his grandkids again, she thought. "He was . . . a nice man. He was going to retire to Wyoming."

"He may not have been dirty, but he wasn't able to protect you. He let Ishmaru close enough to kill him with his barehands. It could happen again." He paused. "And your friend Alan wants you to come in?"

"Yes."

"It would mean hours and hours away from —"

"Be quiet," she said harshly. "I've heard all your arguments. I know what you want. I have to think."

Noah dropped down in the chair by the window. "Whatever you want."

Sure, as long as it suited him, she thought bitterly.

Coup.

Joshua will be alone.

The police can't be trusted when there's this much money involved.

The only way you'll be safe is to help me go public with RU2.

She spun to face him. "Who knows about this place in the mountains?"

"No one."

"Absolutely no one?"

He nodded. "I handled everything myself."

"And there will be no one there but us?"

"Just your family and me."

"Then I'll go. I'll do what you want." She added, "But I want one promise from you. Nothing must happen to my son and Phyliss. Whatever happens to you or me, they must not be hurt."

"Done," he said instantly.

"I mean it," she said fiercely. "Don't be glib. This isn't negotiable. I'm holding you responsible for their safety."

"Dare I ask what would happen if I failed you?"

"You'll learn the true meaning of barbarism."

He smiled. "I told you that you had good instincts."

She moved toward the door. "I'm going to go and try to explain this mess to Phyliss and Joshua. After that, I think we'd better get out of the area. Alan said that the police are looking for me. We'll drive to West Virginia?"

He nodded. "It's the safest way to travel. No records and we'll need my jeep anyway to get up the hills."

"We'll take both cars. I want a way out if I don't like the setup. How long will it take us?"

"Three days." He stood up and moved toward the bureau. "It will only take me a few minutes to pack and settle up the bill. Can you be ready to leave in twenty minutes?"

Twenty minutes to explain to Joshua and Phyliss why they were fleeing from their home like criminals? She wasn't even sure herself that she was doing the right thing. "I'll be ready."

Noah waited until the door closed behind her to pick up the telephone receiver and punch in Seth's number.

"Ishmaru is free," he said when Seth picked up the phone. "He wasn't there when the police arrived."

"Son of a bitch. I knew I shouldn't have listened to her."

"Oh no, you should have killed him in front of her and Joshua."

"You malign me. I would have sent the kid away. Is she going to the cabin?"

"Yes. We're starting right away. We're driving and should be there in three days."

"What about Ishmaru?"

"Forget Ishmaru."

"He's hard to forget." Seth paused. "Kate Denby has guts. She doesn't deserve to have that bastard butcher her."

"I'm taking her away from here. She won't be in any danger. Just make sure you're at the cabin when we arrive."

Seth hesitated. "I'll be there."

"Seth."

"I promise. I'll be there."

Noah was marginally satisfied. Seth never broke his word. He hung up the phone. He had not liked lying to Kate, but he hadn't wanted anything negative affecting her decision. Seth had obviously scared her, and maybe a fait accompli would be best.

He started tossing clothes into his duffel. He could feel the adrenaline racing through him. It had been hard as hell to play a waiting game this past week. Now he could *move.*

Everything was falling into place at last.

Noah was wrong.

Seth snapped the cover back on his cellular and slipped it into his back pocket.

It would be a big mistake to forget Ishmaru. From what Kendow had told him, Ishmaru would never give up now that he'd suffered a defeat. Noah was so blinded by his desire to get RU2 completed that all he could see was the plan he'd been formulating for months. He couldn't see that Kate Denby was in just as much danger now as she had been before.

Or he didn't want to see.

But Seth could see it and it left a nasty taste in his mouth. She hadn't volunteered to be sucked into this, and Noah should be thinking about her first. Her and her son, Joshua. The kid was another innocent bystander. God, he hated it when kids became involved.

When obstacles appeared, they had to be dealt with immediately or they grew out of control. Ishmaru should be dealt with now.

But where to find him?

When a beast was wounded it returned to its lair.

Where's your lair, Ishmaru?

Kendow might know. Or he might know someone who did.

He took out his cellular again and punched in Kendow's number.

"You fool," Ogden said coldly. "It was only one goddamn woman and you couldn't get the job done."

He should not be speaking of Kate in such a manner, Ishmaru thought. She deserved better than this disrespect. "I'll do it. Be patient."

"I'm not a patient man. I want her found and I want her dead. Did you get her records?"

He was tempted to lie but great warriors did not lie to vermin. It was beneath them. "No, only the two pages I faxed you. The others weren't at GeneChem. She must have them with her." He paused. "But you have another problem. Noah Smith is still alive. He didn't die in the explosion."

There was a silence at the other end of the line. "How do you know?"

"I heard them talking. The woman and the man who came later. She was on her way to join Smith at his motel."

Ogden muttered a curse. "They're together?"

"So it would seem. Don't worry, it will only make things easier for me."

"Nothing's easy for a fool who —"

"Enough," Ishmaru said softly. "I will hear no more. Locate them and let me know. I'll take care of the rest." He replaced the receiver before

Ogden could answer.

He would have to kill Ogden, he thought objectively. But not right away. Ogden provided a service. He was the quiver that held Ishmaru's arrows, the pony that bore him in his search for glory.

He was the scout who pointed the way to coup.

Ishmaru took the threaded needle he'd laid in readiness beside the phone. First he must take care of this trifling wound, and then he would return to his medicine cave to refresh his powers. But he could not stay long. Kate was waiting.

Pain seared through him as he plunged the needle into his flesh and brought it out on the other side of the gaping wound.

He wanted to scream.

He did not scream.

He plunged the needle in again and took another stitch.

See how I suffer for you, Kate?
See how worthy I am of you?

"Idiot." Raymond Ogden crashed the phone down and glowered at William Blount sitting in the chair across the room. "And you're another one for recommending the son of a bitch."

Blount shrugged. "You needed someone who you could trust not to talk. You didn't complain about his work on Smith's plant."

"He fumbled that job too. Smith's still alive and Kate Denby's with him."

"Not good," Blount said. "But not terrible either."

"What do you mean? Do you think Smith's going to wait around and let us take another swipe at him? He'll go underground until he's ready to surface."

"Then we'll just toss out a net and find them."

"How?"

"It's a small world." Blount smiled slightly. "Everyone is connected to everyone else. We just have to find the appropriate connection and follow it." He rose to his feet. "I'll make a few calls."

"You're damn right you will." Ogden stood up, moved over to the mirror, and straightened his tuxedo jacket. "But not only to your mob friends. I can't run the risk that they'll screw this up too. I have to protect myself and widen the scope."

He didn't like that, Ogden thought as he watched Blount's expression in the mirror. The young punk liked to feel in control. Well, he wasn't in control. Ogden ran the show and he wasn't about to let the bastard think anything else. He'd never liked the prick anyway, with his perfect teeth and uppity airs. He'd hired Blount as his assistant because he was the illegitimate son of Marco Giandello and the connection was useful for getting things done. But it wasn't like the old days; now the dons sent their kids to college and they came out like Blount with his gleaming smile, Armani suits, and veiled contempt. Well, let him sneer. Ogden might not have gotten any further than eighth grade, but he had built a pharmaceutical empire and he was the one who paid Blount's salary and pulled the strings. "I want you to call Ken Bradton of Bradton Mutual Insurance, Paul Cobb of Undercliff Pharmaceutical, and Ben Arnold of Jedlow Laboratories. Arrange a meeting for two days from today."

"Is that discreet?" Blount asked. "I thought we agreed that the fewer people who knew about RU2, the better."

We. The little turd thought he actually had a hand in Ogden's decisions. "If Smith goes public, I've got to be ready for him. I don't swing a big enough club to squash RU2 by myself."

"It would be more discreet to allow my father to handle the matter."

And let those dago creeps get a stranglehold on Ogden Pharmaceutical? Not a chance. "We'll do it my way." He straightened his bow tie. "I have to make an appearance at the governor's fund-raiser tonight. I'll be back home in a few hours and I want you to tell me that meeting is set."

"It's almost midnight here now and Ken Bradton is on the East Coast."

"Then wake the bastard up. Wake everybody up." He turned away from the mirror. "Tell them I said if they want to save their asses, they'll be here in two days." He started for the door. "And while you're at it, call Senator Longworth in Washington and tell him I want him here too."

"For the meeting?"

159

"No, a day later. In private."

"Are you sure he'll come? This is going to be a hot one for any politician."

"He'll come. He likes money and I know where the body's buried." He gave Blount a sardonic smile. "You two will get along great. He's big on discretion too."

"I meant no offense." Blount's perfect teeth shone in a brilliant smile. "I'm sure you know best, Mr. Ogden."

"You don't make things easy," Robert Kendow muttered as Seth got into his car at Los Angeles airport. "You always expect results overnight. These things take time."

"I don't have time. I have to be somewhere three days from now. I made a promise." He leaned back in the seat. "And one of those days is almost over. Where does Ishmaru stay when he's here?"

Kendow gazed at him in exasperation. He had known Seth Drakin for over ten years, and his single-mindedness was nothing new. When he had first met him, he had been fooled by that easy, low-key manner and thought his formidable reputation blown up out of all proportion. He had remained blissfully ignorant until he saw him in action. Drakin was easy only as long as he got what he wanted. Cross him and he became both difficult and lethal.

"Ishmaru," Seth prompted. "You said he still lives here in L.A."

"I said I'd seen him here several times. I don't know where he lives."

"He was raised here. Does he have family or friends?"

"No family. Friends? You've got to be kidding. The bastard's psycho."

"There has to be someone." Seth smiled. "I want him, Kendow. I'll be most unhappy if you don't help me."

Kendow instinctively tensed. Seth's tone was soft but he had heard it before. He took a deep breath. "I'm trying. There's a man he used to know. Pedro Jimenez. A total slimeball. When Ishmaru first started out, Jimenez handled the contracts for him."

"He doesn't now?"

He shook his head. "Ishmaru left him far behind. But he probably knows more about Ishmaru than anyone else in town."

"Where is Jimenez?"

"Still in East L.A." Kendow grimaced. "It's a great recruiting ground for shooters. He has two young Hispanics under his wing now."

"Take me to him."

"I haven't located him. He moves around a lot." He added hurriedly, "I'm supposed to meet a man tonight. I promise you that you'll see Jimenez tomorrow. I can't promise you that he'll talk. He's smart enough to be scared of Ishmaru like everyone else."

"Oh, I think he'll talk," Seth murmured. "I've always been surprised how obliging people can

161

be when they're given a chance."

Beads of sweat coated Jimenez's forehead. "I can't help you, senor. I told you that I don't know where he is."

Seth studied him for a moment. The plump little man was every bit the slimeball Kendow had called him. Seth would have to press just a little harder. The bastard knew he'd just as soon break his neck as look at him. Seth had made sure of it during the ten minutes he'd been in the bar. "I think you do know. You must have had to contact Ishmaru to set up his jobs. I doubt if you hung a red flag out the window."

Jimenez gave him a sickly smile as he shakily lit his cigar with an ornate initialed gold lighter. "That was a long time ago."

"You haven't seen him lately?"

He shook his head emphatically.

Seth believed him. Jimenez had about as much backbone as a squid. "Or heard anything?"

Jimenez moistened his lips. "Someone saw him yesterday afternoon."

"Here?"

He shook his head. "He never goes in bars. He says liquor dirties his soul."

"Who saw him?"

"Maria Carnales. She runs a shop a few blocks from here. He always buys his incense from her."

"Incense."

Jimenez shrugged. "I never asked him what he uses it for. I never asked Ishmaru nothing.

162

Why don't you go ask her if she knows where he is?"

"Because you know." He leaned forward. *Press hard. Let him see the edge.* "And you're going to tell me."

"He'd kill me."

Seth smiled.

"I tell you, he'd kill me if I told you."

Seth reached out and gently, almost caressingly touched Jimenez's jugular. "And what do you think I'll do if you don't?"

Jimenez slammed the car door shut and pointed at the woods stretching before them. "There's a cave about a mile from here. He calls it his medicine tent. He has it camouflaged with branches." He stuck out his chin. "I'm not going any farther."

"Yes, you are." Seth started down the path. "I may need you."

Jimenez reluctantly followed him. "Why would you need me?"

Seth lifted his brows. "Why, to stake out for the tiger."

Seth heard him half swearing, half praying behind him.

He should have left him at the car, Seth thought; he'd probably be in the way. But he wouldn't trust the worm not to turn. Jimenez was terrified of Ishmaru, and Seth couldn't be sure that he'd impressed him enough.

It was getting dark, the shadows were gathering

on each side of the path.

He stopped, listening.

Nothing.

"What is it?" Jimenez whispered.

"Just checking."

He moved quickly down the path.

He could hear Jimenez's strangled breathing behind him.

He stopped again.

"Goddammit, what do you hear?"

"Nothing." It was what he smelled. Incense. Charred oak. "The cave's up ahead, isn't it?"

"I don't remember. It's been years."

Seth drew his gun. "Stay here. Don't move."

"I want to go back to the car."

"Not a step." He faded into the shrubbery and moved parallel to the path.

The shrubbery was thick, the camouflage so well done he wouldn't have known the cave was there.

The smell of incense was strong, overpowering.

Before the cave were the ashes of a burnt-out campfire surrounded by stones.

The mouth of the cave was dark.

Ishmaru wasn't here. But he'd been here. The signs were recent. Seth judged no later than this morning. He'd built a fire, burned his incense. . . .

And what else?

"Jimenez." He didn't answer. "Jimenez!"

Jimenez was breaking through the underbrush, his gaze fixed warily on the opening of the cave.

He breathed a sigh of relief. "He isn't here. Can we go now?"

"Give me your lighter."

Jimenez handed him his gold lighter. "We should leave. He's gone and he won't be back until he needs it again."

Needs? "Come with me."

"I don't want to go in there."

"Come anyway." He strode into the cave with Jimenez on his heels.

The incense smell was stronger here. Very strong.

He lit the lighter.

Jimenez whimpered.

Scalps. Seven or eight of them crowning poles driven into the ground in a circle.

Scalps. Of course. A scalp had been considered a badge of honor by Indians, and Ishmaru had made his Indian heritage his religion.

He turned to look at Jimenez. "You knew about this."

"No, I —" He swallowed. "It had something to do with nightmares and power. I don't know. He called them the guardians. He'd sit in the center of the circle for hours and burn incense. At first he wanted to take a scalp every time he was out on a contract, but I convinced him not to do it unless it was safe and didn't get in the way."

"Very sensible," he said sarcastically.

"Can we go now?"

"Not yet." His glance had fallen on a small cardboard box in the corner. He knelt beside it.

Watches. Jewelry. A pocketknife. More trophies?

A book, well thumbed and faded with time. *Warriors.* Obviously Ishmaru's primer.

As he stood up he brushed against one of the poles. He put his hand out to steady it.

Long silky blond hair.

This scalp wasn't like the others. It was fresh. And it was a child's.

Seth stared at it, trying to control the rage tearing through him.

Evidently Ishmaru had found a new source of power on his trip to Dandridge.

"There's no use staying here and waiting," Jimenez said. "He was never here for more than twenty-four hours. He said he never needed more than that to —" He broke off as he saw Seth's expression. "I never had anything to do with this. I told you, I tried to keep him from —"

"Shut up." He turned away and shoved the box with his foot toward Jimenez. "Gather all the scalps and put them in the box along with everything else that you can find of Ishmaru's."

"You want me to touch them?" He shook his head. "He won't like it. He'd regard it as desecration."

"You can either gather them or join them," Seth said with soft violence. "And I don't particularly care which."

Jimenez moved quickly toward the poles.

Five minutes later he was holding the heaping cardboard box. "Now what?"

"Now we go." He lit the dry grass and branches on the cave floor with Jimenez's lighter. The flames leaped high.

"Why?" Jimenez wailed.

"I wanted it gone." Not that he'd be able to forget what he'd seen. He didn't want to think that Ishmaru could ever come back here. He wanted to hurt the bastard.

"This was his special place. He'll go crazy," Jimenez sputtered.

"I hope so." Seth watched the flames a moment before he turned to go. "Come on."

"What are you going to do with all this stuff?"

He didn't answer.

It wasn't until they reached the car that Jimenez spoke again. "Can I have my lighter back?"

"I must have lost it somewhere back at the cave. Maybe in the fire. Afraid it's too late."

Jimenez's eyes widened. "What do you mean? That lighter had my initials engraved on it." His voice went shrill with panic. "What if Ishmaru comes back and finds it? He'll think I did this."

Seth turned to look at him. "Oops."

They were calling his flight.

Seth quickly finished typing the address into the label machine he'd picked up at a drugstore on the way to the airport. He pulled the *Warriors* book out of the small cardboard box before sealing it. He might need it later.

He pressed the address label on the box, added the stamps he'd purchased from the airport post

167

office, and headed for the postal box down the hall. He was barely able to squeeze the box into the opening.

Second call for his flight.

He stripped off his gloves and stuffed them in his back pocket. No other fingerprints but Ishmaru's and Jimenez's were on the box, which was now on its way to the L.A. district attorney's office. He had little faith they'd catch Ishmaru, but maybe it would be a wake-up call. Even if they managed to nail only that bastard Jimenez, it would be a plus. He'd been tempted to kill the asshole himself. Seth had thought he had seen everything, but the sight of that little girl's silky —

Last call for his flight.

Don't think about it. He couldn't do anything for that poor kid, and Ishmaru was still out there. He had a job to do.

He hurried toward his departure gate.

Noah's cabin was set far back from the road, screened by trees and shrubbery. Kate wouldn't have even been aware the place existed if she hadn't been closely following Noah.

"Are we here?" Phyliss asked.

"I guess we are." Kate rolled to a stop behind Noah's jeep. "It's about time." It seemed as if they'd been winding through bumpy back roads for hours. She glanced at Joshua sleeping in the backseat and decided not to wake him. Let him sleep. It had been an exhausting trip, emotionally as well as physically. She'd rouse him when they had a bed in which to settle him.

Kate got out of the car and looked up at the cabin. Actually, it was larger than her house back in Dandridge but it was built of logs and stone and appeared rustic enough to be called a cabin. A wide deck wrapped around it. "How many rooms does it have?"

"Seven." Noah pulled his duffel out of the jeep. "Kitchen and living room combo, three bedrooms, two baths. Plus the lab at the back."

"I'll start to unpack," Phyliss said as she got out of the car.

"Don't bother," Noah said. "You're not staying."

Kate froze. "What?"

He started climbing the steps leading to the deck. "I'm moving Phyliss and Joshua to the ranger station four miles from here."

"Why? There's obviously plenty of room for all of us."

"You'll be busy."

She followed him up the steps. "Not too busy for my son. He stays with me."

He looked at her. "No, he doesn't stay with you. I made you a promise to keep your son safe. I intend to keep it."

"By separating us?"

"Think." He lowered his voice so that it would be audible only to her. "We're the primary targets. We'd be first on the list. Joshua and Phyliss are much more likely to be hurt if they stay close to you."

But she didn't want to be separated from Joshua and Phyliss. The very idea made her feel isolated and shaken. "You said this place is safe."

"As safe as I can make it." His lips tightened. "There's no way I can assure you that you'll get out of this alive, but the boy *will* survive. We've had enough innocent bystanders suffer."

She couldn't help but be swayed by both the logic and the passion of his argument. "I don't like having them there by themselves."

"They won't be by themselves. I told you I'd have them guarded."

She frowned. "By the forest ranger?"

"Well, of sorts." He paused. "Actually, Seth persuaded the forest ranger to take a vacation and let him take over."

She went rigid. "Seth?"

He tried the front door and found it open. He called, "Seth."

"He's here?" she asked in shock.

"Damn right, I'm here. You took long enough. I was getting bored." Seth rose from the easy chair across the room. "Good to see you again, Kate. How's Joshua?"

"Okay," she answered automatically as she watched him come toward her. It was the first time she had actually looked at him. His hair was very dark, cut close to subdue a tendency to curl. He was in his middle thirties but moved with the same youthful springiness as Joshua. His face was as lean and angular as his body and dominated by a wide mobile mouth and light blue eyes.

"What the hell are you doing here?"

"I was invited." He looked at Noah. "You didn't tell her?"

Noah shook his head. "She was skittish."

Skittish? Anger suddenly jarred Kate out of her bewilderment. She whirled on Noah. "You told me no one knew about this place."

"I lied," Noah said simply.

"Because I was 'skittish.'"

"His word, not mine," Seth said.

Noah ignored him. "Because I needed you here and you were looking for an excuse not to come."

She flung out an arm at Seth. "An excuse like him?"

"My feelings are hurt," Seth said. "My company is usually sought after by one and all."

"Who else knows?" Kate asked Noah.

"No one." He raised his hand to ward off the charge he knew was coming. "And that's not a lie."

"How could I ever be sure?" It was too much after the exhaustion and terror of the past few days. She exploded. "*Damn* you. I'm out of here."

She turned on her heel, strode out of the house and down the steps. "Get back in the car, Phyliss."

"Again?" Phyliss made a face and climbed into the passenger seat. "Make up your mind."

"It's made up."

"Where the hell are you going?" Noah called from the deck behind her.

She didn't answer as she got behind the wheel.

"Will you listen to me?" Noah called. "I can't let you go like this, Kate."

She started the engine and drove away.

"Testy, wasn't she?" Seth strolled out of the cabin and handed Noah the Springfield rifle he'd taken from the case by the door.

"What am I supposed to do with this? Shoot her?"

"Just the left back tire. She's going slow enough." Seth shaded his eyes with his hand. "And you'd better do it before she reaches the curve or she may go off the road when the tire bursts."

"Since you seem to be orchestrating this, maybe you'd prefer to do it," Noah said sarcastically.

Seth shook his head. "I'm already in deep trouble and I'm going to have to live with the kid and the grandmother. I don't want them shaking in their boots every time I walk in the room." He grinned maliciously. "Besides, I want to see if you've lost your touch. Come on, it's only five hundred yards."

"Six."

"Whatever. The way I see it, it's either a high-speed chase that could send them over a cliff or a neat little bullet on the straightaway." He looked back at the road. "I'd judge you only have forty seconds before she reaches the curve."

No one was better than Seth at judging in this arena, Noah thought. And he was right; it was the only safe way of stopping Kate and she had to be stopped. He lifted the rifle and sighted. He pressed the trigger.

The tire blew. Kate struggled to keep the car on the road. The Honda came to a stop two yards from the curve.

"Not bad," Seth murmured. "Some people never lose it. Did it feel good?"

"No." He tossed Seth the rifle and started down the steps. "And it's going to feel even less good when I get out there and have to face Kate."

Seth smiled. "I think you're lying. I watched you. I bet it did feel good." He headed back into the house. "I'll go get my gear and set out for the ranger station. I'm a peaceable man. I really don't want to hang around if there's going to be a row."

Noah snorted derisively as he jumped into the jeep.

Kate leaned her head on the steering wheel, heart beating frantically. Damn him. Damn the crazy, obsessive son of a bitch.

"My God, what happened?" Phyliss asked after she caught her breath.

"He shot out a rear tire." The sound of the shot and the blowout had come almost simultaneously, but there was no doubt in Kate's mind what had happened.

Phyliss blinked. "He really didn't want you to go, did he?"

"He really didn't."

"Why have we stopped?" Joshua asked sleepily

173

from the backseat. He sat up and looked around. "Are we there? I don't see a cabin."

She was grateful Joshua had slept through everything, but this was no time for explanations. "Stay in the car." She grabbed her purse and got out of the Honda.

Phyliss followed her as she moved to the rear of the car. "Why did you change your mind about staying?"

"He lied to me. There was someone at the cabin."

"Oh, and you were afraid?"

"No." Fear hadn't entered into it. She had known neither Noah nor Seth Drakin would hurt them. But Noah had lied to her. She had felt used and manipulated and then he had used *that* word. Brainless birds were skittish, horses were skittish. Women were not skittish.

"Here he comes," Phyliss said, looking up the road. "What do we do now?"

"Wait." Kate drew the Colt from her purse as the jeep stopped behind them.

"For God's sake, put that up." Noah jumped out of the jeep. "You know I'm no threat to you."

"You shot at us," Kate said coldly. "I'd say that's a threat."

"I had to stop you." He held out his hands. "Do you see any weapon?"

"I see a liar and a man who shot at me."

"I shot at your tire, not at you." He went to the trunk of the car. "Give me your keys. I'll change your tire and you can drive it back to the house." He glanced at the gun. "Put it away. If you weren't so tired, you'd realize that you over-reacted. You know I've no intention of harming you."

"I'd say you're the one who overreacted," Phyliss said dryly.

"Maybe you're right." He grimaced. "I was desperate. There didn't seem anything else to do at the time. I honestly had no intention of harming you, Mrs. Denby." He met her gaze directly. "I promise that I'm going to do everything in my power to see that nothing happens to you."

Phyliss studied him for a moment and then said, "Put the gun away, Kate."

Kate hesitated, then wearily slipped the gun in her bag. She was sick to death of guns. She felt like some half-baked Annie Oakley. She had handled the weapon more in the past few days than she had in all the years since Michael had given it to her. She threw him the trunk keys. "Change it and let us get out of here."

"I want you to come back to the cabin and let me make dinner for you all. Okay, I made a mistake. I should have told you about Seth."

"*And* the ranger station."

He took the spare tire and jack out of the trunk. "But does the fact that you find me untruthful and unscrupulous really alter the reason you came here? You wanted to be safe. I'll keep you safe."

"That could be a lie too."

"Don't you trust your own judgment? You didn't think it was a lie before." He knelt down and began to jack up the car. "Just come back to the house and give yourself a chance to think. You've been under tremendous pressure and, like an idiot, I tossed the last straw at you. I won't do that to you again. Even if you —"

"What happened to the tire?" Joshua was standing beside Noah staring curiously at the hole in the rubber.

"I told you to wait in the car, Joshua," Kate said.

"But it was rocking. Besides, maybe I can help. You taught me how to fix a flat." He touched the hole. "Blow-out?"

Noah nodded. "My fault, I'm afraid."

"Why?"

"I shot out the tire."

Joshua's eyes widened and he took a step back.

"I only wanted to get your mom's attention." Noah made a face. "But she's mad and punishing me by making me change and repair it."

Joshua looked at Kate.

What could she say? She didn't want him frightened. "That's right, Joshua. It's okay."

He looked back at Noah. "Yeah, she always makes me fix what I break." He shook his head. "But I never did anything this stupid. You have to be careful with guns. My dad would have tanned me for doing something like that. He used to take me to the target range, but I never —" He stopped abruptly and Kate saw his hands clench at his sides.

"I was careful," Noah said quickly. "I've done

it before when I was in the service. You were never in any danger, but I guess I was pretty stupid. It won't happen again." Noah took off the tire and laid it on the ground. "It's getting dark. I'd like to finish this job and get back to the cabin and start supper for us. I could use some help."

"Supper," Joshua repeated. Then he nodded vigorously, shifted the tire aside, and knelt beside Noah. "I'll put on the lug nuts, you tighten them. Okay?"

"Okay," Noah said. He looked at Kate. "Okay?"

He wasn't asking only for permission for Joshua to help him, Kate knew.

"We're all hungry, Kate," Phyliss said quietly. "What could it hurt?"

She wasn't sure. In the space of a few minutes Noah Smith had won over Phyliss, who was no easy game, and was now working on Joshua. Not only that, but he had almost convinced Kate that she had compromised Joshua's safety by acting impulsively.

Maybe it was true, she thought wearily. She had certainly not acted with her usual cool deliberation. She had gotten angry and walked out. Perhaps she should have listened and —

My God, what was she doing? She was blaming herself when this asshole had just shot out her tire.

And called her skittish. Somehow that repulsive adjective weighed almost as heavily as the more violent act.

"Please," Noah said softly.

And that was supposed to make everything all right? Not likely.

But she was hungry and tired, and so were Joshua and Phyliss. She wouldn't make them all suffer because she wanted to brain Noah Smith. In fact, it might be pleasant to see him slaving on their behalf. "Okay," she said. "Supper."

"Dessert," Noah announced. "Sorry, I didn't have time to put together anything. We'll have to settle for a store-bought cherry pie." He got up from the table and disappeared behind the breakfast bar into the kitchen area.

"He's good," Phyliss said as she leaned back in her chair. "Steak, potatoes, and pie, homemade biscuits."

"He likes food," Kate told her.

Joshua took the last of his biscuit and mopped up the gravy from his plate. "Did you know he shot out that tire from six hundred yards?"

"No," Kate said. "He told you that?"

Joshua nodded. "He used to do it all the time when he was a sharpshooter in the Special Forces. But he said that was a while ago. All he's been doing lately is target shooting with Seth." He popped the biscuit in his mouth. "He says Seth can hit a bull's-eye from a thousand yards."

"Don't talk with your mouth full," Kate said.

"Sorry."

"And who is Seth?" Phyliss asked Joshua.

"Noah's friend. He was the one who came to

the house that night."

Phyliss looked at Kate. "That was the man? I only caught a glimpse of him."

Kate nodded.

"He lives at the ranger station a few miles from here. Noah said he'd take me there tomorrow." Joshua shook his head. "A thousand yards . . . Dad told me practically no one could do that. And Seth knows all about tracking."

"That's nice." Noah had spent his time well when he'd had Joshua helping in the kitchen while he prepared dinner. He'd not only filled Joshua with admiration and enthusiasm but primed him to renew his acquaintance with Seth. The man never gave up. Kate wondered why she wasn't more annoyed. Maybe it had something to do with the flames crackling in the fireplace across the room, a full belly, and the feeling of cozy isolation in this aerie in the woods. Was he manipulating her again? Probably, but it didn't matter as long as she recognized it and could deal with it. "But it depends on what you track and what happens when you find the quarry."

"Oh, Seth doesn't shoot any animals. He just tracks them and gets them in his sights. Noah says animals aren't fair game for him."

And what was fair game for a man who could hit a target at a thousand yards?

"Noah says Seth would probably take me along if I asked him." He gave her a wary glance. "No guns. I know you don't like hunting. I'd only take my camera. People go on camera safaris all the time. I bet I'd get extra credit when I get back to school."

"We'll talk about it later."

"But it would be good exercise, and you always say I should —"

"Give it a rest, Joshua," Phyliss advised. "Your mom's tired."

He sighed and pushed back his chair. "I'll go help Noah."

Phyliss smiled as she watched Joshua leave. "He's excited. A new interest isn't a bad thing right now. It was this Seth who was here when you arrived?"

She nodded. "Noah wants you and Joshua to move to the ranger station with Seth so he can take care of you. He says it will be safer for you than being with me."

"Don't tell Joshua that or you'll never get him to go."

"I don't know that I want him to go anywhere. And certainly not with a stranger who may be a terrible influence. Maybe I shouldn't even be here." She wearily rubbed her temple. "Have I done the right thing, Phyliss?"

"I don't know. Michael would say you hadn't. Michael would say trust the system. Go to the police." She leaned back in her chair. "But you see so many bad things on television that no one seems to be able to stop. Detectives taking bribes, drugs, children abused." Her lips trembled. "And if they killed Michael and managed to fool Alan and the rest of the force into thinking it was about drugs, I can see how you'd be afraid to trust anyone but yourself. That's why I didn't argue with you about coming. We can't lose Joshua too."

Kate reached out and closed her hand on Phyliss's. "We won't lose him."

"And working to complete this RU2 will make him safe?"

"I think so. It makes sense." She grimaced. "But I don't even know that RU2 is what Noah says it is. I only have his word."

"It would be pretty stupid for him to go to all this trouble if it wasn't." Phyliss paused. "I like him."

"He made damn sure you would. But he lied to me and he'd do it again."

"We all have things that are so important to us we'd lie to protect them." Phyliss smiled. "Even you. You'd lie until you were black in the face to keep Joshua safe. Maybe RU2 is Noah's Joshua."

"Maybe. I'm sorry to have drawn you into all this. You didn't deserve it."

"You and Joshua are my family. It goes with the territory," Phyliss said. "I'll take care of Joshua. You take care of trying to get us out of this mess. Okay?"

"You think I'm going to stay."

"Aren't you?"

"Yes," she said. The knowledge that this would be her decision had been growing all evening. For the first time since Michael's death she felt as if the world had steadied on its axis. They were safe here and it was to Noah's advantage to keep them safe. She could overlook almost anything else. "As long as it's on my terms."

Seven

The air was cool and crisp when Kate opened the door and stepped out on the deck after she had put Joshua to bed.

Noah turned to face her. "Joshua asleep?"

She shook her head. "It will take a while." She glanced at him. "You did a real number on him talking about your friend Seth."

"It was all true." He added soberly, "No more lies, Kate."

"Phyliss said that everyone lies if the stakes are high enough. That doesn't excuse you or make what you did more palatable to me." She looked intently at him. "What would you do if I left right now?"

"Try to stop you in any way I can. But I'm not Ogden. I wouldn't hurt you or your family. If nothing worked, I'd try to get along without you." He added, "And hope that you all stayed alive until I can go public."

She believed him. "Phyliss said RU2 may be like a child to you."

"Maybe. I don't know anymore. At first it was an ego trip, then it was a kind of holy mission, then it turned into something else. If it's my child, it's a child who's already murdered ninety-nine human beings. I expected a fight but not that." He paused. "But the price is already too high to stop. I can't let all those people die for nothing. I have to try. Will you try with me?"

She didn't answer directly. "Who is Seth Drakin?"

"A friend. We were together in the service."

"A friend who can hit a bull's-eye at a thousand yards?"

"I'm not trying to hide anything from you. Seth had a hellish upbringing and he never settled down after we got out of the service. He's been everything from a mercenary to a smuggler."

"And you set him to watch my son?"

"I'd set him to watch my son in the same circumstances. Joshua will never be safer with anyone. He's not what you think. His IQ is probably higher than mine. He's certainly better read and he handles people better than any man I've ever met."

"When he doesn't kill them."

He grimaced. "Talk to him. Let me take you all to the ranger station tomorrow."

She nodded. "But I want it understood that if I decide that the situation isn't what I want for Joshua, you'll give me no argument."

"No deal. I'll argue. Everyone has the right to argue." He smiled. "But I won't push too hard."

She found herself smiling back before a thought occurred to her. "One other thing. If you ever refer to me as skittish or any other demeaning term, I'll crown you."

He shuddered. "I knew that was a mistake the minute it came out of my mouth."

"Big time. And now I want to see the lab."

He nodded.

"And your notes and test results on RU2."

"Now? Wouldn't it be easier if I gave you the computer disk?"

"No, I'll take the papers to bed with me and browse through them before I go to sleep." She moved toward the door. "I need to decide for myself whether you're a genius or some crackpot."

"Oh, I'm a goddamn genius," he murmured. "No doubt about it."

He was a goddamn genius.

No doubt about it.

Kate thrust the last pages back into the briefcase he had handed her and dropped it on the floor beside the bed. She turned off the light on the bedside table, but already a predawn grayness lit the room. She had meant only to glance through Noah's work, but she had been caught, held in thrall by the possibilities.

No, not possibilities. Miracles.

If only RU2 had been available three years ago . . .

Noah had already developed RU2 and was testing it at the time Daddy had forced her to make that hideous decision.

She swallowed to ease the tightness in her throat. It was stupid to look back. What was done was done.

Look ahead. If she worked hard enough, she

could do something more special than she'd ever dreamed.

She could be part of the miracle.

Phyliss, Joshua, and Noah were already at the breakfast bar when Kate came into the room the next morning. "Good morning." She handed Noah the briefcase. "Thank you. Interesting reading."

"Hi, Mom. Noah said to let you sleep. Want some pancakes?"

"Just orange juice." She poured herself a glass and sat down. "You're almost finished?"

Joshua nodded. "We're going over to the forest ranger station."

Noah was frowning. "What do you mean, 'interesting'?"

He was like a little boy begging for praise after winning a contest. Well, he wouldn't get it from her. She would begin as she intended to proceed. After that night of immersion in RU2 she was already intimidated enough by Noah. It would be difficult to hold her own on a professional level. "Actually, very interesting." She sipped her orange juice. "How did you sleep, Phyliss?"

"Like a log," Phyliss said. "And you?"

"Well enough. The country air must agree with me." She glanced at Noah. "I have to talk to Seth Drakin first, but I think we may stay awhile."

A brilliant smile lit Noah's face.

"This is neat." Joshua called down from the

fourth landing of the forest station. "It's like a tree house. Hurry up, Mom."

"I'm hurrying," Kate said. "If I don't get a heart attack first." She glanced back over her shoulder at Noah. "You didn't tell me this place has as many landings as the Washington Monument."

"You're exaggerating," Noah said. "The ranger has to be high enough to sight forest fires."

"If I ever get up there, I may never come down," Phyliss said grimly. "Who needs a Stair-Master?"

"Hi." Seth Drakin was leaning over the top deck, his expression as boyishly eager as Joshua's. "Pretty cool, huh?"

"Awesome," Joshua said as he took the last steps two at a time. "How far can we see?"

"About thirty miles. Good to see you again, Joshua." He handed over the pair of binoculars he was holding. "You can see a big lake to the north."

Joshua frowned. "Where?"

"Here, let me help you focus." He squatted beside him and adjusted the binoculars. "Now?"

Joshua nodded. "Wow. I can even see a bird on that pine by the shore." He crossed the deck and stretched over the rail, the binoculars pressed to his eyes. "And there's a campfire . . ."

Kate was about to tell him to get back from the rail when Seth moved quickly to his side.

"Hey, don't hang over the rail like that. Lyle hates carpentry work and I promised him that I'd treat those rails like they were made of straw."

"Sorry." Joshua backed away. "Who's Lyle? The ranger?"

"Yep." He pointed to the north. "Want to see the cabin you stayed at last night? It looks as close as the next room." He smiled at Kate as she reached the top landing. "You had a late night last night."

"You could see in my bedroom?" she asked warily.

"Well . . ." He smiled mischievously. "Yes."

She tried to remember whether she had undressed in the bathroom or bedroom last night.

"But I'm no Peeping Tom. I just took a peek and then got out."

Maybe. His smile was a little too innocent.

"Could you see my room too?" Joshua asked.

"Nope. You must be on the other side of the house."

"Maybe Mom and I could change and we could signal each other."

"We'll talk about it. I think I have a better idea." Seth turned to watch Phyliss as she struggled up the last steps. "I'm Seth. You must be Phyliss Denby."

"I'm not sure," she said breathlessly. "I was when I started up these stairs. I may have passed into the afterlife." She gazed out over the expanse of forest and the hills in the distance. "But, you know, it may be worth it."

"Campfire?" Noah asked, his gaze to the north.

"A honeymoon couple," Seth said. "I paid

them a visit at five this morning, and they didn't even invite me to breakfast." He mournfully glanced at Phyliss. "All I had was a bowl of Total and a cup of coffee."

"Sounds like a well-balanced meal to me," Phyliss said blandly.

"What kind of grandmother are you?" Seth said in disgust. "That opening should have led to an offer of gingerbread cookies and pot roast for supper."

"Have you been living in a cave for the last thirty years?" Phyliss asked.

"Sometimes." Seth smiled at her. "Okay. We share the cooking?"

"Or work out trades." She returned his smile. "If Kate decides we're to stay."

Seth turned to Kate. "You wouldn't make me stay here alone? I didn't peek, honest."

"We're going to live here?" Joshua asked, his eyes wide with excitement.

Kate said, "You and your grandmother and Mr. Drakin might stay here. Would you like that?"

"It would be cool." He suddenly frowned. "You wouldn't be here?"

"Your mom has to work in the lab at the cabin and there's only one bedroom here." Seth added, "You and your grandmother will share, and I'm going to bunk on the couch in the living room."

Joshua slowly shook his head. "I don't think so. I have to stay with Mom."

"You could keep an eye on the cabin with the

binoculars," Noah said. "I promise to watch over her. I know I fouled up the last time, but I don't do that very often."

"Maybe it would be okay," Joshua said doubtfully. "You're pretty good with that rifle."

"This isn't a set deal," Kate said. "I have to talk to Mr. Drakin first. But if we decide it's the best thing to do, I'll jog over every day to see you." She added, "And you can come to the cabin."

Seth quickly shook his head. "He'll be too busy. I promised Lyle we'd keep an eye out for fires, and Joshua will have to take his watch. But you can come here and help us."

"Is there a phone?" Joshua asked.

Seth nodded. "And I've already programmed the cabin number into it."

"Phyliss?" Kate asked.

Phyliss nodded. "I can handle them."

Kate still hesitated.

"She can't make up her mind until she looks the place over to make sure it's not a hovel," Seth said. "Will you keep watch while I take your mom inside, Joshua?"

"Sure." He raised the binoculars to his eyes. "Do I look for smoke?"

"And anything else that might pose a problem." Seth opened the door for Kate. "Keep a sharp eye on those honeymooners. They weren't paying any attention to their campfire this morning."

"I'm not sure I want Joshua to keep an eye

on those honeymooners," Kate murmured as she entered the station. It was surprisingly cozy, with a denim-covered couch and easy chair, and the kitchenette and breakfast bar across the room.

"He'll probably get quite a few lessons in biology while he's here, but the honeymooners were in the tent the last time I saw them." He turned to face her and the boyishness fell away from him as if it were a hat he discarded. "Okay. You're not sure about me. So ask me questions."

"Will you answer them?"

"Most of them."

"Why does Noah think you can keep Joshua safe?"

"I can shoot, I'm woods savvy, I don't trust anyone, and I made Noah a promise."

"Promises are broken all the time."

He shrugged. "I prefer to keep mine."

"Anything else?"

"I like kids."

She could tell that by the way he'd handled Joshua, but she wasn't sure how much of a kid he was himself. He had shown her a completely different side of the man who had come running up her driveway that night.

"Fifty-fifty," he said as if reading her mind. "Joshua and I will bond but I can keep it under control."

"You're the one who told Noah about Ishmaru."

"That doesn't mean we're buddies. I know a

lot of people. What did you tell Joshua about Ishmaru?"

"The truth."

"Did you tell him you wanted him away from you for his protection?"

"No, do you think I wanted to scare him to death?"

"I think he's more scared about something happening to you." He smiled. "Nice kid. Smart too."

"I don't want him to feel threatened."

"I'll try, but there's no way I can promise. Blindness can be a risk." He stared directly into her eyes. "If you put Joshua in my hands, he's mine. He won't come to the cabin, because that would nullify moving him here. You can visit him here, but not without phoning to let me know so that I can meet you and make sure you're not followed. If I think it's safer to move him, I'll move him. I'll try to let you know, but if I see a risk, I won't do it. Is that clear?"

"Very clear." She should resent his arbitrarily taking over Joshua; he was her son and responsibility. But she didn't resent it. She felt relieved and comforted by the all-encompassing wall Seth was building about Joshua. "But he's not yours, he's mine. And if I think you're not taking proper care of him, I'll push you off this tower. Is that clear?"

He smiled. "I got it." He waved a hand at the door. "Now you'd better go tell Joshua I have your stamp of approval."

She said dryly, "There's no way you'll have my stamp of approval if you let him become a damn voyeur with those binoculars."

It took over half the day for them to unpack Phyliss's and Joshua's belongings and get the two of them settled in the station. It was almost sunset when Kate and Noah got back to the cabin.

She felt oddly flat as she climbed the steps to the deck.

"You're very quiet," Noah said as he unlocked the door. "It's going to be fine, you know. Joshua is happy."

"I know."

"Seth will take good care of him."

"He'd better."

"If you'd had doubts, you wouldn't have left Joshua." His gaze searched her expression. "What's wrong? I want to make things right for you. What can I do?"

"I just miss him," she said simply.

"You only left him ten minutes ago. You spent hours away from him when you went to work every day."

"So I'm not reasonable. This is different. I feel as if I've sent him away to boarding school or something. You couldn't understand."

"No, I don't." He crossed the room to the wall phone in the kitchen. "But I'll see if I can fix it." He pressed a number on the dial. "Two is the ranger station." He spoke into the phone. "Seth, let me speak to Joshua." He held out the receiver to her. "Talk to him."

She took the receiver. "What will I say?"

"Whatever you want to say. Ask him about his first day at boarding school." He moved around the breakfast bar into the kitchenette. "How about spaghetti for dinner?"

"Fine," she said automatically. "Hello, Joshua." She thought quickly. "I was wondering if you'll need another pair of binoculars. . . ."

She hung up the phone ten minutes later.

"Feel better?" Noah asked.

She did feel better. She had known Joshua was just a phone call away, but the brief connection had reinforced the fact and lessened the isolation. "Yes. How did you know?"

"It must be because I'm sensitive as well as brilliant." He looked up from the tomato sauce he was stirring and grinned. "Lucky guess."

She smiled back at him. With a dish towel wrapped around his waist and a smear of tomato sauce on his chin, he appeared very un-geniuslike at this moment. "That's what I thought." She moved around the breakfast bar. "What can I do to help?"

"Get out of my kitchen. I'm very possessive about my dishes."

"You have a secret recipe?"

"Hell yes." He grimaced. "Haven't you noticed? I'm great on secret recipes. But I promise this one isn't another RU2. No catch-22's. It will only delight the palate."

She sensed bitterness layered beneath the lightness of those last sentences. "RU2 may be the single most valuable medical breakthrough in history. It will save millions of lives."

"And has already taken almost a hundred." He paused. "No, *I* took those lives. I created RU2. I knew what the fallout might be and I went ahead with it. Anything that happens is on my head." He took the pot of sauce off the flame. "As it will be on yours if you help me."

She stared at him, puzzled. "Why are you warning me? You did everything but kidnap me to get me to work on the project."

"I just want you to know that — Dammit, I don't know." He shrugged wearily. "I guess I feel guilty and want to share a little of it. Or maybe I want you to tell me to go to hell and walk away."

"And then you'd come after me and convince me to come back."

"Probably."

"Certainly." She said brusquely, "So shut up. You didn't mesmerize me into agreeing to stay. I made my decision. I could have walked away. I didn't." She went to the cabinet. "Does this idiotic culinary possessiveness of yours include setting the table?"

"No." He watched her get down the plates, and a slow smile lit his face. "You don't find me mesmerizing?"

"Sorry."

"Damn." He took the boiling noodles off the stove and moved over to the sink to drain them. "I must be slipping."

She found herself smiling as she set the table. She was beginning to feel comfortable with him, she realized. This wasn't the brilliant scientist whose work astounded her, nor the relentlessly determined man who had shot out her tire. He was more human, vulnerable. He was the Noah who had sat in the diner and smiled at the waitress and made her feel as if she were the most important person in his world.

But Kate wasn't Dorothy; she had to live with Noah for the next weeks. She had to work with him and hold her own.

"Hurry up," Noah said as he poured the sauce over the noodles. "If you're lucky, I'll let you take the garlic bread out of the oven."

"That's slave work."

"Yep."

To hell with putting up barriers and holding her own. She couldn't work in an atmosphere in which she was constantly on guard. As he had said, they were in this together. It would do no harm to be friends. "Take it out yourself. I choose my work." She sat down at the table, spread her napkin on her lap, and announced, "I'm waiting to be served."

When she went to her room that night, the first thing she saw was the hurricane lamp on the windowsill. The candle was lit and casting shadows on the wall. There was a note from Noah beside it.

You really can see this room from the ranger station.

196

Seth thought you could light the candle every night and tell Joshua that it's your way of saying good night.

She smiled as she gently touched the glass globe with her finger. Very thoughtful of Seth. He had not impressed her as the kind of man who would think of the little things. It made her feel more comfortable about leaving Joshua in his care.

She looked out at the darkness and whispered, "Maybe this will work out after all. Good night, Joshua."

Noah waited only until the door closed behind Kate before he dialed Tony at the lodge.

"It's about time," Tony said sourly. "I thought you'd dropped off the planet."

"Did you switch to a digital?"

"Yes, the day after you told me."

"Good. Any more deaths?"

"No." He paused. "What the hell happened in Dandridge?"

"Nothing good."

"I'd say that's an understatement. She killed a policeman?"

Noah went still. "What?"

"There's a warrant out for her arrest in the killing of one Caleb Brunwick. You didn't know?"

Noah muttered a curse. "Of course I didn't know. It's crazy." Not so crazy, he realized. What better way to take Kate out of the picture and discredit her after Ishmaru had failed. "What's the motive?"

"The word is that she flipped after the murder of her ex-husband and blamed the police department. She sent a note to the police commissioner telling them that she had taken a life for a life."

"Forgery."

"And several coworkers testified that she was suffering from exhaustion and depression."

Ogden had woven his net and was drawing it tight. Christ, he had moved faster than Noah had thought possible. "Lies."

"Well then, she'd better get back there and clear it up."

Which was exactly what Ogden wanted her to do. If the frame was good enough, she'd be held. If it wasn't, she'd be set up for Ishmaru again. "What's happening with Ogden?"

"Barlow said he met with three bigwig executives yesterday."

"Who?"

"He was only able to identify one. Ken Bradton."

"Shit."

"And today he paid a visit to an inn on the outskirts of town where Senator Longworth was registered under a phony name."

"He's sure it was Longworth?"

"Longworth isn't hard to spot. He loves the limelight and he's conducted more Senate investigations than Joe McCarthy." Tony was silent a moment. "Ogden's moving and shaking. That Washington connection doesn't look good. What are you going to do?"

There wasn't much he could do, Noah thought in frustration. His hands were tied until the work here was finished. "Wait. Watch. I want you to go to Washington tomorrow. Stay at a hotel outside the city and keep a low profile. I don't want Ogden to know you're in town."

"You mean I can come down from my mountain?" Tony asked sarcastically. "I thought I was here for the millennium."

He didn't have any choice but to expose Tony. Everything was going to hell in a handbasket. "I'll call you on your digital phone tomorrow night and get your hotel number."

"What about Barlow?"

"For the time being, have him stay in Seattle and keep an eye on Ogden," Noah said. "Be careful, Tony."

"Always." Tony hung up the phone.

Now what? he wondered. Should he tell Kate about the warrant? He might be able to convince her of the danger of going back, but her instinct would be to trust her friend Alan and clear herself. In that case, the best they could hope for was a delay for RU2, the worst was that Kate could die. He couldn't accept either consequence.

So he would not tell Kate.

My God, he was digging a deep hole for himself.

Seth contentedly breathed in the clean, pine-scented air as he gazed out into the darkness.

It was good here. Not perfect. Nothing was perfect. But he'd take this corner of West Virginia anytime over that hellhole in Colombia.

He could hear the clatter of china and running water inside the house as Phyliss did the supper dishes. Nice woman. Nice kid. Nice place. Maybe he could stay awhile even after Noah brought order into the chaos surrounding them. Noah had always been good at patiently shaping situations to suit himself. Not like Seth. He had never had the patience. If things didn't happen quickly enough, he'd make them happen and damn the consequences.

And then he'd move on.

Who the hell wanted to stay in one place anyway? This job would be like any other except he was helping Noah. After it was over, he'd get restless or bored or something would happen that would make him leave.

He heard the screen door open and glanced over his shoulder to see Joshua coming out of the house. "Hi. Nice night, huh?"

Joshua came to stand beside him. "It's quiet." His hands clutched the railing. "I didn't expect it to be this quiet."

"It's not really quiet. Listen to the night sounds."

Joshua's hands nervously opened and closed on the rail. "Yeah . . . but it's kind of lonely. It kinda makes you —" He broke off and turned away. "I think I'll go around to the other side where I can see the cabin." He quickly walked away and around the corner.

Too quickly.

He looked as if he were trying to escape from something.

Like the rest of us, Seth thought. Welcome to the world, kid.

But the kid belonged to him for the time he was here, and escapes often led to disaster. It was during quiet moments like these that the shock of displacement and traumatic events tended to hit home.

He followed Joshua.

But he stopped when he reached the corner.

Joshua was sitting on the deck, his shoulders heaving, silent tears running down his cheeks. He had run out here to vent his grief where no one could see him. Seth could understand. He had never wanted anyone to see his tears either.

Should he leave Joshua and go back into the house?

Probably. The kid was proud and wouldn't want anyone to know. He might accept comfort from his mother or a man like Noah, but Seth would only bungle it.

He started to turn and then swung back. To hell with it. So he wasn't Noah. The kid was hurting. He would deal with it in the only way he knew how.

"I'm coming over," Kate told Phyliss over the phone two days later. "Tell Seth. He told me to call and let him know when I was coming."

"He's not here. He and Joshua are on maneuvers."

"What?"

"You heard me. I told him you wouldn't like it."

"Where are they?"

"Near the lake. Ten miles south. He has his pager. Shall I buzz him?"

"No, I'm on my way." She hung up.

"Trouble?" Noah asked.

"Why would you think that?" Her tone dripped sarcasm. "Just because your friend has taken a nine-year-old boy on maneuvers. Give me the keys to your jeep."

"I'll go with you."

"One of you is enough to deal with. Give me the keys."

He shrugged and tossed her the key ring.

Ten minutes later she was bouncing along the rough dirt road that bordered the lake.

No sight of them.

She stopped the jeep and jumped out.

"Joshua."

No answer.

Where the devil were they?

"Seth."

No answer.

Anger ebbed as anxiety flooded her. She moved quickly into the woods. "Joshua!"

"Time to answer. She's worried, Joshua. You never hide from someone when they're worried about you." Seth moved out of the shadows only a few feet away.

"Hi, Mom." Joshua was trailing behind him. "I knew it was you before you called." He glanced at Seth. "Gosh, you've got a super nose. You were right. She does stink."

"I beg your pardon?" she asked coldly.

Seth grimaced. "No offense. Not you in particular. Just human beings collectively."

Joshua giggled. "But we don't stink, do we? We didn't shower last night and we rolled in dirt this morning."

"We stink a little," Seth told him. "It takes a good two days in the field before you wear away the scent of civilization."

"What are you talking about?" Kate asked. "Is this part of these stupid maneuvers?"

Joshua's smile faded. "Are you mad, Mom?"

"She doesn't understand," Seth said quickly. "Why don't you go a little way down the path and let me explain it to her."

"We're not doing anything wrong, Mom. We're just on maneuvers."

"Maneuvers are war games. You know how I feel about —"

"I'll come in ten minutes and I want you to tell me all the scents that you can identify." Seth jerked his thumb. "Hit it, kid."

Joshua grinned and ran down the path.

She felt a hurtful pang as she watched him go. She was being . . . closed out.

"Sorry we weren't at the station," Seth said.

"You didn't tell us you were coming today."

"I didn't know until the last minute." She swung around and attacked. "Maneuvers? He's just a little boy. I won't have him playing games like this."

"It's no game." He raised his hand to cut off her protest. "I'm not going to give him a rifle and a machete. Though I understand his father had no compunctions about teaching Joshua to shoot."

"At targets. And I didn't like that either."

"It surprises me that you'd object." He smiled. "You're a fighter too. I knew that the moment I saw you."

"Battles shouldn't be fought with guns."

"But they are. Look at the evening news."

"Well, my son isn't going to live in a ghetto where he'll have to face that threat."

"No, he lives in a quiet little subdivision where nothing bad ever happens. But his father's been murdered and he thinks his mother may be at any moment."

She felt as if he had struck her. "I did everything I could to keep him safe."

He shrugged. "Things happen. Ghettos don't have the monopoly on bad luck." His expression softened. "Look, I'm not putting the kid through commando training. I'm just trying to make him believe that he can deal with what's happened to him. Right now he feels helpless and worried as hell. He wasn't able to help you when he thought you needed him."

"He's just a child."

"With a king-size sense of responsibility. It must be in the genes." He paused. "He cried the other night."

She stiffened. "What did you do?"

"Ignored it. Pretended I didn't see it. He didn't want me to know. So I didn't know." He shook his head. "I'm not his mother. The only way I could comfort him was to take away his helplessness."

"I should have been there."

"Not if you want to keep him safe. I didn't mean to lay a guilt trip on you. I just wanted you to know that Joshua needs to feel adequate to fight what's going on around him."

"Not this way. I can't —" She stopped as she realized she wasn't thinking. It seemed she had been acting on impulse ever since this nightmare started, and she couldn't afford to do that where Joshua was concerned. "Just a minute." She was silent a moment, trying to clear her mind. "Just what are you teaching him?"

"Nothing violent. Woodlore, how to move silently, how to see and not be seen."

"Then why are you calling it maneuvers?"

"It seemed logical. Joshua feels as if he's in a war."

"Does he?" she whispered, appalled.

"Look, it's natural. There's nothing anyone can do to make him feel any different. He's too smart. For God's sake, he *is* in a war. Telling him that you'll take care of him doesn't make him think he's any safer. You're the one he's worried about."

"But I'm supposed to take care of him. It's my job."

"And you've had to delegate it." He stared intently into her eyes. "Let me do my job in my own way, Kate."

"The devil I will." She gave a weary sigh. "But maybe you're right. Maybe playing these stupid war games will make him feel more secure."

He smiled. "Good, then let's go tell Joshua you're not mad at him." He reached out and took her hand. "If you're good, we might even let you play with us."

She hesitated and then placed her hand in Seth's. He led her down the path in the direction Joshua had taken.

She felt as she had when she was a very little girl and Daddy had led her through Jenkins's woods. Seth's hand was hard, callused . . . and safe. Strange that she felt so safe with a man who plied death for a living. Was this why Joshua instinctively trusted him? She should pull away. She wasn't a little girl any longer. She didn't need anyone to guide her. Yet she didn't want to make an issue of it.

He settled her inner conflict by dropping her hand. "Joshua's just ahead."

"How do you know?"

"I smell him. Prell shampoo. Dove soap. Dead giveaways." He grinned. "One day without a shower isn't enough."

"It had better be. Because I'm telling Phyliss he's not to do without another one."

"Spoilsport."

"Can you really spot someone just by their scent?"

"Sure. Like Joshua said, I've got a good nose. But in the woods, manmade scents stick out like a burning bush. Before I go into the field, I even bury my gear in the ground for a day so it will take on an earth smell."

She made a face. "Pleasant."

"Better than dead," he said cheerfully.

What must it be like to live as he did? she wondered. His life, filled with death and distrust, was as volatile as hers was stable. Or had been stable, she thought ruefully. Nothing about her life was stable any longer. "I guess so."

"I know so." He smiled at her. "There are advantages to living on the edge. You always appreciate the in-betweens. I bet I enjoy life a hell of a lot more than you or Noah."

"Like hitting your thumb with a hammer because it feels so good when you stop?" she asked sweetly. "I believe that's called masochism or maybe just plain nuts."

"Ouch." He broke into a trot and called, "Come out and help, Joshua. Your mom is attacking me."

Joshua appeared from behind an oak tree. "She's still mad?"

"No, I'm not mad," Kate said. "I'm hungry. Did either of you bring any food, or were you supposed to live off the land?"

"Not this trip," Seth replied. "My backpack is down by the lake. But Joshua has to earn lunch. Well? What did you smell?"

"Leaves. Rotting wood. Something minty. Shit." He looked at Kate. "I'm not cursing, Mom. There really was some animal back there."

"I believe I taught you other words for that."

He grinned mischievously. "Seth says you have to be quick in the woods." He looked at Seth. "Did I get them all?"

"No," Seth said. "But you did pretty good for a beginner. Now, go down to the lake and bring back my pack so we can feed your mom. After lunch we'll go find that pile and you'll learn what kind of animal made it."

"Right." Joshua ran down the path at full speed.

"Sit down." Seth gestured to the grass beneath the tree Joshua had sprung from. "You look tired."

"I'm not tired. I only walked a quarter mile. I'm not that decrepit."

"Okay. You're not tired, you're tense. It must come from using all those brain cells." He sat down, stretched his legs out in front of him. "You should follow my example." He leaned his head back against the trunk and closed his eyes. "Never think when you can feel."

"That's why you're such a success in life?"

"Yep." He opened one eye. "Oh, were you insulting me?"

"Yes." She dropped down beside him. "Not that it makes any difference to you."

He yawned. "It makes a difference. But I forgive you."

"Thank you." She paused. "Was it safe to let Joshua go alone?"

"Yes."

"I suppose you would have smelled someone, Tarzan?"

"Or heard them."

"Even Ishmaru?" She shivered. "He thinks he's some kind of Indian warrior."

"Not enough. He's a drugstore Indian. He invented himself. He smells of Mennen aftershave lotion, incense, and sesame seeds."

"You could tell that in the brief time you were kneeling beside him?"

"I paid attention. When you run across someone as weird as Ishmaru, you make a point of remembering everything about him. It could save your neck."

"I see your point." She tilted her head. "What about me? What do I smell like?"

"The first time I saw you, you smelled of a botanical shampoo. Cassia, I think. You must have run out or not brought it with you, because you washed your hair this morning with Prell. No perfume, but you're wearing Opium body powder." He smiled. "Nice. Clean and nice."

"Thank you," she said faintly. "I suppose you know what kind of toothpaste I used too."

"Colgate. Scope mouthwash."

She laughed. "I think I'd hate to have that keen a sense of smell. Not all odors are pleasant."

His smile faded. "No, some aren't pleasant at all." He closed his eyes again. "So we deal with them and then try not to remember."

He was talking about something specific, she guessed. Seth Drakin must have confronted a good deal of unpleasantness in his life.

"Does Joshua have a dog?" Seth asked.

She was startled at the sudden change of subject. "No."

"Want one? I tried to give him to Noah, but he may be too busy to take care of a pet."

"Your dog?"

"Sort of. I picked him up in Colombia. He's in quarantine right now."

And remembering that unpleasantness had reminded Seth of the dog. She felt a stirring of curiosity but resisted the impulse to question him. It wasn't her business, and in spite of his candid demeanor, she had an idea that Seth was not nearly as open and uncomplicated as he seemed. "I think we'd better talk about that later."

"Okay. I didn't think you'd commit. You're too cautious."

" 'Caution' isn't a dirty word, you know."

"No, it's a nice sturdy word. Like 'responsibility' and 'sincerity' and 'duty.' " He yawned. "The bug that bit Noah in the ass. He used to be much more entertaining."

"If you expect me to argue with you, you're going to be disappointed. I took the day off to relax, and that's what I'm going to do."

"Then lean back instead of sitting up stiff as a poker."

She hesitated and then leaned back. The bark of the tree felt rough through her sweatshirt. She was about as relaxed as a tightly drawn wire. She shot Seth a glance from the corner of her eye. The sunlight filtering through the trees lit the sun streaks in his dark brown hair. His eyes were closed, his long, muscular body appeared totally relaxed. All he needed was a fishing pole to look like one of the kids in a Norman Rockwell painting, she thought in exasperation.

But he wasn't a kid. He was very male and she was reacting to that masculinity, she realized in astonishment. The sexual response was sharp, intense, almost animalistic. Where had that come from? It must have something to do with being in the forest surrounded by nature.

"Joshua tells me you're quite a pitcher," Seth murmured.

"Yes."

"Did you play when you were a kid?"

"They didn't let girls in Little League, but my dad played with me. Did you play ball?"

"A little. Sandlot in Newark, New Jersey. I was a catcher. I always thought that catchers were the gladiators of the game. The idea appealed to me."

"War games even then?"

"You're talking about the great American pastime."

She was beginning to relax, she realized. The

sun was warm on her face, and she could smell the grass and earth and the musky odor of Seth a few feet away. Not unpleasant. It seemed to go with the other earth fragrances around her.

"That's right, take it easy," Seth murmured. "You like the woods, don't you?"

"Can you smell that too? There was a forest in back of the house where I grew up. My father and I used to go for long walks every Saturday. They weren't like these though. No hills."

"Did you grow up in Oklahoma?"

She nodded. "About fifty miles south of Dandridge. My father was a G.P."

"What about your mother?"

"She died when I was four. Then it was just me and my dad."

"You got along well?"

"Oh yes, you might say that." She added simply, "He was my best friend."

"You miss him."

"Every day."

He didn't comment further. Thank God, he wasn't one of those people who thought they were required to offer sympathy. "He was a very fine doctor and an exceptional man. I was lucky to have him for my father."

"Another white hat. Like Noah."

Surprise rippled through her. "Yes." She hadn't realized it until this moment, but Noah did remind her of her father. He had the same dedication and strong sense of responsibility.

Do it for Joshua's sake. Don't try to nail me back

to my branch. I've no taste for crucifixion.

She flinched away from the memory, suppressing it as she always did. She had become expert at blocking that thought. It was a matter of survival.

"Noah mentioned that he died of cancer?"

"Yes. Three years ago."

Joshua was coming down the path, lugging the backpack. He waved at her.

She waved back, watching him contentedly. That hurtful memory of Daddy was fading, and the weird intense sexual flare Seth had lit in her had died down as if it had never occurred. Thank God, Seth hadn't noticed. She imagined there wasn't much that he missed. She wouldn't worry about it. She felt safe. The sun was bright. It was hard to believe anything bad could happen today.

"One minute at a time," Seth murmured.

She turned to see that his eyes were open and he was looking at her.

"It's something you and Noah should learn. You let life weigh you down." He smiled, an oddly beautiful smile. "Nothing's all bad, if you take it one minute at a time. Enjoy the moment, Kate."

Eight

Tony called Noah a week later. "There was a minor demonstration at the Supreme Court yesterday."

"Against what?"

"Genetic experimentation and testing."

"Shit. How minor?"

"About five hundred people. But it may be the tip of the iceberg."

"I want to know if there are any more."

"You think Ogden is stirring them up?"

"Hell yes, it's too coincidental."

"I'll be on top of it. How's it going there?"

"Well enough."

"That's a cautious answer."

"Caution is the name of the game. Just see that you follow the rules."

"It's almost midnight. Go to bed."

Kate glanced up from the slide she'd been studying under the microscope to see Noah standing beside her. "In a moment." She looked down at the slide again. "I want to make sure that —"

"Now." He pulled the slide from the microscope. "You're so tired I wouldn't trust your judgment anyway."

"I'm fine." She tried to take the slide away from

him. "And you have no right to interfere."

He evaded her. "Who has a better right? I'm the man who cracked the whip and chained you to the galley oars."

She made another snatch for the slide. "That culture will deteriorate. Give it back to me."

"Take another tomorrow." He pulled her to her feet. "You've done enough today. You don't have to work twenty-four hours a day."

"I haven't. I spent three hours at the ranger station with Joshua this afternoon."

He pulled her toward the door. "How is he?"

"How do you think he is? He's on Treasure Island skipping along with Peter Pan."

"I think you have your stories mixed." He closed the laboratory door firmly behind them. "And I've never heard Seth compared to Peter Pan before. As I remember, when you first met him, you thought he was Jack the Ripper. This new persona would amuse the hell out of him."

He was right. That first image had faded the longer she spent in Seth Drakin's company. It was a little unsettling. The man seemed capable of projecting any personality he chose, and yet he seemed totally genuine. "You know what I mean." She longingly glanced back at the laboratory door as he led her toward the kitchen. "All I need is one more hour."

"I don't trust you. I'd find you in there at dawn."

He was probably right, she thought. The excitement was growing every day, every minute.

215

"You brought me here to work."

"But not to slave until you collapse from exhaustion. What good would you do me then?"

"You can't have it all ways." She looked accusingly at him. "Though you certainly try hard enough."

"Don't we all?" He poured her a cup of coffee. "Drink it and go to bed."

She raised her brows. "Coffee?"

"Decaffeinated."

She should have known. Noah would take care never to waiver from his purpose. This wasn't the first time he had almost physically ejected her from the lab. He had hovered over her like a mother hen for the last two weeks, cooking her meals and then watching her to be sure she ate them, making sure she slept and got out for a walk or run every day. Even if it was only over to the ranger station to see Joshua. "You're making me uneasy. I feel like a virgin being fattened up before she's sacrificed at the altar."

"This must be your night for inaccuracies." He grinned at her. "I think it was animals that were fattened, not humans. And unless Joshua was adopted, you're definitely not a virgin." His smile faded. "I'm doing my damnedest to make sure you're not sacrificed on my altar or anybody else's."

He suddenly looked so tired and discouraged that she felt a surge of compassion. She glanced away from him and deliberately reined in any hint of softness. "Well, the virgins probably got fat anyway. I've heard they were pampered big time." She took a sip of coffee and put it down on the counter. "No more coffee. If it doesn't have a kick, there's no use drinking it."

"I'll try hot chocolate tomorrow night. Go to bed."

She shook her head. "Not yet." She headed for the deck. "I need some air."

He followed her out the door and closed it behind him. "Do you need your jacket?"

Mother hen again, she thought ruefully. He hadn't paid attention to a word she'd said. "No, I won't be out here long. You really can go on to bed."

"I'll wait for you."

She moved toward the deck railing and stared out into the darkness, listening to the night sounds. He remained at the door but she was aware of his gaze on her. "I'm not going to run away."

"I know. You're too excited. I'd have to blast you out of here now."

"I hit ninety-two percent today."

"It has to be ninety-eight."

"Then you should let me go back to the lab tonight."

"No deal."

She had known he wouldn't budge, but it hadn't hurt to try. "I'll reach ninety-eight by next week."

"Good."

"Good? It's stupendous. It's what you wanted, isn't it?"

"And what you wanted."

She nodded. She breathed deep of the night air. "I like it here. I've never been to West Virginia before. All these lovely trees. I've always thought of it as being riddled with coal mines."

"You should see my home state if you like trees. My parents had a summer place north of the city, and some of the forests there are so dense that it's like going into a tunnel."

"Are your parents still living?"

"No, my mother died when I was a teenager, and my father suffered a heart attack twelve years ago." He grimaced. "And I'm afraid I was never on the best of terms with either one of them. My father was always too busy with the plant to pay much attention to my mother or me. She divorced him when I was a boy. He fought and retained custody of me."

"Then he must have cared for you."

"Maybe. I don't know. As his son I was heir to his company." He shook his head. "Christ, how he loved that company. He poured everything he was into building J. and S. I guess there wasn't anything left for anyone else."

"But you loved it too."

"He hooked me early and I never got over it. But I tried damn hard. I never wanted to run a company. I went to Johns Hopkins for my degree, but he cut off funds and pulled me out before I finished." He smiled crookedly. "He told me that a little medical knowledge was a plus for running a pharmaceutical company but I didn't need a degree."

"What did you do?"

"Exploded. Told him to go to hell and did the one thing I knew he'd hate most. I joined the army."

"That's where you met Seth?"

"Seth, Tony Lynski, and I were in the Special Forces together. We were in a unit tapped by the CIA for covert missions." He shrugged. "It didn't take long for me to see that I wasn't cut out for the work. When my time was up, I went home. I made a deal with my father, finished my schooling, and went to work at the plant. After he died, I was all set to hire a management team to take over J. and S. and set up an independent laboratory off the premises."

"Why didn't you?"

"It was mine. The plant, the people . . ."

"They say, given time, we all become our parents."

"You think I became my father? No way. I made sure I didn't keep my nose pressed to the grindstone. Life is to be lived. But I tried to strike a balance. The employees at J. and S. were my people. I had to take care of them." His lips thinned with pain. "I didn't do a very good job, did I?"

"You couldn't know that Ogden would —"

"I'm not asking you to make excuses for me. I know what I did." He opened the door. "It's time you went to bed."

He was upset, so *she* should go to bed? She was tempted to argue with him but instead found herself acquiescing. He was hurting. It would do no harm to let independence lapse for the moment. She stopped beside him and asked curiously, "What do you do when you're not forcing food and coffee on me?"

"Make phone calls. Talk to Seth and fill him in on everything." He paused. "Get ready."

"Get ready for what?"

"Apocalypse. Designed and orchestrated by Mr. Raymond Ogden."

She frowned. "What are you talking about?"

"We'll discuss it when RU2 is ready."

"Why not now? Do you think I'm too 'skittish' to keep my mind on two things at once?"

He flinched. "God, I wish I'd never used that word."

"It should be banished from the English language. Do you?"

"I think you're totally brilliant and as solid as that rock at Gibraltar. I just don't think you need to have everything on your plate while I have nothing to do." He smiled. "I can't just twiddle my thumbs. I'll go nuts. Give me a break, Kate."

"I don't see why —" Oh, what difference did it make? she thought impatiently. She didn't really want to think ahead of the work going on in the laboratory right now. The path was too exhilarating, victory too close. "I'm not going to sit around and let you plan everything, you know."

"It never entered my mind."

"Yeah, sure." She gave him a skeptical glance as she went past him into the house.

"What do you want for breakfast?" Noah called.

"Real coffee."

"No problem. It's permitted at seven in the morning."

"Six."

"The lab door will stay closed until seven-fifteen, so you might as well get the extra hour's sleep. I'll have eggs, bacon, and toast and 'real' coffee on the table at seven." He smiled at her. "And I'll give you a thermos of coffee to take to the lab so you won't have to surface until noon."

"You're too kind."

"I'm trying to be kind, Kate."

The unfamiliar note in his voice made her look at him. She tensed as she met his gaze. Something was suddenly different. A moment before, she had been annoyed and impatient, but now she felt . . . aware.

Oh shit.

What the hell was wrong with her? It was as if all the fear and tumult she had experienced since Michael's murder had ripped away the repression of the past years and left her open and vulnerable. She hadn't felt anything for anyone since she and Michael were divorced, and now she was suddenly drawn to two men. A few days ago she had been sexually aroused just watching Seth Drakin, and now she was feeling something toward Noah.

But this awareness wasn't the same as the other. This was milder, not at all animalistic. More like a warm breeze than a storm of feeling. Maybe it wasn't sexual. It felt more like deep admiration and the need to be close to someone.

But she still wanted him to touch her, hold her.

And he wanted to touch her too. She could see it in the slight tension of his body.

She felt his eyes on her as she moved hurriedly across the living room and down the short hall to her bedroom.

Tomorrow everything would be back to normal. Noah didn't want complications any more than she did. They would ignore that brief moment and concentrate on what was important.

She opened the door of her bedroom.

The hurricane lamp was burning on the windowsill.

She had been so immersed in the lab that she had forgotten to light it for Joshua this evening, she realized guiltily.

But Noah had not forgotten.

I'm trying to be kind, Kate.

Protectiveness, kindness, and warmth. She felt like a needy child reaching out in the darkness. She didn't want to be needy. She didn't want to rely on anyone but herself.

Oh shit.

"Seven on the dot," Noah said when she walked into the kitchen the next morning. He removed the sizzling bacon from the pan and divided it between the two plates on the counter. "You get the coffee. I'm busy."

It was as if that moment last night hadn't happened, Kate thought. Well, what had she expected? Noah to pull her down on the kitchen floor and make wild love to her? Naturally, she was relieved.

And unreasonably deflated. So much for her sex appeal.

"Hurry, I promised to get you in that lab by seven-fifteen," Noah said as he dished up the scrambled eggs.

"Give me a chance." She took down the cups and saucers from the cabinet. "I'm sorry to disrupt your schedule."

"It's your schedule." He carried the plates to the breakfast bar, where he had already set place mats and orange juice. "You're the one who didn't want to leave the lab last night. I'm just trying to accommodate you."

"That will be the day." They had fallen back into the comfortable wrangling of the last weeks, she realized. She poured coffee into the cups and carried them to the breakfast bar. "No toast? What good are you?"

"Damn good." He grinned and moved toward the oven. "Biscuits. I made them from scratch."

"You do know when I turn my work over to you that there's no way you're going to get this kind of service from me?"

"I'll find a way for you to compensate."
She stiffened. "Really?"

"Dammit." He stopped in mid motion. "That blew it, didn't it? Now we'd better talk about it." He put the biscuits down on the cabinet and turned to face her. "I can't have you on edge every minute."

"I'm not on edge."

"The hell you're not." He grimaced. "Okay, I'm human. I want to jump into the sack with you. I've wanted it for quite a while, but that doesn't mean I'm going to give you any grief about it. I've loaded you down with enough problems."

"Quite a while?" she asked, startled.

"You think it struck like lightning? Maybe for you but I've not been as preoccupied." He said lightly, "You're quite a dish, my dear Dr. Denby."

A flush heated her cheeks. Stupid of her to get this disconcerted. Particularly since he obviously thought that moment last night had been purely sexual. Maybe it had been for him. The need for nurturing was seldom a first priority with men, and he wouldn't thank her if she told him that her feeling had been more a craving for comfort and emotional closeness than sex. "It's probably propinquity."

"Probably," he agreed. "And it may happen again. We're both healthy specimens with the usual urges. I just want you to know that it won't affect anything."

"Thank you. I didn't think it would." She sat down and began to eat her breakfast, trying to

ignore a disappointment that was as totally irra-
tional as Noah's dissection of the matter was ra-
tional. He had merely voiced her own thoughts.
They were colleagues and were there to work.
They had no time to establish a relationship,
either sexual or emotional. "But I'm glad we
cleared the air."

"It's been almost four weeks," Ishmaru said
when he got through to Ogden. "You didn't call
me."

"I didn't say I would. I don't need you anymore, you inept prick."

"Where's Kate Denby?"

"I don't know. Don't call me again." Ogden
hung up the phone.

Ishmaru dialed the number again and got William Blount. It was just as well. Blount had hired
him in the first place and respected his power.
Ogden was like a big, clumsy bear, but Blount
had always reminded Ishmaru of a sleek black
snake, clinging to the ground, waiting for his
chance to strike. "Where's Kate Denby?"

"Hello, Jonathan." Blount's voice was silky
smooth. "Mr. Ogden is very displeased with you.
I think we'll have to part company."

"Where is she?"

"We haven't been able to determine her loca-
tion as yet."

"I want her." He paused. "Or Ogden. Or you.
Your choice."

Blount chuckled. "Interesting selection. I wish

I could accommodate you on the first two, but that's impossible at the moment."

"How do I get her?"

"Wait just a moment." Ishmaru heard him cover the phone and then a muffled, "I'll be sure and take care of it, sir. Good-bye, Mr. Ogden." A silence and then he was back on the line. "We've been waiting for them to surface. But perhaps it would do no harm to let you probe a little. The only lead we have is Tony Lynski, Smith's lawyer."

Ishmaru recognized the name. "Lynski was on my list."

"That's right. He disappeared at the same time the plant was destroyed. We've recently tracked him to a lodge in the Sierra Madres, but he'd fled the coop when our man got there."

"You think he knows where she is?"

"Possibly."

"Give me the address of the lodge."

"He's not there any longer."

"Give it to me."

"Very well." Blount rattled off the address. "Good luck. Naturally, if you come up with anything, I'll be sure to reward you handsomely."

He meant himself, not Ogden, Ishmaru noticed. The snake was flexing its coils.

"But it would be best if you'd call my private number. Mr. Ogden might not appreciate your interference. You know I'll give you what you want."

226

"Try to find out more," Ishmaru said before hanging up.

Ogden might no longer point the way to coup, but Blount would take his place. There was always someone who wanted to deal in death and glory. He had suspected Blount to be such a man at their first meeting. Blount had the dark instinct. He was too sly to be a warrior, but Ishmaru could see him as a shaman, sitting in the medicine tent, plotting to gain his own glory.

He looked down at the address in his hand. Ogden had given up. He would not give up. He would find Lynski. He was skilled at finding out information. There might even be more coups to be earned on the path to Kate.

Kate. It was strange how in his thoughts sometimes she was Kate and sometimes Emily. But more and more, Kate was fading and Emily was coming in clearer.

"I'm coming, Emily," he whispered. "Be patient. I'll find you."

Ishmaru.

Kate jerked upright in bed, her heart pounding wildly.

It was nothing, she told herself. A nightmare.

Oh God. Ishmaru.

She got out of bed and stumbled to the window. Joshua . . .

Joshua was safe. Seth and Phyliss were taking care of him.

It had only been a nightmare, blurred and disjointed . . . and terrifying. Joshua was safe. She was safe too.

She didn't feel safe. For the first time since she had come to the cabin, she was afraid. She didn't care if she was being foolish. She wanted Joshua here where she could touch him, not up in the clouds at that damn ranger station.

Crazy. She couldn't call and wake him up in the middle of the night.

She was shaking, trembling. Her hands clenched on the windowsill.

Help me. I don't want to be alone anymore.

Listen to her sniveling. Crying out.

She didn't even know to whom she was crying out.

Seth.

She rejected the thought immediately. She didn't even know from where it had come. Seth was the last person she needed in her life. So there was a strong physical attraction. She had jumped into one disastrous marriage when she had been too blinded by youth and impetuousness to think in her usual cool, analytical custom. She had been lucky Michael had proved as steady as he had been or their relationship could have been even worse. There was nothing steady about Seth Drakin.

Noah?

She felt a warm rush of feeling as she thought of him. Yes, she must have been thinking of Noah. Noah was safe. Noah would help her. They had similar backgrounds, similar goals. He had become a close friend, and that single moment of intimacy between them could turn into more, given time.

Even thinking about him was making the terror go away.

But Noah didn't want her for anything but the work she was giving him. She had hit 96 today, and soon she would be finished with her part.

So what if he didn't want her? It didn't matter. It was only during instances of weakness like this that she needed anyone. It would pass like all the others.

Tomorrow she would be strong again.

Kate was at the breakfast bar drinking a cup of coffee when Noah came into the kitchen at five-thirty the next morning. "I thought I heard you. You're up early." His gaze ran over Kate's gray sweatshirt, pants, and running shoes. "I take it you're not going to work this morning?"

"Sorry to disappoint you," she said curtly.

"I don't believe you're being fair," he said quietly. "I don't recall locking you in the lab lately."

"I don't feel like being fair. I didn't sleep well. I have a headache and I'm tired of pushing myself for your damn RU2." She finished her coffee and set the cup down. "And I want to see my son."

His gaze narrowed on her face. "Why didn't you sleep well?"

"How do I know?"

"I think you do know."

"Maybe you think I had some kind of yen for

you?" Her gaze dismissively went over him from head to toe. "Forget it."

"Ouch." He grimaced. "You are in a foul temper."

"I have a right. I don't have to be sweetness and light every minute of the day." She moved toward the door. "Call Seth and tell him I'm on my way."

"Yes, ma'am."

She ignored his sarcasm as she ran down the deck stairs and into the woods. Under the leafy canopy it was dim and cool.

It was good to run again. She could feel the blood pumping through her body, clearing her mind, driving the tension from her muscles.

She could smell the damp wood and leaves, could feel the damp earth give slightly beneath her tennis shoes.

The path was fairly level for the first two miles and became rougher only during the approach to the higher ground where the station was located.

Her lungs began to labor as she sprinted uphill, but the heady burn was beginning and taking away the pain.

There was no one but herself on the planet.

RU2 faded into the background.

Noah was gone.

Ishmaru didn't exist.

"I'm glad you're so eager to see me, Kate."

Ishmaru.

She stopped as if struck by a bullet.

"Hey, I didn't mean to scare you." Seth was

jogging toward her. "You're pale as a ghost."

Of course it wasn't Ishmaru. That nightmare must still be with her. "You startled me. You usually don't meet me until I reach the last mile."

"I saw you eating up the path and thought I'd join you." He grinned. "Race you to the station." He spun around and dashed ahead of her.

"You're cheating," she shouted as she took off after him.

His only answer was a whoop and a laugh.

Peter Pan, she thought resignedly.

He was sitting on the steps when she reached the station.

He yawned. "What kept you?"

"You cheated." She glowered at him, trying to catch her breath as she dropped down beside him. He looked flushed and glowingly alive, and it didn't improve her temper that he wasn't even breathing heavily. "And I should have had a handicap. Climbing all those flights of steps must give you lungs of iron."

"Yep." He flexed the muscles of his right arm. "I'm a true man of steel." He stretched his legs out before him. "But you're pretty fast." He gave her a sly glance. "For a woman."

"Is that supposed to annoy me?" Her breath was beginning to steady. "I wouldn't give you the satisfaction. How's Joshua?"

"Great. We went hunting yesterday afternoon. He got a shot of a deer from only four yards away." He shook his head. "But I'm having trouble getting him to be patient about having

231

the film developed. He has a stack from the last couple weeks."

"Can't you mail it in?"

He shook his head. "No contact. Noah's orders."

"And you always obey Noah?"

"Sure. It's his game. Besides, he's usually right." He stood up and pulled her to her feet. "But don't tell him I said so."

"Don't worry, I won't. He has enough confidence in his own omnipotence."

He gave a silent whistle. "Noah said you were having a bad day."

"You discussed me? And what did Noah decide was wrong?" she asked sarcastically. "That I had PMS?"

"No, he said that you were overworked, under tremendous pressure, and even though you have more guts than any woman he'd ever met, your temper was bound to come out occasionally." He paused. "Disappointed?"

"Yes. She wanted to retain the edge that anger had given her. "Are you sure you didn't make that up?"

"I wish I had. It sounds pretty good, doesn't it?" He grinned. "Would I score a few points with you if I agree with him?"

Oh shit.

She was feeling that same tingling sexual urgency she had experienced that day in the woods. One moment she had been irritable and wanting to strike out, and the next she was wondering what it would be like to have him crouched over her, in her. What the hell was wrong with her? It seemed as if all her emotions were out of control today.

He was staring quizzically. "Well, would I?"

"No." She started up the steps. "You don't need points with me. You have Joshua and Phyliss in the palm of your hand."

"You underestimate them." He caught up with her on the steps. "Phyliss is too canny not to see through me, and Joshua is a bright kid. He'd dump me in a minute if I did something that disagreed with the way you brought him up. You did a good job with him."

"Thank you." She gazed at him curiously. "What do you mean about Phyliss seeing through you? What is there to see?"

"All the holes." He grimaced. "Do you think a man who's been a mercenary for all these years is normal? You have to be a little twisted. After I got out of the army, I could have gone back to a normal life like Noah and Tony. I didn't do it."

"Why not?"

He didn't answer. He was looking up the stairs. "I bet I can beat you to the top."

"Why not?" she repeated.

He glanced at her. "You're beginning to see through me too. Maybe it's time I moved on."

"Do you always move on when you feel exposed? What about Noah? He's known you for years."

"I'm comfortable with him. Noah's got a little

bit of me in him. Without the holes, of course."

"Well, you'll find yourself with quite a few more holes if you move on and leave my son unprotected."

He burst out laughing. "God, I like you, Kate."

She liked him too, she thought resignedly. It was hard not to like Peter Pan. "I mean it, Seth."

He sobered. "No chance. I'm crazy about the kid."

She smiled. "You have good taste."

"Then do you want to marry me and set up housekeeping?"

"What?"

"I'd probably foul up raising a kid of my own. You've saved me the trouble."

She chuckled. "You'd run scared if you had the slightest glimmering I'd take you seriously."

"You never know." His gaze went beyond her to the top platform, where Phyliss was standing at the rail watching them. He called, "Phyliss, I just proposed to Kate and she laughed at me."

"Because she has good sense."

"Then I guess you won't marry me either?"

"No, but I might adopt you. I need a challenge in my declining years."

"No way." He shuddered. "You'd plug all my holes and make me walk the line." He added, "And I haven't noticed you declining. Next time you feel yourself slipping, call me. I want to watch."

Kate smiled with amusement as she saw the look of perfect understanding they exchanged. It wasn't the first time she'd witnessed this byplay between them. They were as comfortable together as if they'd known each other for years. She'd never seen Phyliss that easy with Michael, she realized. There had been love, but mother and son had been miles apart in character. Michael had never had Phyliss's sense of fun and acceptance of life.

"Is Joshua up?" she asked as she reached the platform.

Phyliss shook her head. "It's only six. Something wrong?"

"No, I just wanted to see him. Nothing's wrong." It was the truth, she realized. Nothing was really wrong that she couldn't handle. She felt calmer now that she was here. The shadow of Ishmaru was fading. Any threat seemed far away. This crazy yen she had to go to bed with Seth was controllable. The tension that sparked between her and Noah could be worked out. Everything was coming back into perspective. "Why don't you fix us some breakfast while I go wake up Joshua?"

"She was really on edge," Phyliss said to Seth as they watched Kate reach the bottom of the steps and set out in a run. "Did she talk to you?"

"Well, she threatened my life if I didn't do right by her boy." Seth smiled as he leaned on the rail. "I told her that you'd keep me in line."

"Liar." Phyliss glanced at him. "Not that I couldn't if I put my mind to it."

"I know you could. You're stronger than I am. You could blow me away."

She studied his expression. "Do I detect a sober note?"

His gaze went back to Kate's retreating figure. "I've liked being here with you and Joshua," he said haltingly. "It's been . . . nice."

"Good God, am I in line for another proposal?"

"Nah, you've got too much sense." He shrugged and continued awkwardly, "I just wanted you to know that you're — I've never met — You're a special person, Phyliss."

"I know. Do you have anything else to impart?"

"No."

"Then stop wading in this weird maudlin tripe and go wash the dishes. It's your turn."

He let his breath out in a sigh that was half exasperation, half relief. "I did them last night."

"And I cooked breakfast this morning." She smiled. "Stop arguing. You can't win them all, Seth."

He scowled as he headed for the door. "No, but I'd like to win one."

Noah was standing on the deck when Kate reached the lodge.

"Feel better?" he asked.

"Yes." She ran up the steps. "Much better. I spent the day with people I love and I got in a good run. Nothing like a run to exorcise your demons."

"And was I one of your demons?"

"Maybe." She smiled. "But if you were, consider yourself exorcised too."

"I don't want to be one of your demons, Kate."

"I told you —" She broke off when she saw that his expression was grave. Bring it out in the open, she told herself. She couldn't live with all this inner turmoil. It would get in the way of her work. She shook her head. "You're not. I've been behaving like an ass. Sorry. I'm usually not into denial."

"Denial?"

"I've been alone for a long time. You're here. I've been feeling . . . I don't know. The whole world is spinning around me and I guess I need to hold on to someone." She held up her hand as he opened his mouth to speak. "I know it's inconvenient. I know it's the worst possible time. Don't get me wrong. I'm not propositioning you. I just wanted to be honest. You deserve honesty."

"Do I?"

"Yes, you've been straight with me ever since we came here." She shrugged. "So now it's said and I can go back to work." She changed the subject. "What's for dinner? I'm starved."

"Roast duck." He didn't move. "You're right, it's the wrong time." He added softly, "But it won't always be this way, Kate."

She glanced back at him and warmth flooded through her as she saw the gentleness in his expression. This was what she wanted. Not a few wild, sensual moments in the woods with Seth Drakin. She needed gentleness, security, and a solid relationship.

But not now, she thought. It was too soon for both of them.

Maybe sometime.

A lingering promise.

Just maybe . . .

"I've done it," Kate announced as she breezed out of the laboratory four days later. "And you've got it. Over to you, Dr. Smith."

Noah's face lit with eagerness. "Ninety-eight?"

"On the nose." She flopped into the easy chair and stretched her legs out before her. "My disk and the paperwork are on the lab table."

"You do know I'm going to have to pull you back into the lab when I reach the final phase?"

"I thought you would, but that's down the road. If you need any explanations, I'll hang around for a day or so. After that you'll have to make an appointment. I'm going to spend more time with Joshua and Phyliss."

"You're glowing." He smiled. "Congratulations, Kate."

"Thanks." She felt as if she were doing more than glowing. She was incandescent. "I don't know why I'm so excited. I've known it was coming for days."

"But now it's here. You've done something very special."

"I know. Break out the champagne."

"No champagne. How remiss of me. Can I make you a cup of coffee?"

"Not good enough." She jumped to her feet. "I feel like I'm going to float away. I'm going for a run. Want to come with me?"

"Sure, why —" He broke off. "You go on. I'd better go in and take a look at your notes. I might be able to start work later tonight."

She felt a little of the shine leave her. She should have known he wouldn't want to wait even one day to move RU2 closer to completion. "Suit yourself." She took off her lab coat and threw it on the chair. "See you."

She ran out of the cabin and down the steps. Forget it. It didn't make her accomplishment any less important because she couldn't share it.

But she could. She could share it with Joshua and Phyliss and Seth. She didn't need Noah.

She set off for the station at a brisk run.

Nine

"Come out of there, Noah," Seth called as he threw open the door of the lab. "It's time you got off your butt and helped me."

Kate looked up from the centrifuge in alarm. "Is something wrong?"

"Hi, Kate. No, nothing's wrong. I just need to talk to Noah."

"I'm busy, Seth," Noah said. "We're getting close to —"

"On the deck," Seth interrupted. "Now." He turned and left the lab.

Noah shrugged at Kate. "Sorry, I'll be with you in a minute."

"Okay, what's the matter?" Noah asked as he came out on the deck.

Seth scowled. "You need to spend some time with Joshua."

"Is that what this is all about? That's your job."

"And I'm doing it. Since you pulled Kate back into the lab with you, he spends most of his time with me." He was silent a moment before he muttered, "It's not good for him, dammit."

"Why not?"

"He . . . likes me. For God's sake, he's beginning to think I'm some kind of role model."

Noah started to laugh.

"It's not funny."

"I'm sure Kate would agree with you."

"You're damn right she would. Kate knows what's best for Joshua. So do something about it. Distract him, take him for walks, tell him no one in his right mind would want to be like me."

"Do you think it would do any good?"

"I don't know," he said gloomily. "Maybe not. I'm too damn charismatic."

Noah struggled to smother a smile. "I realize that's always been a problem for you."

Seth grimaced. "I tell you, we've got a situation here. The kid's just lost his father. He's vulnerable. He doesn't need to attach himself to someone who's going to walk away from him. You handle it."

"What makes you think I won't walk away from him when this is over?"

"You couldn't desert a charging rhinoceros if you thought it needed you. You're sickeningly upright and responsible these days."

"I resent that. Though you've been remarkably steadfast yourself for the past few weeks."

"Short-term. Always short-term."

"That's what I thought when I took over J. and S. You find it sneaks up on you." Noah smiled. "By God, I think I may have found a way to rope you in, Seth."

"No way. Next you'll have me dressed in an Armani suit and carrying a briefcase like Tony. Hell, maybe we'll join the same racquet club."

"Tony would not be amused."

Seth grinned mischievously. "Then it would

almost be worth it." His smile faded. "Sure, I like the kid, but not enough to stick around and play doting uncle. Besides, when this is over, Kate will hand me the pink slip and wave good-bye."

Noah shook his head. "She likes you, Seth."

"As long as I protect her son. When I'm no use to her, she'll find me an 'inconvenience.' My God, you should know that better than me. She's even more responsible than you are, Noah."

"I don't find you an inconvenience."

"Yes, you do. Why else would you try to change me to fit into your mold?"

"It could be because you're my best friend and I'd like to see you more than once or twice a year."

Seth glanced away quickly. "Then accept me the way I am."

"I would if I thought you were content with your life."

"Look, I'm no whiz kid who's going to invent something that's going to rock the world. Just leave me to do what I do best."

"And what is that?" Noah studied him. "You know damn well you could be anything you want to be."

"And I want to be what I am. Drop it, Noah."

"Okay . . . for now."

"God, you're stubborn. You've been at me for fifteen years. When are you going to give up?"

"When I have you in the racquet club." He smiled. "And I won't even make you wear an Armani suit."

"It would come." He made a face. "Kate would make it one of her top priorities."

Noah went still. "What does Kate have to do with this?"

"Come on, I've known you too long. I've watched you with Kate. There's something there, something good."

Noah was silent. "Possibly. We'll have to see."

"You're getting as cautious as Tony," Seth said in disgust. "What more do you want? You and Kate could be Siamese twins. You're both disgustingly dedicated, boringly loyal, abysmally solid people. You fit like the proverbial glove."

"We're not that much alike."

Seth snorted.

"My business, Seth." Then Noah quietly repeated Seth's words: "Drop it."

Seth shrugged. "It's my business too if I'm looking after your future stepson."

"Jesus, we're not even talking about —" Noah shrugged. "There's no use talking to you, is there?"

"Will you come over to the station tomorrow and take Joshua out?"

Noah frowned. "Can it wait? In a few days we'll be finished. We're within a hairsbreadth of getting the combination right."

"No, it can't wait. I've waited too long already. One day off won't hurt you. Let Kate take over."

"You're overreacting."

"The hell I am. If you don't forget about RU2 for one day, I'll come back here and pull you out by the scruff of your neck. Get your nose out of those test tubes and help me."

"Okay. Okay. It's not that I mind spending time with Joshua. It's no chore."

Seth forced a smile. "And I know you'll find it nearly impossible to find anything negative to say about me, but try to disillusion him a bit." He turned and ran down the stairs and jumped into his jeep. "I've got to get back. Eight tomorrow morning."

Noah watched him until he disappeared from view. It was clear Seth was writhing beneath the bit. Or maybe it wasn't clear at all. Maybe Peter Pan was having growing pains. At any rate, he was unsettled, and any instability that was even remotely connected with RU2 was dangerous.

Jesus, couldn't he think of anything but how it affected RU2? he thought wearily. Seth was no threat; he was the one person Noah could trust in this world.

But he still had to consider all the ramifications of RU2. Too many people had died. RU2 had to come first. It had to be protected.

But was he protecting it? he wondered suddenly. Had he done enough?

He moved toward the telephone and punched in Tony's number in Washington.

"I need you to do something for me," he said when Tony answered.

"Hello to you too," Tony said sourly. "I am doing something for you. I've been sneaking around dealing with politicians and lobbyists. I deserve a medal for wading through all this crap."

"May I remind you that most politicians are also lawyers."

"No, you may not. I'm not in the mood."

"What's happening with Longworth?"

"Nothing. Or as much nothing as possible with that windbag."

"Any more demonstrations?"

"One yesterday at the FDA. I was going to call you to tell you about it. It was smaller than the last one, but they hauled in a couple celebrities to spearhead it. How close are you to finishing?"

"I don't know. Soon."

"It better be damn soon. I'm sick of this business. Why don't you send Seth here and let me out? I'm not doing anything but watching and waiting."

"I need Seth where he is. You'll have to bite the bullet." He smiled as he heard Tony's groan of frustration. "But I'll give you something else to do to keep you from overdosing on all the bull-shit."

"Anything."

"You may not be as enthusiastic when I tell you what it is."

"Time for bed, Joshua," Phyliss said, then frowned at Seth. "Put away that guitar. You know he was supposed to be in bed an hour ago."

"Sorry." Seth meekly set the guitar on the platform. "Time got away from us."

"Fifteen more minutes, Grandma? I've already

got my pajamas on," Joshua pled. "And I've almost got that chord down."

"It will still be there tomorrow."

"You never can tell," Seth murmured. "Haven't you ever heard of the lost chord?"

"I've heard of procrastination." She jerked her thumb toward the door. "Bed."

"I've still got to say good night to Mom." Joshua cast a last longing look at the guitar before getting to his feet. "I'll go get my binoculars."

"Remember to wash your face and brush your teeth."

"Yes, ma'am." He disappeared into the house.

Phyliss lingered, her gaze on Seth. "You okay?"

"Sure." He took up the guitar again and struck a chord. "Why shouldn't I be? A little restless maybe."

"You didn't look restless when I came out here. You looked . . ." She shrugged. "I don't know. Melancholy."

Christ, she was sharp. "Melancholy?" He pretended to think about it. "Oh, I like that. It sounds damn sensitive. I don't think I've ever been accused of that before."

"You are sensitive."

"Really? Would you like to know how many men I've killed, Phyliss?"

"No, but if you were as tough as you'd like me to think, I don't believe you'd remember the body count."

"I probably don't." He struck another chord. "But I'm good at estimating."

"Stop evading and tell me what's wrong."

She had cut through his evasions like a bulldozer. Kate did the same thing. The two women were alike in many ways. "How do I know? You tell me. You seem to be able to read my mind."

"No, I can't read your mind. You're too good at closing people out. But you do let out little snippets every now and then." She frowned. "Did you find out something when you were at the cabin? Are we still safe here?"

"As far as I know. I don't like the length of time it's taking them to complete the work on RU2. It's always better to keep on the move when someone like Ishmaru is after you." He shrugged. "But that's Noah's decision. He's the sheriff. I'm just the hired gun in town."

"And that's the way you like it?"

"Sure."

"I think you're lying to me. I don't see you as a hired gun."

"No?" He cast her a glance. "You think I resent Noah?" He shook his head. "He's the closest thing to a brother I've ever had. We have our differences, but I love the bastard."

"Then why are you —"

"I've got them." Joshua came out on the deck, waving the binoculars.

"Good." Seth stood up and propped the guitar against the rail. "Come on." He strolled around the corner to the north railing. "We'll just be a minute, Phyliss."

"You're never 'just a minute.' If you haven't

got Joshua inside and in bed in ten minutes, I'm coming back out to get you." She went into the house.

Seth grimaced. "Tough."

Joshua nodded with a conspiratorial smile. "Yep." He dropped down on the deck and crossed his legs tailor fashion. "But we've got ten minutes." He leaned against the wall. "Listen. Is that an owl?"

"Yes. He's in that sycamore tree. Third branch from the bottom."

"I can't see him." Joshua lifted the binoculars. "There he is. I see his orange eyes. It's dark. How did you see him without the binoculars?"

"Practice. Sometimes creatures more unfriendly than owls perch in trees."

"Like snakes? I read about anacondas. They live in South America. Did you ever wrestle with an anaconda, Seth?"

"Do you think I'm stupid? Why would anyone want to wrestle with an anaconda?"

"Well, they wrestle alligators down in Florida. My dad told me so."

The last sentence came easily, Seth noticed. Maybe some of the pain was dulling. God, he hoped so.

"Well, I bet your dad wasn't dumb enough to wrestle alligators. He sounds like a pretty cool dude."

"He was." A silence fell between them. "You were talking about men hiding in trees, weren't you?"

He should probably deny it. You didn't talk to kids about death and violence. Noah would deny it.

He wasn't Noah. He had promised Joshua honesty. "Yes."

"Snipers?"

"Sometimes. But that's during wars. There aren't any snipers here."

"I know that." Another silence. "What are we going to do tomorrow?"

"I'm going to be busy, but Noah's coming over. I think he wants to take you fishing."

Joshua frowned. "What are you going to be doing?"

"I have some telephone calls to make."

"Couldn't you do that at night?"

"No." He looked straight ahead. "You don't need me. You and Noah get along fine."

"Yeah." Joshua was silent a moment. "Maybe you could make your calls in the morning and we could all go in the afternoon."

"I think you'd better go without me. I may get tied up."

"Okay." Another silence. "Does he really want to go with me?"

"Sure. Why shouldn't he?"

"It's just . . . he always seems busy."

"So is your mom. But she likes to spend time with you. Or maybe you think she's faking it."

"Mom doesn't fake anything," Joshua said fiercely. "She never lies."

"Okay. Okay. I'm just trying to point out that

249

you're a pretty awesome kid."

Joshua suddenly grinned. "I know *that.*"

"And you'll like getting to know Noah better. He's pretty awesome too."

"Not as awesome as you."

Oh shit. "Sure he is. Just in a different way." He paused. "A better way."

Joshua shook his head.

He'd done his best. He'd just have to leave it to Noah. "Our ten minutes is almost up. You'd better say good night to your mom."

Joshua stood up and raised the binoculars. "The candle's lit. But I don't see her. She must be working again tonight."

"But she lit the candle. And she'll know you saw it and said good night."

"Yeah. The flame is pretty, it's not flickering at all tonight. It's real steady and strong."

Like Kate, Seth thought. Steady and strong and burning bright.

"Say good night, Joshua."

"G'night, Mom. Sleep tight."

Seth's gaze traveled to the cabin and the candle he could only barely discern without binoculars.

Strong and bold and burning bright . . .

"Good night, Kate," Seth said softly.

"Have a good evening, Mr. Blount." The security man at the parking garage smiled ingratiatingly. "See you tomorrow."

"Thank you, Jim." As Blount moved down the aisle of cars to his reserved space, he felt a tiny burst of pleasure at Jim's servile tone. It didn't have the element of fear his father's presence evoked, but it was still satisfactory. The people here at Ogden Pharmaceuticals knew he had the power to hire and fire, to destroy at will. His father had not held as much power at the same age. He had been a stupid punk running numbers in the slums of Chicago.

And soon Blount would hold more power than his father had ever dreamed.

He unlocked his Lexus and got into the driver's seat. He had chosen the car with great care. Nothing flashy or too expensive like his father's Rolls. Boasting substance and sleek good looks, it was the car of a young man on his way up in the legitimate business world. Not that there was much legitimate about Ogden, but perception was everything, Blount had found. Perception and the ability to outthink the fools who —

"Don't move."

Blount froze, his gaze flying to the rearview mirror.

Ishmaru.

He stifled the panic that jolted through him and smiled at the slimy little bastard who had risen from the floor and was now sitting in the backseat. "This isn't necessary. Why didn't you call me? I could have met you for a drink."

"You sent me on a wild-goose chase."

"What do you mean? I gave you all the information I had about Lynski. I told you it was a dead end."

"It was a dead end because you sealed Lynski's cellular phone records."

"The cellular company proved intractable. We're still working on it."

"I think you have the records. I think you know where Lynski is right now."

"And not tell you and Ogden?"

"Where is he?"

"Really, Ishmaru, that would be very foolish of me. I know how badly you want —" He inhaled sharply as he felt the blade of a knife dig painfully into his nape. "Don't be hasty. I was going to tell you eventually. I was waiting for the right time. Lynski's using a digital phone now. We can't listen in on digital, and I haven't been able to gain access to his new phone records yet. We don't want just him. We want Smith and the woman. If you blunder right now, you'll mess up everything."

"I won't blunder. He'll tell me what you want to know. Where is he?"

Blount broke into a sweat. If he told him, Ishmaru might think his usefulness over and cut his throat. If he didn't, the crazy dick might still do it. "Perhaps you're right. Maybe waiting isn't the way to go. But there's always a chance that Smith and Dr. Denby have split up. If they have, you'll need my help to locate the woman." He could feel the blood dripping down his neck, and he added quickly, "I'm working on a few leads now that look promising. Naturally, I'll be at your disposal. After all, we're on the same team."

"Where is Lynski?"

"Brenden Arms Hotel. Georgetown. He's registered under the name of Carl Wylie." The knife in his flesh was not withdrawn. His hands clenched on the steering wheel. "Yes, by all means, go to Lynski, but keep me informed. In the meantime I'll work on the other lead I have. Okay?"

Silence. "Okay."

The knife wasn't there anymore. He felt sick with relief and rage. Damn the bastard for making him feel this weak and ineffectual. "But give me a few days to see if I can find out any more information from the phone company. It won't hurt you to just watch him for a day or so. Will you do me that favor?"

"Maybe." Ishmaru was getting out of the car. He stood beneath the harsh lights of the parking garage, staring without expression at Blount. "Don't lie to me again."

"It wasn't really a lie. I was just waiting to —"

Ishmaru walked away, ignoring him as if he were a fly he'd just swatted. Rage tore through Blount. He'd have the fucking asshole killed. He'd call his father and tell him to — No, that was his father's way. Blount knew that you didn't kill because of anger. You killed because it was smart.

He took out his handkerchief and dabbed at his bloody neck. How had Ishmaru gotten into the garage anyway? He'd fire that incompetent jerk in Security. He felt a little better at the decision. After all, his power was still intact.

This was only a setback. He'd regain control. He'd find a way to use Ishmaru to get RU2.

And then he'd castrate the fucking jerk and have him tossed in Puget Sound.

Ten

"I'm scared," Kate whispered. She thrust the results of the last test at Noah. "You look at it."

"Coward." He drew a deep breath and studied the results.

"Are you going to stare at it all day? *Tell me.*"

"Give me a chance." He lifted his gaze and smiled. "Bingo."

Joy surged through her. She launched herself into his arms, almost knocking him down. "You're sure? No mistake?"

"Read it yourself." He picked her up and swung her in a circle. "We did it!"

"What if we made a mistake? We should run another test."

"You said that the last time. Don't worry, half the labs in the world will be running tests on our RU2 before they start using it. That's why the antirejection factor had to be so high."

"I know that." She stepped back and smiled up at him. "And it's not our RU2, it's yours."

He shook his head. "It's ours. I told Tony that I wanted the patent papers changed to show both our names on the application."

She stared at him, stunned. "I can't let you do that. I was only in on the project at the end."

His brows lifted. "You don't think you made a

major contribution?"

"You're darn right I did. I'm proud as the devil of my work, but I didn't create RU2."

"You almost died for it. That should count for something." He put his hand over her mouth when she opened it to protest. "It's settled. Tony should have the paperwork completed by now. He gets cranky when I make changes."

She turned her lips away from his hand. "I won't take credit for something I didn't do. File the patent with my name and I'll issue a press release stating that you're just being overly generous to a colleague." Her smile had an element of malicious mischief. "Then the world really will think you're Saint Noah. I'm sure you'll love that."

"I can stand it."

She went still as she met his gaze. Something was there, something good and sweet and exciting.

The promise . . .

His hand gently brushed her cheek. "Kate . . ."

Yes, this was right, she thought, this was good. Not that primitive sexuality she'd experienced when she was with Seth. This was sensible and had substance.

He stepped back and smiled. "Not yet. I refuse to seduce you when you're riding this high. We've got all the time in the world now."

Yes, they had time. She smiled back at him. "You know you're adding fuel to my story. Not only Saint Noah but a monk to boot."

"Ouch. You wouldn't do that to me?"

She felt a slow warmth move through her. "No, I wouldn't do that," she said softly.

He took a step forward and then stopped. He gave a low whistle. "I think I need to throw up a few barriers. Let's go telephone Seth and the others and share the news. Then I'll create a dinner for all of you that will make you —"

The phone rang.

"Saved by the bell." He grinned as he moved toward the phone. "Christ, I can't believe I said that."

"Neither can I," she said dryly. "No one has ever wanted to be saved from me before. I'm hardly some femme fatale."

"You come close enough." He picked up the phone. "Hello."

She looked at him inquiringly.

"Tony," he mouthed silently.

Tony Lynski. She felt a ripple of uneasiness. She knew Noah talked to him frequently, but he represented the outside world. The world they would soon have to face again now that RU2 was complete.

"No, I haven't changed my mind," he said into the phone. "Do you have them ready? Okay, I'll meet you at your hotel tomorrow afternoon."

Her eyes widened in shock.

She watched him hang up the phone. "You're leaving?"

"Just for the day. I have papers to sign."

"Couldn't he come here?"

257

"He could, but I don't want even Tony to know where we are."

"Because of me?"

"I promised that you and your family would be safe. I don't want to take any chances."

"Does that mean you're taking a chance?"

"For God's sake, what do you want me to say? I don't think anything will happen, but it could."

"Then stay here. It's crazy to leave when you don't have to. I don't want you to change the damned patent."

"It's not only the patent. I have some other papers to sign too." He added quietly, "I have to go, Kate."

He wouldn't change his mind, she realized in panic. He was going and she couldn't stop him. "Then you're a fool." She walked away from him.

"Does this mean you won't eat my dinner?" He added coaxingly, "It's going to be world-class."

"Screw your dinner. If you won't be —" He wouldn't listen to reason from her, but Seth might be able to persuade him. "Okay. Call Seth and tell them to come."

"He won't listen, Kate," Seth murmured from the doorway at the end of the evening. Phyliss and Joshua were already going down the steps. "I tried. I even offered to go and get the papers for him."

"It's crazy," she said fiercely. "He doesn't have to take the risk."

"He'd have to take it sometime. We can't stay here forever."

"Then go with him. Protect him. Isn't that what you're here for?"

"No, I'm here to protect Joshua and Phyliss, and while he's gone, you're included in the package." His lips curved in a sardonic smile. "I know you'd rather I put my head in the noose, but Noah won't oblige."

She hadn't meant that at all. She just didn't think of danger in connection with Seth. He seemed to be able to handle anything. "I don't want anyone to go. I merely thought that two would be —"

"I know," Seth said lightly. "I'm dispensable. Noah's not."

"No one's dispensable." She impulsively put her hand on his arm. "I'm sorry, Seth. I was upset. I spoke without thinking."

"That's when the truth always surfaces. It's okay. I know where your priorities are." He glanced back at the kitchen, where Noah was loading the dishwasher. "I can't force him to let me help, Kate. I'm not even sure that I should try. He can take care of himself a hell of a lot better than you. He'll be okay."

"You can't promise that." She shivered. "Ishmaru is out there."

"No, I can't promise a damn thing." He turned and started down the steps. "Good night. I'll check in with you tomorrow."

She had an uneasy feeling that she had hurt

him. Maybe not. It was hard to see beyond that tough, mocking persona to the complex man who lay beneath. One minute she felt she knew him very well, and the next he confounded her. Thank heaven Noah was as solid as Seth was mercurial. She was never entirely comfortable with Seth.

No, that wasn't true. She had been comfortable with him at times, and he could be as soothing as a summer wind. He was just not . . . steady.

"Hey, do I get help with these dishes?" Noah called.

"Sure." Another opportunity to talk to him, perhaps persuade him. Though God knows hope and time are running out. "I'll be right there."

Noah left at five the next morning.

Kate watched the glowing red taillights of the jeep until it disappeared around the curve of the road.

He was gone.

Her hands clenched into fists at her sides.

Dammit, why wouldn't he listen?

She went inside the cabin. Keep busy, too busy to think. He had promised he'd call when he reached Lynski in Washington so that she'd know he was safe. That was only a matter of hours. She'd make coffee and then go into the lab, check the results again, make several copies of the disks and documentation. By the time she was finished, she should hear from him.

She was being too negative. Noah wouldn't have gone if he'd thought it was risky. RU2 was too important to him to jeopardize. Lynski had been in contact with them for weeks, and there had been no threat. Noah said Lynski had taken every precaution when he had reached Washington.

There was no reason to think Noah would not be safe.

It was Noah Smith going into the hotel.

Ishmaru hadn't been sure when he'd seen him go by in the jeep. Smith had been very careful. He'd circled the block three times before he'd pulled into the hotel parking lot. Even now he was looking from side to side trying to spot any threat. Very smart.

Not smart enough. Ishmaru's hands tightened on the steering wheel of the delivery truck he had parked in the alley by the hotel. A rush of excitement was exploding through him. He hated to admit that bastard Blount was right, but here was Smith strolling into the trap and he'd had to stake out Lynski for only a few days.

And where Smith was, Kate could probably be found.

The joy that went through him was close to ecstasy.

Come out, Smith. Go back to her.
I'll be right on your heels.

Noah finished signing the papers and handed the pen back to Tony. "Is that all?"

"It's enough," Tony said. "Too much. It's a

big damn mistake." He folded the papers and tucked them into his briefcase.

"But they're tight?"

"Iron tight. I'll put them in a safe-deposit box at First United Bank of Georgetown."

"Right away."

"As soon as you leave here."

"Don't wait. I have to call Kate and tell her I'm on my way back to the cabin. Go now."

"What's the hurry? I told you there hasn't been a sign of any surveillance. Why not have a drink with me?"

"Another time." He smiled. "Thanks, Tony."

"I just did my job. How's Seth?"

"At the moment he's feeling trapped. He's scared you'll insist he join your racquet club."

"No chance. I'd throw away my racquet and take up glassblowing if he even came near the place." Tony turned toward the door. "Will you be here when I come back?"

"No, I have to get back to Kate."

"Umm, that's interesting." His smile faded. "Here's another thing you'll find interesting. Yesterday Longworth introduced a bill to give the government power to regulate genetic research, experimentation, and product control."

"Shit."

"He slipped it into a package of welfare programs that the president is clamoring for."

"How much time do we have?"

Tony shrugged. "It depends on how much exposure the bill gets and lobbying done for and against it. I've notified the big genetic research labs. Maybe they'll stir things up."

"I can't count on it."

"Then you'd better move fast." He opened the door. "I'll be in touch."

Noah stood there for a few minutes after the door had closed. Damn straight, he'd better move fast.

Noah picked up Tony's digital phone. A minute later Kate answered.

"I'm coming home," Noah said.

"Everything's all right?"

"It could be better. Longworth introduced a bill that will stop genetic research in its tracks."

"Damn. Well, we'll have to find a way to handle it." She paused. "But I was asking about you. Are you safe?"

"I'm fine. Everything's finished and I'm on my way home. I should be there by midnight."

"Be careful, it's raining cats and dogs here. You'll hardly be able to see the highway."

"Midnight."

"Good." Her voice was a little throaty as she added, "I might even be persuaded to fix you a snack."

"No snack. We never had our own personal celebration. I think it's time. I'll bring champagne."

There was a silence at the other end of the phone. "Just bring yourself, dammit."

She hung up.

A smile lingered on his lips as he replaced the

receiver. Home and Kate and the —

Pain sliced through his back.

"Jesus, what's —"

Something struck him in the neck.

He stumbled and fell to the floor. Oh God, the pain . . .

He instinctively rolled over to face the attacker.

Ishmaru. Standing there smiling, a bloody knife in his hand. The bastard had stabbed him, he realized through the haze of agony.

Ishmaru bent and retrieved the gun from Noah's coat. "Now we're going to talk. And if you tell me where to find Kate soon, you may not have to suffer long."

"Go . . . to hell."

Ishmaru sat down beside him. "I was going to follow you, but there's always a chance of losing someone in traffic. I didn't want to take that chance. When I saw Lynski leave, I knew it was a sign. It's much safer to have you tell me where Kate is."

He was bleeding, dying.

All for nothing . . .

No, RU2 wasn't nothing.

Ishmaru's knife plunged into his right arm.

He clenched his teeth to keep from screaming.

"Tell me," Ishmaru whispered. He pulled the knife out.

He was going to pass out. No, fight the bastard. . . .

"Tell me."

He lunged upward, hitting Ishmaru in the chin.

He fell back, his eyes glazing. My God, the bastard had a glass jaw. Lucky . . .

He was on his knees, then on his feet. Had to get out of here before Ishmaru —

Christ, he hurt.

He staggered toward the open door. He was in the hall. He could see the elevators up ahead. He had to get to the elevators. Had to get to Kate . . . had to get to Seth.

RU2 . . . Too many people had died. . . . His people.

RU2 . . .

He didn't see Ishmaru in the doorway behind him.

He didn't hear the bullet that tore through his heart.

Ishmaru ran forward, cursing.

Why didn't he realize he couldn't escape? He was Ishmaru, the warrior. The punch had stunned him but only for a few moments. Then he had been forced to end it too quickly. And with a gun, he thought with disgust. No coup.

The elevator door opened and a hotel maid started to wheel her cart from the cubicle.

She saw Noah's body. She saw Ishmaru coming toward her with a gun in his hand.

She screamed. The next instant the elevator doors closed as she frantically punched the button.

The bitch would rouse the entire hotel.

He knelt and rifled through Smith's pockets.

Car keys, wallet, slips of paper. He took them all and stuffed them into his jacket pocket.

No one expected to die. They almost always left behind clues to their lives. He doubted if Smith was any different.

He ran toward the exit door at the end of the hall.

"Where's Seth? I've got to talk to Seth."

"Who is this?"

"Lynski." A pause. "You're Kate."

"Yes."

"I've got to talk to Seth. Give me his number."

"What's wrong?"

"Everything's wrong. Everything in the whole damn world has gone to hell."

Panic soared through her. "Where's Noah? Is he on his way back?"

"Give me Seth's number."

She rattled off the number. "Dammit, tell me what's wrong. Is Noah hurt?"

"Noah's dead."

He hung up the phone.

The receiver dropped from her hand. It couldn't be true. She had spoken to Noah only a few hours ago. He had said he was safe. Noah was coming back tonight. They were going to celebrate. The promise was going to become reality.

The promise . . .

Tears were streaming down her cheeks. She shouldn't be crying. It couldn't be true. Noah couldn't be dead. All that brilliance and dedication gone.

And the man himself, strong, kind, caring . . .

Michael, Benny . . .

And now Noah?

No, it was too much. It couldn't be true. She sank down on the couch and curled up in the fetal position. She would stay here and Seth would come and tell her it was all a mistake.

Seth would come. . . .

Ishmaru impatiently tossed Smith's wallet on the floor of the car.

Nothing there to help.

His car keys followed.

Nothing was left but a stick of gum and a narrow slip of paper.

A credit card receipt from a gas station. This one was issued by Pine Mountain Gulf. An address and phone number in West Virginia were listed at the top.

"I've got you, Smith," he murmured. It was surprising how even the most careful people goofed up on the little things. Credit card receipts were always useful. Everyone stuffed them in their pocket or purse without thinking, because they were afraid of credit card fraud.

Smith had probably filled up close to his point of origin to avoid stopping on the way. It gave Ishmaru a place to start, and most of the time that was all he needed. He would ask questions and search and soon he would have Kate.

He started his truck and swung onto the Belt-way.

I'm coming, Kate.

"Why the hell didn't you hang up the phone?" Seth asked as he came through the door. "I thought you'd —" His gaze found her. "Christ." He fell to his knees beside the couch and gathered her in his arms. He was wet, she thought dully. It must still be raining. It didn't matter. He was here now. He would tell her everything was all right.

He was rocking her back and forth as if she were a little girl. She felt like a little girl, bewildered, lost.

"You're stiff as a block of ice," he said.

"He's not dead," she whispered. "You came to tell me it was a mistake. Isn't that right, Seth?"

"It's not a mistake." His voice was unsteady, his eyes glittering with moisture. "Noah's dead. Ishmaru killed him."

Ishmaru. She should have known it was Ishmaru. He was the nightmare, the nemesis. "He kills everybody. Michael, Benny . . . all those people at Noah's plant. But I didn't think . . . Not Noah. I hoped he couldn't kill Noah."

"He must have caught Noah off guard." His arms tightened around her and he pressed her face into his shoulder. His voice was thick with pain. "I can't think of it without —" He broke off and a moment later he pushed her away. "Listen, Kate, I can't let you fall apart like this.

268

We can mourn later. There's too much to do now. Ishmaru is still out there."

Of course he was. She was beginning to think he could never be stopped. He would just go on and on until —

"Kate." He shook her, hard. "Tony isn't sure how much Noah told him. There were knife wounds on —" He stopped when she flinched. "I don't think he told the bastard anything, but I have to take precautions."

"Yes, of course," she said dully.

He muttered something beneath his breath. "Joshua. Ishmaru may be coming after you and Joshua." His tone hardened. "Do you want to lie here in a stupor while he slices up Joshua as he did Noah?"

Shock seared through her. "Joshua." She pushed away from him. "Ishmaru's coming here?"

"We don't know."

Joshua might be in danger. She had to think. Easy to say. She felt as if her mind were frozen. "I'm sorry. You'll have to help me. I'm having trouble functioning."

"I wonder why. I'm not doing so well myself." He moved toward the kitchen. "I'll make you some coffee. Go wash your face and start packing."

"Joshua . . . You should go back to Joshua."

"He and Phyliss are packing. We'll go by and pick them up. Hurry."

"You should go back to them. Ishmaru . . ."

"Even if he knows where we are, it will take him at least four hours to get here." He gave her a cool glance over his shoulder. "Move."

The last word was like the crack of a whip, startling her into motion. He had changed, she thought as she hurried toward her bedroom. The gentle Seth who had rocked her and comforted her was gone as if he had never existed. Everything about him now was hard and sharp. Even the way he walked was different. The loping stride that had reminded her of Joshua was now tense, crackling with energy.

This was the man she had first met in her driveway. The man she had thought of as Jack the Ripper. Noah had laughed about that and teased her, but he had known that Seth could be like this. He had counted on it.

Noah . . .

She pushed aside the pain. She mustn't think of Noah now; she must think only of Joshua and Phyliss. She took her suitcase from the closet and began throwing clothes into it.

"Ready?" Seth asked when she joined him ten minutes later. He handed her a cup of coffee and screwed the top on a large thermos. "Where's the stuff for RU2?"

"I packed it up earlier." She set her suitcase down and took a sip of coffee. "I wanted to keep busy while Noah was gone. It's stacked in the corner of the lab."

"I'll go get it. Take your suitcase and the thermos to the jeep."

"I want to drive my car."

"No. One car. I need you all close, where I can see you." He disappeared into the lab.

She took another sip of coffee, then set it down on the counter and picked up the thermos and her suitcase. It was heavy but she welcomed the effort it required to lug it down the steps and stow it into the back of the jeep. It was still raining sheets and she was soaked by the time she climbed into the passenger seat. Thank God, Seth wasn't pampering her. She needed to keep in motion to stop thinking about —

What was keeping Seth? She had set everything neatly in the corner. Or maybe it only seemed that he was taking too long.

Seth was coming down the steps, his arms laden with boxes and briefcases. He set them on the front seat. "Check them. Is everything here?"

She went through the boxes, the briefcases, the disks. "Yes."

He picked up the boxes and stowed them in the back. Then he was in the driver's seat, pulling out of the driveway.

"Where are we going?" she asked.

"We're heading for White Sulphur Springs. I told Tony to meet us at a motel there."

"Why?"

"He said he had to see us."

"What if Ishmaru follows him?"

"Then I'll kill the son of a bitch."

"Lynski or Ishmaru?"

271

"Maybe both." He stopped the car as he reached the main road. "You're sure you have everything?"

"I told you I did."

"Just checking." He pulled something out of his jacket pocket. "Here we go."

The explosion rocked the car as the cabin blew up behind them.

She gazed in shock at the flaming wreckage. "What happened?"

"A little plastic in the right place." He put the control back in his pocket and started the car again.

"You blew it up?" she whispered.

"Some computer whiz might have been able to retrieve something from the lab. Noah died for that damn RU2. Do you think I'd let anyone steal it from him now?"

The glare from the fire cast his face in stark relief and was reflected in his blue eyes. She had never seen a more coldly savage visage.

"No, I don't suppose you would." She shivered and looked away from him.

She had lost Noah.

And she had lost the Seth she had come to know.

It took only thirty minutes to pick up Phyliss and Joshua and load their luggage into the car. They were both silent, shaken as they climbed into the backseat.

"There's a fire," Joshua said. "The cabin's on

fire. I saw it from the house. Should we call Lyle?"

"I already did before I locked up the station," Seth replied. "I told him to come back and take over his job."

"Will it cause a forest fire?"

"No danger. It's raining so hard, it will be out before we're ten miles from here."

Joshua moistened his lips. "Did *he* do it?"

"No, I did. Ishmaru's nowhere near us, Joshua."

"Then why are we running?"

"So he won't get near us." Seth started the car. "It will be okay."

"Will it?" Joshua whispered. "He killed Noah."

"Seth said it will be okay, didn't he?" Phyliss slid her arm around Joshua's thin shoulders. "He always tells us the truth."

Joshua sat straight and stiff on the edge of the seat. His hair was wet and plastered around his face, and in the dashboard lights his features looked gaunt and wizened. Not a child's face, Kate thought. My God, what had she done to him?

He stared at Seth. "Seth?"

Seth met his eyes. "It's okay for now, but it's not over. But I — We can handle it, can't we, Joshua?"

Joshua slowly nodded and sank back against the seat. "Sure."

Blunt honesty instead of comfort. It wasn't how Kate would have handled Joshua's fear, but maybe Seth's way was better. She wasn't sure,

Kate thought wearily. It did seem to work. Anything that worked was a plus right now.

It was almost a totally silent ride to White Sulphur Springs. They reached the Dinmore Motel on the outskirts of the city at dawn the next day. Seth moved with lightning efficiency in getting a room for Phyliss and Joshua and a separate one for Kate. After settling them in he handed the key to Phyliss. "Lock the door. Take a shower and change, but don't go to bed. We may be moving on after I talk to Tony."

"Right," Phyliss said. "Can I go to that convenience store on the corner and get us something to eat?"

Seth shook his head. "Stay inside until I come for you." He said to Kate, "You come with me." He turned and left the room.

"I'll come back as soon as I can," Kate said.

"Don't worry about us. You're the one who looks like she's been run over by a truck," Phyliss said.

That's what she felt like, Kate thought — squashed flat by a truck with razor-sharp treads.

"Go on, Mom," Joshua said as he moved toward the bathroom. "Seth must need you."

She smiled shakily. "And Seth knows best?"

He gave her a sober look. "Seth's smart. He knows about stuff like this." He disappeared into the bathroom.

"He's right," Phyliss said. "I think we should trust Seth right now, Kate."

"I guess we should." She leaned forward and

kissed her cheek. "Thanks, Phyliss."

"For what?"

"For putting up with this mess I've gotten us into."

"Don't be stupid. You're blaming yourself for something you couldn't prevent. Did you kill Michael or Benny or Noah? When something happens, you have to react. That's all you did. React in the way you thought best for everyone." She made a face. "Now get out of here. I want to get out of these clothes and dry off."

"Okay." Kate left the room.

Seth was waiting outside. "I'll let you relax and clean up as soon as I can." He took her arm and guided her down the walkway. "Tony's in Room 34, according to the desk clerk. We'll get this over as quickly as possible."

"And then?"

"We'll see." He stopped before a door and knocked. "I have a few ideas."

Which was more than Kate had right now. She was acting purely on automatic. She'd had too much time to think about Noah on the drive here. Noah . . .

The door was opened by a tall, heavyset man dressed in khakis and a striped shirt. "It's about time."

"Tony, this is Kate Denby." He pushed her into the room. "I'll be back in a few minutes. I want to look around."

"I wasn't followed. Do you think I'd make that mistake again?" Tony Lynski asked bitterly.

"I'll check myself. If you hadn't made it the first time, Noah would be alive now."

"Bastard," Tony muttered as the door closed behind Seth. He turned to Kate, his face twisted with pain. "But he's right. I wasn't careful enough. I should have known Ishmaru was watching me."

Did he want her to argue with him? She didn't know what she felt toward Tony Lynski right now, but it wasn't the impulse to comfort. "What happened to Noah?"

"Ishmaru killed him in my hotel. He was found near the elevators outside my hotel room."

"I know that. What happened to his —" She stopped to steady her voice. "What happened to his body?"

"The morgue. There was no identification on the body. Ishmaru must have taken it. They'll list him as a John Doe."

She flinched. Somehow that horribly impersonal disposal was almost as terrible as the murder itself. "And you let them take him?"

"I came back as he was being put into the coroner's wagon. I didn't know what the hell to do. There was a cop asking questions of everyone in the building, and I gathered what information I could."

"John Doe."

"Do you think I liked it? But I had to get to Seth before I made any decision." He paused. "Noah cared about you. He could hardly wait to get back."

"Why weren't you with him when it happened?"

"He sent me to deposit the documents he signed in a safe-deposit box."

The patents. So Noah's death was her fault too. "You weren't there to help him. No one was there."

"I couldn't know that —"

Seth came into the room. "The area's secure. You did something right, Tony."

Tony drew a deep breath. "Was that necessary?"

"No, but it felt good." He looked around the room, spied a coffeemaker on the desk, and moved toward it. "Why the hell didn't you give her something hot to drink? Can't you see she's almost shell-shocked?"

"You were only gone — Oh, what the hell." He threw himself into a chair. "Get it out of your system."

"I can't." He poured coffee into two mugs, brought one to Kate, and pushed her down in the other chair. He took a sip from his own cup before he said, "Not without breaking your neck. Why are we here?"

"Because Noah would want you here," Tony said. "He came to Washington because I'd drawn up some documents for him to sign."

"The patents," Kate said. "I told him I didn't want them changed. I told him —"

"One document was the patents." Tony looked at Seth. "The other document was a new will

277

leaving all his possessions, including RU2, to you, Seth."

Seth froze. "What?"

"You heard me. He decided he hadn't made adequate provisions for protecting RU2 in case something happened to him. So he left it in your hands."

"*My* hands?"

"I told him he was crazy. I told him you were the last person he should trust with anything important." He smiled crookedly. "He wouldn't listen. Noah never listened to me."

"*Goddamn* him."

Kate stared at Seth in shock.

"I won't take it." He hurled the coffee mug against the far wall. "He can take his RU2 and shove it. He couldn't catch me in that trap when he was alive, and I won't let him do it to me now."

"A nice adult display of gratitude," Tony said sourly. "Now why don't you pull out a gun and shoot somebody?"

"Don't tempt me."

"Well, I did what Noah would have expected of me." He leaned back in the chair. "What do you want to do?"

"I'll tell you what I'm going to do. I'm going to find Ishmaru and gut him."

"About RU2?"

"I don't want it. I won't take it."

"You mean you don't want the responsibility."

"Can you blame him?" Kate said. "For God's

sake, find a way to let him out. He doesn't have to die too."

"The will's iron tight. He's got it whether he wants it or not." Tony smiled. "If I'd known you'd be this upset, I wouldn't have argued with Noah."

"I'll sign it over to Kate."

"You can't. It's yours for life." Tony was obviously beginning to enjoy himself. "I guess that means you inherited me too. What are your instructions? Shall I call a board meeting to —"

"Damn you to hell." Seth tore open the door and slammed it behind him.

"Drink your coffee," Tony told Kate. "He'll be back once he cools down. Jesus, it felt good to needle him for a change." His smile faded. "I guess that's pretty immature. Noah's dead. I shouldn't be —" He shrugged. "What can I say? I'm human."

"Yes." She lifted the cup to her lips and found her hand was shaking. She carefully set the cup on the table beside her. "Why Seth? Why did Noah will everything to Seth?"

"That's what I asked him. He said Seth could do the job." He grimaced. "If he doesn't decide to sell RU2 to some Colombian drug lord."

"He wouldn't do that. He blew up the cabin to make sure no one would get hold of it."

"Who the hell knows what Seth will do? He's always been a wild card." He shook his head. "It was a mistake. Everything's falling apart. Noah's dead and we're helpless. RU2 is heading for the trash heap."

She jumped to her feet. She couldn't handle this and she couldn't sit here any longer. She felt as if she were being smothered by the heavy blanket of his words. "I need some air. Tell Seth I went for a walk."

"I'm sorry. I guess I wasn't very tactful. I'm having trouble dealing with —"

The door closed behind her, shutting out his words. She drew a deep breath, but it didn't help. She still felt the heaviness dragging her down. She jammed her hands into the pockets of her jacket and started walking toward the highway, her mind spinning.

Noah's dead.

RU2 is heading for the trash heap.

Ishmaru.

Joshua.

Seth is a wild card.

We're helpless.

Helpless . . .

Two hours later Seth met Kate as she was returning to the motel.

Relief rushed through him. "I can see how you'd have trouble taking Tony for very long, but couldn't you let someone know where you were going?"

"I didn't know." She shot him a cool look. "And I didn't see you handing out maps when you stormed out in your little tantrum."

"It wasn't a tantrum. I was —" He shrugged.

"Okay, I lost it. Tit for tat. But you should have —"

"You said it was safe. Was that a lie?"

"No, but you never —" He stopped, studying her. When he had last seen her, she had been wooden, lethargic, almost dazed. She was not like that now. Her eyes were bright, her lips firm, and her manner cutting sharp. It was as if a wind had blown over her, clearing all the cloudiness away.

But leaving what behind?

"For how long?" she asked.

"What?" He was so absorbed by the change in her that he'd lost track of the conversation. Safe. She was asking how long they'd be safe. "I don't think we left any trail, but there are usually loose ends somewhere. A few days maybe."

"And then we run again?" She emphatically shook her head. "No way. I'm through scurrying and hiding and standing by and watching Ishmaru kill people I care about. I'm tired of that asshole threatening my family and not being able to do anything about it."

He smiled slowly. "You're angry. I haven't seen you this angry since that first day at the cabin."

"I wasn't angry then. Not like I am now." She walked faster, her words coming fast and vibrating with emotion. "I *won't* be helpless. Tony said we were helpless, but that's a lie. You're only helpless if you give up. I'm not giving up and neither are you. Do you hear me? You won't sell RU2 to some scum of a drug lord and you won't run away from this."

He lifted a brow. "And what would you do if I did?"

She stared at him. "Haunt you, hurt you, whatever is necessary. I won't let you go. I need you. I'm not going to be a victim anymore."

"Even if it means dragging me kicking and screaming along with you."

"I *won't* be a victim," she repeated.

He considered her for a moment. "You need a shower and a few hours' rest. We'll talk when you're not so upset."

"I'm not upset. Everything's crystal clear for the first time since this started."

"We'll talk later."

She shrugged. "It won't make any difference." She walked on ahead of him as they entered the motel parking lot.

He watched her moving purposefully, back straight, stride strong.

Strong and bold and burning bright.

No, it wouldn't make any difference. Not to the Kate he was looking at now. No softness, no uncertainty, just rage and determination.

And Seth knew from experience there was no more lethal combination.

Eleven

"Come in." Kate was toweling her hair dry when Seth knocked on the door six hours later.

"I told you to lock your door," Seth said as he entered the room and closed the door behind him.

"I locked it while I napped. I knew you'd be coming soon, and I was in the shower."

"That's not good enough."

"Okay." She threw the towel aside and ran her fingers through her damp hair. "I'll remember next time."

"You're being very meek."

"I'm being sensible. You know more about this. I'll learn from you. I told you I needed you." She sat down on the bed and drew her terry robe closer about her. "I'm damned well not going to do anything that will get me killed." She met his gaze. "But I'm not hiding anymore."

"What about Joshua and Phyliss? Are you going to risk them?"

"Of course not. I've been thinking . . . Noah said that they were most at risk when they were with me."

"That's true."

"Then if I become visible, they can't be any-where near me."

He shook his head. "You won't allow Joshua out of your sight."

Her hand clenched on the tie of her robe. "I will if it will save his life."

"It's not necessary," he said roughly, "I'll get Ishmaru."

"And after you kill him, Ogden will send someone else. I want this over. We have to go public with RU2."

"You go public. I don't want anything to do with it."

"No, you just want to go and gut Ishmaru and then disappear into the sunset. I'm not going to let you do it."

"And how are you going to stop me?"

"I'm not going to have to stop you. You like Joshua. You're not going to let him die. You're not that callous."

"I let Noah die. He was my best friend."

"And you're so angry with yourself that you want to kick everyone in sight."

"Maybe."

"Not maybe." She shook her head wearily. "Look, I don't care what you do after RU2 is accepted and my family is safe. You can go to Tibet or back down to South America and get scalped by a headhunter. That's your choice. I just have to have your help now. Will you give it to me?"

"I've been to Tibet. It doesn't appeal to me."

"Will you help me?"

He looked down at the floor. "Since you put

284

your plea in such caring terms, I don't see how I can refuse."

Relief surged through her. She hadn't been able to believe Seth would abandon them, but she couldn't be sure. As Tony had said, he was a wild card.

"But Ishmaru is mine. No questions, no arguments. I'm taking him down."

"No arguments." She shuddered. "I stopped you once when you had a chance to kill him. I wish I'd let you do it."

"It was my mistake. I knew it was the wrong thing to do when I left you." He shrugged. "But you were already scared of me, and I knew Noah was more afraid of not getting what he needed from you than he was of Ishmaru."

"He told you that?" she whispered.

He nodded. "He told me everything that was going on with RU2. It was the intelligent thing to do. Keeping your allies in the dark is a good way to get them axed." He moved over to the coffeemaker on the bureau. "Coffee?"

She nodded absently. "Then you know everything that Noah knew." A sudden thought occurred to her. "About me too?"

"Most things. About your background, the way you thought." He didn't look at her as he poured coffee into the mug. "Don't worry, he didn't tell me how you were in bed."

Shock went through her. "He told you he went to bed with me?"

"Not exactly. I just assumed . . ." He shrugged.

285

"You were a matched set. Throw a man and woman together and you get combustion."

"Well, the combustion never occurred. We were too busy to — It would have gotten in the way."

"RU2 again. How clinical and practical of both of you." He smiled. "You know, Noah was a damn fool."

She felt a ripple of disturbance. "It wasn't Noah's sole decision."

"But you were alone and vulnerable and not obsessed with RU2. I'd bet a nudge would have sent you over."

"This is none of your business, Seth."

"I'd have nudged and damned the consequences." He moved across the room and handed her the mug. "But then, I'm philosophically opposed to denying myself."

"Enjoy the moment?"

"Right."

"Well, Noah had other priorities."

"I know. Like saving mankind." He held up his palms and pretended he was weighing. "Saving mankind? Sex?" Suddenly he fell to his knee with his left hand on the floor. "Sorry, Kate." He sighed. "Sex wins every time."

She hadn't smiled since last night, but she found herself smiling now. "You're being ridiculous."

"I just wanted to establish the fact that I'm not Noah. I'll never be either a monk or a saint, and I'm definitely not a white hat. Not black either, but maybe a dirty brown." He sat on the floor and crossed his legs tailor fashion. "I won't try to spare you or use you, and I'll be as honest as I can. Which is more than you got from Noah."

She frowned. "What do you mean?"

"He didn't tell you that you were wanted for murder in Dandridge."

"What?"

"The officer in the black-and-white. You were supposed to be unbalanced and angry at the police department because of your ex-husband's death."

She shook her head. "That's crazy."

"No, it's a very clever way of keeping you tied up and discredited if you try to go public with RU2. Some nice sums must have changed hands."

"No one could possibly — Alan must have tried to tell — It doesn't make sense."

"The charge wouldn't hold water, but it's an obstacle. It makes sense."

He was right, she realized dazedly. They had done the same thing to Noah after the plant explosions. Implicate the victim — that was their strategy. "How long did Noah know this?"

"Since the night you arrived at the cabin. He needed you to work on RU2, and he was afraid you'd bolt back to Dandridge and try to clear yourself."

"I might have." She moistened her lips. "But he had no right to keep it from me. It wasn't right."

"He needed you." He shook his head. "We both loved the bastard, and there's no use blaming him now. He just got caught up into something that dwarfed everything else around him." His lips thinned. "He's even trying to protect it from beyond the grave."

"Yes." The shared patent, the will. Seeming acts of kindness and generosity but chaining them both to RU2. Chaining her, at least. She doubted if anything could chain Seth for long. Well, it had to be long enough to make sure Joshua and Phyliss were safe. "I don't blame him. He meant well."

"Saint Noah."

She had called him that, she remembered with a pang. "He was a good man."

"The best." He glanced away from her. "But he wasn't a saint, he was human like the rest of us. He made mistakes."

"What kind of mistakes?"

"He sat on his hands and waited until Ogden marshaled his forces. Now it's going to be all the harder for us."

"We had to complete the formula for RU2."

"And I could have been in Washington cutting the ground from beneath Ogden."

"You had to protect Joshua."

"There were other solutions, safer solutions. Noah just wanted to keep you happy so that you'd work harder. He knew stashing Joshua near you would do that."

"Safer solutions?"

"We were in the middle of the woods. It's hard to keep watch over anyone."

"You did it."

"But I'm bloody wonderful. It's not the way I would have handled it, but Noah was running the show. He's not running it any longer." His gaze shifted back to her. "And neither are you, Kate. If you want me, it's got to be my way."

She stiffened. "The hell it will."

"I won't say I won't consult you. You're smart and you're savvy about RU2. I'm just telling you that I won't take a backseat again."

He meant it, she realized with frustration. "I don't like backseats either. I let Noah handle everything and now I find myself wanted for murder and —"

"Choose, Kate."

She stared at him a long time before she reluctantly nodded. "As long as I can see sense in what you're doing and it doesn't threaten my family."

"Good." He rose to his feet. "Now get dressed while I go get Tony. We have some strategy to plan if you're going to go public. It's not going to be pretty."

"The apocalypse," she whispered.

"What?"

"That's what Noah called it."

"He tended to be negative after the explosion at his plant." He moved toward the door. "It's not the apocalypse."

"What is it then?"

"Just a war," he said wearily. "Just another war."

"You're going to go public," Tony repeated. "Without Noah?" He cast a glowering look at Seth. "With him?"

"That's right," Kate said. "And we'll need your help."

"You're making a mistake to trust him."

"I don't think so."

"I've promised her I won't sell RU2 to my friendly local drug cartel," Seth said. "I wonder what put that idea into her head? That sounded remarkably like you, Tony."

"It was." He glared at Seth. "You've always been bad news."

"Well, I'm your bad news now. You've got to work with me."

"I don't have to do shit."

"You'd rather Noah died for nothing? You'd rather Ishmaru skips away?"

Tony was silent.

"Come on," Seth said quietly. "Noah was your friend. You may not believe I'm capable of taking Noah's place, but you know I can get Ishmaru."

"Maybe."

Seth stared at him.

"Okay, you're good at what you do." Tony shook his head. "What the hell. Things can't get much worse."

"I take it that's an affirmative?"

"What do you want from me?"

"A hell of a lot. First, information. What's happening with Longworth?"

"I told Noah about the bill he introduced."

"Nothing else?"

"How the hell do I know? I've been occupied for the last twenty-four hours."

"Fill me in on the patent situation. Have you filed?"

"Not yet. Noah brought me the final procedure when he came to change the patent to include Kate. The documents are in a safe-deposit box."

"I want you to go back to Washington and file them. Do you have someone in the patent office you can trust to do it confidentially?"

"Hell yes. I have someone in every patent office here and every major country in Europe. Noah had me on the road for the last six months."

"Why Europe?"

"He knew that it might not be possible to overcome the opposition here. It's easier to get a drug approved abroad."

"Then why didn't he plan to file there?"

"You know Noah. He was patriotic as hell. He wanted the U.S. to have the benefits. It takes years for the FDA to accept foreign drugs."

"His people . . ." Kate murmured.

"Yeah," Tony said. "That's what he said."

"We'll file in Europe," Seth said. "Which country is best?"

"Holland. Amsterdam's average rate of approval is three months to the FDA's three years."

"And the pharmaceutical companies in Europe

haven't had a chance to mobilize against RU2. We'll go for it."

"No," Kate said.

They turned to look at her.

"We try Noah's way first. We try to protect his people. Our people."

"It's not smart," Seth said. "We'll all be a hell of a lot safer in Holland."

"You said you could keep Joshua and Phyliss safe."

"But you'll be exposed, a target. It's not smart."

"I don't care if it's smart. Those butchers who killed Noah are trying to stop RU2 dead in its tracks. I don't want them to get what they want." She smiled bitterly. "So your challenge is to keep them from hitting the bull's-eye. Noah died for RU2. We have to try to do it his way."

He gazed at her for a long moment. "Four months. If we don't make big strides in that time, I'm not going to let you beat your head against the wall. Noah wasn't stupid. He wouldn't have set up the mechanism if he didn't think there was a risk of RU2 not being accepted here."

She nodded. "Do you think I don't know the problems? I want testing to start as soon as possible, and even if we manage to stop that bill from going through, the FDA is going to be supercautious. But we can at least try to get rid of the obstacles Ogden's put in the path."

Seth turned to Tony. "Go ahead and file in Washington."

"You want to keep it secret?"

"Only for twenty-four hours. I don't want any convenient fires destroying records until we go public."

"And how do we do that?" Kate asked.

"The *Washington Post.*" He asked Tony, "Who's smart and hungry?"

"Zack Taylor, Meryl Kimbro . . . you name it. Everyone wants to be a star."

"You choose, then."

"Meryl Kimbro. She's more open than Taylor."

"Arrange a meeting for Kate and me tomorrow night, nine o'clock."

"Where?"

"Any hotel." He raised a brow. "Disappointed? I'm no Deep Throat, and parking garages are too damp and gloomy."

"A parking garage might impress her more."

"She'll be impressed enough when Kate gets through with her." He took Kate's elbow. "Get stirring. When the papers are filed, call me on your digital."

"Where will you be?"

"Near here. We have some security arrangements to make."

"Much good that will do you. There won't be any place safe when you open that can of worms."

"Not for us. Joshua and Phyliss." He held open the door for Kate. "And you're wrong. I know a safe place."

"Where is this safe place?" Kate asked as they walked toward Phyliss and Joshua's room.

"It's kind of hard to explain. I prefer you see it." He stopped outside the door. "I want a moment alone with Joshua."

"Why?"

"He's not going to like you leaving him. But I think he'll accept it more easily if the news comes from me. Take Phyliss for a walk and explain things."

"I should be the one to tell him."

"This isn't a case for maternal duty. Do what's right for the kid. You can talk to him later."

She gave up the battle. Maybe he was right. He certainly had Joshua's complete confidence. "How long do you need?"

"Twenty minutes."

She nodded. "Okay."

"No." Joshua's hands clenched into fists at his sides. "I'm going with you."

Seth leaned back in the chair and waited. Let him get it out.

"She *needs* me."

"Yes, she does."

"Then tell her that she has to take me."

"She wouldn't listen. She thinks this is the best way to make sure you're all safe."

"What about her? She's not . . . He hurt her. He almost killed her."

"But he didn't. She was too much for him."

"He *hurt* her."

That memory clearly haunted him. "He won't hurt her again."

"He killed my dad. He killed Noah."

"He won't hurt your mom. I won't let him."

"I need to be there. I need to help you. Tell her."

"No."

Joshua's eyes widened.

"I won't do it because she's right. You should be as far away from her as possible. If she has to worry about you, she won't worry about herself. You'd be a danger to her."

"I'd take care of her."

"Think, Joshua."

"I don't want to think. I want to go with you."

"Even if it means you may get her killed?"

There was a silence. Seth could see the struggle taking place, but he knew he couldn't help Joshua.

"You're telling me the truth?"

"Have I ever lied to you?"

Another silence.

"You'll take care of her? You promise you won't let anything happen to her?"

"I promise."

Joshua nodded jerkily. "Okay."

Seth sat looking at him, knowing how agonizing that decision was for Joshua. He wondered if he would have been able to handle the trauma that had been thrown at the boy when he was Joshua's age. The kid was wounded, but Seth could almost see his resilience and strength growing every day. He wanted to reach out and . . .

He didn't reach out. Joshua didn't want comfort. He wanted Kate safe and Seth's promise that he would keep her that way. Joshua had made an adult decision, and Seth would not treat him as a child at that moment.

God, he was proud of him.

Kate stared at the huge southern mansion in disgust. "This is your safe place?"

"Sort of. That's the Greenbriar Hotel, the main attraction of this resort. There's also a fine golf course."

"I don't play golf," Phyliss said from the backseat. "Tennis?"

"Yes, but I'm afraid you won't be playing. Ping-Pong okay?"

"Well, it was good enough for Forrest Gump." She slid her arm around Joshua's shoulders. "How about it, Joshua?"

"Why are we here?" Joshua whispered. "It doesn't look . . . it's not like the ranger station."

He meant it didn't look safe, Kate thought. He was right. "What the devil are we doing here?"

"You'll see." Seth turned down a side road, and the hotel was soon lost to view. Three miles later he pulled into a turnout screened by shrubs and stopped the car.

"I thought you said the woods weren't safe," Kate said.

"This is just the window dressing." He got out of the car and approached a group of large rocks. "Come on."

Kate slowly got out of the car, followed by

Phyliss and Joshua. "Window dressing?"

He lifted a smaller rock, revealing a control panel, and punched in a code. Two of the large rocks parted.

"Open sesame," he intoned.

"Like Ali Baba's cave," Joshua said. "Neat."

"You won't find any genie in a bottle here." He started down the ramp. "Wait. I'll be right back."

Phyliss warily stared down into the darkness. "Take your time. I'm not in any hurry."

Light suddenly illuminated the interior, and a moment later Seth was climbing the ramp toward them. "I had to kick on the generator. Go slowly. The main areas are being flooded with oxygen, but it won't be ready for another five minutes."

The ramp was wide and curving, the sides of the tunnel smooth concrete. "It's like a bunker," Kate murmured.

"Right the first time." The last curve of the ramp had taken them to a large steel door that resembled a bank vault. "That's what it was designed to be."

"A bunker?"

"During the cold war, Congress didn't like the idea of being blown to bits in case of an atomic attack. So they secretly built a bomb shelter to stay in until it was safe to return to the upper world."

"I remember seeing something on one of the news shows on television about that," Phyliss said. "It became public knowledge only a few years ago."

"I can see why," Kate said dryly. "Their constituents wouldn't appreciate their representatives saving their own necks while the rest of the country went up in flames."

Phyliss was frowning. "But there was something else . . ." Her gaze suddenly went to Seth. "The hotel was going to open it to the public. Maybe give tours."

"I'm surprised they didn't set up an amusement park and sell tickets. But I guess the Greenbriar has too much class."

Kate drew a deep breath and spoke very precisely. "You're settling Phyliss and Joshua in the middle of a tour site?"

Seth grinned. "It might not be a bad idea. Didn't you ever hear about hiding in plain sight?"

"It would be a lousy idea and I won't —"

"Easy." He punched in a code on the door panel. "I didn't think you'd go for it. This isn't that facility. Congress's hideaway is over a mile away. There's a tunnel linking the two facilities, but no one knows about it. No one is going to run a tour through here." The steel door lumbered open. "The lights go on automatically when the door is opened, but the control panel is on the left as you enter." He entered the facility and turned to face Phyliss. "No dishes here. Throwaway paper plates, so water isn't wasted."

"I should have known. You'll do anything to avoid housework."

Joshua looked around him. "It's like a house."

A bachelor's pad, maybe, Kate thought. All sleek black and white modern furniture and lots of mirrors. It was too cool for her taste, but the white velvet couch across the room looked comfortable. Joshua evidently was finding it so as he bounced on the cushions. "How much room is there?"

"A kitchen, storage area, two bedrooms, and an exercise room." He smiled at Joshua. "With a Ping-Pong table."

"Neat." Joshua jumped off the couch and went exploring.

"Why doesn't anyone know about the tunnel?"

"Because Jackson made sure that it wasn't included in any of the blueprints. He hired people he trusted . . . well, not trust. Actually, he hired people he had something on to build this little bit of heaven."

"Jackson?"

"Lionel Jackson, a senator who was involved in the building of the bomb shelter. He wasn't sure that the air and food would last long enough in the main facility. Too many people to share it. So he built himself an escape hatch and this little safety net to come home to while his fellow congressmen were suffocating or starving to death."

"Charming," Phyliss said.

"He was charming. He was elected to the Senate for twenty-four years."

"And is he likely to show up here?" Kate asked.

"He died eight years ago."

"Without telling anyone about this place?"

"He told his son, Randolph. There came a time when it was necessary that his pride and joy have a hideout. Randolph was as charming as his father but not nearly as smart. He got the daughter of a New York Mafia boss pregnant and then beat her to death in a fit of rage. Lionel decided his son needed to be out of sight until he could smooth things over. He hired me to bring Randolph down here and guard him." He shrugged. "I did my best."

"They found him here?"

"No, he got bored. One day I came back from getting supplies and he'd flown the coop. The stupid bastard went back to New York. He lasted one day." He gestured around him. "So you might say I inherited the place."

"Have you used it since then?"

"Once or twice." He smiled. "But I never brought anyone else here. No tours. No unexpected visitors. It will be like living in Fort Knox."

"Just what I always wanted," Phyliss said.

"Best I can do," Seth countered. "I'll spring you as quickly as I can." His gaze went to Joshua, who was back and prowling around the living room. "You're going to have your hands full. He's excited now, but in a few days he's going to go stir-crazy."

"We can't go out at all?"

"No," Kate said sharply. "Please, Phyliss. I have to know you're both safe."

"I wish we could be as certain about you." She

turned to Seth. "You take better care of her than you did that senator's kid or I'll cut your throat."

"Yes, ma'am. I'll have Rimilon bring fresh food and supplies and set them inside the tunnel. You take one trip to the surface to pick them up and meet him and then you stay behind that locked door."

"Wait a minute," Kate said. "Who's Rimilon?"

"He served under me in South America and Tanzania. I called him yesterday when you were sleeping and told him to meet us at the fork in the road at four o'clock." He checked his wristwatch. "Forty minutes. We don't have much time."

"I don't like him knowing they're here."

"And I didn't like the idea of relying only on a steel door to protect them. Rimilon is good."

She smiled sardonically. "Like you?"

"Hell no. He's good, not magnificent. You don't get magnificent every day." His smile faded. "I can trust him, Kate."

"Can you? I don't seem to be able to trust anyone anymore."

"I'm not overflowing with the milk of human kindness myself. But I have leverage with Rimilon, and leverage translates to confidence."

"What kind of leverage?"

"He knows I'd kill him if he betrays me," he said simply.

She watched him as he moved across the room toward Joshua. Toughness, humor, and a streak of deadly violence. He was still an enigma, but she no longer felt at a loss with him as she had the first time she'd encountered that lethal side of him. The other facets of his character were still there; he was just more than he had first let her see.

"You take care of yourself," Phyliss said.

Kate turned back to her. "I'm leaving my medical bag in case you need it. I feel guilty about this. I don't see any other way. I'm going to worry."

"Of course you feel guilty. You're one of those people who think the world rests on their shoulders."

"Joshua is my responsibility."

"Granted. But he's mine too. Loving someone carries a price tag. Don't insult me by assuming you're the only one who can keep him safe."

"Sorry." She gave Phyliss a quick, hard hug. "I hope it will be over soon."

"It may not." Phyliss shrugged. "At first I thought it would only be a matter of time before everything returned to normal. I'm not sure now. It may never be the same. I've just got to deal with it."

Kate felt a rush of guilt. "I didn't know all this —"

"I know you didn't," Phyliss interrupted. "But I don't think you're thinking so much as reacting now. While you and Noah were working, I had lots of time to think about this. Even after the first threat is over, there are going to be repercussions." Her smile was sad. "We're stuck in

Oz. We're not going to be able to go back to Kansas, Dorothy."

"That's not true. I'll find a way to —"

"Come on." Phyliss took her arm. "I need to talk to Seth before you leave. There are things I have to know."

Kate let her lead her across the room to Seth and Joshua. Phyliss had changed, she realized. She had always been strong, but now there was a subtle difference. She had usually been content to let Kate make the decisions, but now she was taking control. Why was she surprised? Kate wondered wearily. Everything was changing.

"I want to know how all the controls work," Phyliss said.

"That's not necessary. It's still state-of-the-art technology. Just press buttons. Everything's pretty much automatic," Seth said.

"I've had too many appliances blow up to trust automation, and oxygen pumps are a tad more important than a coffeemaker. I want to know how to jury-rig everything if it becomes necessary." She put a hand on Joshua's shoulder. "And I want Joshua to learn too."

There was both affection and pride in Seth's smile. "Good idea." He turned to Kate. "It will take a few minutes to go over everything in depth."

She nodded. "I'll go up to the car and start bringing down their luggage."

He walked her to the door. "Satisfied?" he asked in a low voice. "It's the best I can do."

303

"Nothing would satisfy me right now, but I suppose a shelter that would repel an atomic bomb is fairly safe." She made a face. "But it won't keep me from worrying."

He turned back to Phyliss and Joshua. "That goes with the territory."

She hugged Joshua. "I'll be back soon," she whispered.

Joshua nodded. "I know you will." His arms tightened around her fiercely. "You mind Seth, Mom. Do you hear me? You mind Seth. He'll take care of you."

Tears stung her eyes. "I'll be fine." She brushed his forehead with her lips and released him. "And you take care of Phyliss."

"Sure. Seth said that was my job." He turned to Seth and thrust out his hand. "Good-bye."

Seth gravely shook it. "Good-bye, Joshua."

So grown-up, Kate thought with a pang. He was caught in the barbed net Ishmaru and Ogden had woven, and his childhood was being torn away from him.

Damn them.

She turned away and strode quickly into the tunnel.

She heard the heavy vault door slide closed behind her as Seth caught up with her. "Okay?"

"No," she said shortly. "I'm not okay. I'm scared and angry and I want my life back." They had reached the surface and she watched Seth close the entry. She shook her head as she saw the rocks shift smoothly into place. "It's incredible. You'd never know it was here."

"That should make you feel better." He strode over to the jeep and got in. "Come on. We have to meet Rimilon."

Rimilon was waiting at the crossroads. He didn't look like a mercenary, Kate thought as he got out of the Volkswagen and walked toward them. Or maybe he did. What did she know? He was a squat, powerfully built man in his early forties. His hairline was receding and he was wearing khakis, a Ralph Lauren sport shirt, and Nike tennis shoes. He'd fit in very well with the golf aficionados at the resort only a few miles away.

He nodded politely at Kate when Seth introduced them. "I don't think you need me," he told Seth. "God, you gave me directions and I still had trouble finding that tunnel entry."

"A little insurance never hurts." He handed Rimilon a slip of paper. "If you see anything out of the ordinary, call me."

Rimilon smiled. "Whatever you say."

"Exactly." He met his gaze. "I'd be very annoyed if anything unpleasant happened here. I'm holding you responsible."

Rimilon's smile faded. "Okay. Okay. Lighten up. I said you didn't need me, I didn't say I wouldn't be careful. You know I don't make mistakes."

"Don't start now." Seth nodded and started the car. "When you deliver the supplies, intro-

305

duce yourself to Phyliss and the boy so they'll know who you are, but your job is to guard the entrance."

"Right." Rimilon hurriedly backed away from the jeep. "Fine."

Kate was silent for several minutes after they had reached the highway. "He was afraid of you."

"Was he?"

"You know he was."

"Good. Leverage."

He had told her Rimilon knew Seth was capable of killing him, but she had not expected that flicker of fear in Rimilon. "I thought you were old military buddies. Why should he be afraid?"

"Namirez is probably still on his mind."

"Namirez?"

"A mutual acquaintance." He glanced at his watch. "We have a long trip. Why don't you try to take a nap?"

The subject was closed. He wasn't going to talk about Rimilon or this Namirez. Well, it didn't matter. Let him keep his secrets. She wasn't concerned about his past, only the present.

She closed her eyes. "Wake me if you get tired, and I'll take over."

A laboratory.

Ishmaru climbed over charred and fallen timber, his boots sinking into the mud. There wasn't much left, though he could tell the cabin had been more than a weekend getaway.

But nothing he could salvage to find Kate, he

realized in frustration.

Lynski?

He had probably split when he had come back and found Noah Smith.

Dead end.

Maybe not. Blount had said he had another lead.

And what Blount knew, he would tell him.

But he was still filled with rage that he'd wasted all this time for nothing. He *needed* to find her. He needed to count coup now so that he could go back to the cave. Since he'd killed Smith two days ago, the nightmares had started coming again, more horrible than ever. The soul he'd taken must have been very strong.

He could not bear another night. He would have to go to the cave.

He needed the guardians.

Twelve

Seth and Kate checked into the Summit Hotel in Washington, D.C., in the early hours of the morning. It was very luxurious, very large, and very public.

"Not exactly your average safe house," Kate observed dryly as the doors of the elevator shut and he punched the button for the twelfth floor. "I expected something a little smaller and more discreet."

"Once you go public, any cover you might have had is blown anyway. This hotel is run by a Japanese conglomerate. They're very proud of their service . . . including their tight security."

"And you're going to rely on that security?"

"No, but it's a start." The elevator stopped and they moved down the hall. "I have a few other ideas."

"I'm sure you do."

"I've arranged a two-bedroom suite. Large sitting room with bedrooms on either side. You don't open the door for any hotel employee. I'll try to give you as much privacy as possible, but at night the doors to my bedroom and yours stay open. Understand?"

"Perfectly."

The suite was large and airy, the furniture elegant. As distant from the cozy comfort of her home as could be imagined, Kate thought.

Seth put down the duffel he was carrying that contained the RU2 research documents. "Tony will put this in a bank vault, but we may need it tomorrow when you talk to the reporter." He opened the adjoining doors and checked the locks. "I know you want to shower and get to bed, but the porter should be bringing the other bags soon. I'll stay here until he leaves."

She shrugged. "Whatever you want."

His brows lifted. "You must be tired."

She was tired and lonely and worried. She didn't want to be in this luxury hotel facing weeks of separation from her son. She wanted to be home with Joshua. "I'll survive."

He smiled. "That's what this is all about."

"Will Tony be staying here at the hotel too?"

"Yes, it's more convenient, but don't expect to see much of him. I guess you've caught on to the fact that he disapproves of me."

"It would be hard to miss." She sat down on the sofa. "I'm a little surprised he's helping us."

"He loved Noah." He took a chair opposite her. "And he loves seeing me in this position. He knows I'm hating it. He didn't want Noah to involve me from the beginning. My way of making a living offends him." He paused. "Which brings up something I have to ask you. Is there anything in your present or past that Ogden can use to hurt you?"

She stiffened. "What?"

"Don't freeze up on me. I have to know. We all have skeletons in our closets. I just have to make sure that no one's able to rattle yours. Is there anything I should know?"

No one must ever know.

"No." She jumped to her feet. "You wait for the bags. I have to go to the bathroom."

There was a knock on the door.

"Saved by the bell," Seth said. "Now you don't have to run away."

"I don't know what you mean."

"Don't worry, I'm not going to force you to confide your sins. Though I damn well should." He walked to the door and paused with his hand on the knob. "Just remember that whatever you've done, I've done worse. Anytime you want to talk to me, I'll be here."

She didn't answer.

He shrugged and let the porter in.

"It's a bunch of bullshit," Meryl Kimbro said flatly. She clicked off her tape recorder and rose to her feet. "And believe me, after covering Washington for eighteen years, I'm an expert on bullshit."

"Wait." Tony jumped to his feet. "You need to take time to —"

"But what if it isn't?" Seth asked softly. "What if it's all true?"

Her glance shifted to him. "No proof. You can't pin Ogden or Longworth or this Ishmaru. We'd be sued."

"Then don't mention them. Go for the story on RU2."

"And give you free publicity on a drug that's not been approved by the FDA."

"It could save a hell of a lot of lives."

"If your claims are true. There have been four demonstrations this week from anti-genetic-research groups. The paper doesn't need to take that kind of static because of an untested drug."

"My claims are true," Kate said quietly. "I'll give you documentation."

"Which I wouldn't understand."

"Take it to a scientist who would."

The reporter hesitated. "Not interested. Bullshit." She walked out of the hotel room.

"I guess that's that," Tony said. "I'll go down to the next name on the list."

"No," Kate said. "Wait."

"Why?"

"The woman's a professional. We've aroused her curiosity. She won't be able to walk away from it."

"She just did."

"I like her. I think she's honest. I've got a feeling . . . Give her twenty-four hours before you approach anyone else."

"I don't think that —"

"Twenty-four hours." Seth smiled at Kate. "I have a great respect for instinct."

Tony shrugged. "You're the ones on the hot seat."

Meryl Kimbro called the next afternoon. "Okay, you've got me. I want to see the RU2 documentation."

"What changed your mind?" Kate asked.

"I called Dandridge and checked out your story. By the way, you're not wanted for murder anymore, but they do want you for questioning."

Relief poured through Kate.

"A Detective Eblund went to bat for you and knocked the legs from the case. It apparently was pretty damn flimsy anyway."

Bless Alan. "Nonexistent."

"And I went to the city morgue and viewed the John Doe they carted from that Georgetown hotel."

Kate flinched. John Doe. The idea of Noah being treated so impersonally still made her cringe.

"If he's not Noah Smith, he's close enough to be a twin. They thought I was crazy when I asked them to run a fingerprint match with the Noah Smith who died in that explosion, but I think they'll do it. The rest of the story may be bogus, but I've got enough to make it worthwhile to go a little further. I'll pick up the RU2 stuff in forty minutes."

"No, I'll go with you when you check it out."

"You don't want to let it out of your sight? Okay, no problem."

Kate turned to Seth after she hung up the phone. "Well, I'm not wanted for murder any

312

longer and she's going to check out RU2."

"Then we've got her," Seth said. "I'll bet we get our story in tomorrow's paper." He paused. "And everyone will know exactly where you are. Are you sure that's what you want?"

"No, but that's what we've got to do." She made a face. "At least it's not all bad. I won't have the police breathing down my neck."

"Then hang on to your hat. The roller coaster ride's about to begin."

They were gone!

Ishmaru wanted to shriek with agony as he walked into the cave. He knelt, pawing desperately through the blackened remnants.

After fifteen minutes he found only one charred pole. After an hour he unearthed a gold lighter. Nothing else.

No sign of the guardians.

He rocked back and forth, his arms wrapped tightly around his body. He waited in terror for them to come.

They were closing in, swooping about him, howling in the darkness.

"Stay back," he whimpered. "Do you hear me? Stay back."

He bolted from the cave.

He didn't stop until he reached the edge of the forest. He sank to the ground beneath an elm tree. Who had done this? Who had robbed him of his strength?

Emily.

Who else but another spirit would know that spirits could weaken him? He had angered her and she had struck back.

Rage tore through him. *You'll suffer, Emily. You'll suffer for setting them loose.*

He looked down at the gold lighter he still clutched in his hand. The metal was damaged and charred, but the initials were clear. Jimenez. The clumsy fool had even left a mark to point the way, but wait. Hadn't there been signs in the cave of someone else digging, searching? She had used Jimenez as a weapon to inflict this terrible blow. The coward would never have dared do this unless driven.

No matter who the messenger, it was Emily who had done this to him.

The newspaper story was on the front page. It focused almost entirely on RU2, Kate, and the John Doe whose fingerprints had matched those of Noah Smith. No mention of Ogden or any conspiracy.

"Not even an 'alleged' reference to Ishmaru," Kate said.

Seth shrugged. "She's careful but I'll bet she keeps digging. And she makes us sound fairly sane and respectable. That's more than the tabloids will do. Two days from now every rag in the supermarket will have a story about that bogus warrant issued against you and my very disreputable background."

Kate's gaze was still on the newspaper. "What

do you think? Is it enough?"

Seth shook his head. "We need to stir things up more. Let me think." He moved over to the window and looked down at the traffic below. "It's still a risk for you to go out in public. Ogden's goons probably won't touch you since you've gone public, but that doesn't mean he won't stir up those demonstrators."

"I've faced that kind of threat before. I want it over. What do I have to do?"

"Call Meryl Kimbro and tell her we're going to pay a visit to Senator Longworth this afternoon. I'll call the television stations."

"He won't see us."

"When you come surrounded by newspaper reporters and television crews, he'll see you. Politicians don't like to appear evasive in public."

"You know as well as I do that I won't be able to persuade him to bow out on that bill."

"But if you come off sympathetic enough, it may deflate his balloon."

"And then?"

"Then we pay a visit to Senator Ralph Migellin."

"Another politician?"

"But Ralph Migellin is that rare breed — an honest and respected politician. He's also an idealist. If we can pit him against Longworth, it will stall the bill."

She shook her head. "How do you know so much about the Washington scene?"

"You'd be surprised how useful knowing the

players is in my line of work." He turned to face her. "And Ralph Migellin was never on any payola list I ever saw." He moved toward the door. "Change clothes. Try to look professional, intelligent, and sexy as hell."

"You don't ask much."

"No, I don't. You can do it with your hands tied behind your back." He grinned at her over his shoulder. "But leave off the bondage. S and M isn't that palatable to Middle America."

Kate was taken aback when she opened her bedroom door an hour later. Seth was wearing a well-cut brown suit and a silk tie that appeared both discreet and expensive. She had never seen him in anything but jeans or khakis, but he carried the formal clothes with surprising elegance.

"Stop staring." He grimaced. "I do have my civilized moments."

"You look very . . . nice."

"I look like a lawyer. But you can be damn sure the suit isn't Armani."

His vehement tone puzzled her. "Armani?"

"Never mind." His gaze ran over her. "You look good in black, but the suit's a little too stern. You need to soften it."

"I'm not trying to win a fashion award," she said dryly.

"Wear the jacket open so the silk blouse shows." He was unbuttoning the jacket as he spoke. He fluffed her hair. "There. Perfect." He saw her face begin to cloud and added, "Relax. If I'm willing to sacrifice myself on the media altar, you shouldn't mind. Even Marcia Clark cut her hair and bought a new wardrobe for the Simpson trial." He led the way out of the suite.

"I have no intention of doing either." But she left the jacket open anyway. "Why are you suddenly so concerned about appearances?"

"Because the media is about to shred us and have us for breakfast. But a picture can sometimes speak more than a story."

"Our work on RU2 stands alone. It shouldn't need anyone to —" She stopped. Nothing stood alone in this hype-driven world. Everything was questioned. "Okay, I'll smile for the camera."

"You don't have to smile. After what's happened to you, no one expects you to be anything but serious. Just show them you're a human being as well as a scientist. This is your show. I'm just here for backup." He took her arm. "And stand close to Longworth. He's a big man and next to him you'll look fragile as hell. It won't hurt to have him seen as a bully out to get the courageous little woman."

"I've been fighting that 'little woman' image all my life."

"Do what you like, but we need all the weapons we can get."

Sure, give her a choice and then tell her she's going to deep-six the battle if she makes the wrong one. "Are you sure you weren't in politics yourself?"

"Closest I ever came was bodyguard to a Colombian judge, and that didn't last long."

"Did he get killed too?"

"No, he decided to take the bribe the cartel offered him, and I became unnecessary." He punched the elevator button. "But I kept him alive for eight months before he caved in. Not bad."

William Longworth was distinctly uncomfortable, Kate noted. He had a smile pasted on his face, but he was very pale and the fingers he was tapping on the desk were trembling slightly.

Strange. From what she had heard about the senator, he was seldom visibly shaken. The reporters surrounding them shouldn't have upset him; he loved the media.

But this interview had not gone his way, Kate thought with fierce satisfaction. She had been able to give facts, and he had been able to supply only rhetoric.

"If RU2 is the miracle Dr. Denby claims, will you reconsider your support of the bill controlling genetic research?" Meryl asked the senator.

"Certainly not. Genetic research is dangerous. It should be kept in firm, guiding hands. My constituents would never forgive me if I allowed it to go unchecked. If this RU2 is a miracle drug, which I doubt, then it should be controlled and tested until there is no doubt of its safety."

"The FDA has the most painstaking testing in

the world," Kate said. "Why not leave it in their hands?"

"Naturally, we'll rely on their expertise. But the decision should lie with the American people."

"You mean you," Kate said. "Congress is notorious for gridlock. Are you going to let thousands of people die while you haggle in committees?"

Longworth cast a sad look at the TV cameraman. "You see? Reckless impatience. The American people deserve more." He smiled at Kate. "I'm sure you mean well, young lady, but you're backing the wrong horse. The public regards fooling around with genetics as dangerous and against the will of God." He stood up and leisurely walked to the window. "See for yourself."

Kate had no chance. Reporters rushed to the window, knocking her aside. Seth reached out to steady her and then pushed through the mob gathered around the window.

A huge crowd milled in the street below. Kate caught glimpses of the signs they were carrying.

Stop Them

Save Our Babies

We Don't Want Their UnGodly RU2

Bless You, Senator Longworth

"How did he manage to get a crowd this size on such short notice?" Kate muttered. "We only called him this day."

"Rent-a-mob?" Seth took her elbow and guided her away from the window. "Come on. We might as well leave. Longworth's checkmated us. Those reporters are going to focus on the demonstrators."

"Then all this was for nothing?"

"No, they'll air some of the interview." He held open the door for her. "You were great. Kind of reminded me of a machete chopping through a balloon."

"I thought I had him." She glanced back at Longworth, who was chatting genially with Meryl Kimbro. As she watched, Longworth raised his gaze and met her own. He smiled triumphantly before returning his attention to the reporter. "I'd like to push the bastard through that window."

"Too many witnesses."

"It seems impossible that anyone could be swayed by that bag of wind. He's . . . he's . . . some kind of obscene joke."

"Easy. It's over. He won the ball game, but you had your innings. Now we go on to the next step." He opened the door. "Tony's waiting downstairs in Senator Migellin's limousine. We'll go out the back way. The mob may recognize you from Kimbro's story."

Tony was standing beside a long black limousine over a block away. He waved frantically when he saw Seth and Kate. "What the devil happened? This demonstration is really going to impress the senator. Why not just burn the American flag?"

"He's inside?"

Tony nodded.

Seth opened the car door and all three got into the car.

"You're Kate Denby?" Ralph Migellin smiled. "You've caused quite a stir." His gaze went to the crowd in the next block. "I didn't bring out that many people at my last rally."

"Seth Drakin." Seth shook his hand. "Thanks for coming."

"It was the only way to meet you unobtrusively. I'm not sure I want to be involved with this RU2. It could be very detrimental to my career." He shrugged. "But sometimes a man has no choice. I hope this isn't one of them."

"Tony has explained everything to you?" Seth asked.

Migellin nodded. His gaze returned to the crowd. "Would I face that kind of opposition?"

"Yes," Seth said.

"Well, at least you're honest." He turned to Kate. "And would your RU2 be worth it? Is it the miracle you claim?"

"Noah Smith thought it was worth it," Kate said. "He died for it."

"I'm asking what you think."

"Oh yes, it's a miracle. But I've put myself and my family at risk. If something happened to them, I don't know if I could say it was worth it. I'm not that selfless."

"But you're here."

"Because I was angry and tired of being pushed around. Not because I'm particularly noble."

"And will this RU2 save as many lives as you claim?"

"Probably more. Our estimates are based on

the major diseases. More research will probably provide a bigger picture."

"I see." Migellin stared at her for a moment before heaving a resigned sigh. "I'm afraid I believe you. Too bad. I was looking forward to a peaceful campaign year." He took out a notebook from his pocket, scrawled something, and handed it to Kate. "However, I'm not completely convinced we even have a shot. I'd like you both to meet me at my country place tomorrow afternoon. I have some people I'll want you to meet."

"Who?" Seth asked.

"Frank Cooper for one. He's head of the Gray Panthers. The retired citizens' lobby is a very powerful influence here in Washington." He smiled. "And they're very concerned about their health."

Kate felt a rush of relief. He was going to help them. "You'll try to block Longworth's bill?"

"I didn't say that. I'll need support and you'll have to get it for me. Be there tomorrow. I'll make a decision then."

"We can't," Seth said. "Arrange it for day after tomorrow."

Kate's gaze flew to him. "Why not?"

"Noah Smith is being buried tomorrow afternoon."

Migellin nodded. "I understand. Where is he being buried? I'd like to attend."

"Mount Pleasant Cemetery outside the city. I want to avoid the media."

"Not much chance. There are leaks everywhere

in this town. But I'll be there."

"Why?" Kate asked. "You never met Noah."

"He was a brave man. I would have liked to have known him. Now all I can do is pay my respects." He added, "Then my country place day after tomorrow at three. I'm afraid I have to get back to my office now. May I drop you at your hotel?"

"That would be kind," Kate said. "The Summit." She watched him as he told his chauffeur their address. He *was* kind. As different from Longworth as day and night. He gave her a warm feeling of security and comfort. It was good to know that not all politicians were like that pompous bastard.

Her gaze shifted to Seth. He never failed to surprise her. Today he had been smooth and self-effacing, letting her have the spotlight. Yet she had always been aware of him in the background, supporting, guarding.

He turned his head and met her gaze. "Okay?"

She nodded. "It's been a crazy day, hasn't it?"

He smiled. "I've seen worse."

Tony left immediately after Migellin dropped them off. Up in the suite, Seth ordered dinner.

"The food won't be here for another forty minutes," he told Kate. "Go take a shower and get comfortable. You look beat."

She felt beat. She kicked off her heels and discarded her jacket. "Why didn't you tell me about Noah's funeral?"

"I just arranged it this morning. I thought you needed to concentrate on Longworth."

"I didn't even know you were thinking about —"

"It bothered you that Noah didn't have proper burial. I could see it when Tony was telling us about it."

"Didn't it bother you?"

He shook his head. "And I don't think it would have bothered Noah. Dead is dead, and all the formalities don't mean crap. But it mattered to you."

"Yes, it mattered to me." She tried to steady her voice. "Thank you."

"No problem." He moved toward his bedroom. "Take your time. I'll be back for the waiter. I just have to phone Rimilon and make sure everything's okay."

She nodded and headed for the bathroom.

Moments later she was standing beneath the warm spray of the shower. Noah was going to be put to rest. They were going to be able to say good-bye to him with the dignity he deserved. It was one of only two good things to come out of this nightmare of a day.

The pounding water was soothing and she gradually began to relax. She was used to working in a laboratory, not facing the media and defending her work. And Longworth and his blasted mob of —

Stop thinking about it. It was over. As Seth had said, they had to go on with the next steps. Easier for Seth than for her. He seemed as pliable as a Gumby toy, perfectly at ease in any situation. God, they were so different.

She had put on jeans and a sweatshirt and was blow-drying her hair when Seth knocked on the bathroom door. "Dinner."

"I'll be right out."

When she entered the sitting room, Seth was at the table, straightening napkins and taking off the serving domes.

Noah.

He looked up and saw her face. "What's wrong?"

"Nothing." She came toward him. "You just reminded me of Noah. He was always fussing with the table settings. He was never happy with the way I did it."

"Forget it," he said. "I'm nothing like Noah. I'm not a gourmet cook and the only food I prepare is K rations in the field. Room service is just fine with me."

His tone was so sharp it startled her. She sat down at the table and picked up her fork. "Sorry."

"What are you sorry about? That he's dead? You can't bring him back by trying to see him in every man you meet."

Anger flared. "Don't worry, I wouldn't make that mistake with you. Noah was kind to me."

"That's why you're so happy and free from worry. That's why your son is living in a bomb shelter."

She sat back and looked him in the eye.

"What's eating you? Noah was supposed to be your friend."

"He *was* my friend but he's dead, dammit. I don't have to pretend that he was perfect. I won't —" He broke off and Kate could see a myriad of expressions struggling across his face. "Oh, what the hell." He sat down across from her and viciously speared a piece of tomato in his salad.

"I think you're being unfair. Noah did what he thought was right. He may have involved you in this against your will, but did it ever occur to you that by willing you RU2, he probably made you a billionaire?"

He didn't answer.

"And he died for something he —"

"All right, he's perfect," Seth said. "Drop it, okay?"

"No, it's not okay." She shrugged. "But I'll drop it. I've no desire to argue with a sulky little boy."

"Little boy?" His gaze lifted to her face. "That's not what this is about, Kate."

She went still when she saw his expression. She couldn't look away.

"I'm not at all like Noah," he said softly. "You're vulnerable, you're lonely, and we're going to bury my best friend tomorrow. It doesn't matter. If I thought I could nudge you into bed tonight, I'd do it."

She could only stare at him. She was suddenly acutely aware of his physical *presence*, the power of his shoulders beneath the chambray shirt, the seductive curve of his wide, mobile mouth, the intensity of the blue of his eyes. She moistened her lips. "Enjoy the moment?"

"You bet." He waited.

She shook her head.

An undefinable emotion flickered across his face. "I didn't think so."

"It's not — We're not — It would be a mistake."

"You don't have to look so damn appalled. It isn't as if you'd mind going to bed with me. I've always known we had that going for us. I didn't ask for a lifetime commitment."

He had known. She shouldn't be shocked. She had already learned he was a man of surprises. "I guess I'm not used to enjoying the moment. I've always had to think and plan." She paused. "Besides, things are too confused. I'm sure you'd regret it if you —"

"The hell I would." He smiled recklessly. "Don't tell me what I'd regret. I wouldn't regret one minute. I learned a long time ago that the only things I regret are the things I didn't do, and I've wanted to go to bed with you since the moment I saw you."

Her eyes widened. "You never said — I never realized."

"Because I thought you and Noah were an item. For God's sake, you were like Barbie and Ken playing in that laboratory. He was my friend. I do have a few scruples. Though if I'd realized he was being so stupid, I probably would have forgotten them."

"He was being sensible."

"Stupid," Seth repeated. He pushed his plate aside and stood up. "I'm going to my room. I think I've done my best to spoil both our appetites."

"We can't let this make a difference. We have too much to do to —"

"Bullshit." His voice was thick with tension. "It's going to make a difference. I wouldn't want it any other way. I want you to know that all you have to do is reach out and I'll be there." He moved toward his room. "Be ready at three tomorrow afternoon."

"You're making this impossible."

"Not impossible. Hard. There's nothing wrong with hard. Nothing at all." The door slammed behind him.

She pushed her plate aside. He was right. She was too upset to eat. She was shaken and angry and disturbed. It was just like Seth to throw a monkey wrench into the works when the situation was difficult enough. Self-indulgent bastard. He was as explosive as a keg of dynamite, as sensual as the goat god Pan, and as selfish as —

Sensual.

She didn't want to think about how aware she had felt that moment after he had told her he wanted her. She didn't want to think about Seth in that way. She didn't need a one-night stand. She needed steadiness and commitment and mutual interests. She would be miserable in a relationship with a wild man like Seth.

I didn't ask for a lifetime commitment.

But that's what she needed. Not to go up in flames that would burn out quickly. She had a career and a son. She would be totally irresponsible to take what —

What she wanted? Did she want Seth? Look at it honestly.

She remembered that day in the forest, the moment that had just passed.

Oh yes, she wanted to go to bed with him.

But that didn't mean she would do it. Adults made choices; unlike Seth, they didn't grab what they wanted without thinking of the consequences.

Maybe tangents are the way to go.

Why had Phyliss's words about Noah's methods popped into her head? Probably because Seth was a tangent in himself. An erotic, powerful departure from everything safe and familiar.

And Kate did not go off on tangents.

"Ready? Tony has the car downstairs," Seth said as soon as she opened the door the next day.

She nodded. "I'm ready."

"Good." He studied her face. "You're trying not to look me in the eye. Don't worry. This is Noah's day. I'm not going to unsettle you."

"You didn't unsettle me," she lied even as a rush of relief poured through her. "But I'm glad you — You're right, this is Noah's day."

There were only a handful of people at the

grave site. Tony, Seth, Senator Migellin, and someone she assumed was an aide. The service, conducted by a minister, was brief.

She could feel tears sting her eyes as she watched the coffin being lowered into the ground.

Someone took her hand and she looked up to see Seth. He was staring at the coffin too, and his eyes were glittering with moisture. "Good-bye, Noah," he whispered. "Nice knowing you."

She had known Noah for only a matter of weeks. He'd been Seth's friend for years. Her hand tightened around his.

"I have to leave." She turned to find Senator Migellin beside her. He squeezed her shoulder gently. "I'm sorry about this. I'm afraid the leak must have come from my office. They even seem to know when I go to the bathroom."

She stared at him in bewilderment. She heard a muttered curse from Seth and followed his gaze to the gates of the cemetery a few hundred yards away.

A crowd was gathered outside the gates.

Demonstrators? My God, couldn't they leave them alone even in this moment?

No, not demonstrators but reporters, cameramen. A TV van was parked at the curb.

"You'd better come back to the city in my car," Migellin said as he started for the gates. "My aides are holding them back. They should be able to manage to get us to the limousine. They're experts at cleaving through crowds." He glanced at Seth. "Unless you want to stop and give a statement? It's your chance away from Long-worth."

He took Kate's arm. "Not today."

No, not today. This was Noah's day. She lowered her head and quickly followed the senator.

It was like being overwhelmed by wasps as soon as they went through the gates.

The crowd swarmed around them. Microphones were thrust in front of her face. She was torn away from Seth.

"Kate!" Seth called from somewhere behind her.

She could no longer see him.

She couldn't see the senator ahead.

She fought to get through, but she was whirled away to the side and thrown hard against one of the reporters.

"Sorry." She straightened. "Please let me through to —"

Ishmaru.

He smiled. "Hello, Kate."

Christ, no.

She flinched back into the crowd of reporters.

She couldn't see him anymore.

But he could be beside her in the crowd.

Or in back of her.

Or waiting until she broke through the crowd.

A hand fell on her shoulder.

She screamed and struck out with her fist.

"For God's sake, Kate."

It was Seth.

"Get me out of here. Get me away . . ."

His arm was around her and he was shoving through the crowd.

A camera fell to the ground.

A reporter cursed.

Where was he?

The senator's car was up ahead. Safety.

But Noah had thought he was safe that last day.

Noah was dead.

She was in the car.

"Now, what the hell made you panic?" Seth asked as he got in beside her and slammed the door shut. The limousine pulled away from the curb and sped down the street.

"Ish . . . Ishmaru." She could barely get the word out. "Ishmaru."

Senator Migellin frowned. "In the crowd?"

She nodded jerkily.

"Pull over," Seth said.

"No." Her hand frantically tightened on his arm. Not Seth. He would die just like Noah. "He'll be gone now. I only saw him for a minute."

"Are you sure you weren't imagining things?" Tony asked. "He must have been on your mind today."

"I wasn't imagining anything," she said fiercely. "I was practically in his arms. He smiled at me and spoke."

"Okay. Okay," Tony said soothingly. "It only seemed bizarre he'd risk coming to Noah's funeral."

"The son of a bitch is bizarre," Seth said. "He's crazy."

"I'll have the chauffeur radio the police to go back and check it out," the senator said, then leaned forward and tapped on the glass.

"Too late," Tony murmured.

"Why didn't you tell me back there?" Seth asked. "Why the hell didn't you tell me when I could have —"

"Shut up," she said. "I was scared and I didn't think of anything but getting away from him. I'm not a macho gun-running idiot who —" She had to break off to steady her voice. "And don't yell at me again."

"I didn't yell." But Seth's voice was taut with tension, and the lines around his mouth even tighter. He turned away from her and stared out the window. "You made a mistake. I could have had him."

"All right, I made a mistake." Kate threw her purse and jacket on the couch. "I should have screamed or told you right away."

"You're damn right," Seth said coldly.

"I was terrified. I didn't think I would be, but he caught me off guard and I panicked. I promise it won't happen again."

Seth didn't answer. He went in his room and shut the door.

He had a right to be angry. They'd had a chance to get Ishmaru and she'd blown it. God, she had acted like a sniveling coward.

Seth came back in the room carrying a pillow and blanket. He tossed them on the couch in the sitting room.

"What are you doing?" she asked.

"I'm sleeping here."

"You don't have to do that. I told you, he caught me off guard. I'm not afraid anymore."

He ignored her. "Call room service and order dinner. I'll phone Rimilon and do the daily check."

He was silent all through dinner. She was glad to escape to her bedroom when it was over. She was not accustomed to an angry, remote Seth. She had not realized how she had leaned on his calm, easy, sometimes humorous support. She took a shower, put on her sleep T-shirt, and got her book. She would go to bed and block him from her mind.

She was still reading after midnight when the phone beside her bed rang.

"It was good to see you today, Emily."

Ishmaru.

Her heart stopped and then began beating double time. "Why do you always call me Emily? My name is Kate."

"Are you still trying to deceive me? We both know who you are. Where's the little boy?"

Her hand tightened on the phone. "Safe."

"No one is safe. We're all on the edge. When you ran away from me today, I was very disappointed. It wasn't like you. I was afraid Emily had left you."

334

Who the *hell* was Emily? "I was startled. Why don't you come here now?"

He laughed. "You want to trap me. No, I'll pick my time. I couldn't believe it when I saw the article in the paper. I was afraid I'd have to search for you for a long time, but there you were. You do know I could have killed you today? But it would have been too fast." His tone sharpened. "I'm very angry with you, Emily. You sent your messenger to take away my guardians."

"I didn't send anyone."

"You sent Seth Drakin to destroy me. Jimenez told me he did it, but I know it was really you. I don't sleep now. But that's all right, it gives me time to think of ways to hurt you. I was going to let you have a warrior's death. I still might, but I want you to suffer first. You shouldn't have taken them away."

"I don't know what you're talking about. Are you afraid to come to me?"

"No, but I want you to come to me."

"Where are you?"

"Not now, soon. Soon you'll come to me. But not until I hurt you as you hurt me."

He hung up the phone.

"Seth!" She was out of bed and running to the sitting room.

"I heard it all." He was replacing the receiver on the extension by the couch. "I picked up the phone at the same time you did."

"Can we trace it?"

He shook his head.

"Then what can we do?"

"Wait for him. You heard him, he wants you to come to him."

"He knew where I was."

"We haven't been trying to hide. We knew that wasn't possible."

"I want you to call Rimilon. I want to know Joshua is all right."

"He asked where Joshua was."

"I don't care. How do we know he doesn't know? He seems to know everything else. Call him."

He sat up and reached for his digital phone. He punched in the number. "I know it's late, dammit. Is everything secure?"

He hung up the phone. "Rimilon's bunking near the entrance and there's been no one near the site."

"I want to talk to Joshua."

He looked at her. "Are you sure?"

"Yes. No." She wanted Joshua to stay safe behind that steel door. She wanted to hear his voice. "No, I guess not."

"Good."

"He's crazy," she whispered. "He kept muttering something about his guardians. I took away his guardians. Dammit, I don't even know what he's talking about."

"I know you don't."

Her gaze flew to his face. Her eyes widened. "But you do, don't you?"

He nodded. "I know."

"He called you the messenger."

"I've been called worse."

"Dammit, what are you keeping from me?"

"I hoped you wouldn't have to know. It's not pretty." His lips tightened. "How the hell could I guess he'd blame you?"

"What did you do?"

"I got his old buddy Jimenez to take me to a cave that he called his medicine tent. He'd go there to refresh his powers or when the dreams became too bad. He'd sit in the middle of the guardian circle and burn incense."

"Guardian?"

He paused and then said curtly, "Scalps. Poles with scalps of his victims affixed to the top."

Her stomach lurched. "God."

"Before I came to the cabin, I went there and burned everything except for evidence I sent to the district attorney's office. I don't know why the bastard connected you to it."

He seemed to blame her for everything, she thought dully. "Why does he call them his guardians?"

"I looked it up in the book I found in his cave. The Plains Indians believed in ghosts. If you kept the scalps of victims near you, they were rendered earthbound and powerless. He probably convinced himself that the circle was protecting him from at least some of his victims."

"I want to see the book."

"You probably don't." He went into his bedroom. He came back with the book and handed it to her. "He turned down pages and underlined. You'll probably want to skip the passages on methods of scalping."

She gingerly ran a hand over the faded cover. Ishmaru had touched this. Ishmaru had pored over this thing. She opened the book and her eye was caught by a yellow highlighted word.

Coup.

There were pages and pages about methods and rites for taking coup on the enemy.

I will have three when you are all dead.

She slammed the book shut. "You're right, I don't want to read this. Not now."

He held out his hand for the book.

"No, I want to keep it. I have to read it. Just not right now."

"Well, say something," he said roughly. "Swear at me."

"Why? You thought you were doing the right thing. You didn't know it would boomerang. You were right to send those . . . things to the district attorney."

"Bullshit. It's probably the only law-abiding thing I've done in fifteen years." His lips twisted sardonically. "And it hurt you. It hurt both of us. Serves me right."

"Did Noah know what you'd done?"

"No, he didn't want to know anything about Ishmaru after he got you to the cabin. He wanted to pretend Ishmaru didn't exist." He shrugged. "There wasn't anything to be done, so I kept it to myself."

"You should have told me."

"Ishmaru had already spooked you. Telling you about the scalps would have scared you to death."

The thought chilled her to the bone. "I have to know what I'm facing." She paused. Where should she start? "I want to know who Emily is."

"I'll make some calls and try to find out." He hesitated. "I don't suppose you'll forget all this and let me handle it?"

"You can't handle it. I'm the one he wants to hurt. What could you do?"

"What I wanted to do since the beginning. Find him. Kill him."

"Before he finds me . . . or Joshua?"

"Goddammit." He suddenly exploded. "I won't let it happen. Can't you trust me?"

"I can't trust anyone."

His eyes blazed down at her. "Fine. Great." He lay down and closed his eyes. "Then go back to bed."

Just like that. Go to bed. Forget the monster. Wait for him to call again. "Don't give me orders." Her voice was shaking with rage and terror as she turned on her heel. "Don't ever give me — I'll do what I please. I know you think I'm gutless but I won't let —"

His hand was on her shoulder and he spun her around to face him. "Damn you." He pulled her into his arms. "Shut up, okay?"

"I won't shut up."

"Then will you stop shaking?" He buried his

face in her hair. "Will you please just stop shaking?"

"Just turn it off and on? I'm not like you. You could probably sleep after you'd murdered the Pope. I'm human."

"Oh, yes."

"And you don't have to sleep in here. I can take care of myself."

"I'm staying."

"I don't want you here."

"Tough."

"Let me go."

"In a minute." He pushed her away and looked down at her. "I don't think you're gutless. I think you've got too much nerve for your own good. You've just blown up Ishmaru into your own private nemesis. Who could blame you?"

"Then why were you so damn mad at me?"

He cradled her face in his hands. "You almost got killed. I was supposed to keep you safe and I almost let that bastard kill you. And now everything I've done is blowing up in my face."

She stiffened. "You were mad at yourself and you took it out on me? That's just like a —"

"Hush." He kissed her. Soft, gentle, not like Seth at all. "Hush." He rocked her back and forth. "I'll do anything you say, just be quiet and let me enjoy this."

Enjoy the moment.

She was enjoying the moment. Heat was moving over her and she wasn't shaking any longer. Or if she was, it wasn't from fear. She had read somewhere that the desire for sex was most intense after extreme terror. Intense? Oh yes, this was intense all right. She could smell the scent of Seth's aftershave and feel the muscular hardness of him.

"I'm nudging," he whispered. "Can you tell?"

She could tell.

He pushed her away. "But not very hard. I'm feeling too guilty. You'll have to nudge back."

She could back away from him. She could go to her room and be sensible . . . and cold and lonely and scared.

Or she could stay here and enjoy the moment.

She took a step closer and her arms slid around him. "I'm nudging."

She was the same, Ishmaru thought with relief. At the cemetery he had feared she'd changed, but it had only been a momentary slip. She had challenged him. She wanted the battle as much as he did.

But it could not take place here where she was surrounded by people who could help her. She didn't embrace the concept of coup, so the advantage would be on her side. She didn't have to get close. No, he had to draw her to him at the appointed place. But first he had to hurt her. He had to cause her the anguish he faced every night.

The boy? He would certainly be the most logical choice.

He picked up the phone and called Blount.

"Good God, do you have to get me up in the middle of the night?"

"Yes. You said you were working on another lead to get Kate Denby. Have you got it?"

"Ogden wouldn't want me to give you any more information."

"Screw Ogden."

Blount laughed. "My sentiments exactly. He's been more obnoxious than usual since the woman went public with RU2."

"That's your problem. I killed Smith."

"Which did us little good since he'd already designated an heir. We've had to pump up the pressure on the Washington sector, and that asshole Longworth is demanding more money."

Why did Blount think he was interested? "Do you have a way for me to get Kate Denby or not?"

There was silence at the other end of the line. "Yes, but you'll have to follow up on it. It's only a thread."

A thread strong enough could be used to garrote the most powerful warrior. "Give it to me."

"Not quite yet. I'll have to set it up." Blount paused. "And I'll want something from you in exchange."

Thirteen

Seth wasn't in bed when Kate stirred the next morning.

"Coffee." He came into the room, balancing two cups and a carafe. He was barefoot and without a shirt. His hair was rumpled, a stubble darkened his cheeks. He looked sexy as hell when he should have looked like a slob, Kate thought. Women were never that lucky. He sat down on the side of the bed. "I've ordered breakfast but told them to wait for an hour. I thought you'd need time to pull yourself together."

"Thank you." She needed the time. She felt suddenly shy and uneasy. Why did daylight make such a difference? This was the same man to whom she had made love three times last night. Heat tingled through her at the memory. God, she had acted like a nymphomaniac. She hadn't been able to get enough of him. Even now, looking at him, she felt —

She pulled the sheet up higher and took the cup from him. "How long have you been up?"

"Since six."

She glanced at the clock. It was almost ten. "What have you been doing?"

"Thinking." He pulled the sheet down and kissed her breast. "Waiting."

Her heart was beating hard, fast. "What were

343

you thinking about?"

"That you'd probably wake up regretting this." He sucked delicately on her nipple. "And wondering how I could get you to let me stay in your bed."

She tried to keep her voice even. "It could interfere."

"You liked it."

"Of course I liked it. You're very . . . talented."

"So are you. God, are you talented. I had a hunch you were a very sexy lady, but you still surprised me."

"It had been a long time for me."

"Let's see how you are when it's only been a few hours." He took the cup from her and set it on the nightstand. "Purely as an experiment, you understand."

"I haven't finished my coffee."

"It's getting in the way."

"We should talk . . ."

"We can talk while we're occupied." He unzipped his jeans and climbed into bed. "You're more pliable when I'm in you."

He was in her now, moving slowly, tantalizingly. He whispered, "The way I look at it, I'm an asset to you. I'll keep you relaxed."

Relaxed? Her nails dug into his back.

"Everything will be just as it was." He punctuated each word with a thrust. "No strings. We just go to bed together and do this. What's wrong with that?"

She couldn't answer. She couldn't think. She

could feel the rough denim of his jeans rubbing her thighs and Seth inside her. She bit her lip as the rhythm escalated.

"Come on," he whispered. "If I sleep with you, I'll be better able to protect you."

She laughed desperately. "That's pretty lame."

"Well, I just thought I'd throw that in for good measure."

"You have a very good measure as it is." She rolled over on top and smiled down at him. "And I'm enjoying every inch of it."

"The coffee's probably cold," Kate said as she lazily reached over him to get her cup on the nightstand.

"I hoped it would be. That's why I brought the carafe." He sat up and scooted off the bed. "I'll pour you a fresh cup."

"You're being very obliging."

He smiled. "I want to keep on your good side." He topped off her coffee and set down the carafe. "How am I doing?"

Too damn well, she thought. At the moment she wasn't sure if he was Peter Pan or Casanova. "You're very good indeed."

His smile faded. "I didn't set out to seduce you last night."

"It just happened?"

He sat down on the bed again. "I would have backed down if you'd said you didn't want it." He grimaced. "You mad at me?"

She felt too languid and contented to be angry

at anyone. She wondered if his efforts in the past hour had been aimed at that goal. Possibly. It appeared Peter Pan had a touch of Machiavelli. "No, I'm not angry." She took a sip of coffee, then met his gaze. "And you didn't seduce me. I wouldn't let anyone seduce me. That implies loss of choice and it was definitely my choice. You offered me something I wanted, and I took it."

He heaved a mock sigh. "Oh dear, I feel so used."

She smothered a smile. The rascal was impossible. She finished her coffee and gave him the cup. "I need to shower. How much time before we have to leave to meet with Migellin?"

"Two hours. But breakfast should be here any minute." He watched her get out of bed and head toward the bathroom. "Lord, you have a fantastic bottom."

"Thank you." Any uneasiness was gone, she realized. She couldn't remember ever feeling this comfortable with a man before. It was as if they'd been lovers for years. "I'll be out in a minute."

"Kate."

She looked back at him. He was leaning on one elbow and smiling at her. A lock of dark hair had fallen over his forehead, and he somehow managed to look mischievous and sexy at the same time. "How about it?" he asked coaxingly. "Wanna play house with me for a little while?"

"Maybe." She returned his smile. She couldn't help it. "You definitely have entertainment value."

He gave a whoop and slapped the bed. "I've got you."

She shook her head in exasperation and closed the bathroom door. What had she gotten herself into? She had never intended this to happen.

But why not take the only pleasant thing that could be garnered from this hellish situation? Seth himself had said that they would be lovers for just a little while. Last night she had been frightened, haunted by that monster, and he had made it go away. Today she felt stronger, almost normal again, able to cope.

And Seth had given her that gift.

She would keep it and hold on tight until this nightmare was over.

"What do you think?" Senator Migellin asked Kate in an undertone. "Did I do good?"

"Great." Kate's gaze was on the gazebo across the lawn, where Seth was surrounded by the five people the senator had invited. Seth seemed to be holding forth. She wondered what he was talking about. Whatever it was, it must be amusing. "We couldn't ask for anything more. You've gathered almost every health special interest group in Washington. Your Gray Panther, Frank Cooper; Celia Delabo, president of the Cancer Society; Justin Zwatnos of Gay Men's Health Crisis; Pete Randall from the Foundation for Multiple Sclerosis. You've even got Bill Mandel of the FDA. I'm impressed."

"They were impressed by you." The senator

poured her a glass of iced tea. "You were very convincing."

"I just told them the truth."

"But with passion. There's no substitute for passion."

"But is it enough? Will they support us?"

"I hope so."

"If they don't, will you still try to block Longworth?"

"It could be political suicide."

"Will you?"

He smiled. "That passion can be quite ruthless, can't it?"

"I don't want you to be hurt."

"But you'd rather I be hurt than RU2 be put on hold."

"I guess I would." She shook her head. "It's very important, Senator."

"At least you're honest." He looked down at his drink. "There's not much time. Longworth is pushing this bill more strongly than I've ever seen him push anything. He has a lot of people in Congress who owe him favors. He's been around a long time. I've only been in office for eight years."

"But it means lives."

"Did you know that the Capitol switchboards have been flooded with calls about the bill for the past two days?"

"In our favor?"

He shook his head. "Longworth's."

"Dammit." Her hand clenched on the glass.

"Why won't they understand? We're trying to *help* them."

"People parrot what they hear and they're hearing plenty from Ogden and the other pharmaceutical giants. What you must understand is that between Longworth's arm-twisting and the calls from constituents, it's going to be a very tough fight for us."

"Us?" Her gaze flew to his face.

He shrugged. "How can I resist? I've always wanted to go up against that bag of wind."

"Thank God."

"Tomorrow I'll go to work trying to get the bill separated from the welfare package. At least then we'll have a shot. You'd better expect to attend a lot more of these meetings. I'll need all the help I can get." He leaned back in the lawn chair. "So I'd better rest now. I may not get another chance for a while. Do you like my place?"

Her gaze wandered over the English Tudor house, the flagstone terrace that led down to rolling green lawns, the large gazebo on the hill veiled with climbing roses. "It's lovely. So peaceful."

"That's what I wanted. Peace. I grew up in a tenement in New York and had to fight from the time I was a kid. No one appreciates peace like the man who's never had it." He smiled. "And then you come along and throw me into the melee again."

"Don't blame me. I think you would have backed us even if I hadn't tried to persuade you."

"Maybe." His gaze went to the gazebo. "That

young man is rather extraordinary. Do you know he talked me into arranging FBI protection for your public appearances while you're in Washington?"

"No, I didn't. But it doesn't surprise me."

"Before I came to see you, I made sure I had reports on both of you, and nothing in his hinted at this."

"What?"

"He's very charismatic."

"Oh, yes."

"He has those executives in the palm of his hand, and they're not easy." He added thoughtfully, "We had a little talk earlier and he came across as hard as nails, but then I saw this side of him. A combination like that is quite unique. He could be a very dangerous man."

"Not to us."

"I admit I had apprehensions regarding having Drakin in charge of RU2." He turned to Kate. "I suppose you did too?"

"Yes."

"But you're satisfied with his stability?"

Seth was about as stable as a monsoon. "I'm satisfied about his commitment to RU2."

He chuckled. "Nice dodge. I guess that's all we can ask for."

She nodded. "That's all that concerns us."

"What were you talking to them about in the gazebo?" she asked as they were driven home in the senator's limousine.

He shrugged. "This and that. I'd tell them a story about my deep, dark past and then throw in something about RU2 that they could identify with. It kept them off guard and interested." He paused. "I suppose I should confess that I wasn't only planning your seduction this morning while you were sleeping. I called Kendow and he did some checking. Emily Santos was one of Ishmaru's early victims. She's been dead for over twelve years. She was blond and small and she didn't die easy. She took a butcher knife to the bastard. He has a scar on his neck to prove it."

"How did Kendow find out? This Jimenez?"

"No, he'd already gathered the files when I was looking for Ishmaru." He paused. "Jimenez was found dead recently."

She didn't have to ask him how he died. Ishmaru again. "Then he thinks I'm some kind of reincarnation of this Emily Santos?"

"So it would seem."

She stored away the information because she didn't want to think of anything connected with Ishmaru right now. They'd had success today and she had no desire to dissipate her feeling of confidence. She changed the subject. "The senator said you were extraordinary."

"Damn straight. Did you doubt it?"

"No, I just wondered where you learned to handle people so well."

"Twelve foster homes. It took a little while for me to get it right. But the last time I got to stay four years."

"You were an orphan?"

"Not exactly. My father abandoned my mother and me when I was born, but my mother stuck around for another two years."

"She left you?"

"A state agency took me away from her after the welfare worker found out she'd left me alone for almost three days."

"That's terrible," she whispered.

"Yeah, maybe. Shit happens."

"It shouldn't happen to children."

"But it does."

Twelve foster homes. What must it have been like for a child to be bounced from place to place, to face rejection time and time again? No wonder he had trouble settling down.

He smiled. "Don't look so horrified. I was probably better off in the foster homes. I got enough to eat."

"And you learned to handle people."

"Sometimes you handle them. Sometimes you walk away. Sometimes you just get rid of them."

"Were you 'handling' me this morning?"

"Doing my damnedest." He took her hand and raised it to his lips. "But you're not easy. You'll only let me go so far and then you back away." He licked her palm. "I'm having to work at it."

"You don't *have* to do anything."

"True. My choice." He laced his fingers with hers. "But I've never minded working for what I want. It makes it more fun."

"Tell me, is 'handling' the same as manipulating?"

His smile disappeared. "No way. Not in this case. Even if you let me, I wouldn't manipulate you. Haven't I been honest?"

He had been honest. He had seduced, coaxed, persuaded, while being perfectly honest about what he was doing. It was difficult to resent anything he did when he was so open about it. "Yes, you've been honest."

"Then you have nothing to worry about. You're smart enough to see right through me if you put your mind to it."

Instead of her hormones, she thought ruefully. She found she was having difficulty separating the physical from the mental. "The senator was right, you're a dangerous man."

"Yep, but you like that about me too. Same as those people back at the gazebo. It excites you to get close to the dark." He grinned mischievously. "Want to get *really* close?"

She looked at him warily.

"Ever done it in the backseat of a limousine?"

Her eyes widened in shock. "No, and I don't intend to do it now."

He sighed. "I didn't think you were ready for that yet. Oh well, maybe the senator will lend us his car later. We'll be working pretty closely with him."

It was strange how quickly you could become accustomed to lying naked in a man's arms, Kate

353

thought lazily as she listened to the steady beat of Seth's heart beneath her ear. Sometimes it was exquisitely arousing; at other times, like the present, it was just comforting and nice.

"Move," Seth whispered. "I need to get a drink of water. Sex is thirsty work."

She reluctantly rolled over and watched him go to the bathroom. A minute later she heard the toilet flush and he came out with a glass in his hand. "You always drink water afterwards. Weird."

"Well, I used to smoke, but when I quit I had to have a substitute. It's an oral thing."

"When did you quit?"

"Five years ago." He finished the water and set the glass on the nightstand. "In my line of work there are too many ways to get killed as it is without committing suicide."

She cuddled close to him as he got back into bed.

"Did I tell you how much I like you curling up against me like that?" He pulled the blankets over both of them. "Kinda like a puppy with its favorite bone."

"Was that a pun?" She gently nipped his shoulder. "Well, I've got to admit you are my favorite —"

Puppy. The word was triggering a memory. "How's your puppy?"

"Fine. I called the quarantine center and checked on him last week. They said he's put on weight. He was half starved when I picked him up in that village."

"What village?"

He was silent so long she thought he wasn't going to answer. "Just a village. I don't know if it even had a name."

"What were you doing there?"

"I'd had a report from one of my men, and I went to check it out."

"And you saw the puppy and liked him?"

"Yeah, he was a survivor. I like survivors."

"Survivor?"

He kissed her lightly on the nose. "Hey, you don't want to hear this."

"Don't I?" She suddenly knew she did want to hear it if it would let her know Seth better. "Why was the puppy a survivor?"

He shrugged. "Everyone else in the village had been butchered." He glanced at her. "See, I told you that you wouldn't want to hear."

"Who did it?"

"José Namirez. He wanted to control his little corner of the world and hired me to help him do it. It wasn't a complicated situation. The only real impediment was a local drug lord, Pedro Ardalen. He'd set himself up as a sort of feudal baron with an army to match. It took us three months to clean them out. The villagers were all too frightened to refuse Ardalen when he marched in and demanded sanctuary."

"And then?"

"Namirez wasn't content with winning. He wanted to make examples. I'd told him when he hired me there were to be no reprisals."

"And he did it anyway."

"He did it anyway." He kissed her cheek and whispered, "So I shot him."

She went rigid. "Just like that."

"Exactly like that." He raised his head to look down at her. She could see the cool glitter of his light eyes in the dimness of the room. "Happy? Do you feel as if you know the real me now? Isn't that what you wanted?"

"Yes."

"And you didn't like what you heard. Well, that's me, Kate. I won't lie to you. If you don't want to hear unpleasant truths, then don't ask me questions."

"Maybe I won't."

A troubled silence fell between them.

"Do you want me to leave you alone?" Seth asked.

"No."

"Good." He drew her closer. "I would have had to try to seduce you into letting me stay, and I'm plumb tuckered. Christ, you exhausted me."

"I didn't see any signs."

"I was afraid I'd lose my macho image. You're a tough critic."

Her uneasiness was slipping away. That other Seth was gone again and she could keep him at a distance. There were deep valleys and chasms between them, but as long as she didn't probe, didn't question, she could keep the Seth she wanted.

She didn't have to accept that other, darker Seth.

She received the package the next day. The porter brought it to the suite after breakfast.

It was the size of a shirt box and was wrapped in red-and-white-striped paper and pasted with gold stars. Happy wrappings. Bright, celebratory stars.

She opened the box.

A Little League baseball shirt.

And a note.

Right size, Emily?

She whimpered.

"It doesn't mean anything," Seth said. "He can't know where Joshua is. He knows you're vulnerable about anything connected with your son. He's trying to scare you."

"He's succeeding." She closed her eyes. *Please, God, keep Joshua safe. Don't let any of this touch him.* "Phone. Make sure."

Her fingers dug into the baseball shirt as Seth placed the call.

A few moments later he nodded as he hung up. "Bluff. Phyliss and Joshua are both safe."

Her fingers relaxed. Safe.

But for how long?

She was vaguely aware that Seth was on the phone again. "The package appeared on the concierge's desk addressed to you. No way to trace it."

She hadn't thought there would be.

"There's always Amsterdam," Seth said quietly.

Hope flared and then died. "It wouldn't stop him. He'd follow us. And as long as I make myself an open target, he may focus on me and not Joshua." She hurled the box into the wastebasket.

God, she hoped she was telling the truth.

Another box came the next day. It held a baseball cap.

This time the note said, *I'm looking for him, Emily.*

Two days later the package was long and cylindrical.

A baseball bat with *Joshua* burned into the wood.

I'm getting closer.

"I'm going to tell the desk to hold all packages," Seth said. "I'll pick them up at the desk myself."

"No." She carefully laid the bat on the table beside the door. Her hands were shaking only a little, she noticed. Strange. She felt as if she were falling apart.

"What do you mean?" Seth said harshly. "Look at you. This is killing you. You've been balanced on a tightrope since that first package."

"He'll know when I stop opening them."

"He's not a mind reader."

"He'll know." She had the feeling he knew every breath she took. "He's enjoying what they do to me."

"I'm not enjoying it."

"If the threat keeps him satisfied, maybe he won't act." She moved heavily toward the bedroom. Don't think about it. Block it out. She could get through this. "I have to finish getting dressed. Migellin's arranged some sort of luncheon for me."

"It can't go on, Kate. You can't go on."

"Yes, I can. I can do anything I have to do to keep my son safe."

"We've got the statement from Lila Robbins." Blount placed the document on Ogden's desk. "But it cost us a bundle." He sat down in the chair in front of the desk. "And it will cost us more if you want to bring her to trial as a witness."

"We'll worry about that later. This may be enough to give to the media. What details does she give?"

He shrugged. "Three years ago she was a nurse at Kennebruk Hospital in Dandridge. Kate Denby's father was admitted by his daughter in September. He had cancer and was terminal. Robbins said Kate Denby was very stressed. She overheard the father pleading with her to give him an overdose. He was transferred to a private hospital and died there two days later."

"And she thinks Denby did it? Any proof?"

"None. Though she said anyone at Kennebruk would testify that the man was nowhere near death."

"It's so *good*," Ogden said. "A woman who

would kill her father would be considered loony as a hoot owl."

"Or desperate," Blount said. "Mercy killing might arouse a certain amount of sympathy in some quarters."

"Bullshit. No one would trust the word of a woman who's been covering up a murder for three years. Was there an autopsy?"

Blount shook his head. "Denby was the attending physician and she signed the death certificate. He was cremated."

"All very convenient. Why didn't the nurse come forward before?"

"She said that it isn't that unusual for doctors to commit mercy killings in terminal cases. Everyone on staff usually just looks the other way. It was only when she read about the murder of the policeman that she even remembered Denby's father. When our man showed up on the scene, she decided to make a little money for herself."

"It's all hearsay. It might make the rag sheets, but it's not enough to be really valuable. What's the name of that private hospital she had him transferred to?"

"Pinebridge."

"What have you found out from them?"

"Nothing. I thought Robbins might be enough. Our man was becoming a little too visible."

Ogden scowled. "Well, it's not enough. We have to have the Denby woman completely discredited. Now that she's linked up with Migellin, she's beginning to become a major pain in the ass. In two weeks she's managed to get two major television interviews, and that bastard Migellin has cut the bill out of the welfare package. How the hell are they managing it?"

"Drakin?"

"Don't be stupid. The man's practically a criminal and we've gotten stories about his background into eight magazines this month."

"He certainly appears to be irresponsible enough to scare off most people," Blount murmured. He'd been very interested in the dossier Ogden had ordered on Drakin. He just might be the key that would open the treasure trove. Thank God, Ogden couldn't see it. "I'm sure the setback is only temporary. So I should send someone else to Pinebridge?"

"I said so, didn't I?"

"Just verifying. I want to make sure I don't misunderstand you." He smiled. "Actually, I thought that might be your decision, and I know just the man to send."

"No," Ishmaru said. "I'm not ready yet."

"What do you mean? This is what you wanted."

Blount didn't understand. Ishmaru had watched Kate go about town for the last few days. She was suffering. He didn't want it to stop. Every move from now on must be carefully orchestrated to bring about the maximum effect. "I've decided to do the job you want me to do. It may fit into my plans." He paused. "If you find her son for me."

"I told you we haven't been able to locate him."

"You haven't tried hard enough. Bug their hotel room."

"We've tried. Drakin is too sharp."

"The telephone."

"They're using digital. It would take a truckload of equipment to do the job, and Ogden won't authorize it now that they've already gone public."

"You'll find a way to get around it."

"Besides, that hotel is a skyscraper. The range wouldn't be —"

"I want to know where the boy is."

Blount sighed. "I'll do my best."

"Not your best. Find him."

Everything was going very well, Kate thought as she watched Senator Migellin ply the congresswoman from Iowa with coffee and charm. He was good at this kind of thing.

And so was Seth. She glanced at the corner of the terrace where he was standing with a few members of the Senate. These afternoons at Migellin's country house had become commonplace, and Seth and Migellin used these relaxed occasions to brilliant advantage. She wished she could say the same for herself, she thought ruefully. She was too blunt and impatient. She'd found her best course was to make herself available for questions on RU2 and otherwise keep her mouth shut. Particularly lately, when she'd found it difficult to barely hold herself together.

Migellin glanced at her over the congresswoman's head and smiled.

Did he need her?

No, he was leaving the congresswoman and coming toward her.

She frowned. "Is something wrong?"

"I don't know. Is there? You look a bit . . . frayed."

"I'm fine."

He studied her face with concern. "You're sure?"

She wasn't sure of anything except that she had to get through this day. She hadn't received a package this morning, and she didn't know whether that was bad or good. She nodded. "Thank you for asking. You can go back to the congresswoman now."

He grimaced. "I needed a breather from hammering sense into that woman's head. First-term representatives are harder than seniors. They haven't learned that you have to bend to play the game."

"You don't bend."

"I wish I could say that was true. But I do try to stand tall on the important issues."

"Are we swaying any votes?"

"Oh yes, I got Wyler and Debruk this week." He gently put his hand on her shoulder. "It's still not a sure bet, but we're doing better."

She smiled at him. "That's what I told Seth."

"He's certainly doing his share." He squeezed her shoulder and released it. "And now I'd better get back and do mine."

"When is the bill due up for vote?"

"Next week. Unless we can stall it again."

Next week. Panic tore through her. It was too soon. Longworth was wheeling and dealing just as hard as they were. They needed to do more work before they risked a vote.

"Did you know the bill was due to be voted on next week?" she asked Seth when he joined her before lunch.

He nodded. "Migellin told me."

"How can you be so calm? It's too soon, dammit."

"Migellin may be able to stall it. He's very popular. Even his political adversaries like and respect him."

How could they help it? He was as down-to-earth as Abraham Lincoln, with Jack Kennedy's class. "I wish we hadn't had to draw him into this. He said it might hurt his career."

"Second thoughts?"

"No, RU2 is worth it. I suppose I'm just not as tough as Noah."

"Oh, you're tough." His hand brushed her cheek. "Hold on for another hour and we can go back to the hotel." He turned and moved across the terrace toward Migellin.

Hold on. Smile. Talk to them. Don't think of the package that might be waiting for you back at the hotel.

364

"A call for you, Dr. Denby." Migellin's servant, Joseph, was at her elbow extending the portable phone.

She tensed. It could be Tony. It could be Meryl Kimbro. She was often in touch these days. It didn't have to be —

"I found him, Emily," Ishmaru said.

There was a click as he hung up the phone.

Panic raced through her. It was a lie. He only wanted to frighten, torment her.

"Oh, and the gentleman said there was a package for you in the foyer," Joseph said. "Shall I bring it?" He didn't wait for an answer but hurried off.

Seth. She wanted to scream his name. *Come to me. Help me. Tell me he's lying again.*

He was still talking to Migellin. She would have to go to him.

She started across the terrace.

Joseph was coming toward her, smiling and carrying a package. Red and white stripes, a scattering of gold stars.

She stopped, frozen, as she stared at it.

She couldn't hear anything. Everyone seemed to be moving in slow motion. Joseph was still smiling as he handed her the package.

Seth had raised his head and was looking at her. She saw his eyes widen when he saw the box. He started toward her. "Kate, don't —"

She couldn't hear him anymore. The box. She had to open the box. She reached out and lifted the lid.

Hair. Blood. Soft, silky brown hair. A cowlick. *Joshua.*

She plunged down through the agony into darkness.

"Come back to me, dammit."

Seth. His voice was sharp, demanding.

"Kate. Wake up. I won't have this."

His tone was so compelling that she opened her eyes.

His face was twisted with pain, his eyes glittering.

Something was wrong. He was hurting. She should try to — *Joshua.*

She closed her eyes, tight, tighter. *Shut it away. Shut it —*

"Kate, it wasn't him."

He was lying. She had seen —

"It wasn't Joshua. I swear to you." He thrust his phone at her. "Joshua's on the phone. Talk to him." He held the phone to her ear. "Okay, don't talk to him. Listen."

"Mom, what's wrong? Seth said you're sick."

Joshua's voice. A miracle. "Joshua?" she whispered.

"Mom, you're scaring me. You sound funny. What's wrong?"

She swallowed. "Nothing. Nothing. I was just missing you. Are you okay?"

"Sure. I'm kinda bored. When can we leave here?"

"Soon, I hope." Oh God, the tears were running down her cheeks, and her voice was thickening. She couldn't talk anymore. She thrust the phone back at Seth.

She heard him murmuring to Joshua, and a minute later he hung up. He returned the phone to his pocket. "Convinced?"

She nodded. "I couldn't believe —"

"Shh, just relax."

She looked around the shadowy bedroom. "Where are we?"

"Still at Migellin's. You've been out for over four hours."

"That horrible —"

"Don't think about it."

"It was the cowlick. Joshua has —"

"I know. This child was younger but the hair was very similar." His tone hardened. "Goddamn his soul."

"He killed a little boy just to do this to me?" It was hard to believe such evil existed. No, not really hard. Not when she knew about Ishmaru.

"Will you be all right if I leave you for a while? Migellin's downstairs with the police and they want a statement. He's trying to keep them from bothering you. Maybe I can substitute."

"I'll be okay. Thank you."

He squeezed her hand and stood up. "I won't be long. Try to take a nap."

It shouldn't be a problem, she thought drowsily. She felt as if she'd been knocked on the head. Besides, if she stayed awake, she would have to think of the contents of that box and the agony of the parents of that little boy. She wasn't capable of facing that yet. Instead she would lie here and think of her and Joshua playing baseball in the backyard. Those were good moments, but they seemed so long ago.

Joshua . . .

Kate was still sleeping when Seth returned two hours later.

God knows she needed it.

He stood looking down at her. The lines of strain and fear on her face were still present, and he realized that he had never seen her when those lines were gone entirely. No wonder. Their time together had been fraught with threat and anxiety from their first meeting.

He fought back the wave of tenderness and moved toward the window. He didn't want this. He didn't want the agony of worry. He didn't want the tenderness. He sure as hell didn't want the chains that went with both.

His fault. He had known from the beginning that she was going to mean too much and he'd dived in anyway. He hadn't cared that she'd never want more than they had now.

Grab the moment.

Yeah, sure. So what was he going to do now?

He was going to stop soul-searching and get to the business of keeping her alive, he thought impatiently. Something about all this had been nagging at him. Deciding to play his hunches, as he'd learned to do a long time ago, he started to leave.

He would go down and talk to Joseph before taking Kate back to the hotel.

He glanced back at her as he reached the door and again felt that bittersweet wave of tenderness.

Sleep well and heal, Kate.

Fourteen

Seth and Kate didn't reach their hotel until after three in the morning. In spite of Seth's efforts the police had still been there when she woke and insisted on taking a statement. Their manner had been sympathetic, but the questions totally merciless.

"You've been very quiet." She tossed her handbag on the couch in the sitting room and kicked off her high heels.

"I've been thinking."

"I'm going to take a shower and go to bed." She headed for the bedroom. "You'd think after all that sleep that I'd feel rested, but I —"

"Wait."

She glanced at him over her shoulder, caught his expression, and then slowly turned to face him. "What is it?"

"A hunch. Just a hunch. But we may not be going to bed anytime soon."

She tensed. "What kind of hunch?"

"I thought it a little odd that Ishmaru had staged his latest drama at Migellin's place instead of the hotel. Delivering the package to the country must have been more difficult for him to manage."

"What are you getting at?"

"He knew what it would do to you. He'd know

I'd have to call Joshua."

"So?"

"The telephone. When a digital call comes from a high-rise, it ranges from hard to impossible to listen in or trace it. But in the country there's practically no interference."

"But you said that it would take a truckload of high-tech equipment to monitor a call."

"I checked with Joseph. There was a large telephone truck parked by a telephone pole down the road from Migellin's for most of the day." He paused. "I called the telephone company and they had no record of a truck being in the neighborhood."

The panic was building again. And she had thought the nightmare over for a little while. "You're saying that Ishmaru knows where Joshua is?" she whispered.

"No, the call was short. I doubt if it was traceable even with state-of-the-art equipment."

"But you're not sure."

"I put Rimilon on alert." He met her gaze. "And I'm going down there tonight."

"I'm going with you." She thrust her feet back into her heels. "Why didn't you tell me before?"

"Because it may be for nothing."

"I don't *care.*"

"And if we go, there's a good chance that we'll be followed. The shelter won't be safe anymore."

"What difference does it make? I'll never feel secure about contacting Joshua and Phyliss again. And being able to check on them was the only thing that made life bearable this last week. I'd rather have Joshua here where I can protect him. I couldn't stand not being able to know what was happening."

"Neither could I. Okay, go pack an overnight case and call valet parking and have the car brought around while I see about hiring a helicopter." He smiled. "Let's go get your son."

"Want to play Ping-Pong?" Phyliss asked as she got up from the table and started collecting the paper plates.

Joshua listlessly shook his head.

"Checkers?"

"You always win."

Phyliss grinned. "Why do you think I want to play?"

Joshua got up from the table, wandered into the living room, and flopped on the couch.

Phyliss frowned as she watched him. Something was wrong. He had been quiet all day, even before he'd spoken to Kate, and now he was downright surly. Joshua was never surly. There was no way he could have been overjoyed about being locked up in this dungeon, but Joshua had been as good-natured as could be expected. More than could be expected.

Phyliss dumped the plates into the disposal and followed him into the living room. "How about poker?" She sat down beside him. "Be a sport. I'm bored."

He didn't answer. "What do you think Mom's doing now?"

"What she has to do."

"She sounded scared. Maybe Ishmaru is after her."

"Seth told you she was fine."

"Maybe he lied."

Her uneasiness increased. Seth was beyond reproach in Joshua's eyes. "What reason would he have?"

"I don't know. I should be helping him. I shouldn't be here."

"And leave me alone? I need you, kid."

He shook his head as if to clear it. "I shouldn't be here . . ."

He was acting sluggish, strange.

No, not now. Let her be wrong.

She scooted nearer and drew him close. "Maybe it won't be much longer." Oh God, his head resting against her arm was burning hot.

"Grandma, I should be helping Seth . . ."

"Later," she whispered. "Just rest now."

The Japanese doorman smiled widely as Seth and Kate came out of the hotel. "Taxi?"

"No, we're expecting — There it is." Seth stepped into the driveway and hailed the young boy driving their car.

"Ah, your car." The doorman took Kate's overnight case and escorted her to the car. He opened the back door and placed the case on the floor inside. He bowed low. "I hope you will return to the Summit. It was our pleasure to serve you."

Seth pressed a bill into his hand before getting into the driver's seat. The doorman was still bowing and smiling when they reached the street.

"How long will it take us to get there?" Kate asked.

"A couple hours. But the advantage is that we can set down in a field nearby."

"Will they be able to trace the flight?"

"Maybe. Maybe not. I'll file a fake flight plan. We may get away with it."

Yokomoto carefully held the white braid on his doorman's uniform sleeve away from the public telephone. "You've picked them up?"

"Loud and clear. Is the bug on the car?"

"No, an overnight case. Do not lose them."

"Not likely. The transmitter I gave you was mega-powerful."

Such a tiny instrument. Technology was truly a wonderful thing. "You will remember me to Mr. Blount?"

"You'll get your money."

Such a lack of delicacy and tact deserved no answer. Yokomoto hung up the phone.

"I've been trying to call you," Rimilon said as Seth jumped out of the helicopter.

"We couldn't use the digital. What's happening?" Seth asked.

"Other than the kid being sick, nothing. Easiest assignment you ever gave me."

"Joshua's sick?" Kate was terrified. "What's wrong?"

"I don't know. Mrs. Denby came up top and said I should call you. She looked kind of scared."

Kate was off across the field at a dead run.

She heard Seth say to Rimilon, "Check out the helicopter for bugs, homing devices, anything you can find."

"You think you were followed?"

"Check. I don't want to take any chances." He caught up with Kate. "Easy. Kids get sick."

"Joshua's never sick. It doesn't make sense. And why should he be sick now? It's too coincidental. What if Ishmaru —"

"Be reasonable, Kate. Ishmaru couldn't have anything to do with it unless he was able to blow germs through that steel door."

"I don't feel like being reasonable," she said fiercely. "My son's sick."

Phyliss met them at the vault door. "Thank God. I don't think he's any worse, but he's still burning with fever. I didn't want to call you, but I didn't know what to do. I can't get the fever down. I've been bathing him with lukewarm water for the past five hours."

"Get my medical bag, Phyliss." Kate hurried toward Joshua's bedroom.

He was pale, his skin flushed. She sat down on the bed beside him.

"How you doing, baby?" she whispered.

"Not so good." His voice was hoarse.

"You're going to be fine. We're going to get

you well in no time."

He looked beyond her shoulder to Seth. "I stayed, Seth. I took care of Phyliss."

"I know you did." Seth came closer. "Now it's time for us to take care of you. Hang in there, sport."

"My head hurts . . ."

"I've got something for that." Kate opened the medical bag Phyliss set on the bed. "But first I've got to examine you. Okay?"

He nodded and closed his eyes. "Neck hurts . . ."

"What is it?" Phyliss asked when Kate came out of the bedroom.

"I don't know. I don't like that neck ache." She shook her head. "I can't tell without tests."

"Hospital?" Seth asked.

She nodded. "And right away. I've taken some blood samples. Where's the closest hospital?"

"In White Sulphur Springs. Fifteen minutes by helicopter."

"Let's do it."

"I'll get Joshua." Seth moved back toward the bedroom. "You're coming too, Phyliss. I don't want to leave you here alone."

"I wasn't going to let you leave me. But what's different? I've been down here for weeks."

"Things are changing."

"What does he mean?" Phyliss asked Kate.

"We've been under surveillance. It's possible we may have been followed."

"Damn." She shook her head. "I'm sorry about Joshua."

"It's not your fault." She handed Phyliss her coat. "You're moving out of here for good."

Phyliss heaved a sigh of relief. "Thank God. It was like being buried alive. But Joshua was great."

"So were you."

Seth was carrying Joshua out of the bedroom, wrapped in blankets.

"Let's go. Get the door, Phyliss."

Rimilon met them at the helicopter. He held up a tiny metal device. "On the bottom of the overnight case. Very high powered."

"But no sign of anyone?"

Rimilon shook his head. "Not yet. So the tunnel is probably safe. Where are you going?"

"White Sulphur Springs Hospital." He handed Joshua up into Kate's arms. "Stay here for another couple hours and watch and then go there."

Rimilon stood to one side while they took off, the tornado of wind from the helicopter blowing his sparse hair into a wild tangle.

"It's meningitis," Kate said as she came into the waiting room. "I put him on antibiotics. He'll be okay."

"Where the hell did he get meningitis?" Seth asked.

"Who knows? The incubation time for the virus is variable. Days, weeks, months." Her knees felt weak; she collapsed on a chair. "And we were lucky, it could have been a more deadly form."

"How long will it take him to recover?" Phyliss asked.

"It seems to be a light case. A few weeks. He should be able to leave the hospital in a day or two." She raised a shaking hand to her mouth. "I was so afraid . . ."

"Kids get sick," Phyliss said.

Seth had said that too. Didn't they know she knew that? "But I thought . . . Everything's been going wrong. Everyone around me is —"

She wouldn't say the word. She didn't want to even think of that word in connection with Joshua. She turned to Seth. "What happens now? How do we keep them safe?"

"I'll have to work on it."

"Work fast." She closed her eyes. God, she'd sounded like a bitch and Seth had been wonderful. "I'm sorry. I know you'll do the best you can. I'm just so afraid that —"

"You need some sleep." Seth turned away. "No one's leaving the hospital. I'll arrange to get you and Phyliss a room here. Rimilon will be on guard in the hall."

"What about you?"

"I'll stay with Joshua."

She shook her head. "No, I'll do it."

"He'll need you more later."

"Are you crazy? I've been without him for weeks and he's *sick.*"

He held up his hands in surrender. "Okay, I'll come with you."

"It's not necessary. He'll be sleeping."

"Maybe not. But I'd kind of like to stay anyway."

Seth couldn't persuade Kate to leave Joshua until nearly dawn and then only because she decided she had to go to the lab and check to see why Joshua's latest blood results hadn't come back.

"Why don't you take time to shower and change? I won't leave him," Seth said.

"Maybe."

She wouldn't do it, Seth thought as the door swung closed. She'd been hanging over Joshua all night, and she'd be back here as soon as it was possible.

He could use a shower himself, he thought wearily as he leaned back in his chair. It had been a hell of a twenty-four hours.

"Seth." Joshua's eyes were open. He whispered, "I blew it, didn't I?"

"It's like being shot from ambush. Not your fault."

"You're not mad?"

"No problem. We'll get through it."

Joshua frowned. "Really?"

Seth smiled. "Really."

"I'll be ready to go back real soon."

"I don't think that will be necessary. The danger has lessened. How would you like to stay at the same hotel with your mom and me? Maybe in the suite next door."

He smiled eagerly. "Could I?"

"You're still not going to be able to go out, but at least you'll be aboveground."

He yawned. "And I could see Mom?"

"Every day."

"Good." He closed his eyes. "I missed her."

Seth could see he was about to drift off. "She missed you."

"Will Grandma be . . ."

He was asleep. Seth sat back in the chair. Funny. He could see a lot of himself in the kid. Nah, he had never been as steady as Joshua. That was all Kate. Or maybe it was all Joshua. Seth had always believed that people were born with their own special souls. If that was true, Joshua was lucky. He'd drawn a winner.

He should go and tell Kate that Joshua had woken up.

No, this was one of the good times. He'd sit here for a little while with Joshua and enjoy it.

"Mr. Drakin?"

Seth looked up to see a dark, heavyset young man smiling at him from the doorway with Rimilon hovering behind him. "I'm William Blount. May I have a word with you?"

"I'm busy."

Blount glanced at Joshua. "He's sleeping. I won't take more than a minute of your time."

"Who are you?"

"At present I'm employed by Raymond Ogden."

Seth stared at him for a minute and then rose

to his feet. "Ten minutes. In the hall, right outside."

"As you wish." His smile widened. "Though I'm no threat to either you or the boy. What do you think I am? A monster?"

"There seem to be quite a few wandering around."

Blount glanced at Rimilon. "Can we dispense with this gentleman? I need a bit of privacy."

Seth nodded at Rimilon and the man moved to his former position a few yards down the hall.

"Thank you," Blount said.

Seth closed the door and leaned back against it. "What do you do for Ogden?"

"Oh, this and that. My title is personal assistant. I assure you I'm in his deepest confidence."

Seth waited.

"You're still afraid that I mean you harm." Blount shook his head. "Will it put you more at ease to know that Ogden knows nothing about your whereabouts at this time? My man reported only to me."

"How did you find us?"

"A bug. We were right behind you when you landed in that field. We landed a few miles away and arrived just in time to see you take off again without our little device. A huge disappointment. But your friend Rimilon obligingly left a few hours later, and we followed him here. You mustn't be angry with him. I have good people and we were very careful."

More careful than Rimilon, Seth thought, trying to control his rage. Even if Blount's men were experts, Rimilon should have made sure he wasn't followed. He didn't usually make mistakes like this, and Seth would make goddamn sure he didn't make another even if he had to break the bastard's neck. "And you didn't report any of this to Ogden?"

"Ogden and I are not in agreement on a number of things."

"Such as?"

"He wants to destroy RU2."

"And you don't?"

"Why should anyone destroy a goose that could lay a golden egg? Do you know how many people would be willing to pay a fortune to be treated with RU2? Illness falls on rich and poor alike. Fortunately, the rich can pay handsomely to be saved from the grim reaper."

"And what do you want from me?"

"You now own RU2. What if we opened a large clinic in Switzerland? We're talking about billions."

"Are we?"

"I've investigated your background thoroughly. This fruitless battle to get RU2 accepted must be very distasteful. That kind of commitment isn't for you. You like to move around. Now all you have to do is supply the RU2 and leave the rest to me. You don't even have to show up at the clinic."

"I could hire a business manager for that. Why do I need you?"

"We both know that once the success of RU2 is demonstrated, it will be impossible to keep samples from being stolen. It could be a more lucrative black market than cocaine. You need a powerful organization to discourage such thievery."

"And you have such an organization?"

"My father is Marco Giandello."

Seth masked his sudden flare of interest. "And he's committed to the plan?"

"I've discussed it with him in depth. It's not exactly his field of preference, but he's willing to back me. We're a close family."

"So I've heard," Seth said dryly.

"Don't misunderstand me. My father would be far in the background. This would be a legitimate enterprise." He paused. "Are you interested?"

"I could hardly help but be interested. What about Ogden?"

"I'll part company with Ogden as soon as it's convenient for us. It's not a bad thing to be in his confidence."

"Can you get him to call off Ishmaru?"

"I'm afraid Ishmaru is out of his control. He's become obsessed. Pity."

"More than a pity. I find him . . . inconvenient. I want him out."

"I can arrange that."

"Tell me where he is and I'll arrange it."

He shook his head. "Ishmaru still has his uses." His smile became smug. "But I've been able to sidetrack him. I made a deal."

"Was part of the deal telling him where we are?"

"Oh yes, but he won't bother you. He wants Kate Denby." He frowned. "Or maybe the boy. I'm not sure."

Seth reined in his fury at the casual statement. "That's reassuring."

"And he's promised that within a few days he'll be on a plane out of Washington."

"Going where?"

"I can't share all my secrets. Let's just say removing Ishmaru is my gesture of goodwill. Will you think about my proposal?"

Seth slowly nodded.

A flicker of excitement showed in Blount's expression. "I knew a man of your character would see the advantages."

"You mean lack of character, don't you?" Seth shrugged. "I'm making no promises. Let me think about it. Where can I get in touch with you?"

Blount quickly handed him a card. "It's my private line in Ogden's office."

"This isn't a Seattle number."

"No, Ogden rented a house in Virginia. He wanted to be near Washington during this crucial time."

Seth thrust the card in his jeans pocket and opened Joshua's door. "Until I make my decision, I trust that there will be no more incidents like the Noah Smith death?"

"That was Ishmaru. Though Ogden wasn't displeased until he found that Smith's death did him no real good. He doesn't want any martyrs now that you're all in the public eye. It would focus too much attention."

"And what do you want?"

"I want my clinic in Switzerland. Would I cut off my nose to spite my face?"

"I had to be sure." He smiled. "I believe I'll be in touch, Mr. Blount."

"I'll look forward to it." He turned and moved down the corridor toward the bank of elevators.

Seth's smile lasted only until the elevator doors closed. *"Son of a bitch."* He wheeled and turned to Rimilon, who was down the corridor, leaning against the wall. "Stay here. Don't let anyone in to see the boy."

"No one? What about the nurses or —"

"No one," Seth tossed back over his shoulder as he ran down the hall. *Kate.* Ishmaru knew where they were. He could be in the hospital right now. Watching. Stalking.

Kate had gone to the lab. Where the hell was the lab?

Kate wasn't in the lab. She was standing at the nurses' station, talking to the head nurse.

She turned as Seth approached. "Is he awake? I've just been —"

"Ishmaru knows we're here."

She felt the blood drain from her face. "How do you know?"

"I'll tell you later. I don't want you wandering about the hospital. Come back to Joshua's room."

"Where else do you think I'd go?" She pushed past him and hurried down the corridor. A hospital was such a public place. People came and went. . . . Were there windows in Joshua's room? Oh God, she couldn't remember. One window. No fire escape.

Rimilon smiled as he saw her. "Don't worry, he's fine, Dr. Denby. I just took a peek."

She must look as terrified as she felt.

Joshua was sleeping.

Or was he?

She went limp with relief as she saw the steady lift and fall of his chest.

"Stay here," Seth said in a low voice behind her. "I want to alert Security and then try to find —"

The phone on Joshua's bedside table rang.

She went rigid.

"Christ." Seth started toward the phone.

"No." She was there before him, picking up the receiver.

"How sick is he, Emily?"

Fear lanced through her. "Damn you, leave my son alone."

"Did my little joke at Migellin's amuse you? The cowlick was hard. Do you know I had to spend three days at that elementary school to get a perfect match? It was close, wasn't it?"

"Leave . . . him . . . alone."

"Oh, I intend to leave him alone . . . for now. I wanted you to suffer and I've accomplished my purpose. I think our battle will be much more

386

enjoyable if you know while I'm killing you that you can't prevent your son from dying. It will increase both your pain and your will to live. No, you first, then him. I never meant it any other way." He paused. "But there has to be another coup before our battle. Someone who will mean something to you. I've gone to too much trouble."

"Then come and get me."

"Not before I've planned everything perfectly. You took away the guardians, but if I destroy you, I'll still be able to keep the dreams away. I know you're helping them to get through to me."

"You're insane."

"So insane I've managed to have you dance to my tune. It was pleasant, but now it's time for the coup. Guess who I've chosen?"

He hung up the phone.

"What did he say?" Seth asked.

"He wants a coup, but he doesn't want it to be Joshua." She moistened her lips. "He said it's not time. He told me to guess who —" Her gaze flew to his face. She whispered, "Oh God, Phyliss."

"Shit." He ran out the door.

She followed at a dead run.

Phyliss was alone, sleeping, unable to defend herself.

They'd been so afraid of the threat to Joshua that they'd forgotten how unpredictable Ishmaru could be.

Let it not be too late, she prayed. *Not Phyliss . . .*

They turned the corner. Two rooms down.

Seth burst through the doorway and turned

on the light. "Phyliss!"

Phyliss opened her eyes and yawned. "Time to get up? How's Joshua?"

Kate's heart was beating so hard that she could hardly get her breath to speak. "Fine."

"Good. I'll take my turn at watching him as soon as I have my shower." She frowned as she sat up and swung her legs to the floor. "Why are you staring at me, Seth?"

He cleared his throat. "I was just thinking how wonderful you look."

"Bull. No woman my age looks good in the morning. You know, it's a good thing this is a hospital. Because you're really sick." The bathroom door closed behind her.

Seth shook his head. "Damn, I was afraid. I couldn't think —" He stopped as he saw Kate reach over to the other side of Phyliss's pillow.

A piece of notepaper lay mere inches from where Phyliss's head had rested.

Not her either. Not yet. Guess again, Emily.

Seth turned away from the waiting room coffee machine, handed Kate a cup, then sat down in the chair opposite her. "How do you feel?"

"How do you think I feel?" She shivered and quickly took a sip of hot coffee. She couldn't seem to rid herself of the chill. "I was scared to death."

"So was I."

"How did you know that Ishmaru was here?"

"I had a visitor." He related the details of Blount's visit. A smile lit his face as he ended with "Good, huh?"

She felt a sinking sensation at Seth's excitement. "No, damn you. You're not going to do it."

The smile faded from his face. "I meant the fact that Blount may have been telling the truth about Ishmaru being out of the picture for a while, not Blount's clinic. I told you I'd stay with you on RU2."

"I know you did but —"

"But you thought I'd deal with the people who murdered Noah because it would mean shucking responsibility." His hand tightened on his cup. "For God's sake, don't you know me better than that?"

"Sometimes it's hard to read you." But she could read him well enough to realize that she had hurt him.

"They say no one knows you better than the one you sleep with." He added bitterly, "Maybe I should look deeper into my motives. Could be I'm worse than I thought."

"Stop it." She couldn't stand his pain. She reached out and covered his hand. "I'm sorry. I shouldn't have said it. It was stupid."

"It was stupid." He took his hand away. "But if you thought it, you should say it. It's no surprise. I've known how you've felt."

"I spoke without thinking. I've been through hell tonight. And how am I supposed to forget that you threw a fit when you found out you'd inherited RU2?"

"We've been working and sleeping together. I'd have thought you'd remember that too." He tilted his head. "But maybe you don't want to remember. Do you find me threatening, Kate?"

"Threatening? I don't find you —"

He waved his hand impatiently. "Forget it. I didn't mean to make you defensive. It's not important. Anyway, I think Blount was telling the truth about Ishmaru. He thinks he's got him bottled up. But Ishmaru is too erratic; we'll still have to be careful."

He had changed the subject and she was relieved. He'd made her feel guilty and unsettled and a little afraid.

Afraid?

She asked quickly, "What about Blount? Can he be a danger?"

Seth nodded. "He's no judge of character, but I'm sure he's more cunning than Ogden and just as dirty. He's also got his dear old dad to pull into the play." He shrugged. "But I've stalled him for the time being. Like you, he thinks he's made me an offer I can't refuse."

It was a barbed dig and it hurt. Everything he said to her today seemed to hurt. "How long do you think we have before Blount becomes suspicious?"

"A week is reasonable. Maybe two if I can push it." He looked up. "But I saw a few possibilities in Blount's setup."

"What possibilities?"

"You wouldn't approve. I think I'll keep them

to myself until I see how playing the game your way will go."

"We're doing very well. Senator Migellin has been wonderful."

"Yes, I'd say the chances are fifty-fifty now."

"No more than that?"

"When we started, I'd have said more like twenty-eighty."

"Well, I think we're doing better than fifty-fifty. I think we're winning." She met his gaze. "We're going to win, Seth."

He smiled. "Because you won't have it any other way."

"You're damn right."

"I'm going back to Joshua." He finished his coffee. "We're taking Joshua and Phyliss back to Washington with us."

Joy surged through her. "Is it safe?"

"As safe as anywhere now. This area's no longer secure, but there's a chance we may have a reprieve from Ishmaru." He stood up. "We'll make it safe. I'll put them in the suite next door and install Rimilon in the same suite with them."

She made a face. "Phyliss will love that."

"She'll love it if it protects Joshua. Rimilon can be unobtrusive when he tries." His lips tightened. "He'll try hard. He wants very much to please me right now."

With mixed emotions she watched him walk out of the waiting room. No one had ever managed to throw her into wild confusion the way Seth did. He was like a tornado, touching down and scattering her composure to the four winds. In this one conversation he had driven her from anger to remorse and then piled on guilt, sympathy, and God knows what else.

Fear.

The thought jumped out at her.

Seth had said she felt threatened by him. It wasn't true, of course. Seth would never hurt her.

Except by being Seth. Except by disturbing the calm serenity of her life.

Except by leaving her.

Oh God, yes, it would hurt when he left her.

The realization sent a ripple of shock through her. But only because she had grown accustomed to having him in her bed. He was so damn good . . .

And he was wonderful with Joshua, wonderful with Phyliss.

And he was good company. As she had told him that first morning after they'd made love, he had great entertainment value.

But that was all.

She couldn't let it be more. Seth would never lack confidence in his own worth, unlike Michael, but neither would he ever have Michael's steadiness.

Why was she comparing them as if she had a choice?

Seth would leave her. It was only a matter of time after RU2 was accepted that he would move on.

See how that hurt? So admit that he is a threat.

Protect yourself. Don't let him come any closer.

She pushed her cup away and got to her feet.
Go to Joshua. He and Phyliss are your life.

Don't let Seth come any closer.

They arrived back at the hotel in Washington three days later.

"Everything okay?" Seth asked after Kate came back from settling Phyliss and Joshua in the suite next door.

She nodded. "Though Rimilon seems to be a little cowed by Phyliss."

"Aren't we all?" He took off his jacket and tossed it on the couch. "I called Migellin. He wants us at his house tomorrow afternoon. He's having one of his get-togethers."

She gave a ghost of a smile. "After what happened the last time, I'm surprised he can persuade anyone to come."

"On the contrary, I'd bet they're tripping over each other to come and see you. The ones who were there when you opened that package will be able to dine out on that story for months."

"I can't imagine that." She shuddered. "I can't even talk about it."

"Then don't." He picked up his suitcase and started to carry it into the bedroom.

"Wait."

He stiffened and then turned to face her.

She took a deep breath. "I don't want to sleep with you anymore."

He smiled sardonically. "I did scare you, didn't

I? I made you think. I should have kept my mouth shut."

"It's beginning to be too complicated."

"And heaven forbid you have to deal with complications."

"You don't want complications either."

"But the difference between us is that I know I can't hide from them." He took a step closer. "Why did you decide to get rid of me? You liked the sex too much? It's like a drug, isn't it? You lose control and you don't like to lose control. You like everything to be smooth. Or maybe I wasn't comfortable and steady like Noah and your father."

His eyes were glittering, his lips tight, and she felt a jolt of uneasiness. "Be reasonable. There's no cause to be angry."

"I am angry. I don't like to be kicked out when I haven't done anything. Hell, I've been a goddamn saint. Almost as holy as Saint Noah." He grasped her shoulders. "It's not *fair*."

"I know it isn't," she said helplessly. "But I can't help it."

She watched emotions flicker across his face. He was silent a moment. "Neither can I. I told you, I don't react well to rejection. I connive and manipulate and do anything I have to do to avoid it." His hands dropped from her shoulders and he headed for his bedroom. "Okay, I'll be nice and tame. I'll go to my lonely bed and leave you to yours. I'll smile and pretend everything is hunky-dory. But don't think it's over. I won't let it be over. In a month I'll be back in your bed."

She shook her head. "It wasn't supposed to last forever. You wouldn't want that."

"Don't tell me what I want." The door slammed behind him.

She flinched as if he'd struck her. His intensity frightened her. That dark, violent streak had never been turned on her before.

And not only frightened, she also felt raw and guilty and lonely.

Very lonely.

She forced herself to read Ishmaru's *Warriors* before she went to sleep that night. She had put it off, but she could do so no longer. He was coming closer. She had to try to rid herself of fear and find a weakness.

And for the first time since she and Seth had become lovers, the nightmare came again.

She awoke panting, sweating, weeping.

Seth.

Seth wasn't there.

But Ishmaru was, invading her sleep as he'd invaded her life.

And he'd not been stalking her.

He'd been after Seth.

Someone close to you. Guess again.

She hadn't even considered a threat to Seth. Seth was strong, smart, dangerous, able to fend off any threat.

Noah had been strong and smart too.

She wanted to run into Seth's room and be

with him, protect him.

Don't let him come any closer.

Stop shaking. Seth was far more able to protect himself than Noah. Go back to sleep.

Guess again . . .

Blount was supremely satisfied.

He'd read Drakin correctly. It was only a matter of time before the man came into his camp.

And with him would come money and power.

He hummed softly as he unlocked the door and entered his office. He always arrived two hours earlier than Ogden, who usually came in around ten. Blount's diligence impressed Ogden. And the two hours gave Blount time to scan any documents Ogden chose to keep locked in his drawer.

The subterfuge wouldn't be necessary very much longer. He was on his way. He had Drakin, and Ishmaru was cooperating beautifully.

Yes, he was very satisfied with how things were going. He picked up the phone. Now he had to check on only one more detail. . . .

Fifteen

He would come to the gazebo.

Blount had said he always watched the sunset from the gazebo on the hill when he was at his country place. The bastard had better be right. He didn't have time to stalk. He had a reservation on the nine o'clock flight to Oklahoma.

In other circumstances what he was about to do might have been a pleasure. He had watched Migellin on TV and the man impressed him as being strong in spirit. He must have the soul of a warrior, or Blount would not be wanting to get rid of him.

He had watched the guests depart one by one. Emily and Drakin had been the last to go, and Migellin had smiled at her and she had looked at him with affection.

He was coming up the hill.

Faster. Come faster. I'm waiting for you.

He was wearing a gray sweater, and the breeze was ruffling his hair. He looked relaxed and contented.

Ishmaru was suddenly contented too.

Migellin was important to Emily and he was strong. He would fight. It would be worth the delay to confront such a man, and in the end it would be the same.

Coup.

"How you doing?" Kate came into Joshua's room and plopped down on the bed.

He scowled at her. "Grandma won't let me up. I feel fine."

"Tomorrow."

"What's the difference between today and tomorrow?"

"Twenty-four hours. Now tell me what you did today while we were at the senator's."

He nodded at the guitar by the bed. "I practiced 'Down in the Valley.' I'm getting pretty good." He brightened. "You want to hear it?"

"You bet." She handed him the guitar and stood up. "Wait a minute and I'll get Seth. He'll want to hear it too."

"He's already heard it. He came to see me before dinner." His forehead was wrinkled in concentration as he began to pluck the chords. "He said he'd teach me another song tomorrow. Maybe 'Yankee Doodle.' "

She curled up in the chair across the room and watched him. Thank God, children were so wonderfully resilient. They were better at handling adversity than grown-ups were. Lock them up and they'll learn to play the guitar. She remembered reading the diary of Anne Frank years ago and being impressed at how life went on even under that terrible threat. In a way, Joshua's situation was the same.

He looked up. "You listening?"

"Every note. You're pretty hot stuff."

He grinned and looked back down at the chords he was making. "I'm getting there."

She rested her head on the cushion, listening to the soft music. Peace. Love. Togetherness. It was like the times they'd had together before all this began. The calm in the eye of the hurricane.

Well, she'd take it.

Enjoy the moment.

"Migellin is dead," Tony said as soon as Seth opened the hotel room door. "His wife found him in the gazebo earlier this evening."

"How?"

"Stabbed. There was a note beside him saying this is what happens to all heathens who tamper with God's natural order."

Kate felt as if she'd been stabbed herself. She turned to Seth. "Ishmaru?"

"Probably. Or maybe Ogden pumped up one of those fanatics to do it."

"You don't believe that."

"No, but I hoped you might. Ogden didn't want martyrs, and a dead Migellin will loom pretty damn large."

"He loomed pretty large in life too." She tried to steady her voice. "I suppose we don't have to guess anymore about the coup. Ishmaru wanted it to be Migellin."

Seth turned back to Tony. "What do the police say?"

"Not much yet. The place is crawling with FBI and CIA too. A senator of Migellin's stature could be a target for terrorists." He paused. "But it's the note that will be all over the press. I don't know whether that's bad or good for us."

Kate said, "I can't see anything good about any of this. A decent man is dead, and if it's Ishmaru, he'll come after us now."

"He didn't before. He wants you to come to him."

"And Migellin was simply an isolated incident? I don't think so."

"I don't know. I'm just telling you not to jump to conclusions. Let me look into it."

"Look into it all you like." She pushed past him. "But I'm going to go to my son."

"He's safe, Kate. You know he's well guarded. Rimilon is always —"

"I don't know anything anymore." She knocked on the door of the adjacent suite. "I just want to be with my son."

Phyliss opened the door. "Kate?"

"Migellin's dead. He's dead, Phyliss." She went into the suite and closed the door. "Is it okay if I stay with you awhile?"

"Don't be an ass." Phyliss drew her close. "Come on. Tell me about it."

"She's pretty shaky," Tony said.

"Can you blame her?" Seth asked.

"No. I felt pretty shaky myself when I heard about Migellin. I liked him."

"So did I." He went back in the suite. "Come in. There are a few things I want you to do."

"What? You know without Migellin our chances of stopping that bill are zero."

"Maybe. Where's that pet snoop you keep on a leash?"

"Barlow? Still in Seattle."

"Bring him here. I may need him."

"Migellin was our only hope. What can —"

"Just bring him." Seth sat down and reached for the phone.

"Who are you calling?"

"My old buddy Blount."

Blount answered the phone on the second ring. "I was expecting your call, Drakin. You've heard about Migellin? What a pity. Ogden is ranting like a bull. It's very amus—"

"Why?"

There was a silence. "Migellin was an obstacle. Even if you withdrew your opposition to the anti-genetic-research bill, Migellin would have continued. He was that kind of man."

"So you made him a martyr."

"You sound like Ogden. We don't have to worry about that. There may be a backlash against the pharmaceutical companies, but that won't affect us. Once the bill is passed, it will put RU2 on the back burner for at least ten years. The less RU2 out there, the more profit we'll reap. Supply and demand. You know Migellin's support will disintegrate now."

"Yes, I know that."

"And once you bow out, the bill will be passed in a heartbeat."

"Very clever. I hadn't looked at it that way."

"That's my job. To keep you from having to deal with these niggling little details. That's why our partnership is going to work." He paused. "And it will be a partnership, won't it, Drakin?"

"I'm drawing closer to a decision now that Migellin's out of the way."

"I thought that might spur you."

"But partners should trust each other. You lied to me about Ishmaru being off the scene. It was Ishmaru, wasn't it?"

"Of course, I told you we'd made a deal. But he hopped a plane afterward just as he promised. Don't worry about Ishmaru. His usefulness is almost over. My father knows how to handle vermin like him."

"That's very reassuring."

"We should meet and discuss how we'll proceed."

"Not yet. We need to let the furor about Migellin's death die down."

"I guess I'm a little impatient. You're right. You'll contact me after the funeral?"

"You can be sure of it." He hung up the phone.

"Well?" Tony asked.

"I want to know everything there is to know about Ogden, Blount, and Marco Giandello. Fast."

"What good is that going to do? You'll just be spinning your wheels now that Migellin's dead."

"Then let me spin them."

He stared at Seth in surprise. "You're not going

to give up, are you?"

"Knowing your opinion of me, I realize that must astound you."

"It does. Why?"

"Because some things are worth digging in for the long haul."

"RU2?"

"I'm afraid I'm not that noble. I operate on a more personal level."

"Kate?"

"Kate, Noah, Migellin. I'm pissed off. Big time."

Tony gazed at him warily. "And what are you going to do?"

He smiled. "Why, what I do best. What else?"

Pinebridge.

Ishmaru smiled as he walked down the long driveway toward the impressive front entrance of the small hospital. He had a good feeling about Pinebridge. It was located in the countryside outside town and was surrounded by woods.

The appointed place?

Ah, Emily, you little devil, you're even more than I anticipated. It took a divine viciousness to kill your own father. Of course, he could have done it, if his father had not died before Ishmaru had found the true path. But not many others were capable of such an act.

She must have left a trail; everyone left trails. Records in the office, someone on the staff who had seen something. There would be a trail and he would be able to use it to draw Kate to him. He would offer the evidence as bait and Kate would come.

A gray-haired woman in her fifties looked up with a smile when he entered the personnel office. "May I help you?"

"I hope *I* can help *you*. My name is Bill Sanchez. The Valmeyer Employment Agency sent me here about the orderly job."

"Oh yes." She leafed through the papers on her desk. "But I thought they were going to send . . ." She found the paper for which she had been looking. "A Norman Kendricks."

"I came instead." He smiled. "Norman couldn't make it. He isn't well."

Another funeral.

Would they never stop?

Driving rain beat against the ornate lid of the flower-heaped casket.

In spite of the weather the grave site was crowded with people. Congressmen, foreign dignitaries, the vice president and his wife.

Not like Noah's funeral, Kate thought. Migellin deserved this tribute, but so had Noah. She glanced at Seth. Was he thinking about Noah too? No, his face was wet with rain, but she saw no sorrow. His expression was tight, hard, and reminded her vaguely of the night he had come to get her after Noah's death.

She had been afraid of him that night.

The service was over and the crowd was shifting, moving, gathering in little cliques now that the moment of unity was over.

Seth took her arm, carefully sheltering her with the black umbrella as they fell behind the mourners walking toward the cemetery gates.

"Noah should have had a funeral like this," she said. "It doesn't seem fair."

"Noah wouldn't have wanted anything this grand. Migellin probably wouldn't either."

"I guess you're right." Migellin had been a man of simple tastes. "We'll have to think about what to do now."

"If you're ready to pull your head out of the sand."

She couldn't resent the comment. It was the truth. She had barely seen Seth in the last few days. She had stayed with Phyliss and Joshua, closing everything else out. She had been driven back to the womb. "I'm ready. We can't stop the vote from going through now, can we?"

"It would take a miracle and there aren't that many to go around."

"There must be something we can do."

"There is. I want you, Phyliss, and Joshua to take the next plane for Amsterdam."

She stiffened. "You're giving up."

"There was always the possibility that we couldn't ram RU2 through here. We'll file in Amsterdam."

"And let Ogden and Blount and all those other bastards win?"

"I didn't say that."

"That's what you meant."

"Sometimes we have to take what we can get. It may be impossible to get support for RU2 now, but Ogden and Blount won't win."

"How can —" She stared at him. She whispered, "You're going to kill them."

"Dead men don't win."

"*No.*"

"I've had Tony make arrangements for you to leave for Amsterdam day after tomorrow. Rimilon will go with you and take care of security."

"And leave you here to commit murder."

"Execution."

"You're the one who'll be executed."

"If I'm stupid. I'm not generally stupid."

She wasn't going to be able to convince him, she realized in panic. "I'll go to Amsterdam, but only if you'll go with me."

"I'll join you there shortly."

"If you're not killed or arrested."

He glanced at her. "It's got to end, Kate. I tried to do it your way and it's not working. There's no way the law will get them. They used Ishmaru and that psycho won't talk. Noah's dead. Migellin's dead. I won't let Ogden and Blount live."

Her hands clenched into fists at her sides. "*Damn* you."

"Why are you surprised?" His voice roughened. "You should have known I couldn't stand this. Do you know how often I've wanted to leave you all and go after Ishmaru? I couldn't do it. It was too dangerous to leave you. I still can't do it, but

I can get Blount and Ogden."

"I don't want you to —"

"You'll be safer in Amsterdam." He acted as if he hadn't heard her. "No demonstrators, and I'll take care of Ishmaru once he surfaces here."

"You're not listening. I won't go there unless you go."

"You'll go. You'll do what's best for Joshua and Phyliss. You know you will."

"Don't *do* this."

He smiled. "Don't look so scared. I don't always barge in and shoot people."

"You did with Namirez."

He shrugged. "There are more subtle ways. I have a few ideas."

She looked at him in despair. "I wish I'd never brought you into this."

"But you did. So now you have to shut up and take the consequences. It's my game now."

"The hell it is. I won't let —"

"A sad occasion. It must be particularly sad for you, my dear."

Kate's gaze flew to Senator Longworth, who was coming toward them accompanied by a small, plump woman. Beneath the shadow of the umbrella his mournful face appeared as pale and gaunt as one of the stone effigies around them.

She stiffened. "It's a sad day for everyone, Senator Longworth. Migellin was a very special man."

He nodded. "Too bad his last cause had to be

the mistake for which he'll be remembered."

"It wasn't a mistake. He was committed to —"

"Now, don't get upset." He held up his hand to stop the flow. "This is a day of truce. I wanted to show you that there was no animosity on my part for the problems you've given me. I don't believe you've met my wife, Edna?"

The small woman huddled next to Longworth murmured a soft "How do you do."

"Edna is a little shy." Longworth beamed down at her. "But we've been together twenty-six years and she's a real trooper. One of the old guard. Not one of those Hillary Clinton–type upstarts."

Kate nodded politely to the woman. Edna Longworth was obviously the quintessential "little woman." She couldn't help it if she had linked her life to an asshole.

"What do you want, Longworth?" Seth asked.

"I told you, I wanted to express my —" He stopped as he met Seth's gaze. "There are reporters outside the gates. I thought it wouldn't hurt either one of our objectives to be seen together now. Sort of an enemies-joined-in-sorrow sort of thing."

Kate stared at him incredulously. "Screw you."

"No need to be abusive," Longworth said. "After all, you're the one who's lost. I merely wanted to —" He looked down at his wife, who was tugging at his arm. "What is it, Edna?"

"They said no. You promised if they said no that we'd go back to the car. You promised."

"We'll go shortly."

"It's raining," Edna said stubbornly. "You promised."

To Kate's surprise he gave in. "Oh, very well." He turned back to Kate. "My wife doesn't like the rain. Sweet things tend to melt, you know." He took his wife's arm and walked ahead of them toward the gates.

"He thinks he's beaten us," Kate said. "I wanted to slap him."

"I believe you slapped him down fairly thoroughly," Seth said.

"Did you see how he treated his wife? My God, he was patronizing." She whirled on Seth. "I don't want him to win. I don't want RU2 to go down the drain."

"Then think of a way to save it."

"We'll think of a way to save it. You don't have to go after —"

"No, Kate." His quiet tone was implacable. "Drop it."

She would drop it. What did she care if he got himself killed or arrested? He was a stupid, violent man who deserved whatever happened to him. She couldn't help him if he wouldn't listen. She would drop it.

For now.

"Mr. Drakin?" The man standing in the doorway was small, dark, and dressed in a neat gray suit. "I'm Frank Barlow. I have a report for you. I believe you told Mr. Lynski that —"

"Come in." Seth glanced over his shoulder at

Kate curled up on the sofa. No need for her to hear this. She had been upset all afternoon. "This won't take long." He took the detective into the adjoining room and closed the door. "Sit down."

Barlow sat down in the chair by the window and opened his briefcase. "You asked for a report on Ogden. There isn't much more than what I gave Mr. Smith before."

"What about Blount?"

"He keeps his nose very clean, but there's no doubt he arranged for the bombings at J. and S. Ogden doesn't have the contacts."

"Giandello?"

"Crime boss. Smart enough but clings to the old ways. Vice. Drugs. Gambling. Doesn't like to dip into anything new."

"Blount is his son. What's their relationship?"

"Close enough. At least on Giandello's part. He prides himself on his family. He's very protective of Blount. Even though he's illegitimate, Giandello put him through school, visited him frequently, gave him a fancy car for graduation."

Seth wasn't learning much he didn't already know. He tried another tack. "What kind of man is he? What pushes Giandello's buttons?"

Barlow frowned. "What do you mean?"

"Is he hot-tempered? Is he afraid of anything? Does he have any pet peeves?"

"He was hot-tempered enough to dismember one of his more ambitious competitors," Barlow said dryly. "But as I said, he's smart. He doesn't attempt anything he can't carry through." He glanced down at the paper in front of him. "He doesn't like Jews, Nazis, blacks, or homosexuals."

"Just your ordinary, clean-cut American entrepreneur," Seth murmured.

"Anything else?"

"Hell yes, we're going over these reports until I know more about them than their mother." He sat down and took the pad from Barlow. "We'll start with Blount."

Seth had said it wouldn't take long, but it had already been an hour.

He had shut the door and closed her out. For weeks they had shared everything, done everything together. It felt strange and unsettling to be alone again. That it had been her choice made no difference.

Kate got up and went into the bedroom. She would go to bed and forget it. She was used to being alone.

But not in the way Seth was alone. She had Joshua and Phyliss. Seth had no one.

His choice. He had no desire for ties of any kind. Like a magnet, he drew people to him, but then he cut them off once they'd entered his circle.

Or didn't he dare keep them? How many times had he put down roots only to have them torn up? Well, she could do nothing about it. He was what he was and she was what she was and the difference was staggering.

But what they'd had together . . .

She undressed and slipped into bed. Go to sleep. Forget that closed door.

She couldn't forget it. She kept remembering her nightmare. Seth in danger. Seth being pursued by Ishmaru. She was still awake when she heard the door of Seth's room open and then the door to the hall close. She lasted another twenty minutes before she couldn't stand it any longer.

She got out of bed and a moment later she was opening Seth's door.

It was dark, but she could dimly see Seth on the bed across the room. "Could I come to bed with you?"

"Do you need to ask?"

"Yes." She flew across the room and slipped beneath the covers. She lay there beside him, not touching him. "I think I do. You were very angry with me when I —"

"Kicked me out," he finished. "Hell yes, I was mad. But I got over it. Sort of. Why are you here? I take it that it's not my fantastic sex appeal."

"You said you'd be back in my bed in a month."

"And you wanted to save me the trouble?"

"Maybe." She paused. "Who was that man?"

"Ah, the truth outs. You're trying to seduce me into telling you all my secrets."

"Who is he?"

"A private investigator. Barlow. Tony says he's good. He'd better be."

"Why do you need him?"

"Information."

"What kind of information?"

Seth didn't answer.

She turned to face him. "Why won't you tell me?"

"Because if you don't know, you can't be charged as an accessory."

"I hate this," she whispered. She laid her head in the hollow of his shoulder. She could hear the beat of his heart beneath her ear, strong, solid. Home. "I'll help you."

He stiffened against her. "What?"

She was almost as surprised as he. She hadn't known those words would tumble out, but now that they were said, she knew they were inevitable. "You heard me. If you have to do this, I'll help you."

"Why?"

"The same reasons you have."

"Kate."

He wasn't buying it. He knew her too well. She felt tears sting her eyes. "Dammit, I just don't want you to have to be alone."

He was silent and then his lips brushed her forehead. "Hey, that means you like me."

"Maybe. A little."

"More than a little. Big. It takes big to offer to become an accessory." He gently stroked her hair. "Particularly since you're so sure I'll be caught and sent up the river." He added in a mock gangster snarl, "How do you think you'll look in prison gray, kid?"

"Stop joking. I know they're murderers themselves, but I believe in the law. And I resent death. I always have. It's a defeat. This whole thing scares me."

"But you're willing to do it anyway. What about Joshua?"

"That's what terrifies me the most. I know he has Phyliss." Her arms tightened around him. "But I have to be there for him. I don't want him to have to rely on her. So you think of a good enough plan to make sure that he doesn't."

"I'll do my best." His voice was unsteady. "Go to sleep, Kate."

She was too frightened to sleep, too terrified of the act to which she had committed herself. She needed to be closer to him. She lifted herself on one elbow and bent down and kissed him. "Not yet . . ."

Sixteen

A note was propped on the bedside table when Kate woke.

Don't panic. I'm not trying to shut you out. I've just gone to do a little reconnoitering. Be back tonight.
Seth

What reconnoitering? He had denied trying to shut her out, but he'd told her nothing about what he was planning to do.

Was that because she hadn't asked him? She should have asked him. He had realized her reluctance and would not willingly involve her.

Well, she would ask him tonight. She didn't want to think about it right now. She would much rather try to come up with a way to get RU2 back on track. There must be a solution. Something was nagging at her, nibbling at the edge of her consciousness, just out of reach.

She swung her feet to the floor and headed for the shower. She would spend the day with Joshua and Phyliss. Maybe they would go swimming in the indoor pool. Whenever a problem stumped her, she usually tried to get completely away from it and clear her mind. It was amazing what the subconscious would do if you let it alone.

"Why are you here, Drakin?" Marco Giandello leaned back in his executive chair. "I don't believe we have business."

"I was under the impression we did. Your son offered me a deal and your participation was an integral part of it."

"You deal with my son. This is his game."

"I've no desire to close him out. I just want assurances before I commit myself that you'll be on board."

Giandello smiled. "I don't believe in all this DNA stuff, but my boy thinks it's worth a shot. It's a good thing for a son to try to make his own way in the world. I don't mind lending him a hand."

"I'm relieved. The situation is too volatile. I needed a little insurance." He paused. "Your son *is* being careful with Ogden, isn't he?"

"What? I guess so. Why?"

"Nothing. I just heard Ogden has a violent temper. He's not going to be pleased when he finds out your son has been dealing behind his back. He has a lot to lose."

Giandello stiffened. "My boy knows how to take care of himself."

Seth held up his hands. "No offense. I just don't want anything to interfere with the deal. This whole RU2 mess has been a major pain in the ass for me. All I want to do is go back to South America with a potload of money and live like a king." He grinned as he rose to his feet.

"And let you and Blount take care of all the headaches for me. I feel much better now. I hope you won't mention this visit to Blount. He might resent me running to Papa. It implies a lack of trust."

"I don't keep secrets from my son."

Seth shrugged. "Well, whatever you say. Goodbye, Mr. Giandello. Thank you for seeing me."

Giandello waited until the door closed before he picked up the phone and called his son.

"What the hell do you mean bothering my father?" Blount said when Seth called him from the plane on the way back to Washington. His voice was shrill and without its usual smoothness. "This is between you and me, Drakin."

"Easy. I'm a careful man. I had to make sure that you were telling me the truth. As you said, without protection the well could run dry. But your father reassured me. I'm ready to commit."

A silence. "I never doubted you would. I knew you were a man who knew which side his bread was buttered on." The smoothness was back and with it extreme satisfaction. "I just wish you'd trusted my word. We need to meet and discuss this."

"My thought exactly. How about three this afternoon at the Washington Monument?"

"Too public."

"Better than a restaurant or hotel. There are paid informers all over Washington. Nothing but tourists at the Monument."

"Very well." He chuckled. "It doesn't really matter if we're seen together anyway, now that the deal's struck. The Washington Monument at three."

"The Washington Monument at three."
"Who is this?" Ogden demanded.
"Just be there."
"I don't pay attention to anonymous calls."
"You will if you want to catch Judas in the act."
"Judas?"
Seth hung up the phone and leaned back in the seat. Not a bad few hours. He had set the top in motion. Now all he had to do was keep it spinning.

Kate supposed she should get out of the water. Joshua would stay in the water as long as she did, and they had already been here in the pool for over two hours. Not that he looked tired. It was as if he'd never been ill. But appearances could be deceiving and there was no sense taking risks.

"One more lap." She splashed water in his face. "Race you."

She beat him.

"You cheated. I wasn't ready."

"I'll take a win any way I can get it." She pulled herself onto the ledge and gave him a hand up. "I'm tired of you beating me."

"Well, maybe it's because you weigh more. You have more to pull through the water."

"Thanks." She threw a towel at him. "Just for

that you can run around the other side of the pool and get Phyliss and Mr. Rimilon. It's time for lunch."

"Okay." He jumped to his feet.

"And bring my robe," she called after him.

She watched him streak away from her. Not even a sign of weakness. He looked as healthy as before his illness, thank God. She had been scared to death that night. . . .

Well, that was part of the territory if you cared about someone. She pulled off her cap and stood up as Phyliss, Rimilon, and Joshua approached. "Ready for lunch?"

"Why not?" Phyliss tossed Kate her robe. "You should need a mega-bunch of calories the way you were tearing through the water all morning. Thinking?"

Phyliss knew her so well. "For all the good it did me. I was hoping that —" She stopped. Could it be? It was too wild an idea. But what if —

She strode toward the door. "I'll meet you upstairs. I have to make a call."

"Who?" Phyliss called.

"Lynski."

"This wasn't a good idea." Blount frowned as he watched schoolchildren pour out of a bus. "How are we going to talk with all these brats tearing around?"

"We'll walk by the pond. You can't say anyone's paying any attention to us. Besides, you said it didn't matter."

Blount's expression lightened. "It doesn't. I guess I'm used to worrying about Ogden. No more." He fell into step with Seth. "You'll have to file RU2 somewhere in Europe. We'll have to have drug approval or we won't be able to open the clinic."

"I already have plane reservations." He cast a casual glance at the black limousine coasting slowly by them. Ogden?

"What about Kate Denby? Her name is on the patent."

"I can prove that Smith did the majority of the work."

"That's what I thought."

"But it would be better if we can come to some kind of agreement with her." He looked out at the pond. "And unless you want to have a court battle with her heirs, you'd better keep Ishmaru away from her until we can work a deal."

"I told you Ishmaru was no problem." He smiled. "And Denby may not be a problem either if Ishmaru finds what he's looking for. It seems the good doctor hasn't been nearly as good as she should have been."

Seth tried to keep his expression impassive. "That's hard to believe. She's a bloody Jonas Salk. She wouldn't let up on me until she and Migellin roped me in." He kept the next question carefully casual. "What's she supposed to have done?"

"Try murder." Blount nodded as he saw his expression. "I was surprised too."

"That cop in Dandridge? That was a pretty lame effort on your part. They dropped the case."

"No, this took place years ago. But that recent warrant against her will look nasty in court."

"Another court case. That's no solution to the problem."

"I don't care about her," he said impatiently. "What about RU2? I'll want my lawyers to draw up an agreement before you leave for Europe."

"I prefer my own lawyers."

"I admit I expected that to —"

"You sniveling little prick." Raymond Ogden spun Blount around to face him. His fist crashed into Blount's lips. "You damn slimy bastard."

Blount fell to his knees.

Ogden kicked him in the stomach. His face was livid with rage. "Pack up and get out of my house. You're through." He kicked him again. "And don't think you're going to get away with anything. I'll stop you. You don't have the gumption to make it in the big leagues, you prick."

"Oh dear, he was annoyed, wasn't he?" Seth murmured as he watched Ogden stalk back to his limousine.

"Bastard." Blount wheezed, trying to get his breath. "How the hell did he know I was —"

"Oh, I told him." Seth helped him to his feet. "It seemed the thing to do."

Blount's eyes widened. "You told him? You set me up?"

"Well, we did have to meet and I thought I'd kill two birds with one stone."

"You wanted him to beat me up?"

"I wanted to see you cut your ties with him. Irrevocably. I think this is irrevocable, don't you?"

"I think I'm going to break your neck," he said through his teeth.

"Understandable." He looked beyond Blount. "But this little contretemps seems to have attracted a crowd. You should really wait until there aren't any witnesses."

Blount took out his handkerchief and dabbed at his lip. "I told you I didn't care if he saw us together. I was going to do it in my own time."

"I'm afraid I'm not very trusting. You're crossing Ogden. Who's to say you won't change your mind and cross me? No, I had to make sure before I committed myself." He beamed. "But now all the impediments are out of the way."

"I'm going to remember this."

"I'm sure you will, but the deal is too sweet for you to scrap because of a few bruises." He brushed a speck of dust from Blount's jacket. "You'll need a place to stay. I'll get you a suite at my hotel for the next few days until we leave for Amsterdam. I'll even come to Ogden's place in a few hours and help you with your luggage."

"I don't need —" Then Blount smiled maliciously. "Yes, by all means come and pick me up. Ogden's supposed to be home this evening. Maybe he'll decide you need a few bruises too."

"You'd wish that on me?" He made a clucking

sound. "And I thought we were getting along so well."

"Shut up, damn you," Blount snarled. He strode past him toward the street.

Seth followed more leisurely. The top was spinning merrily. Just a few more turns . . .

"Well, you look satisfied," Phyliss said as she came into Kate's suite. "What brought this on?"

"I'm not satisfied. I'm excited." Kate hung up the phone. "I played a hunch and I'm not sure if it's going to pay off."

"Are you going to share it?"

Kate shook her head and held up crossed fingers. "Not yet. I'm afraid I'll jinx it. Where's Joshua?"

"Changing." She turned to the door. "And that's what I've got to do. Where will we eat lunch?"

"Here." She moved toward the bathroom. "I'll shower and change. You and Joshua order for all of us. Just a sandwich for me."

"You need more than a sandwich after that workout."

Before she closed the door, she called, "Okay, a salad."

The waiter came with the food as she finished blow-drying her hair. She quickly put on slacks, tailored shirt, and sandals.

"Kate."

"Coming." She breezed into the sitting room,

brushed a kiss on Joshua's forehead, and sat down in the chair across from him. "What did you order?"

"Chili dog."

She flinched. "All this healthy food on the menu and you ordered a chili dog?"

He grinned. "You said I should order what I wanted. Besides, chili dogs are healthy. The meat's protein and the onions are vegetables and —"

"Okay, okay."

"You gave in too easy. You feeling all right?"

"Great." She did feel great. She had the first scrap of hope since Migellin's death. Hope was an amazing upper. "But Phyliss may not feel so great if you have a bellyache later."

"I can handle it," Phyliss said. "I'm having a chili dog too."

Kate gave a mock groan. "I'm surrounded by —"

The phone rang.

Seth?

"I'll get it." She jumped up and reached for the phone on the table.

"Do you know where I am, Emily?"

Her heart stopped and then started double time.

"You're not answering. Do you know who this is?"

"Ishmaru."

"I knew you wouldn't forget me. Just as I can't forget you. Particularly where I am now. It's so pretty here. All these trees and shrubs and wood-land paths. I had a vision about you and a forest. I have many visions, you know. All true warriors do."

Her hand tightened on the receiver. "What do you want?"

"I want you to come to me."

"Screw you."

"You mustn't refuse me out of hand. I've just spent a few interesting days in the records office. The facts were very cleverly hidden, but I dug them out. I know everything. You've been a naughty girl, Kate."

"I don't know what you're talking about."

"Because you haven't asked me where I am. I'll tell you anyway. Pinebridge."

He hung up the phone.

She closed her eyes as waves of terror washed through her.

"Mom?" Joshua was beside her, his eyes wide with fear.

Her arm automatically slid around him. "It's okay. It's okay, Joshua."

"It's not okay. You said Ishmaru."

"It will be okay. It will be fine." She turned to Phyliss. "I've got to go." She grabbed up her purse. Was the gun in it? Yes, Seth always made sure she went nowhere without it.

"Where are you going?" Phyliss called as she ran toward the door.

She couldn't tell her. She had promised.

No one must ever know.

But Ishmaru knew now.

Dear God, he *knew*.

"Take care of Joshua, Phyliss."

The door slammed behind her.

Disaster.

Seth knew the moment he walked into the hotel room.

Joshua was sitting on the sofa, stiff as a poker, and Phyliss looked almost as shell-shocked.

Kate.

"Where's Kate?"

"Gone," Phyliss said. "Why weren't you here? Where the hell were you?"

"I had something to do. Are you going to tell me where she is or yell at me?"

"Ishmaru," Joshua whispered.

His heart lurched. "What happened?"

"She got a phone call and ran out of here."

"How long ago?"

"Two hours maybe."

"You're sure it was Ishmaru?"

"She said the name and I saw her face. It was Ishmaru."

"Where did she go?"

"She wouldn't tell me. She just said to take care of Joshua."

"What are you going to do?" Joshua asked accusingly. "You promised you'd take care of her."

"I will take care of her." He crossed the room and grasped Joshua's shoulders. "Listen to me, Joshua. I won't let anything happen to her. I'll find her and bring her back to you."

"You don't even know where she is."

"I'll find out. Trust me. It will be okay."

"That's what she said. But she was scared. I could tell she was scared."

Seth was scared too. Jesus, he had never been this scared before. "I mean it. I'll bring her back."

Joshua just looked at him. Seth couldn't blame him. It was hard to comfort someone when you needed comfort yourself. He released Joshua's shoulders and walked out of the room.

Rimilon was outside in the hall.

"Where the hell have you been?"

"I saw you get off the elevator and went downstairs to see if I could find out anything from the doorman. She ran right by me. It's not my fault. I tried to stop her. You told me that my job was to take care of the other two."

"What did you find out from the doorman?"

"She took a cab but he didn't hear the destination."

Shit. He strode past Rimilon toward the elevators.

Okay. Be cool. Think.

Why the hell hadn't she waited for him?

Kate.

Dammit, close out the emotion or he wouldn't be able to help her.

But first he had to find her.

He could find her. He had only to find Ishmaru.

And Blount knew where Ishmaru could be found. He had time. Blount had mentioned Ishmaru had hopped a plane after Migellin's death.

Unless he had changed his mind and come back to Washington.

He didn't even want to think of that possibility. He had to assume he had time, that Kate was flying somewhere to meet Ishmaru.

So it was only necessary to add a new equation to the mix. Keep the top spinning and make sure that he found out where Kate was meeting Ishmaru before it stopped.

The cut on his lip stung like hell.

Blount scowled at his reflection in the mirror. The lip was swollen too. Damn Ogden to hell.

And damn Seth Drakin too. He was a marked man. Just as soon as the clinic was up and running, the bastard would die. He'd let his father handle it. It was fitting. Like to like. Scum to scum.

He scraped his aftershave, deodorant, and toothbrush off the vanity into his overnight kit. Except for the open bag on the bed, his luggage was packed and ready. He'd call a taxi and then he'd be out of here. He wasn't about to sit around and wait for Drakin. Though it was a shame he wouldn't have the chance to push the prick into Ogden's path.

Ogden was probably stinko by now. He'd seen the servant carrying a fresh bottle of vodka into the library when he'd crept down to the office to retrieve his belongings. He'd also taken the opportunity to pluck a few files that would prove troublesome to Ogden too. Nothing too incriminating; he kept those in his private safe. But the newspapers would be glad to hear about that land deal for the plant in India. It would be —

"Am I late, Blount?"

He stiffened, then turned to see Drakin standing in the bathroom doorway. "How did you get up here?"

"Not through the front door. I thought it might prove awkward. I climbed the tree outside the window and jumped onto the balcony."

"You went to a lot of trouble."

Drakin smiled. "Not so much. Did that dossier you have on me mention that I was a cat burglar at one time?"

"No." He looked like a cat burglar now in that black sweater, jeans, and sneakers, Blount thought.

"Then of course it isn't true. Because you know everything about me. Right, Blount?"

"I know enough." He pushed past him into the bedroom. "And I have no intention of sneaking out through a window. We're going downstairs and out the front door. Grab that suitcase."

"Not yet." He leaned against the doorjamb. "You'll have to rein in your impatience. Because you know something else that's very important to me. Where's Ishmaru, Blount?"

"I don't have time for this."

"You have all the time in the world. I want to know where Ishmaru is. Is he here in Washington?"

429

"I told you he wasn't."

"Kate Denby got a call from him. He might have come back."

"I don't think so. What difference does it make? Let Ishmaru kill her. She's more trouble alive than dead. We can handle the inheritance problems."

"Let Ishmaru kill her," Seth repeated softly. "Is that what you said?"

Blount stiffened warily. Something was wrong. Something was very wrong about the way Drakin was staring at him. . . .

"Is that what you said about Noah and Migellin?"

"Get out of here, Drakin. Jump out the window or walk out the front door. I don't care." He moved toward the open suitcase on the bed. "I'm not going to stand here and let —"

Drakin's arm had encircled his throat from behind. "Where's Ishmaru?"

He couldn't breathe. He tore futilely at Drakin's arm. His hand touched rubber — no, latex. Drakin was wearing latex gloves like a fucking doctor.

"Ishmaru?" Drakin said.

"He's working at a hospital — Pinebridge."

"Where?"

"Near . . . Dandridge."

"Good." He released him and stepped back. "That's all I needed to know."

Rage seared through Blount. "You bastard." He lunged toward Seth.

Drakin wasn't there. He had whirled aside and when he faced Blount again he had something in his hand. The brass Chinese foo dog statue from the table.

"Come on." He motioned for Blount to come at him again. "One more time. Just once and it will be over."

A sudden chill banished Blount's anger. The prick wanted to kill him, he realized in astonishment. He didn't move. He had no intention of rushing Drakin again. His gun was in the open bag on the bed. When he moved, it had to be for the gun. He forced a smile. "What's this all about? I know I lost my temper, but that's no reason for us to do anything rash. The deal is what's important."

"Is it?"

"Okay, I told you where Ishmaru is. Now we can take up where we —" He leaped for the suitcase on the bed and grabbed the gun. He raised it as he turned toward Drakin.

He had no chance to use it.

Drakin swung the statue with precision and hit the exact spot on the left temple, killing Blount instantly.

Done.

Seth got a towel from the bathroom and wiped the statue. He had worn gloves, so none of his fingerprints were on it, but it would look as if the statue had been wiped clean by someone not wearing gloves. Someone who had picked up the statue on impulse and struck Blount.

He dropped the statue beside the body.

He quickly rifled through Blount's suitcase.

Ogden's files. He'd thought Blount wouldn't be able to resist a little revenge after the way Ogden had beaten and humiliated him. Blount's body would be discovered and Ogden would go through the suitcase before the police were notified. He took the files and slid them under the mattress. Then he opened the door to the hall and left it ajar.

Anything else?

He surveyed the room. No, nothing else. Time to get out. Actually past time. He had to get to Kate. He moved across the room toward the balcony.

Let Ishmaru kill her.

The hell he would.

Pinebridge

It was after midnight when Kate parked the rental car in the parking lot and got out.

It looked the same, Kate thought as she walked up the long driveway toward the hospital. The lights shone soft and welcoming and the lawns were green and tidy.

No, it wasn't the same. It would never be the same. Ishmaru was here.

She had half expected him to appear ever since she had gotten out of her car.

She pushed open the door. The lobby was deserted at this hour of the night.

Where are you? You called me. Now where are you?

"He's not here. I've already checked at Administration."

She stiffened in shock as she saw Seth get up from the chair by a potted fern. "What are you doing here?"

"Having a nervous breakdown," he said grimly. "I didn't even know if you'd come here first. I thought he might have told you to meet him somewhere else."

"Go away, Seth. I don't want you here."

He ignored her. "I described him and the clerk said they'd hired the man as an orderly. He's going by the name of Sanchez. He was on duty this afternoon but he's off this evening."

"Go away, Seth."

"No." He took a step closer to her, his voice low and intense. "Dammit, you don't have to hide anything from me. What do I care if you killed someone? I *know* you. They must have deserved it."

"How did you —" None of that was important now. She couldn't stand here arguing. She had to find Ishmaru. She strode past Seth to the elevators and punched the button.

Seth followed her into the elevator. "For God's sake, let me help you, Kate."

"I can't. He told me to come alone." She pressed the button for the fourth floor. "This is my business. Let me do it."

"Where are you going? He's not in the hospital. His quarters are in the bungalow at the rear of the building."

She didn't answer. The doors swung open and she strode quickly to the nurses' station.

The nurse on duty was dark and plump. Kate didn't recognize her.

She smiled pleasantly. "I'm sorry, it's far too late for visitors."

"I'm Dr. Denby. Is Charlene Hauk on duty?"

"Charlene's working the day shift. She's on at six A.M." She glanced at the clock. "She's probably sleeping."

"Get her out of bed. Tell her Kate is here." She moved quickly down the corridor. "Right away."

Seth fell into step with her. "Where the hell are we going?"

"I think I know where Ishmaru is." She turned left and stopped in front of 403. She drew a deep breath. "Stay here."

She pushed open the door. The room was dark. "Ishmaru? It's Kate Denby."

No answer.

Seth pushed her aside and faded to the left of the door. The next minute the room was illuminated. It was empty except for the figure huddled under the covers on the bed.

It was too good to be true.

She strode into the room and pulled back the sheet.

No one was in the bed. Only blankets rolled

434

to resemble a figure.

Agony wrenched through her as she stumbled away from the bed.

Seth's hands were on her shoulders, comforting, supporting. "Who was supposed to be here, Kate?"

"Daddy." Tears were running down her cheeks. "Daddy."

Her legs wouldn't hold her. She dropped down in the wheelchair by the bed. "Daddy."

Seth dropped to his knees in front of her. "Talk to me. Tell me what's happening. I can't help if you don't talk to me."

"You can't help," she said dully. "No one can help. Ishmaru has him. He took him away."

"Kate." She looked up to see Charlene in the doorway. Her hair was mussed and she was wearing a sweater over her robe. "What are you doing here?" Her gaze went to the bed. "Christ, where's Robert?"

"When did you see him last?"

"I went off duty at three but I came back at six and gave him his supper. We have a new LPN and I didn't trust her to make sure he ate. But he's still got to be on this floor. Everyone knows Robert. He couldn't just wander around the hospital. But I'll call Security right away."

"No."

"We've got to find him, Kate. You know how fragile he's been lately."

"I'll find him." She forced herself to rise to her

feet. "Go back to bed, Charlene. I'll bring him back."

"Don't be silly. I can't go to bed. I love Robert. We all do, Kate."

Seth's gaze was searching the room, skipping over the soft peach walls adorned with several framed pictures obviously drawn by a child, the colorful crocheted cover on the bed, and came to rest on the Tiffany lamp on the bedside table. An envelope was propped against the base of the lamp. He picked it up and handed it to Kate.

Emily

Ishmaru was the only one who called her Emily. She tore open the envelope.

We're in the woods in back of the hospital. At least, I am. I don't know if he'll survive a night in the open. He seems weak. Not like you. Come to me. Find me.

Seth took the note from her hand and scanned it. "Bingo." He turned toward the door.

"No." Kate was there ahead of him. "He wants me. If he sees you, he might kill him. I'm the one who has to go."

"Bullshit. I'm not letting you go alone."

"What on earth is happening, Kate?" Charlene asked as they went past her.

"Don't do anything," Kate called back to her. "Do you hear? Nothing."

"Well, are you going to tell me about your father?" Seth asked quietly as the doors of the elevator closed.

Talk. It didn't matter now. Maybe it would

436

help to keep her from flying apart. "He has advanced Alzheimer's."

"Christ."

"He's helpless." She had to stop to steady her voice. "He's like a baby. He couldn't defend himself from a cockroach much less Ishmaru."

"You told me he was dead."

"That's the way he wanted it. He'd treated hundreds of Alzheimer's patients. He knew what was in store for him." She moistened her lips. "You have to understand. My father was a very special man. He was warm and kind and had a deep sense of personal dignity. He had thousands of friends. Everyone loved and respected him. He always told me that Alzheimer's was probably harder on the family than it was for the victim. He couldn't stand the thought of what it would do to all of us. He didn't want Joshua to see him deteriorate. He didn't want anyone to know. He wanted them to remember him as he was."

"So you faked his death."

"I didn't have any choice. He didn't even tell me he was sick until he disappeared one day. Pinebridge was his practicing hospital and he was on his way home and he suddenly didn't know where he was going. He pulled over to the side of the road. I found him still in the car two days later. He checked himself into another hospital the next week. His chart said he was suffering from cancer. It was a setup. When I got to the hospital, he told me what I had to do. He'd made his plans. He'd even talked to the administrator

437

here at Pinebridge and arranged for care."

"And they agreed?"

"They loved him. They even made sure most of the staff who took care of him were people he hadn't worked with and wouldn't recognize him. Later . . . he was so changed that no one would — You'd have to have known him. He's like a shell now, and before he was so bright and quick that —"

The doors of the elevator opened and Seth started for the front entrance.

Kate stopped him. "No, there's a back entrance that faces the woods."

"You know this place well."

"I should." She led him toward the rear entrance. "Even when I couldn't talk to him anymore, I still came every week to consult with the doctors or just watch him."

"I can't see you going along with all this."

"Neither did my father. So he used pressure. He didn't believe in suicide, but he could have changed his mind. I didn't want to take that chance." She swallowed. "He made me promise to fake the death and then go away and forget him."

Seth shook his head. "And he believed you?"

"Maybe. I don't know. I did almost everything he wanted. I faked the death and I set up the money I inherited as a care fund for him. I didn't tell anyone."

"But you couldn't leave him alone here."

"Don't you understand? I *loved* him. I couldn't

do it. For the first year I visited him every week. He got worse the second year. He didn't know me, but he knew there was some reason he should be upset at seeing me." She blinked back tears. It still hurt. God, it hurt. "He cried. I cut the visits down to once a month."

Seth's hand closed on her arm.

"The first year he started to write a book. He was excited, he felt productive. The second year he couldn't even read what he'd written. Do you know what that did to him? What it did to me?"

"I can imagine."

"No, you can't. No one can who hasn't been there."

"How did you keep the visits from Phyliss?"

"I lied. I got very good at lying."

"Jesus, how did you take it? Without anyone to talk to."

"I promised him no one would ever know. I promised him. . . ."

She stood on the top step and stared out at the woods. A level meadow extended from the building to the edge of the forest. That forest had always looked green and peaceful and inviting. But not now. Ishmaru was there.

"Let me go after him, Kate."

"I can't. Ishmaru will kill him. Stay here."

"Dammit, I can't stay here."

"You will," she said fiercely. "If you don't, I'll never forgive you."

"You won't have the option if he kills you. Trust me. I can do this."

She shook her head.

"I'm coming. It's your choice whether I barge in with you or we have a plan."

He was determined, she could see with frustration. He would do what he said, and she couldn't afford to have Ishmaru see her with anyone.

"Good. Give me ten minutes before you go in." He gazed out at the meadow. "The lights from the hospital make that approach too visible from the woods. I'll go into them a mile north and try to locate your father."

"How?"

He smiled crookedly. "I have a great nose, remember? Patients in hospitals have a strong antiseptic smell. His room reeked of it. It should stick out like a flare."

"Ishmaru will be with my father."

"Then I'll take him by surprise, before he can hurt anyone."

She gazed back at the woods. "Ten minutes."

He was gone.

She watched him run around the corner of the building. She started down the steps. She had gotten rid of him and it didn't matter that she had lied. Not if it meant he would live. Ishmaru could kill him in ten minutes. She would not let that happen.

No more deaths, Ishmaru.

It has to end.

But how? The moment she entered the woods, he would be in control and she would be just another victim. She had to discover a way to shake him, dominate him.

Dominate *him?* When he'd been dominating her life since Michael's death?

He'd terrified her so much she hadn't been able to function. She was terrified now.

Get rid of the fear.

Find a solution.

Think.

Remember.

Suddenly the answer came to her; sure, swift, clear.

Of course.

Simple.

Seventeen

It was Emily.

Her golden hair shone in the moonlight as she walked across the meadow toward him.

Come, Emily, let me send you back to the dark land.

Let me have my reward.

Just a few yards more and into the trees.

He was here.

She could sense him ahead of her in the darkness. Her hand tightened on the gun in her hand. She entered the woods. The leafy darkness enfolded her. "Ishmaru."

No answer.

She went a little farther until she came to a small glade. She stopped, her gaze searching the trees ringing the open area.

"Ishmaru."

No answer.

"You wanted me here. Now stop hiding from me."

"Put down the gun. It's not a fitting weapon."

"Where's Kate's father?"

"Kate's father?" There was a silence. "At last you admit you're Emily?"

"Of course, you always knew it. Where is he?"

"Why do you care, Emily?"

442

"Kate and I are joined." The words came with surprising ease. "I have to care about what she cares about. I have to protect what she needs protected."

"Unfortunate. Such a delicate man. One twist of my hand and I could break his neck. Put down the weapon."

Was he standing in the darkness with his hand around her father's neck? She couldn't take the chance. She laid the gun down on the ground.

"That's right. Neither of us can claim coup with those clumsy guns."

Her gaze strained to pierce the veil of trees. "Where's Kate's father?"

"I set him free."

Her heart lurched. Dead? Did he mean he was dead?

"He was in the way."

She whirled as she saw a flicker of movement to her left.

"You have a good eye." His voice came from her right. "Yes, I was there. I move quickly, don't I? I've trained myself to run like the wind, and I'm stronger than I was when we fought before, Emily. But you might have brought some shaman gifts when you came back."

It was a good opening. Make him uncertain. Take control. "I brought many gifts back. Why do you think you weren't able to kill Kate's son?"

"It was my choice. I wanted to see her suffer, see you suffer."

"You may have thought the choice was yours,

but it was mine. Since the first time you saw Kate, every thought you've had, every act you've taken has been guided by me."

"Liar."

"Why should I lie? Spirits have no need of lies."

"Because I have more power," he said harshly. "You fear me."

"Did I fear you before? Did I fear you the night you killed me?"

"No, you fought like the bitch you are." He paused. "You *cut* me."

"I wasn't strong enough to kill you then, but I am now. I've been waiting a long time to take you with me to the dark land. Do you know who will meet you there?"

"I don't want to hear this."

She could hear the fear in his voice. "The guardians."

He took a long breath. "Ah, you're very clever. But you can't make me afraid. I've been waiting too long for this. It should be a remarkable encounter."

"With me in the open and you skulking like a coward in the trees." Was there a darker shadow beside that pine?

"No, I suppose it is time. I'm coming out."

"Wait." She had no weapons and he was stronger. He would have the advantage and she would be helpless. "That's not how a warrior would do it. They'd stalk and pursue. Or do you think I'd get away from you?"

"I think you want to try."

Why had she made the suggestion? Run in these woods? She could barely see two feet in front of her. But neither could Ishmaru. "Won't that make it more enjoyable for you?"

A silence. "Yes, I didn't get to track you before. It's such an exquisite pleasure. Yes, run and let me catch you."

She went still as another thought occurred to her. Hope surged through her. Maybe . . .

"Do I get a head start?"

"I hear the eagerness in your voice. You're glad the waiting is over, aren't you?"

"Do I get a head start?" she repeated.

"I'll count to ten."

She ran forward and then turned left.

No paths.

Look for a landmark.

All the trees looked alike when you were streaking past them, she thought in despair.

No, that gnarled willow was different.

The willow.

And there was a moss-covered rock to the left.

"You're making too much noise. You're making it simple for me," Ishmaru called from behind her. "But you're fast, very fast. And you run easily, like a warrior."

Her heart was beating too hard. She had to keep her breath under control. Pretend this was just another morning run.

Yeah, sure.

Her feet were suddenly wet. Water splashed on her jeans. She was running across a brook.

Another landmark.

"But I'm faster. I'm getting closer. Can you tell?"

Of course she could tell. He sounded as if he were right behind her.

"The little girl was fast. The one who told me you were Emily. I remember how her yellow hair flew behind her. It took me almost five minutes to catch her."

What little girl? Kate wondered wildly.

"But there never was any doubt. She was the sign. Are you getting tired?"

She was getting tired and his voice sounded as strong and even as when they had started.

And he was closer, much closer.

He would be on her any minute.

Please, I have to run faster. Help me . . .

She *was* running faster, her breath was easier. She felt suddenly stronger.

Adrenaline? She didn't know or care. She'd take it.

She pulled ahead of him, one yard, two yards.

She ran on, leaping over logs and shrubs in her path. Her vision was clearer. Her eyes must have adjusted to the darkness.

He was still close but he was panting, she realized with savage pleasure.

"Better hurry," she taunted over her shoulder. "And don't look behind you. You don't think the guardians would let me fight you alone?"

He made a groaning sound deep in his throat.

But using fear as a goad may have been a mistake. His pace increased. He was close behind her again. Too close.

She'd be damned if she'd let him pounce on her as if she were a frightened rabbit.

That branch by the path.

She stopped, scooped it up and swung it at him as he caught up with her.

He grunted with pain even as he grabbed the branch. "Good. I didn't expect that." He jerked the branch away from her. "You've drawn blood. My turn."

His hands closed on her throat.

She kneed him in the groin.

"Ugh." His hands loosened and she was off again. She darted to the right of the path and then several yards later she crossed the path and started back the way she had come.

He was behind her again.

Run faster. Can't stop. Not now.

She crossed the brook.

She heard him splashing behind her an instant later.

Keep going. Keep going.

The moss-covered rock.

He was muttering something under his breath.

The gnarled willow tree.

Now she had to go faster. It was time for the sprint.

"*No,*" Ishmaru called as he realized her destination. "No, you mustn't do it."

The hell she wouldn't. She was in the clearing.

She dove for the pistol she had laid on the

ground. She rolled over.

He was standing right above her.

She pulled the trigger.

She saw him flinch but he still stood.

She pulled the trigger again, and again and again.

Why didn't he fall?

He was looking at her almost sorrowfully. "Not right." A thin stream of blood trickled from his mouth. "This . . . is . . . not coup."

She shot him again.

He fell to the ground. She rose to her knees and looked down at him.

His eyes were open, staring up at her.

"Not coup . . ." He stiffened, his gaze focusing on something beyond her right shoulder. "No, I don't want — Don't take —"

He whimpered, terror contorting his features. *"Emily."*

Kate felt the hair stand up on her nape. She sat staring straight ahead. She wouldn't turn around and look at what Ishmaru had seen. It couldn't have been Emily. It was his imagination fostered by her own words.

Kate's words or Emily's words?

Ishmaru's eyes were closed now and his muscles lax.

She had to be sure.

She touched the pulse in his throat and then sat back on her heels.

Dead.

Death had always been the enemy for her, but she felt no remorse as she stared at him. She would do it again. If he opened his eyes, she would shoot him as if he were a poisonous snake.

Everything had happened so quickly that it was hard to believe. Ishmaru was dead. The nightmare was over.

No, not really.

Where was her father?

"Kate."

There was a crashing in the underbrush and Seth burst into the clearing. He skidded to a stop and then walked slowly over to where she knelt beside Ishmaru.

"Dead?"

"Yes."

He jerked her to her feet and pulled her into his arms. "Damn you." His voice was unsteady. "Damn you for lying to me. I nearly went crazy when I heard those shots."

She leaned against him. He felt so good. It was okay to lean now, to take from him. "He was waiting for me. I knew it wouldn't be a question of having to hunt him out." She closed her eyes and whispered, "But Daddy wasn't with him. I think he killed him."

Seth shook his head. "I found him wandering around in the forest in circles. I caught the scent right away, but he led me away from here."

Relief surged through her. "Thank God. Where is he?"

"I left him back on the trail when I heard the shots."

"We have to go get him."

"In a minute." His arms tightened around her. "I need this." An instant later he pushed her away and moved back into the shrubbery.

She followed him but he was moving so swiftly that she fell behind.

He was standing in the trail with her father in his arms when she came upon him.

Alarm tore through her. "Is he hurt?"

"It's okay. He's barefoot and his feet are pretty cut up. It's better if he doesn't walk."

"Can you manage?"

"Sure, he doesn't weigh anything."

No, he looked thin and fragile as a child in Seth's arms.

She took a step nearer and laid her hand on his cheek. His eyes were open but he didn't seem to see her. "Daddy?"

He didn't reply.

Familiar pain rushed through her. He hadn't spoken in months. "It's going to be all right, Daddy. You're safe now."

Did he hear her? Did he know what she was saying?

"We'd better get him back to the hospital, Kate," Seth said gently.

She blinked back stinging tears. "Yes, you're right. It's chilly out here."

She turned and walked ahead of him down the path.

They were out of the trees and crossing the meadow toward the hospital when she heard her father's voice.

She glanced eagerly over her shoulder, but he wasn't speaking. He was making a soft, whimpering sound.

"Shh." Seth crooned to him and half rocked him as he walked. "I'm here. It's okay."

Her father seemed to understand. He became still in Seth's arms.

Peace flowed through her. Seth was here. Everything was okay.

"There you are, Robert." Charlene pulled the cover over his newly bandaged feet. "You'll be right as rain in a few days. Better than you deserve for going off with strangers." She turned to Kate. "I called the police like you told me. There's a Detective Eblund waiting at the nurses' station."

"Thanks, Charlene."

"No problem." She left the room.

Seth moved over to the bed beside Kate, his gaze on her father's face. "Will RU2 help him?"

"That's what I hoped when I was working with Noah. But I don't know. I don't think so. Maybe if we'd started treatment earlier, but there's been so much damage done already." She shrugged helplessly. "He's very fragile now and we don't know exactly how RU2 is going to act on certain diseases. We need more tests."

His hand closed comfortingly on her shoulder. "You'll get them in Amsterdam."

451

"God, I hope so." Her hand covered her father's. "We're going to try, Daddy," she whispered. "Do you remember you told me I couldn't nail those leaves back on the trees? Well, we're doing it now and they're going to grow back strong as can be. You'll see. You just have to hang on and get stronger."

"We should go."

She reluctantly released her father's hand and stepped back. "I know." She turned and moved toward the door. "Good-bye, Daddy."

"Does he hear you?" Seth asked as they moved down the corridor toward the nurses' station.

"Sometimes I think he does. Sometimes I think he's just gone away." She swallowed to ease the tightness in her throat. "I hope he has. I hate the idea of him being held prisoner inside himself. I kind of like the idea of him floating around, being the man he used to be."

"Then that's the way you should think of him."

"I talk to him, you know. Is that crazy? If he's not back there, then he must be with me. He loved me. I think he still does."

"Then he has good taste."

She drew a long, shaky breath. "I'm sorry. I'll stop this. Sometimes it gets too much." They were approaching the nurses' station. "There's Alan."

"Are you okay? Do you want me to handle this?"

"Of course not."

He smiled slowly. "I should have known. Do

you mind if I stay while you handle it?"

"No." She reached out and took his hand. "I want you to stay with me. I want that very much."

Alan Eblund turned away from the desk as they approached. "You sure know how to cause a ruckus, Kate."

"Hello, Alan." She kissed his cheek. "Thanks for everything. I heard you went to bat for me."

"It was a frame-up. It would never have gotten to court." He shrugged. "I just punched a few holes in it. But you must have made some pretty powerful people mad."

"RU2."

"Yeah, I've been following you on TV." He glanced at Seth. "Drakin?"

Seth extended his hand.

Alan shook it and turned back to Kate. "Are you sure it was Ishmaru?"

She nodded. "No doubt. How much trouble am I in?"

"If it's Ishmaru, I don't think you'll be held. Self-defense. We've learned a lot about him from a bulletin issued by L.A.P.D. in the past weeks, and his record speaks for itself. But you'll have to come down to the station and make a statement." He shook his head. "But this business with your father . . . insurance fraud and falsifying government records."

"I never touched the insurance money. I don't expect to have a problem there."

"I'll talk to the district attorney about the forged records. It may be okay."

"I couldn't do anything else, Alan."

"You broke the law." He suddenly smiled. "But the D.A. is up for reelection and it's a crime of compassion. I don't think he'll be a hard-ass."

"Will it take long? I have to get back to Joshua. I don't want him to hear about this from the media."

"I wouldn't worry about him minding you blowing Ishmaru away," Seth said. "He'll probably give you a medal."

"He won't give me a medal for lying to him about his grandfather. Everything's going to come out now. I have to tell him first." Lord, it was going to be difficult.

"I'll get you out of there as soon as I can," Alan said. "But no promises, Kate. You stirred up a storm here. There are a covey of reporters in the lobby right now."

"I'll call Phyliss and tell her to hide the morning papers and keep the TV turned off," Seth said. "Go on, Kate. I'll join you as soon as I get through talking to her. Don't worry, I'll take care of everything." He added dryly, "If you'll permit me to handle this little item. I wouldn't want to interfere."

Kate wasn't allowed to leave the station until after dawn. Alan whisked her and Seth out the back of the station and dropped them off at the airport.

"Kate." He stuck his head out the window as

she and Seth were stepping onto the curb. "This RU2 . . ."

She turned back. "What about it?"

"Is it really what you claim?"

She smiled. "You're damned right."

"Then don't give up. Give 'em hell."

"I will."

"Nice guy," Seth murmured as they entered the airport. "For a cop."

"He's nice, period. No qualifications."

"Whatever you say." He stopped her as she started for the ticket counter. "No, not that way. We have to go to the opposite end of the terminal that serves private jets."

"You rented a private jet?"

"How do you think I got here ahead of you?"

"I guess I didn't think at all. I just wanted you to go away."

"You made that clear. I felt most unwant—"

"My God." Kate clutched his arm. "That's Ogden." Her gaze was fastened on the TV screen in the passenger lounge. Ogden was stepping out of a police car onto the curb. "What's happening?" She broke away from Seth and walked closer to the screen so she could hear the voice-over.

"No charges have yet been filed against Ogden. His lawyers insist that the pharmaceutical tycoon is totally innocent and was only brought in for questioning in the murder of William Blount. Mr. Ogden himself has no comment." The screen switched to a commercial.

"Blount is dead." She turned to stare accusingly at Seth. "Reconnoitering?"

"Well, sometimes one thing leads to another." He took her arm and led her away from the screen. "It might have ended with reconnoitering."

"But it didn't."

He didn't answer.

"And Ogden is being held for his murder."

"I don't think they'll hold him. There's not enough evidence. Only enough to make it interesting."

"Interesting?"

He smiled. "Like I said, sometimes one thing leads to another."

"You look like hell," Phyliss said when they entered the hotel suite. "Go into my bedroom and brush your hair and put on a little rouge. You don't want to scare Joshua. He's going to be upset enough."

"Where is he?"

"In his room reading."

"He hasn't found out anything?"

"No, but he's not dumb. When I wouldn't let him watch TV, I had to swear on a stack of Bibles that you and Seth weren't dead or in a hospital."

"Thanks, Phyliss." She glanced at Seth. "I want to talk to him alone."

He nodded and turned to Phyliss. "What do I have to do to get you to go down to the lobby

456

with me for a spot of lunch?"

"Take a shower and use a little deodorant."

He flinched. "Stabbed to the heart again. Why do I put up with you?"

Kate scarcely heard them as she moved toward Joshua's room. She was almost as nervous as that moment when she'd walked across the meadow toward Ishmaru.

Understand, Joshua.

I didn't want to do it.

Just try to understand.

"You lied to me." Joshua stared stonily at the wall over her shoulder. "You told me you never lied to me. You told me it was wrong."

Kate flinched. "It is wrong. What I did was wrong. There's no excuse for it. I didn't see any other way."

"And Grandpa lied to me by making you lie."

"He didn't want you hurt, Joshua. It's a terrible disease."

"He shouldn't have done it," he said fiercely. "I wouldn't have stopped loving him. You didn't."

Why wouldn't he look at her? "No, I didn't. But it's been hard for me."

"Then you should have let me help. It's better when there's two. I could have helped."

"I promised him, Joshua."

"You should have told me. You should have let me help."

"All right, I was wrong. He was wrong. Will you forgive us?"

He was silent.

"Joshua?"

At last his gaze shifted to her face. "I want to see him."

"No, Joshua. He's not the same. I told you how he is now."

"I want to see him. Will you take me?"

She stared at him in frustration. She wasn't sure if it would be better to let him face what his grandfather had become or allow his imagination to create an even more horrifying scenario. Either would be traumatic for a boy of his sensitivity.

She abruptly stood up and moved toward the door. "Get ready. I'll tell Seth."

They arrived in Dandridge the next day and were at the hospital by midafternoon.

Kate stopped outside the door of her father's room. "Do you mind if I go in with you, Joshua?"

He shook his head. "I told you, it's always better if there's two." He hesitated, his gaze on Seth.

"Right." Seth smiled down at him. "I'll wait out here in the hall."

Joshua nodded jerkily. "It's just that you don't know my grandpa."

"No offense taken."

Kate gave Joshua a worried glance as she opened the door. He was pale and he'd been silent most of the journey. God, she hoped she was doing the right thing.

Her father was lying on his side facing the window. Did he see anything? If he did, did he know what he was seeing?

She gently nudged Joshua toward the bed. "I've brought Joshua, Daddy. He wanted very much to see you."

No response.

Joshua walked slowly across the room until he stood next to the bed. He set his Braves duffel on the floor.

"Joshua's my son, Daddy. Remember?"

No response.

"He doesn't have to talk," Joshua said. "Sometimes I don't feel like talking either, Grandpa." He stood looking down at him. "You shouldn't have done it. It doesn't make any difference. I could have come with Mom and we could have gone for walks and stuff. I could have told you all kinds of things. And you wouldn't have had to talk. I could have told you about my baseball team and school and the movies I saw." He paused. "And Dad. He died, you know. You wouldn't have had to do anything."

No response.

"Maybe I can still do some of that. Mom says that RU2 could help." He stopped and blinked rapidly. "But even if it doesn't, I want you to know I'll be thinking about you and maybe that way I can be with you."

Help him. Please say something, Daddy.

No response.

Joshua reached down and unzipped his duffel. "I brought you something. I thought maybe you might look at it and think of me sometimes too." He brought out his baseball glove, the glove that always hung on his bedpost at night. He laid it on the bed beside his grandfather. "It's a real good glove. I used it when we won the Little League championship. I played good that day. I wish you could have seen me."

No response.

Kate felt as if she couldn't take much more.

"That's all." Joshua picked up his duffel. "G'bye, Grandpa. I'll be seeing you." He frowned as he looked at Kate. "Stop crying, Mom. It's okay."

"Yeah, I know." She tried to smile. "Want to go now?"

He nodded. "I guess so."

She ushered him toward the door. "Good-bye, Daddy. I hope you —"

"Mom." A brilliant smile was lighting Joshua's face.

She followed his gaze.

Thank you, God.

Her father's hand was resting on Joshua's old baseball glove.

"They let him go." Kate tossed the newspaper down in front of Seth the next morning. "Ogden's free."

"I told you so."

"And you're not worried?"

He shook his head.

"Well, I'm worried."

"Look, the police think he did it, but they don't have enough evidence."

"But the case is still open."

"Probably not for long." He changed the subject. "I picked up the airline tickets. We leave tomorrow at noon for Amsterdam." He paused. "If you're sure that you still want to go. The major threat is over now."

"I want to go. I want to get Joshua away from this madhouse, and I want to start tests on RU2. We've done our best to do things Noah's way. Even if we manage to stop the bill from going through, it may be years before they'd let us do any in-depth tests." She shook her head in frustration. "All that wasted time. It drives me crazy. I want to *do* something."

"What were you talking about to Tony on the phone this morning?"

"I asked him to get me some information." She picked up her handbag. "I'm going out for a few hours."

He glanced up from the paper. "Where?"

She smiled sweetly and opened the door. "Reconnoitering."

"Kate!"

"You do manage to attract publicity, young lady." Senator Longworth beamed at her. "But unfortunately it's the wrong kind. Shooting a man is hardly a way to prove to the public that you're

461

a stable authority on anything. Not that you had a chance before."

"May I sit down?"

"Of course. Forgive my bad manners. I was just surprised to see you. You've come to tell me you're giving up the fight?"

"I've come to tell you that I'm leaving for Amsterdam." She paused. "And that as long as I'm alive, I'll make sure that you're not given one drop of RU2."

His eyes widened. "I beg your pardon?"

"Isn't that one of the perks Ogden promised you? That he'd find a way of getting you RU2 after the battle was won? You've fought so hard, Longworth. Even Migellin commented on it. It wasn't only for money and political prestige."

He laughed. "This is nonsense. You wouldn't catch me within ten feet of an untested drug."

And he was doing his best to make sure RU2 remained untested. Kate smothered her rage. "Not in public."

His eyes narrowed on her face. "What are you trying to say?"

"That you have AIDS, Senator."

He laughed again. "You're really reaching."

"I'm a doctor. The first time I met you I noticed that you didn't seem well. You appeared pale; your hands shook. I chalked it up to nervousness, but you're a pro. You shouldn't have been nervous. And later at the cemetery your wife appeared very concerned about you being exposed to that little shower. She didn't strike me

462

as being the type to go against you in anything."

"And you've built your case on that bed of sand?" he scoffed.

"No, it was all purely speculative. A shot in the dark. Even if you were ill, what were the chances of it being something we could use? But we have a very good private investigator. I turned him loose and he unearthed a little clinic in Maryland where you undergo treatment. Sunnyvale Physicians Care. Sound familiar?"

"No."

"It should. You're a major stockholder. But you only acquired it last year. Raymond Ogden is also on the board. Did he persuade you that you needed his help to keep your illness secret?"

"AIDS carries no stigma these days. People understand that anyone can get it."

"Do they? Then why do you hide it? Because you're a politician and you know that there's still plenty of prejudice out there to ensure that you wouldn't be voted back into office."

"I'm *not* ill."

"Not critically. You may last for years. You could be cured." She paused. "With RU2. But you're not going to get it. I don't care what Ogden promised you." She glared at him. "You're not going to deny help to everyone else and then sneak back to your little Sunnyvale for a dose yourself. No way. I'll watch you die by inches first."

"I don't know what you're talking about."

"I'm telling you that you drop the bill and

support RU2 or you'll die. Simple." She stood up and moved toward the door. "You back out or no RU2. Not for you. Not for your wife."

"My wife?"

She stopped at the door and looked back over her shoulder. "She didn't tell you? Six months ago she went to a Dr. Timkin here in town. Don't worry, she used another name. She tested HIV positive." For the first time she noticed a break in his control. "You really didn't know."

"I've been careful," he muttered. "She shouldn't be — Why wouldn't she tell me?"

"Why don't you ask her?"

"Pretty heavy reconnoitering," Seth said.

"Well, I didn't knock anybody on the head."

"You might as well have."

"I did feel like smashing him. How could anybody be that selfish, that cruel?"

"Years of practice?"

"Be serious. I'm worried about this."

"It seems to me you've got most of the bases covered. Good work."

"Luck." She shook her head wonderingly. "My God, how lucky. I played a hunch and hit the jackpot. Or RU2 hit the jackpot. Maybe sometimes the good guys do win. It kind of makes you believe in guardian angels."

"And who's our guardian angel? Noah?"

"Maybe." She suddenly frowned. "It's still a gamble. Ogden has so much influence over

Longworth. He might convince him that he can still get him RU2."

"I really wouldn't worry about Ogden."

Seth smiled.

Quivering rat.

Ogden crashed down the telephone. Did he have to handle everything himself? That bastard Longworth caving in at the first sign of trouble. Didn't he have enough to worry about with the police on his ass twenty-four hours a day? He couldn't even go back to Seattle.

Longworth would have to be shoved back in line. It shouldn't be a problem. Sometimes things had to be handled in person. Longworth had been too cowardly to tell him in person that he wanted out. He'd always been able to bully Longworth into doing whatever he wanted. It just took sheer force of presence.

He picked up the telephone. "Have my car brought around."

He grabbed his black overcoat from the hall closet. It always made him look imposing. Not that he needed to look imposing. He was imposing. He'd be able to manipulate Longworth with no —

His black limousine was pulling up in front of the door.

He didn't wait for the chauffeur to get out. He opened the door himself. "Senator Longworth's, George."

The limousine slid silently away from the house.

Someone was in the front seat beside the chauffeur, he realized with annoyance. He'd told George he wasn't to give any of the servants lifts into town.

"You can just let your friend out here, George. And tomorrow you can pick up your —"

"It's not George," the man in the passenger seat said. "His name is Dennis." He turned around in the seat.

"Hello, Ogden," Marco Giandello said.

Eighteen

"Almost packed?" Phyliss asked.

"Almost." Kate carried another armful of clothes from the bureau to the suitcase on the bed. "How about you and Joshua?"

"Joshua's packed." She paused. "I haven't started."

"You'd better hurry. Seth's giving last-minute instructions to Tony, but he should be back soon."

"What instructions?"

"You don't think I've given up trying to push through the testing on RU2? It's not going to be a piece of cake even now that Longworth has come out in support."

"It would go faster if you were here to push it yourself." Phyliss smiled. "You're A1 at pushing."

"I need to be in Amsterdam. I can probably start testing there within three months. There's not much time left for some people."

"Like your father."

She nodded. "But not only Daddy. I'm not that selfish." She closed the suitcase. "Scat. You need to start packing."

"I'm not going anywhere."

Kate turned to face her. "What?"

"I'm staying here."

"Why?"

"I'm going to ram RU2 through the roadblocks those idiots are putting up. I'm good at pushing too."

"Why didn't you tell me this before?"

"I didn't know until I started thinking about it. In a way, Michael died for RU2 too. Maybe I'll be able to make some sense out of it if I make sure that RU2 is all it can be."

"But Joshua will —"

"Joshua will miss me. You'll miss me too. Even that scamp Seth will miss me. You'll all have to suffer. I have things to do with my life."

Kate gazed at her in dismay. "I never meant to keep you from doing what you wanted to do."

"You didn't keep me from doing anything. It's easy to fall in a rut with people you care about. It's time I got out of the rut." She smiled. "So I'm going to get me some executive duds and give Tony so much work to do that he'll be begging you to come back."

"I don't know what I'll do without you."

"You have Joshua. And I think you can have Seth." She paused. "If you want him. Do you want him?"

"It's a complicated situation."

"Do you want him?"

Seth gently cradling her father in his arms. Seth teasing Joshua. Seth quietly holding her and talking. Seth in bed. Face it. Stop hiding. Be honest with yourself as well as Phyliss. "Oh yes, I want him. No doubt about it."

"He won't be easy but he'll be worth it. You

never like easy anyway."

"What are you talking about? I was perfectly content with my life before all this happened."

"You mean you forced yourself into a mold because you were tied to Dandridge by your father. People with very strong wills can talk themselves into anything. I told you once that nothing was ever going to be the same for us. That doesn't mean it can't be good." She gave Kate a hug. "Now stop looking so woebegone. This is the right thing for me to do."

Kate nodded, her arms tightening around her. "I know. I just —" She wasn't behaving well at all. She took a step back and said brusquely, "When Seth comes back, we'll have to brief you, and we'd better set up a conference call every week to discuss any problems."

"Two calls the first month. After that I should be rolling." She moved toward the door. "I'll go break the news to Joshua."

Kate was sitting on the bed, staring at the suitcase, when Seth came in a short time later.

He stopped. "What the hell's wrong now? Has Longworth gone back —"

"Phyliss isn't going with us. She's decided that she has to move on. You should sympathize with that. Isn't that what you always do?"

"What are you talking about?"

"If Phyliss has her way, RU2 will get approval here before Amsterdam."

"If anyone could do it, she could. You have

469

a problem with it?"

"Only because I'll miss her. We're a family."

"It's not as if you won't see her again."

"Not for a long time." She raised her gaze from the suitcase to look at him. Gypsy. Peter Pan. Machiavelli. Nurturer. He was all of those things and Phyliss was right, he would never be easy. What the hell? Most good things weren't. She stood up and squared her shoulders. Go for it. "So I've decided you've got to take up the slack."

He gazed at her warily. "What?"

"You heard me. My family is slipping away. Phyliss is gone. Someday Joshua will leave. Daddy . . ." She drew a deep breath. "So you've got to be my family. I figure if you don't do anything stupid, you should be around for at least another fifty years."

"Fascinating. I feel like a replacement part in a dishwasher."

"Shut up. Do you think this is easy? What if you get tired of me? What if you get bored? What if you decide to run away from us?" She went into his arms and laid her head on his chest. "Well, I won't let you go. I'll follow you. It's time you had a family too. You'll get used to us."

"It's a possibility."

"And you can stop being so damn enigmatic. I know you love me and I think you know I love you."

"Oh yes, but I wasn't sure you'd admit it. I thought I had my work cut out for me. I figured I wouldn't get you to this point for another six months." His arms tightened around her. "Do you think I don't know I'm not what you want in a man? It doesn't matter. Get used to the idea. You're stuck with me. I'm here for the long haul. But I won't change. You'll have to accept me as I am."

"I have accepted you. You're what I want."

"And when did you make this momentous discovery?"

"When I saw you holding my father in your arms," she said simply.

He pushed her away from him and cradled her face in his hands. His voice was tense. "What if you change your mind? I told you how I react when I'm pushed away. I wouldn't be fair or accommodating. I'd manipulate and scheme and use every dirty trick I know to stay."

"Dammit, I'm not going to change my mind. I admire you. I respect you. I love you. And you're not getting away from me. So will you marry me?"

"Is that in the deal?"

"That's in the deal. I want an official stamp on my family."

He smiled slowly. "I'll have to think about it."

Happiness surged through her. It was going to happen. "I'll give you until we reach Amsterdam. After that I'll find myself a Dutchman."

"Oh, it won't take that long. Okay, I'll marry you." He kissed her. "On one condition." His eyes were gleaming and his expression alight with mischief.

"I can hardly wait to hear it," she said warily.

"My dog. You'll have to adopt my dog too. Poor mutt. I hate to put him through that hassle again. Do you happen to know what the quarantine restrictions are in Holland?"